MOUTH-WATERING PR___
AND HER *KEBAB K___*

ON T___

"Just what I like, a cast of ___
members, and suspects in an enjoyable mystery.___
Book Critiques

"A wonderfully diverse and entertaining read."—*Reading Is My SuperPower*

"The perfect amount of mystery, humor, and romance."
—*Devilishly Delicious Book Reviews*

ONE FETA IN THE GRAVE

"With engaging dialogue, an eclectic cast of characters, and a perfect beach setting on a cold winter's day, this was a delightfully charming adventure."—*Dru's Book Musings*

"Top notch!"—*Lisa Ks Book Reviews*

"The pacing of the clues, the red herrings, the revelation of the secrets are all well-placed and make for entertaining reading."
—*The Cozy Pages*

STABBED IN THE BAKLAVA

"This novel should be at the top of the to-be-read list for culinary mystery readers, not to mention those who appreciate their reads full of intrigue, romance, and humor."—*Kings River Life*

"With a warm cast of characters and an ingenious main character, this is a series that will prove delightful for cozy fans."
—*The Parkersburg News and Sentinel*

"A fun cozy mystery that continues a great series. Grab a plate of hummus and some baklava for dessert and sit back and enjoy."
—*Carstairs Considers*

Readers Selection Fresh Pick!—*Fresh Fiction*

HUMMUS AND HOMICIDE

"Clever and charming . . . A culinary delight that will have readers salivating over the food and hungry for literary answers."
—*RT Book Reviews*, 4 Stars

"Likable characters and colorful kebab restaurant setting may whet the appetite of devotees of foodie mysteries."—*Library Journal*

"A delectable read."—Shelley Freydont, best-selling author

"With a great heroine and an interesting setting, this is a fun start to a new cozy series."—*The Parkersburg News and Sentinel*

The *Kebab Kitchen Mystery* Series by Tina Kashian

Hummus and Homicide

Stabbed in the Baklava

One Feta in the Grave

On the Lamb

Mistletoe, Moussaka, and Murder

MISTLETOE, MOUSSAKA, and MURDER
A Kebab Kitchen Mystery

Tina Kashian

KENSINGTON BOOKS
KENSINGTON PUBLISHING CORP.
www.kensingtonbooks.com

KENSINGTON BOOKS are published by

Kensington Publishing Corp.
119 West 40th Street
New York, NY 10018

All Kensington titles, imprints, and distributed lines are available at special quantity discounts for bulk purchases for sales promotion, premiums, fund-raising, educational, or institutional use.

Special book excerpts or customized printings can also be created to fit specific needs. For details, write or phone the office of the Kensington Sales Manager: Attn.: Sales Department. Kensington Publishing Corp., 119 West 40th Street, New York, NY 10018. Phone: 1-800-221-2647.

Kensington and the K logo Reg. U.S. Pat. & TM Off.

First Printing: October 2020

ISBN-13: 978-1-4967-2607-0
ISBN-10: 1-4967-2607-3

ISBN-13: 978-1-4967-2608-7 (eBook)
ISBN-10: 1-4967-2608-1 (eBook)

10 9 8 7 6 5 4 3 2 1

Printed in the United States of America

For my parents, Anahid and Gabriel.
Some of my favorite memories are of growing up and
working in the restaurant.
I miss you both every day!

Chapter One

"Let me get this straight. You want me to run into the freezing Atlantic Ocean in the middle of winter?"

Lucy Berberian's lips twitched as she gave her best friend, Katie Watson, her most convincing look.

"That's right," Lucy said. "This year's Polar Bear Plunge is to benefit the Ocean Crest senior center."

It was early December and the two friends were decorating a seven-foot Christmas tree and hanging wreaths and mistletoe throughout Kebab Kitchen. Lucy scanned the restaurant, noting the cozy maple booths, the tables covered with white tablecloths, and the neat stack of menus on the hostess stand. It was early morning and Kebab Kitchen wouldn't open until the lunch shift, when it would serve its Mediterranean specialties. Through the large bay window was a lovely view of the Ocean Crest beach and the boardwalk, now covered in a sprinkling of snow. The Ferris wheel and old-fashioned wooden roller coaster on the boardwalk pier stood motionless and wouldn't operate until the start of the summer season. But the small town was just as lively as ever and gearing up to celebrate the holidays. Festive parties, boardwalk craft shows, a town Christmas tree lighting, and much more was planned.

Katie removed a bell ornament decorated with glitter from a stack of boxes and hung it on one of the branches of the artificial tree. "This year's Polar Bear Plunge may be for a good cause, but I'm still not certain I want to—"

Lucy reached into a box and pulled out a string of lights. "Of course you do! Don't be a crab. It's only a quick dip in the ocean. Don't you want to help the seniors fundraise?"

"Yes, but—"

"My landlady, Mrs. Lubinski, told me the seniors are excited about the renovation, and they're planning a dance to celebrate before construction begins. Plus, your grandma will have a nice new facility to play designer purse bingo in."

Katie pursed her lips. "You're using my grandma as leverage?"

"Absolutely."

Katie let out a puff of air. "Fine. You drive a hard bargain."

"Good, because if I'm going to freeze my butt off, I want my best friend by my side."

Lucy managed to untangle the string of lights and plug one end into the closest electrical socket, only to find that just half the string lit up. *Ugh.* "One light must be bad. Why does this happen every year?"

"It wouldn't be Christmas decorating without a bad string of lights." Katie stood on tiptoe to hang a reindeer ornament near the top of the seven-foot tree.

Katie was much taller than Lucy, who was only five-foot-three inches. The two had been best friends forever, but were opposites in appearance. Katie had poker-straight

blond hair, blue eyes, and skin that sunburned easily, whereas Lucy had dark curls, chocolate-colored eyes, and an olive complexion that resulted in a summer tan that lasted long after fall. Lucy's Armenian, Lebanese, and Greek ethnicity definitely contributed to her ability to tan.

"I'm flattered you want me by your side when we run into the ocean, but why not your hot chef-turned-fiancé?" Katie asked.

As if on cue, the kitchen doors swung open and Azad Zakarian walked out carrying a loaded tray. No matter how many times Lucy saw the restaurant's head chef, her heart did a pitter-patter. He was tall, dark-haired, and dark-eyed, but it wasn't just his good looks and lean build that attracted her. He had a certain confidence, especially in the kitchen, that she found compelling.

Nothing like a skilled chef in the kitchen, her mother often said. Over time, Lucy had grudgingly come to respect her mother's opinion.

"Hi, Katie. You're just in time to taste test today's specials." Azad pointed to each dish on the tray, "Moussaka and chicken shish kebab as entrees; and the appetizers are octopus with olive oil, fennel, and lemon; tabbouleh salad; and spicy black bean hummus, artichoke hummus, and our traditional hummus. The pita bread is hot from the oven."

Katie's face lit up like the star that topped the Christmas tree. "Bill's going to be so jealous," she said, referring to her husband, an Ocean Crest detective.

Both Lucy and Katie picked up a small plate and fork and tasted each dish. The shish kebab was delicious, the tabbouleh nicely tart, and the hummus smooth with sesame seed puree, lemon, and garlic. But it was the moussaka, the layers of eggplant, ground meat, and béchamel sauce, that melted in her mouth. Azad had outdone himself.

"Oh my gosh!" Katie said. "It's all so good, but the moussaka is fabulous. I could devour all of it."

Azad's grin transformed his face into something even more striking. He picked up the tray and his muscles flexed beneath his chef's coat. "I'll pack a take-out container for Bill and some of the cops at the station."

"They'll love it." Katie set down her empty plate. "Hey, Azad. Are you going to do the Polar Bear Plunge?"

Azad shook his head. "Someone has to hold down the fort here. I'll be in the kitchen and Lucy's parents agreed to help run the restaurant. But I promise to take a break and get to the beach as fast as I can with hot chocolate and towels for you both. Now, if you'll pardon me, ladies, I'll leave you to your decorating. I need to finish preparing for today's service." Azad disappeared into the kitchen.

"You're a lucky lady," Katie said as she reached for some fake mistletoe. "Bill can't boil water."

Lucy hadn't always been so lucky, especially in the romance department. But since leaving her Philadelphia job at a law firm, a lot had happened, in and out of the kitchen.

The sleigh bells above the door chimed and a slim blonde stepped inside. With a heart-shaped face and blue eyes, Susan Cutie was dressed in a mauve blouse and a stylish skirt that emphasized her slim waist. She was the owner of Cutie's Cupcakes. Since returning to Ocean Crest, Lucy had been hooked on Susan's lemon meringue pie. Lucy's fondness for pie and baklava, combined with working in a restaurant all day, inspired her to jog the boardwalk three times a week.

"Nice tree," Susan said as she picked up an ornament that had fallen from a low tree branch and handed it to Katie. "I heard you are doing the Polar Bear Plunge. I came to tell you that Jake and I also just signed up to do it."

"You signed up together? Things must be heating up in the bakery with your new boyfriend," Katie said.

Susan's face turned a shade red. "Jake's been wonderful, and he's taking me out for a romantic dinner tonight. I need to thank Lucy's mom for introducing us."

Lucy rolled her eyes. "My mom already thinks she's quite the matchmaker. This will encourage her to no end."

Angela Berberian was a fixture in town and had been head chef of Kebab Kitchen for thirty years before retiring. Lucy's mother had tried to play matchmaker between Lucy and Azad for as long as Lucy could remember. Of course, that meant Lucy had avoided giving Azad a second chance after he'd broken her heart after college. But time, and Azad's help with the restaurant, had a way of changing a lady's mind.

"If you and Jake get engaged, I'll have lots of tips for you," Katie said. "I've been taking my role as Lucy's matron of honor seriously."

Lucy shot Katie a sideways glance. "A bit too seriously." Her friend had been even more gung ho than her mother. Lucy hadn't seen that coming. She'd always assumed her mother would be too meddling.

"Nonsense. It's never too early to start looking for reception halls. Not to mention bands, florists, and wedding gown shopping. I've been looking at catering halls online."

"We haven't even set a date yet," Lucy protested.

Katie waved a dismissive hand. "Reception halls fill up. You need to plan months in advance. As soon as we're finished here, I'm taking Lucy to one of the sites today."

Lucy looked at her in surprise. "Today?"

"Yup. I already made an appointment," Katie said.

Lucy turned to Susan. "Take your time, Susan. There's no pressure to get engaged."

A dreamy look crossed Susan's face. "It doesn't seem like pressure when you're in love. Does it, Lucy?"

"Susan's right," Katie said. "Love is what matters. As for the perfect wedding, what can go wrong when you plan in advance?"

Lucy held on to the handle above the Jeep's door as Katie took a turn a bit too fast. "Jeez, Katie. Slow down. What's the rush?"

"You still haven't gotten used to my driving, have you?" Katie asked as she sped down Ocean Avenue.

"I don't think I ever will." Katie had a tendency to drive like Mario Andretti. Even worse, she'd often glance from side to side, sometimes waving at people on the sidewalk. Lucy wanted to turn her friend's chin back to the road.

Katie pushed through a yellow light. "Don't get your panties in a twist. We're almost there."

"Where are we headed again?" Lucy's mind had gone blank a few blocks back from Katie's driving. Self-preservation had kicked in.

"I told you. The Sea View was closed for renovations, but reopened about six months ago. We need to check it out to see if it would be good for your reception."

"I still don't see why we couldn't wait to visit."

"I'm saving you time. Azad works all day in the kitchen. Would you rather go by yourself?"

Good point. It was much nicer to tour possible wedding reception halls with a friend. This way, if Lucy really loved the place, she could bring Azad to look at it later. Thankfully, he was easygoing when it came to wedding planning. He'd often said he wanted her to be happy and would like whatever she liked. He also deferred to her about setting a date, which suited Lucy just fine.

"I have another reason for visiting this place," Katie said as she halted at the second of the two stoplights in the small town. "The township employees and their families have a holiday party at Rocco's Ristorante every year, but Rocco retired without notice and moved to the Virgin Islands."

"The Virgin Islands? Wow! I know the restaurant business can be stressful, but that's a big life change." She couldn't image her parents just closing shop and taking off for the Caribbean.

"Tell me about it. Rocco abandoned a lot of people who had events booked. I need to find a new venue for our holiday party and fast. I was tasked with pricing the Sea View. Since the renovations, we hope the owner, Deacon Spooner, cuts the township a deal to help promote his business."

Katie worked for the Ocean Crest town hall and handled everything from collecting real estate taxes, to issuing dog and cat licenses, to handling zoning applications, and more. Her duties had expanded to being in charge of the township holiday party.

They came to the edge of town. "I had no idea you were in charge of finding a new place for the township holiday party. Why didn't you tell me earlier? I would have happily come along," Lucy said.

"I want you to focus on your wedding—whenever it may be—and I'll focus on town business."

They left Ocean Crest and arrived at their destination less than five minutes later. Katie slid into a spot and thrust the Jeep into Park.

Lucy opened the door and stepped out. Her gaze was

drawn to the building before her. An old, two-story manor house, it had eight white columns and looked like an elegant Southern plantation house. "Wow. I didn't know this place existed."

"The renovation must have cost a pretty penny," Katie said.

They walked up the stone driveway, opened the double front doors, and stepped inside. A large chandelier in the vestibule cast a kaleidoscope of color on the floral, patterned carpet.

"Hello?" Lucy called out.

No answer.

Katie shrugged. "Let's check out the catering hall. Someone has to be around."

They pushed through a set of doors and entered the dining room. "From the looks of things, they are getting ready to have a party tonight," Lucy said, gazing at the dozen tables set up around the room.

Each was covered with alternating pink or white tablecloths and set with silver-rimmed china and flatware. Matching pink-and-white napkins were folded into elaborate swans. Flower arrangements of pink and white carnations with baby's breath in vases graced each table, along with tea lights in glass holders. A wooden dance floor gleamed with polish, and an elevated stage showcased where a band could set up and play. The floral carpet they had seen in the entrance hall was repeated here. In the corner was a bar, the counter glossy and recently polished. Large windows were covered with custom gold drapes held back with gold tassels.

Lucy spotted a set of double French doors. Curious, she walked to them and turned the handle. "Oh, look!" she cried out when the doors opened to reveal the view.

A brick patio overlooked the pristine Jersey shore beach and the Atlantic Ocean. It was a cold but clear day, and the cloudless sky was an endless blue line in the horizon. The ocean stretched on forever and the waves were capped with white peaks. A light dusting of snow covered the sand.

Snow on the beach was a sight to see. The Jersey shore tourism bureau had been working hard to create winter events that would draw tourists to the area year-round. It seemed to be working. Tourists had been traveling to Ocean Crest in December just to see snow on the sand and the boardwalk.

After spending eight years in Philadelphia working as a lawyer for a big city firm, Lucy would never get tired of the sight. The patio would be ideal for a lovely wedding reception cocktail hour.

Katie joined her on the patio, and the two stood gazing outside when a deep voice made them jump.

"You were looking for me?"

Lucy whirled to find a middle-aged man approaching. Of average height, his thinning, fair hair was styled in a bad comb-over, his face pockmarked. He held a clipboard in one hand. Dressed in a navy suit with a floral tie that looked like it matched the carpet, he extended his free hand. "Deacon Spooner."

Lucy shook his hand. "I'm Lucy Berberian, and this is my matron of honor, Katie Watson. I'm interested in having a wedding reception here."

"My price depends on the number of guests, the date, and your menu selection. Alcohol is not included and you need to arrange to have everything delivered." He pulled a sheet from the clipboard and handed it to her.

Lucy's eyes nearly popped out of her head as she took in the figures. "That much?"

His gaze traveled around the ballroom. "We recently renovated."

The price was well above Lucy and Azad's budget. Azad wanted her to be happy, but not at *this* cost. If the other reception halls were this pricey, they would have to host a backyard wedding.

Katie took the paper from Lucy, and her brow furrowed as she studied the numbers. "Are you negotiable? I work at the Ocean Crest town hall and we are looking for a venue to hold our annual holiday party. Can you offer a discount if we have both events here?"

Deacon scoffed. "Why does everyone want something for free?"

"Not free," Katie argued. "Just a reasonable price."

He snatched the paper from Katie's hand. "Time for you two to go."

Lucy and Katie gaped in astonishment as Deacon Spooner turned his back and caromed through a door in the corner of the dining room that must have led to his office.

"Wow. I wasn't expecting Deacon Spooner to behave like that," Lucy mumbled beneath her breath.

"What a jerk. I feel bad I made you come here," Katie said.

"It's not your fault. How could you know?" Lucy asked.

Together, they departed through the double doors and walked toward Katie's Jeep.

"He must only deal with rich people. Who else can afford that price?" Katie said.

"And it didn't even include liquor," Lucy added.

"We have to make a list of other places."

"Isn't your township holiday party soon?"

Katie worried her bottom lip. "In two weeks. It puts me in a bit of a bind."

"I'll help you, just like you're helping me," Lucy vowed.

They were almost to Katie's Jeep when a voice shouted out, "Stop! Don't you two go anywhere."

Lucy spun around to see a tall man barreling toward them in the parking lot. "Who's that?"

Katie shook her head, looking just as perplexed as Lucy. "No idea."

The man halted before them. He was even taller up close, about six feet five inches. He was about the same age as Deacon Spooner, but more fit, and he wore a golf shirt, khakis, and brown suede shoes. His pencil-thin mustache made him look like Clark Gable, but without the movie star glamour. He flashed a grin and stuck out a hand. "I'm Norman Weston, co-owner of the Sea View."

Katie spoke up first and shook his hand. "I didn't know Mr. Spooner had a business partner."

"He never tells anyone. I overheard part of your conversation. You work at the town hall?" He looked at Katie.

"That's right," Katie said.

"I was at Lola's Coffee Shop and heard through the grapevine that your holiday party at Rocco's fell through. I'd be happy to hold it at the Sea View for a reasonable price," Norman said.

Lucy wasn't surprised he'd learned of the doomed Rocco's and the township employee holiday party. Lola's Coffee Shop was one of the heartbeats of Ocean Crest. Townsfolk loved two things: coffee and gossip.

"That's wonderful! But what about your partner? Mr. Spooner doesn't seem the agreeable type," Katie said.

Norman waved a dismissive hand. "Despite what Deacon

thinks, he doesn't have full control over the business. I have a say, too."

"Good news." Katie glanced at Lucy before turning back to Norman. "But what about Lucy's wedding?"

Norman smoothed his mustache. "I'll revisit the quote Deacon gave you."

Even though Norman Weston's offer was kind, Lucy wasn't positive she wanted to have her reception here. Deacon had left a sour taste in her mouth.

"That's kind of you," Lucy said. "But if you don't mind my asking, why the difference between you and Mr. Spooner?"

Norman stilled. "Let's just say that business partners have a way of bringing out either the best or the worst in each other."

Based on Norman's tone, Lucy believed it was the latter in their case.

Chapter Two

"I've decided to run into the ocean alongside you and Katie tomorrow," Eloisa Lubinski said.

Lucy stared at her landlady in shock. It wasn't just the woman's outfit that caught her attention—a flamboyant flapper dress complete with feathered headdress and dancing shoes—but the fact that Eloisa Lubinski was in her eighties.

Lucy set down her purse on her kitchen table. Her eccentric, elderly landlady occupied the first floor of her beach home and rented the second floor to Lucy. She'd asked to come upstairs to chat, and now Lucy knew the reason. "You sure you want to participate in the Polar Bear Plunge?" Lucy asked.

Eloisa shot Lucy a challenging look. "What? You don't think a senior citizen can't freeze her boobies alongside you?"

Whoa! Eloisa's breasts were definitely *not* something Lucy wanted to picture in her mind. *No. No. No!* How did one erase a mental image?

Lucy cleared her throat. "I didn't mean to offend you. I was just wondering why."

"Why not? I'm not getting any younger, and if others are willing to do it to raise money for the senior center, why shouldn't I? I'll benefit from the place more than all of them."

"I just figured you'd wait with Azad on the beach, holding hot chocolate and a warm towel."

Eloisa raised a tweezed eyebrow. "Azad will be on the beach?"

Oh brother. Her landlady had a fondness for Kebab Kitchen's chef, and it wasn't for his culinary talents.

"He has to work up until the last minute, but he said he'll take a break from work to be there," Lucy said.

"*Hmm.* Maybe he'll want some company."

"I'll be sure to tell him." Lucy shot her a sidelong look. "That is if you decide not to jump in."

"I'm thinking about sitting this one out now. I'll let you know."

Before moving into the second floor of the widow's beach home, Lucy had been living in Katie and Bill's guest bedroom. When her brother-in-law and real estate agent, Max, had first shown Lucy this place, she'd been hesitant. But the rent was in her budget and it was a short walk to Kebab Kitchen, and she'd decided to give it and her landlady a chance. Lucy had packed her bags and taken the outdoor restaurant cat, Gadoo, with her. She hadn't regretted it.

A low growl drew Lucy's attention. Eloisa's shih tzu had awakened Gadoo, and the cat swatted at the dog. Gadoo's razor-sharp claws just missed the canine. Lucy had no doubt that if Gadoo wanted to slice the dog's nose, he would have. After circling the couch and eyeing each other, the two settled down together on the cushion.

"Cupid and Gadoo have been getting along nicely," Eloisa said.

Getting along "nicely" was a bit too strong to describe

their relationship. Gadoo tolerated the shih tzu. Sometimes the cat even let the dog share his cat bed. The dog's overbite and topknot may have looked adorable, but the shih tzu's appearance and name were deceptive. He wasn't exactly as loving as his Roman namesake, and he had a tendency to growl at people, especially Lucy.

A car honk sounded, and Eloisa peered out the window. "That's Edna. We're dancing tonight. If we don't get there early, all the senior men will be taken. Not many still kicking."

That explained the flapper dress. Eloisa turned toward the door that led to her own downstairs living area and whistled for Cupid. The little shih tzu reluctantly left the couch and trotted over to her side.

"Good sharing, Gadoo. I know Cupid can be a bother sometimes," Lucy said.

The black-and-orange cat blinked his yellow eyes. After refilling his food and water bowls, Lucy poured herself a mug of decaffeinated green tea and cracked open the balcony door. The cat jumped off the couch and joined her on the patio.

Most evenings, Gadoo could be found outside on the patio or visiting Kebab Kitchen, where Lucy's mother still left out cat food for the feline.

It was a cold December evening, but Lucy wore a heavy sweatshirt and jeans. She loved this view, morning or evening, and it had been another bonus when deciding to move here. Eloisa's home was oceanfront, and Lucy sat outside every morning with a mug of coffee and took in the magnificent view. Now, the moon cast a shimmering glow on the ocean. The calming sounds of the waves and the scent of salt air was brisk and refreshing. A breeze blew on her cheeks. Unlike in the spring and summer seasons, she couldn't stay outside now for long, but she wouldn't give up this time. Gadoo wound his body around her feet and purred. She rested her feet on the railing and watched the grass on the sand dunes dance in the breeze, then the dark beach beyond.

A movement below caught her attention, and she focused to see a man walking in front of the sand dunes. He was dressed in black, and from this distance, she couldn't tell if he was wearing sweatpants or jeans. Exercising at night in the cold seemed odd, but who knew? Maybe it was the only free time he had. Or maybe he was like her and enjoyed the beach no matter the season. He headed across a walkway to the beach and disappeared from sight. She dismissed him from her thoughts and sipped her tea and relaxed.

She could see the blinking red and green lights of the neighbor's Christmas tree. All throughout Ocean Crest, homes were festively decorated. Soon the town would have its annual Christmas tree lighting in the park, as well as other numerous holiday parties and festivities planned for the season.

Thanks to Katie, Kebab Kitchen's Christmas tree was decorated. As for Lucy's apartment, Azad said he'd help her select a tree, and he and Lucy could decorate it together.

After a half hour, Lucy's cheeks felt red and her fingers tingled with cold. She reluctantly decided it was time to go inside. She needed a good night's sleep to prepare for the Polar Bear Plunge. Just as she slid the patio door closed, Cupid started barking downstairs.

Gadoo's ears perked up.

Eloisa wouldn't be home for at least another hour, and Cupid often barked at a stray cat or a passerby. She didn't know how much comfort she could offer the agitated shih tzu, but she also knew his high-pitched barking would keep her up.

She cracked the door that led to Eloisa's downstairs living space. "Enough, Cupid!" She used the command Eloisa often issued to calm the dog down.

Cupid kept barking.

She'd have to calm the dog herself. Halfway down the stairs, she called out to the dog once more. But rather than cease, his barking escalated.

Then she heard it. Or rather, she heard *someone.*

Booted footsteps sounded on the front porch. Then Lucy heard the squeak of the front door as somebody else entered the dark, empty house with her.

Lucy had called 911 as soon as she'd realized a burglar was in the house. Thankfully, Katie's husband, Ocean Crest Detective Bill Watson, had been driving by and was the closest officer to the scene. He'd been promoted to detective a couple of months before. Tall and handsome, with blue eyes, Bill was just as imposing in a gray suit and blue tie as he'd been in an officer's uniform.

Lucy stood next to Bill on the front porch as he faced the intruder. "Who are you?" Bill asked, his tone serious.

"Vinnie Pinto. And I wasn't breaking in. Eloisa Lubinski gave me a key."

Vinnie was older, although she couldn't discern his exact age. He was one of those people who could be either sixty or eighty. Of average height and weight, with a full head of salt-and-pepper hair, he had a hawkish nose that looked like it had been broken more than once in a bar brawl. He was dressed in dark clothes—black jacket, sweatpants, and running shoes. Lucy wondered if he'd been the mysterious man walking on the beach. He might have watched her sitting on the patio, thought she was preoccupied, and then headed back to the front of the house to break in.

"We haven't been able to reach Mrs. Lubinski to verify your story. Ms. Berberian is her tenant and she does not know who you are," Bill said.

Vinnie shot Lucy a menacing look. "You're the one who called the cops on me?"

Lucy straightened her spine and glowered back. "You're the one who broke in."

"I already told you and the officer. I didn't break in. Why else would I have a key?" He dangled the key in front of both Bill and Lucy.

Good question. A thought occurred to her, and she shook her head. "You could have stolen it."

"Eloisa and I are longtime . . . friends. I wanted to surprise her."

"Well, you surprised me instead." Lucy found it hard to believe Eloisa would be friends with this man, or anything else for that matter. Even more unbelievable was that Eloisa would give him the key.

"You said you wanted to surprise Mrs. Lubinski. Why?" Bill asked.

Vinnie shifted his booted feet on the driveway. "We're both in the Polar Bear Plunge tomorrow. I thought she'd like to know."

"You are?" Lucy asked, surprised.

"Why not just call her?" Bill asked.

"I called the house, but there was no answer. Last I knew, Eloisa doesn't have a cell phone."

Lucy was beginning to wonder if he was telling the truth. He could have called when she was sitting outside on the patio with Gadoo and she didn't hear the downstairs phone ring. It was true that Eloisa didn't carry a cell phone. She claimed she'd survived all her life without one just fine and didn't need to learn new technology.

Lucy's parents, Angela and Raffi, were stubborn when it came to new technology like the new computerized inventory for Kebab Kitchen, but she was grateful they owned cell phones.

"We'll have to confirm your story with Mrs. Lubinski. Until she returns, you can sit with me at the station."

Vinnie glared at him. "Are you arresting me?"

"Not yet. But I'm still taking you to the station for more questioning," Bill said.

"I want a lawyer."

"That's your prerogative."

Just then, headlights flashed and a car turned into the driveway. Lucy's heart pounded. "Mrs. Lubinski's home! Now we can confirm your story." There was only one way to solve this mystery. Lucy started down the driveway.

Eloisa stepped out of the car and waved at her friend as the car pulled away. She carried her feathered headdress and her shoes. She started up the driveway and raised a high heel in greeting when she spotted Lucy. "My heel broke, so I had to call it an early night." Eloisa halted and frowned when she noticed the two men. "What's going on?"

Bill spoke up first. "This man used a key to get into your home. Lucy called the police. He claims you two are friends and that you gave him a key. Do you know him?"

Eloisa joined the trio on the porch. She squinted from the bright porch light and shot the man a pointed look. "What are you doing here, Vinnie?"

Vinnie shook his head. "Hey, Eloisa. Just tell them you gave me the key."

Quick as a teenager, Eloisa reached out to snatch the key from his fingers. "I did."

"You gave him permission to enter your house?" Bill asked.

"I most certainly did not."

"Then why does he have a key?" Lucy asked.

Eloisa sighed. "He was my property manager a long time ago. I fired him." She turned to Vinnie. "Last I heard, you were driving a trash truck around town."

Vinnie nodded once. "I still am."

"What's this funny business of you showing up here, then?" Eloisa asked.

"I heard you were going to be one of the ocean plungers tomorrow. So am I."

"So? That's what you came here to tell me? You could have visited in the morning like a normal person. You're lucky Cupid didn't bite you," Eloisa said.

"Who's Cupid?"

"My mean dog."

Vinnie scowled at that.

It was the first time Eloisa had called Cupid mean. Did she really realize the shih tzu was scary, or had she said it for show? Some people put out signs, "Beware of Dog," even if they didn't have a dog. Was Eloisa trying to scare Vinnie? As far as Lucy was concerned, Cupid's growl was frightening, even if he was only ten pounds.

Eloisa looked to Bill. "Thank you for your help, Officer, but I won't press charges."

"Are you certain?" Bill asked.

"Thanks to Lucy, Vinnie didn't make it much farther

than the front door. I'm also happy to have my key back," Eloisa said.

Bill's furrowed brow said he didn't agree, but had to accept her decision. "Visit the station right away if you change your mind." Bill's gaze swung to Vinnie. "You're lucky to get a reprieve, but you should know the cops regularly patrol the town. I'll escort you home."

This seemed to irk Vinnie. "I don't need an—"

"It's not a request," Bill said, his tone stern.

Vinnie opened his mouth, then shut it. He followed Bill to the unmarked police car and climbed into the back. Bill drove away.

Once Lucy and Eloisa were back inside the house, Eloisa brewed tea for both of them. They sat at her kitchen table with steaming mugs. Gadoo curled up in an empty wicker chair by Lucy, and Cupid settled in his dog bed in the corner.

Lucy cradled her mug. "What do you suppose Vinnie Pinto really wanted?"

Eloisa sipped her tea. "Cash. Jewelry. Vinnie has a gambling problem. It's why I fired him as my property manager years ago."

This information didn't help settle Lucy's nerves. "Are you sure you don't want to press charges? All you have to do is call Bill and—"

"I don't need to do a thing. Vinnie's obviously in big trouble. If he's in that much debt to think to rob me, his bookie will do a lot more damage than the law." A satisfied expression crossed her wrinkled face. "I say let nature take its course."

Chapter Three

A cold sea breeze blew across the beach. Lucy and Katie stood huddled together with a crowd of brave "polar bears." It had snowed last night and about an inch of snow covered the sand.

Not for the first time since arriving that morning, Lucy eyed the ocean and wondered what the heck she'd been thinking to sign up for this year's Polar Bear Plunge.

"The water temperature is only forty-six degrees," Katie said, her nose red from the cold.

They both wore bathing suits beneath sweatshirts and sweatpants. They also each wore running shoes, not flip-flops. Unfortunately, they weren't going jogging on the boardwalk and would have to take off their clothes soon.

Lucy shivered and rubbed her hands up and down her arms. "Why did you have to tell me? I didn't check for a reason."

"Hey! You dragged me into this, remember? I'm afraid you're going to have to tear my sweatshirt off."

"That's Bill's job. I wouldn't dream of depriving him of the pleasure."

"He's the smart one and is at work. Fifty bucks says he's

sitting at his desk inside a heated police station drinking hot coffee."

"Stop whining. It's for a good cause. We run in and run out. People have been doing this for years. How bad can it be?" If her voice hadn't wavered, Lucy might have believed it herself.

Katie shot her a cynical look. "Sounds like you're convincing yourself more than me."

Lucy shifted her feet. Even if Katie was right, she didn't have to point it out, did she?

The town mayor, Theodore Magic, also the owner of Magic's Family Apothecary, walked to the head of the crowd carrying a bullhorn. Well into his seventies, Theodore was short and thin, with a shock of white hair and wrinkles and age spots on his face and arms. Instead of his pharmacist's coat, he was dressed in khakis, a turtleneck, and a warm down vest. Lucy was jealous.

"Welcome to Ocean Crest's annual Polar Bear Plunge!" Theodore spoke into the bullhorn. "A special thank-you to our brave Plungers. We have forty-six of you, and that's an all-time high. This year's event is extra-special because all your donations will benefit the renovation of the town's senior center."

The large crowd burst into cheers. The onlookers stood to the side, ready to show their support with towels, sweatshirts, and warm drinks. Lucy scanned the group until she found Azad. He'd left Kebab Kitchen early to be here for her. He waved and Lucy waved back. Eloisa stood next to him, dressed in a full-length, white faux fur coat with black spots that resembled Cruella de Vil's dalmatian coat.

Smart lady for skipping this one.

A series of flashes made Lucy blink. Stan Slade had

parked the *Town News* truck on the beach and the head reporter was taking pictures with his news crew. Short and stocky, with black-rimmed glasses, Stan was a heavy smoker, and a cigarette dangled from his lips as he held his camera. She hadn't had a rosy relationship with the reporter in the past, but she was grateful for his presence today. Any publicity toward raising money for the senior center would go far. Other than the news van and police SUVs, no other cars were permitted on the beach.

One by one, the Plungers began to take off their clothes and shoes. Friends and family members came forward to take the items.

"Oh no. We're out of time," Katie said.

Together, Lucy and Katie removed their own running shoes and socks. Barefoot, Lucy stepped on the snow-covered sand. The shock of the cold was jarring. She sucked in a breath and gathered her courage. Next, they stripped off their sweat suits. Dressed in a one-piece Speedo swimsuit, gooseflesh prickled all over Lucy's skin.

Azad and Eloisa approached to take their clothing.

"I'm proud of both of you. Remember, I have towels and hot chocolate waiting. Good luck!" Azad gave Lucy a quick peck on the lips.

"I'm glad you convinced me not to swim," Eloisa said, then winked at Azad. "Plus, I just had my hair done." She patted her bleached-blond hairdo with her free hand.

Lucy was too cold to think of a comeback. Instead, she scanned the group of swimmers. She was surprised to see many local business owners and their employees. The Polar Bear Plunge would benefit town seniors, and all the businesses contributed, whether in direct donations or by raising money by swimming. Ocean Crest residents helped one another.

Susan Cutie stood alongside her boyfriend, Jake Burns. Lean and handsome, with light brown hair, blue eyes, chiseled features, and a diamond stud in his left ear, Jake was always quick with a smile. His charm helped with his Boardwalk Brewery business.

Lucy recognized other locals as well. Ben Hawkins, the town barber, Harold Harper, a boardwalk shop owner, and Candy Kent, owner of Pages Bookstore, and many more were all looking cold and ready. She was taken aback to see Deacon Spooner. The arrogant catering hall owner was the last person she'd expect to participate.

"Time for the swimmers to approach the water," the mayor called out. All forty-six brave people trailed behind Theodore to gather just out of reach of the surf.

Lucy's toes curled in the cold, wet sand. "It's like ripping off a Band-Aid. Make it quick and the pain will fade."

"Where'd you hear that crap?" Katie asked, her gaze never leaving the ocean.

"I just made it up."

"This counts for lots of friend points."

The breeze carried the tang of salt. The sound of the ocean wasn't calming this morning, but ominous, as if to say, *Enter if you dare.*

The mayor raised his bullhorn once more. "When I count down from ten, everyone run for it. We'll all be watching, and the *Town News* will take lots of pictures. Extra points for dunking your heads!"

"I pray I don't suffer a heart attack," Katie grumbled.

"Me too," Lucy said. "I'm starting to doubt the wisdom of signing up."

Katie shot her a disbelieving look. "Just now?"

"Ten . . . nine . . . eight . . ."

Lucy reached for Katie's hand. "BFF forever, right?"

"Seven . . . six . . . five . . ."

Katie gripped her hand. "I'll let you know after this."

"Three . . . two . . . one. Go!"

Lucy and Katie found themselves in the middle of the sprinting crowd. At the first touch of the surf on Lucy's bare toes, she gasped. Then the water hit her ankles and calves, knees and thighs.

Lucy slowed down. "Oh my God! It's freezing!"

"Keep going!" Katie shouted as she tugged her onward.

Lucy gritted her teeth and kept running. Waves hit her stomach, and her gut tightened and her muscles cramped. Then water splashed her chest and shoulders.

Katie gasped, then stumbled, but Lucy pulled her to her feet. "Almost there!"

A tall wave caught them both by surprise and splashed a good amount of water in their faces. Lucy let go of Katie's hand. She sputtered, and both Lucy and Katie would have turned back and run for the beach, but the swimmers behind them were a human wall pushing them forward. The next wave went over their heads.

Lucy caught a mouthful of salt water. "Ugh!" She spit it out and rubbed the stinging water out of her eyes.

"Go back now!" Katie was already ahead of her.

Lucy didn't need any encouragement and fought through fellow swimmers and the waves to reach the shore. She'd never been so cold in her life. In a wild panic, she searched for Azad but couldn't find him.

Would she ever be warm again?

Then she saw Bill holding an outstretched towel for Katie. Wasn't he supposed to be working?

"Lucy!"

She whirled to see Azad sprinting toward her. *Thank my lucky stars!* He wrapped the oversized towel around her and tugged her frigid body into his embrace. She wanted to weep with relief.

"You went in all the way. You're my brave warrior," Azad said.

Warrior? She wasn't sure about that. She felt more like a frozen Popsicle. As for brave, she'd been forced forward by a human wall of wacky swimmers. In her panic to reach the beach, she hadn't been able to identify a single one.

"Thank you," she mumbled against his chest.

He rubbed her arms and her back. He was blessedly warm and she was eternally grateful.

Eloisa hurried up to them and thrust a Styrofoam cup in her face. "Hot chocolate?"

"Thanks, Mrs. Lubinski." Lucy accepted the cup and promptly burned her tongue on the hot drink. She didn't care. At least one body part wasn't numb.

Lucy saw Bill offer hot chocolate to Katie. "Bill left work?"

"He said he couldn't miss watching you two because he doubts Katie will ever do it again."

She laughed. "He's probably right."

"Are you going to do this again next year?" Azad asked.

"No way. Once and done."

"You did good, Lucy." Eloisa patted her head. "I overheard Theodore Magic said they've raised over five thousand dollars for the senior center today."

Lucy smiled at her landlady, the first real smile since

escaping the frigid Atlantic Ocean. "Today's a huge success, then."

And that's when she heard the high-pitched scream.

"What's going on?" Lucy asked.

The piercing scream had made a shiver that had nothing to do with the cold travel down her spine.

"I'm not sure, but it came from over there." Azad pointed to the surf. "Someone's down."

"Lying down? In the freezing surf? Are you sure?"

"Only one way to find out. Come on!" Azad took her hand, and together, they jogged to where Azad had pointed. Katie and Bill were by their side.

A crowd had gathered around a person lying on the beach. Lucy couldn't see much. Her height always put her at a disadvantage in crowds, and she had to shift from side to side to see between bodies.

"Move aside," Bill ordered.

The crowd parted like the Red Sea. Bill may be off duty, but a detective's tone held unmistakable authority.

Lucy gasped and pressed a hand to her chest. A man lay faceup and spread-eagled on the wet sand. His eyes were closed. She couldn't tell if his chest was rising and falling.

Bill knelt down by the man.

"It's Deacon Spooner," Katie said before Lucy could answer.

Bill looked up at his wife. "How do you know?"

"He owns the Sea View. Lucy and I met him just yesterday," Katie said.

The flash of a camera made Lucy jump, and she glanced

over her shoulder to see Stan Slade taking pictures. A cigarette dangled from his lips, a long string of ash ready to fall. Lucy imagined the gruesome image of Deacon splashed on the front page of the local newspaper.

She shivered anew as she crept closer. "What's wrong with him? Is he hurt?"

Bill pressed two fingers to Deacon's neck. His brow furrowed as he met Lucy's gaze. "No. He's dead."

Chapter Four

"I can't believe Deacon Spooner is dead," Lucy whispered to Katie.

They stood with the rest of the crowd on the beach as the paramedics confirmed the worst. The coroner and the police had arrived, and soon after, another town detective, Calvin Clemmons, stepped out of a police Jeep.

Tall, thin, and in his midforties, Clemmons had straw-colored hair, a bushy mustache, and a sharp nose that had always reminded Lucy of a wedge of cheese. Dressed in a plain gray suit, he trekked through the sand in dress shoes. They hadn't been friendly in the past. He disliked her family and held a grudge against her sister, Emma, who had dated him in high school, then dubbed him Clinging Calvin and broken up with him. To make matters worse, Clemmons had never cared for Lucy interfering in murder investigations, though over time, things had defrosted between them.

Lucy and Katie huddled together as Clemmons, along with several other officers, took pictures and processed the area. Azad stood with Lucy and Katie, but Bill had left them to confer with Clemmons.

"We just met Deacon yesterday and now he's gone," Lucy said.

"I can't say he made a good impression, but I still feel horrible," Katie said. "He didn't deserve to die like this."

Azad came from behind Lucy and began to rub the gooseflesh on her arms. "The water is freezing. He probably had a heart attack."

It was entirely possible. When the cold water had first struck her chest, she'd sucked in a desperate breath, and the muscles in her legs had cramped.

Huddled together, they watched as Bill spoke with Clemmons. Eventually, Bill's gaze met Katie's and he came over to them.

"Are you two okay?" Bill asked, his blue eyes examining his wife's face.

"We're both fine. Just a little shook up like everyone else," Katie said.

"You mentioned you both just met Deacon Spooner yesterday. What can you tell me about him?" Bill asked his wife.

Katie shrugged. "Not much. He owns, or rather he *owned*, part of the Sea View. Lucy and I visited to see about possibly having the township employee Christmas party and her wedding reception there."

"Did you know Deacon was going to be one of the participants today?" Bill asked.

"No. But on second thought, it's not surprising."

"Why?"

Lucy spoke up. "All the town businesses are supporting the event by taking the plunge, donating money, or both. I'm here on behalf of Kebab Kitchen."

"You think Deacon was representing the Sea View?" Bill asked.

"Most likely," Lucy said.

"Why? Does it matter?" Katie asked.

Before Bill could respond, Detective Clemmons strode over. His gaze homed in on Lucy. "Hello, Ms. Berberian. Why is it you always seem to be around when there's trouble in Ocean Crest?"

So much for a thawed relationship. Or was Clemmons just horribly lacking in social skills?

Lucy was aware of Azad bristling behind her, but she touched his hand to let him know she could speak for herself. "I'd hardly call today trouble, Detective. Not in the sense that you imply. The poor man most likely had a heart attack."

"You know that for sure?" Clemmons asked.

Even though she had nothing to do with the tragedy on the beach, he had the unnerving ability to make her feel anxious. "No . . . but . . . what else could it be. The water was freezing!"

Clemmons didn't answer. Rather, his lips twitched, and Lucy had the uncanny feeling he was testing her. "Don't panic, Ms. Berberian. For once, I agree with you. But we can't say for certain until it's confirmed by the coroner."

Katie blinked. "Why? Do you think he died by other means?"

Clemmons turned his attention to Katie. "It doesn't matter what I think. There can be no official statement or press release until we have confirmation." He removed a pencil that had been tucked behind his ear. "Now, if you'll excuse me, I have work to do. Meanwhile, I'm asking all the swimmers and spectators to stay until we have everyone's names."

"I'll help with crowd control," Bill said. "I hope we can get this done quickly; these folks probably want to get home and into warm, dry clothes!" He turned to face the crowd, then spread his hands at the group of gaping people. Eloisa, in her white faux fur coat, stood out in the group. "I have to ask you to all step back so the ambulance may leave."

Everyone watched in silence as the paramedics zipped up a black body bag, placed it on a gurney, then wheeled it into the back of the ambulance. The vehicle drove across the sand, followed by the coroner's car.

"Azad, after you give the police your name, can you please take Mrs. Lubinski home?" Lucy asked. "No sense for her to wait on a cold beach."

"You sure?" Azad asked. "I don't want to leave your side."

"I'm sure. This is no place for her, and I'm warmed up now. Besides, Bill will take Katie and me home."

Azad brushed her lips with his. "Just checking you're not still frigid. I'll take Eloisa home." He waved and went to Mrs. Lubinski, offered his arm, and together they spoke with a uniformed officer; then they began the walk to the street.

Once her landlady was safely off the beach, Lucy gave Katie a worried glance. "It had to be a heart attack, right?"

"Right," Katie said. "Still, someone had to see *something*. Maybe even Deacon clutching his chest or calling out for help. Who was next to him in the water?"

"It was so chaotic, I didn't see a thing," Lucy said.

Katie drew in her lips thoughtfully. "The only person I briefly saw near Deacon in the water was Susan Cutie."

"Susan?" Lucy scanned the beach until she spotted the slender blonde. Susan's complexion looked pale as parchment, and she stood unmoving by her boyfriend's side. Jake Burns leaned down to whisper in her ear.

"Susan doesn't look good at all," Lucy said.

"You think she saw something?" Katie asked.

"If she was close to Deacon, it's entirely possible she saw him die."

Noontime rolled around and Kebab Kitchen was busy and bustling.

"Where is my moussaka?" Sally cried. "Table six has been waiting!"

Kebab Kitchen's longtime waitress rarely panicked, and Lucy knew it was due to the extra-brisk lunch shift. The day after the Polar Bear Plunge, every table was filled with locals and visiting tourists. A group of customers waited by the hostess stand to be seated.

"I'll check on the food for you," Lucy said.

"Thanks!" Sally whipped out a pad and headed to another table to take their order. Sally was tall and waif thin, with pixie-style blond hair, and had always reminded Lucy of Olive Oyl from the Popeye cartoon. She was great with the customers, and she, along with Lucy's sister, Emma, were the restaurant's two main waitresses.

Lucy hurried through the swinging doors that led into the kitchen. She found Azad preparing dishes, then placing them on the stainless-steel counter for pick up. Their line cook, a large African American man named Butch, was busy helping. Butch had been with Kebab Kitchen since Lucy was in pigtails.

"Azad, are we out of the special?" Lucy asked.

Azad didn't look up as he worked. "Not yet, but if everyone keeps ordering the moussaka, we will be." He nodded to Butch on his left. "Butch is helping me with more if you want to help serve."

"Thanks." Lucy grabbed a large tray as she hurried out of the swinging doors. Reaching across the stainless-steel counter, she laid plates of steaming shish kebab, pilaf, and moussaka onto the tray and set out for the dining room.

By the soda fountain, she found Sally filling glasses with ice and drinks. "I'll deliver the food to your tables," Lucy said.

Sally shot her a relieved smile, and her festive earrings, red-and-green Christmas lights, swayed. "You're the best."

Halfway to a waiting customer, Emma stopped her. "Is that mine?"

Emma was five years older than Lucy, and the sisters looked alike, with dark, curly hair and petite builds. But where Emma was naturally skinny, Lucy needed to work out to stay trim.

Lucy shook her head. "No, Sally's. But Azad and Butch are putting out more food. I'll help you as soon as I finish delivering these."

Lucy delivered trays of food, poured coffee, chatted with regulars and tourists alike, and refilled the hummus bar with tubs of creamy hummus.

Just as the lunch shift settled down and slowed, Raffi and Angela Berberian swept through the front door.

"Hi, Lucy. We came to give you a break." Her father, Raffi, brushed her cheek with a kiss. Her Armenian father was portly, of average height, and had a balding pate of curly black hair. He'd managed the restaurant for thirty years before handing over the reins to Lucy.

Her parents were semiretired, but they still helped out by relieving both Lucy and Azad when needed. If it weren't for Raffi and Angela, Lucy couldn't have left her duties at Kebab Kitchen to participate in the Polar Bear Plunge, and Azad wouldn't have been waiting with a warm towel.

Angela planted her hands on her skinny hips and eyed

Raffi. "We would have been here earlier if your father hadn't overslept."

Her half-Lebanese and half-Greek mother was short, with olive skin and dark hair that she always styled in a sixties beehive. Today she wore a navy shirt, and the gold cross she never took off glimmered from the overhead fluorescent lights against the dark fabric. She had been a talented chef and a force to be reckoned with in the kitchen before Azad took over as head chef.

"I wouldn't have overslept if your mother hadn't kept me up at night with her snoring," Raffi retorted.

Apparently, her father wasn't in the mood to be criticized. *Oh no.* It looked like her parents weren't having a good day. Lucy knew better than to get involved in their bickering. Her parents had hot tempers, but they loved each other.

Lucy frantically looked around for help from Emma or Sally, but the two women had disappeared into the kitchen. Most likely, they were taking advantage of the lull to clean the large coffee urn before the next rush of customers. Azad and Butch were busy in the kitchen.

Just great. That meant Lucy was alone to deal with her parents.

Angela's lips thinned as she faced Raffi. "My snoring!? You could wake the dead."

"And you sound like Darth Vader," Raffi said.

Angela threw up her hands in the air. "Ugh! You're just making excuses." She turned to Lucy. "The truth is, your father is getting lazy in retirement." She picked up a stack of menus from the hostess stand, began banging them this way and that on a table to straighten them, then placing them back on the stand.

"Mom. Dad," Lucy whined. "No fighting. I've had a stressful week."

Her parents immediately looked contrite.

"You're right, sweetheart, and we're both sorry." Her mother hugged Lucy.

"We heard about Deacon Spooner dying," her father said, taking Lucy's hand in his.

Thankfully, her parents' argument fell to the wayside, and Lucy was glad for their affection. She could use their support and advice.

Angela shook her head. "Mr. Spooner had his quirks, but what happened to him at the Polar Bear Plunge is a shame."

That got Lucy's attention. "You knew him?"

"We've been in business in Ocean Crest for a long time, Lucy. All business owners know one another," her mother said.

Of course they did. After spending eight years in Philadelphia, Lucy was still getting used to the small town again. Gossip traveled faster here than high-speed internet service, and everyone knew everyone. Business folks were all friendly toward one another, too.

"Deacon always thought highly of himself," Raffi said. "He bragged he had grand plans for his catering business, and that the wedding business was lucrative on the Jersey shore. I never doubted him. Many brides want receptions on the beach. Pictures, too."

Lucy just might be one of them, but she kept it to herself. She didn't want to mention her outings with Katie looking at catering halls. Her parents had long wanted her to be with Azad, and Lucy wanted to enjoy her engagement and not rush into a wedding.

"When Deacon didn't get his permit to renovate the

Sea View fast enough, he gave the town engineer an earful," her mother said.

"Really?" Lucy asked. "How do you know?"

"James Galkowski, the engineer, is a regular at Kebab Kitchen," her mother explained.

That was food for thought. Lucy hadn't liked Deacon when she met him, but apparently his personality hadn't impressed others either.

The din of chatting customers had died down. It was the magic time between lunch and dinner, and after a crazy lunch shift, the restaurant was finally calm. Only a few customers remained finishing their meals, drinking coffee, and chatting with friends.

The sleigh bells above the front door chimed once more, and Katie came careening in. Dressed in a floral blouse with amber jewelry and dress slacks, it looked like she'd come straight from work.

"Lucy! Hi there, Mr. and Mrs. Berberian. Lucy, do you have a minute?"

Lucy raised an eyebrow. Katie would call in advance if she stopped by for her lunch break to make sure Lucy had time to sit with her. But it was well past Katie's lunch. Her friend looked frazzled, and Lucy grew alarmed.

"Sure. What's up?"

Katie's gaze traveled over her parents, then returned to Lucy. She sighed and then dropped her purse on one of the tables. "I guess you can all hear what I have to say. It will be on the five o'clock news soon enough."

"Whatever it is, it doesn't sound good," Lucy said.

"It's not. Deacon Spooner didn't die from a heart attack," Katie said.

"What do you mean? Then how did—"

"He drowned."

Lucy's brow furrowed. "Drowned? How? We never went that deep."

Katie shook her head. "No, you don't understand. Deacon *was* drowned."

Her mother gasped and made a cross with her right hand. Her father ran a hand over his balding head.

Lucy merely stared. "How do you know?"

"Bill told me. The coroner's report showed bruising around Deacon's neck and shoulders. He was held underwater."

Lucy gaped. "Held underwater? What are you saying?"

"I'm saying that Deacon Spooner was murdered."

Chapter Five

"Who would do such a terrible thing and drown Deacon?" Lucy asked.

"I don't know," Katie said. "But the organizers of the Polar Bear Plunge were required to obtain a permit for the event and keep a list of names of participants at the town hall. Detective Clemmons came into my office this morning and demanded the original copy. Someone on that list killed Deacon."

They sat in one of the maple booths in a quiet corner of the restaurant by the Christmas tree they'd decorated only days before. For the first time, the twinkling lights and silver and gold ornaments lacked a festive feel and didn't cheer Lucy.

They drank sodas with environmentally friendly paper straws and sat in brooding silence. Lucy couldn't believe the coroner's report had showed Deacon Spooner had been drowned. She'd never have thought his death was foul play.

"This is going to ruin Ocean Crest's Christmas," Katie said.

Lucy pushed her drink to the side. "I hope not."

"Who are you kidding? There's a murderer on the loose. Who'll want to celebrate at holiday parties? And what tourist would visit to see snow on the beach or any of the planned holiday festivities?"

Katie's dour outlook erased whatever hope Lucy had held on to. Tourism was big business at the Jersey shore. The summer season was their bread and butter, but the tourism authority had been successfully advertising fall and winter events throughout all the shore towns.

"I'm still in shock at the news he was murdered. I haven't really thought about all the consequences to the town," Lucy said.

"Well, I have. It's even worse that he was murdered in the ocean. All the evidence was washed away."

"Then it's good that the crime scene investigators have experience quickly processing beach crimes."

Katie's expression was level beneath blond brows. "I know that. But I've also been asking myself why Deacon was murdered the way he was. Drowning someone is very personal. The killer had to hold Deacon down until he stopped struggling. It's different from shooting someone from a distance."

Just the thought made Lucy's gut clench. "I never thought of it that way."

Katie twirled her straw in her drink. "Ever since I learned Deacon was drowned, I can't help but think about it."

"Deacon wasn't very nice when we met him. My parents told me he was arrogant and harassed the town engineer when he didn't approve the permit for the renovations of the Sea View fast enough."

"His business partner was much more down to earth," Katie said.

An image of tall Norman Weston tracking them down in the parking lot came to mind. Norman was certainly friendlier than Deacon. He'd also offered to give them a reasonable quote for both the town holiday party and Lucy's reception.

"They didn't seem to have a rosy relationship, but they survived a renovation together," Lucy said.

"Maybe Deacon had other enemies?" Katie asked.

Lucy contemplated this. "Someone must have hated him enough to want him dead. It's also possible someone saw something suspicious yesterday." Lucy twisted a cloth napkin on the table. "You said you saw Susan Cutie near Deacon in the water."

"I only saw her near Deacon for a brief time."

"I remember that Susan didn't look so great after Deacon washed ashore. Her boyfriend, Jake, was by her side," Lucy said.

"You think the cold got to her? Or do you think she saw something?" Katie asked.

"I don't know. I meant to go over to her to ask if she was okay, but I never had the chance. The discovery of Deacon's body distracted everyone. Do you think Susan knows Deacon was murdered?"

Katie glanced at her wristwatch. "If not yet, then it will be all over the news in a half hour. Why? You thinking of asking Susan if she saw anything suspicious?"

Lucy eyed her friend. "Wait a second. I'm not thinking of investigating. Detective Clemmons is already on the case. Probably Bill, too."

Katie shook her head. "Bill's recently been promoted to detective, but he wasn't assigned to the case. Clemmons is the lead."

"That's my point. Let Clemmons deal with it."

"I'm not saying we should turn into Sherlock and Watson for this crime," Katie said.

"Then what?"

"Only that Susan does make a mean pie," Katie said.

Lucy knew her friend too well. Katie was obsessed with crime-fighting TV shows like *CSI* and *Hawaii Five-O*. Lucy had always suspected her fascination with crime dramas was why she'd been attracted to Bill back in high school, when he'd announced he was going to attend the police academy. Whatever the reason, they had a solid marriage, and Katie's knowledge had helped Lucy solve more than one crime in Ocean Crest in the past.

But this was different. They had no real connection to Deacon Spooner and no reason to get involved in solving his murder. Lucy knew how dangerous it could be to get involved in police business. The authorities could handle this one.

"Fine, but I'm only interested in seeing if Susan's okay." Lucy pushed back her chair.

Katie stood. "That's it?"

"Well, that, and I do have a sudden craving for lemon meringue pie."

Cutie's Cupcakes was located in the center of town in a shopping strip nestled between the barbershop and Magic's Family Apothecary. Susan had decorated her shop with a garland around the door, electric lights in every window, and a Christmas tree that could be seen through the front window. At close observation, Lucy noticed that the tree was decorated with miniature cakes, cupcakes, and cookies.

How clever.

As soon as Lucy and Katie stepped inside the bakery, the delicious smells of baked goods wafted to them. Glass cases displayed cupcakes of every variety—vanilla and chocolate, red velvet, salted caramel, and chocolate ganache. Cookies as large as saucers occupied one shelf inside the case. A separate tall, rotating pie case was in the corner and displayed all types of pies, including apple, blueberry, cherry, boysenberry, coconut cream, and Lucy's favorite, lemon meringue. It was an assault on one's sense of sight and smell and called out to Lucy's sweet tooth.

Working in a Mediterranean restaurant was tempting enough. Lucy couldn't imagine spending her day in the bakery. She'd have to jog the boardwalk three times a day instead of three times a week.

Susan came out from the back room carrying a vanilla frosted cake and a small tray with tubes of colorful frosting. She set down the cake as soon as she spotted them.

"Hi, Lucy. Hi, Katie. Let me guess. A piece of lemon meringue for Lucy, and anything chocolate for Katie."

Susan was pretty and in her thirties, with blue eyes and shoulder-length blond hair. She wore a crisp white baker's coat.

"Yes, for the lemon meringue. You know me so well," Lucy said.

"Good guess for me," Katie said. "But instead of a chocolate cupcake, I'd like a box of your delicious muffins for Bill in the morning."

"You got it." Susan reached into the pie case, took out a lemon meringue pie, and proceeded to cut a large slice.

As much as Lucy wanted the pie, she wanted something else even more. "Susan, there was something I wanted to ask you."

Susan glanced up from placing the pie in a take-out container. "Do you want my lemon meringue recipe?"

Lucy cleared her throat. "Thanks, but I know it would

never turn out as good as yours. I wanted to ask about the Polar Bear Plunge."

Susan's hand trembled, and she stopped closing the take-out lid to look at Lucy. "I heard the official press statement on the news. That detective said it was homicide by drowning. It's horrible."

"Susan, were you near Deacon in the water?" Lucy asked.

Susan glanced down at the pie, then back up at them. Lucy sensed the shift in her friendly demeanor before she spoke a word.

"So what if I was? There were lots of people near Deacon at one point or another. It was hectic in the water," Susan said.

"I know. It's just that you looked kind of pale that day on the beach, standing next to Jake. I was going to go over to you to ask if you were okay, but I never had the chance," Lucy said.

Susan's blue eyes sparked and her mouth drew down into a scowl. "Pale? It was freezing. Not everyone has your olive complexion, Lucy."

Okay. Susan was definitely getting defensive.

"Why are you asking me about Deacon Spooner?" Susan asked.

"No specific reason. We were just wondering if you saw anything," Katie said.

Susan folded her arms across her chest and glared at them. "Just wondering? I know all about your nosy crime-solving habit." Susan raised her chin. "We're friends and both of you know me. Are you accusing me of something?"

Whoa. "No. Not at all. We're just asking," Lucy said.

Just then, Jake Burns emerged from the back room

carrying a different cake; this one wasn't iced. "I saw this back there and thought you could use . . ." He halted when he spotted them. "Oh, hello there, ladies."

Jake gifted them with a charming smile. The diamond earring in his left ear gave him a swashbuckling pirate vibe. He wore faded jeans and a plaid flannel shirt, the shirt pocket embroidered with "Boardwalk Brewery." Jake owned the small local brewery, and his family had been friends with Lucy's parents for years. Angela Berberian had introduced Susan and Jake just last year.

The relief on Susan's face at the sight of her boyfriend was clear. "Hi, Jake. You're just in time to help."

Jake shook his head. "You know I'm not good at decorating, baby."

Susan's eyes never left Jake. "You're good enough, Jake, and I'm backed up and could use your help today."

Susan was obviously using him to avoid answering any questions, but Jake had yet to pick up on her cue.

When Jake held up a hand and continued to shake his head, Susan spoke up once more. "Lucy asked if we saw anything unusual at the Polar Bear Plunge when it came to Mr. Spooner."

Jake's gaze sharpened and his attention turned to Lucy and Katie. "Anything unusual how?"

"Did you notice who was around him?" Lucy asked.

"Not really, no. But I heard about what happened to him, and that it wasn't an accident. Poor guy," Jake said.

Susan laid a hand on Jake's forearm. "It was chaotic and a free-for-all in the water. If what you're really asking is if we saw anything suspicious that could help solve Deacon's murder, the answer is no. I barely knew the guy and didn't pay him much attention." Susan slid the take-out container with Lucy's pie across the counter. A box of muffins soon followed. "Now, if you'll excuse me, Jake will check you out. I have an anniversary cake to decorate." Susan picked up the cake Jake had placed on the counter and headed for the back room just as the door opened.

And Detective Clemmons strode inside.

Chapter Six

"Why are you here, Ms. Berberian?" Detective Clemmons asked.

Lucy opened and closed her mouth at the question. Clemmons was the last person she expected to see here today. Something about the man always made her nervous. Today he wore a seersucker blue suit, completely out of season for the December weather, and a red tie. She became aware of him staring, his mustache and lips drawn downward as he waited for her to answer.

"Pie," she blurted out.

His eyebrow shot up. "Pardon?"

Lucy held up her take-out container. "I stopped by for my usual lemon meringue. Why are you here, Detective? What's your sweet tooth?"

Detective Clemmons let out a sigh and stepped to the counter, where Susan and Jake stood like silent sentinels.

"I have a few questions for both of you, Ms. Cutie and Mr. Burns," Clemmons said.

Lucy and Katie exchanged a knowing glance. *Time to go.*

Susan's face paled, not far from the shade Lucy had noticed at the Polar Bear Plunge. Jake placed a hand on

Susan's lower back, a gesture he'd similarly displayed that day. Lucy couldn't help but compare the two to yesterday.

"What's this about, Detective?" Jake asked.

"Is there a place we can speak alone?" Clemmons said.

"Lucy stays," Susan blurted out.

Lucy started and whirled to Susan. What on earth?

"Lucy's an attorney. I'd like her to stay." Susan met Lucy's gaze, her blue eyes imploring. "You'll stay, won't you, Lucy?"

Well, that was a complete change in Susan's demeanor from moments before. Susan had all but given Katie and her a boot in the rear on their way out.

Questions arose in Lucy's mind. She was no longer practicing law, but managing Kebab Kitchen. Second, she was a licensed patent attorney and had never handled criminal matters. Third, why would Susan want an attorney? She didn't even know why Clemmons was here. He could be asking all the Plunge participants standard questions and checking their names off his list one by one.

For all they knew, Lucy and Katie would be next.

"Lucy?" Susan asked again.

Detective Clemmons turned to Lucy, his expression one of impatience. His brow furrowed. "Ms. Berberian, are you representing Ms. Cutie and Mr. Burns?"

"I . . . I'm . . ."

"Say yes, Lucy." Susan's blue gaze was imploring.

"I'll stay," Lucy said.

"I'll wait outside," Katie said.

Susan walked past Lucy and mouthed the words *thank you*, then proceeded to the front door, locked it, and turned the "Open" sign to "Closed."

"What did you want to ask, Detective?" Jake asked.

"Witnesses placed you near Deacon Spooner in the water during the Polar Bear Plunge."

"What witnesses?" Lucy asked.

"That's not of importance," Clemmons said, his tone terse. "Do you disagree, Ms. Cutie?"

Susan looked panicked. "No, but it wasn't like we planned on staying close to Mr. Spooner. Once the mayor said to go, we all ran into that freezing ocean. All we could think about was getting in and out as fast as possible."

"Why did you do it?"

"Do what?"

"Why did you do the Plunge?"

"Most of the local businesses signed up to support our town's senior center and raise money for the renovation. I did it on behalf of my bakery."

"And I participated to represent my Boardwalk Brewery," Jake said.

"I did it for Kebab Kitchen," Lucy said.

Clemmons glared at her. "I didn't ask you, Ms. Berberian." He turned back to Susan. "Did either of you know Deacon Spooner?"

"Yes," Jake said. "My brewery delivers beer to the Sea View for catering events and weddings."

"What about you, Ms. Cutie?" Clemmons asked.

Susan swallowed and glanced at Jake. He squeezed her hand. "I knew him, too," Susan said, her voice low.

"How?" Clemmons inquired.

"What does it matter? All business owners know each other in Ocean Crest," Lucy said, repeating what her mother had told her.

Clemmons shot her another sour look. "Are you going to keep interrupting me?"

"It's okay, Lucy. I can answer the detective," Susan said.

"I did business with Deacon as well. I made wedding cakes for his brides."

"His brides?"

"Deacon did a lot of wedding business at the Sea View. I made the wedding cakes. Our relationship was strictly business."

"How did you get along in business?"

"Fine, up until recently. I delivered a wedding cake, and a few hours later, I received a call from the wedding planner that the cake was damaged. Deacon claimed I delivered an imperfect cake. I did not. I take pride in my work, and anyone who knows me also knows that I'm a perfectionist."

"What happened after he accused you of delivering a bad baked good?" Clemmons asked.

"We had a disagreement."

"A disagreement?"

"We fought over the phone."

"What happened after that?"

"I had to supply another wedding cake for the bride for free," Susan said. "Thankfully, I had baked one for a different wedding and was able to use that one and bake another to replace the one I sent to Deacon."

"You must have been angry."

Susan hesitated for a heartbeat. "I was. But I certainly didn't murder him over a cake."

"What was that about?" Katie asked as soon as Lucy left the bakery.

Lucy joined her by the Jeep and opened the door. She slid in the seat and reached for the seat belt. "It was awkward for sure. Why do people assume I can represent them in criminal matters?"

Katie looked at her like she was an idiot. "Didn't you spend eight years in that fancy, overpriced Philadelphia law firm?"

Lucy knew that most people thought she was a jack-of-all-legal-trades just because she'd spent almost a decade working in the city. The truth was, she'd slaved as an associate for eight years, trying to meet the firm's required billable hours before finally quitting after she'd been passed over for partner by a male associate a second time and had come home.

"I worked as a patent attorney, for goodness' sake. The closest I got to a crime was trademark infringement for a stinky cologne."

Katie waved a dismissive hand. "Whatever. But Susan asking you to stay during her questioning made her look guilty of *something*."

Lucy leaned back in her seat. "Well, she isn't. She knew Deacon Spooner and supplied the Sea View with wedding cakes. Deacon damaged one and blamed Susan. She had to replace the wedding cake for free."

Katie started the engine. "Not very nice of him, but I'm not surprised from the little we knew about him. Wedding cakes can cost up to five hundred bucks or more."

Really? That was another cost Lucy would have to consider for her own wedding.

"Susan admitted she was mad, but said she didn't kill him over it. I believe her. Killing a man over a damaged cake seems extreme to me," Lucy said.

"You think Clemmons considers her a serious suspect?"

Lucy rubbed her temple. "I don't know. But it doesn't make sense. I've known Susan for years. She may bake a killer lemon meringue pie, but she's not a killer. Someone else did it. The question is, who?"

Katie waggled a brow. "Sounds like you want to find out, Sherlock."

"Don't push it, Katie Watson." The problem was, Lucy had an inquisitive mind by nature. Law school had helped to refine it and taught her to ask questions, even if they were uncomfortable ones.

Still, she didn't know if she wanted to get involved in solving Deacon's murder, even if Susan Cutie had insisted that she stay in the bakery as her "attorney."

Chapter Seven

"How about we go Christmas tree shopping this weekend, Lucy?" Azad asked.

Using a notepad and pencil, Lucy looked up from the shelf where she was painstakingly taking inventory in Kebab Kitchen's storage room. It was the following afternoon, and she was working on her least favorite task as manager. Stainless-steel shelves lined the room and held spices, tahini to make hummus, jars of grape leaves, bags of rice and bulgur, lemons, and fresh vegetables—all the essentials of Mediterranean cuisine. Her father had never computerized the inventory, so everything had to be counted and recorded by hand. It usually took her all evening to complete. If she made a mistake and missed something, there was a likelihood that Azad wouldn't have what he needed to make a certain dish. In the past, Lucy had to rush to Holloway's Grocery in town and clean out their shelves of a specific item. According to Lucy's count, they were missing a ten-pound bag of bulgur.

She tucked her pencil behind her ear and turned toward Azad. "Tree shopping sounds wonderful. It will be my first Christmas in my new apartment and I'm excited."

"Great. I'll help you decorate with Mrs. Lubinski."

"Eloisa just might swoon." Her landlady's secret crush on Azad was not so secret. She'd clung to him like a vine on the beach the day of the Polar Bear Plunge.

Azad grinned. "I like her spirit."

"Careful, or Eloisa might take over the decorating with you while she makes me sit on the sofa with Gadoo and Cupid and act as referee."

Azad chuckled. "Now that would make for an interesting evening."

Lucy smiled as she pointed to an empty spot on the middle shelf. "Hey, do you know what happened to the bulgur?"

"I asked Butch to get it for me. Sorry, but I forgot to put it back."

Lucy shook her head. "It's not your fault. I keep telling my dad we need a computerized inventory system."

"I thought Raffi agreed."

"He claims he hasn't had a chance to look through all the estimates I gave him." She didn't add that the only reason her technology-resistant father had initially agreed to her suggestion was because it would free up her Saturday nights to date Azad. Her mother wasn't the only matchmaker in the family.

Azad leaned against one of the stainless-steel shelves and folded his arms across his chest. Broad shoulders strained against his chef's coat. "You should just do it yourself. You're the manager now."

She was, wasn't she? "You don't think my dad would have a fit?"

"Raffi probably will, but he put you in charge. I say go for it."

Azad's support was one of the reasons she'd fallen for him again after returning to Ocean Crest. He never doubted her ability. As for her propensity to solve crimes, that was a different story. He'd said he understood her need to help others, and he even admired her for it. But he'd also admitted that her crime-fighting escapades had given him gray hairs on more than one occasion.

Azad pushed away from the shelf. "Hey, I've been meaning to ask you about Susan Cutie."

A warning bell sounded in Lucy's mind and she glanced at him. "What about her?"

"I heard Calvin Clemmons is looking at her as a prime suspect in that catering owner's death."

"Where'd you hear that?"

"At Lola's Coffee Shop. Word on the grapevine is that Detective Clemmons made a visit to her bakery to ask her questions. You know how town gossip travels."

Owned by Lola Stewart, both locals and tourists gathered in the cozy coffee house every morning for great coffee and good conversation. Even her father visited every morning, now that he was retired. The coffee shop was also the premier location to hear town gossip. When Lucy had first moved back home, the way gossip spread in the small town used to bother her, but over time, she'd come to appreciate the closeness of the community.

"I know Susan is your friend and this must worry you," Azad said.

Lucy's gut tightened. "She is a friend. But how do you know Clemmons considers Susan a prime suspect?"

Azad flashed her a grin and her eyes were drawn to the sexy dimple in his cheek. "It wasn't just at Lola's. Customers don't just talk to the manager and waitstaff at Kebab Kitchen. Sometimes they ask for the chef and talk town business."

Lucy bit her bottom lip. She had no reason to doubt

what Azad had heard. "The truth is, I've been worried about Susan. I happened to be in the bakery when Clemmons showed up to question her. He has to know she would never drown someone."

How could he consider her a prime suspect already? A damaged wedding cake—even a five-hundred-dollar confection—wasn't sufficient motive for murder. Was there more? Was there something Susan hadn't told her?

According to Katie, Clemmons already had a list of everyone registered for the Plunge. He couldn't have questioned a quarter of them yet. At least he hadn't spoken to her or Katie.

Or was Clemmons working on the basis of a witness who said they'd seen Susan near Deacon in the water that fateful day?

It didn't make sense, Lucy had been in the water. It had been pandemonium, and in her opinion, any one of those swimmers could have reached Deacon and forced him underwater. It wasn't out of the realm of possibility.

Couldn't Clemmons see that?

"I have a feeling about this." Azad interrupted her thoughts. An unmistakable thread of worry laced his voice.

"Don't worry. I'm not doing anything risky."

"That's not what I meant," Azad said.

"Then what?"

"What I mean to say is that I understand. If Susan needs help, that's what good friends are for, right?"

She looked at him in surprise. Was he condoning her helping Susan? Even if that meant sticking her nose in a criminal investigation? "Azad Zakarian, are you telling me to help Susan?"

"I guess I'm saying if you happened to stumble on anything that would help her, that would be okay with me. I also understand that you'd never let down a friend. It's just one of the many reasons I find you irresistible."

Without another thought, she stood on tiptoe and kissed him on the lips.

His dark eyes flashed. "If you do that again, I think I'll skip kitchen cleanup and take you out tonight."

"Don't tempt me."

When Katie came waltzing in the restaurant later that day, Lucy knew there was more on her friend's mind than just the hummus bar for her lunch break.

She waved a copy of the *Town News* in front of her. "Check this out."

Oh no. Lucy's gut tightened with a familiar dread whenever someone thrust the local newspaper in her face. The head reporter, Stan Slade, had a history of reporting stories that affected Lucy—and not in a good way. Katie slapped down the paper on the hostess stand for Lucy to see.

Today's front page featured a picture of Deacon in a body bag being loaded into the back of the ambulance. The coroner was standing behind the gurney, his expression grim. The headline read: HOLIDAY KILLER HAUNTS OCEAN CREST.

Katie's eyebrows drew together. "This will chase away the winter tourists for sure. Stan cares more about selling papers than the town's economy. The mayor had a fit and walked into town hall and started hollering something fierce. Then he headed next door and did the same thing. Bill said the force is under pressure to find the killer fast."

Lucy didn't like this one bit. "I hope that doesn't mean the first suspect that comes to Clemmons's mind, because we both know who's on the detective's radar."

"Do you want to read the full article?" Katie asked.

"No, thanks. I think I get the gist."

For the front page, Stan Slade always selected the picture that held the most impact, whether it was an accurate depiction or not. Not long ago, a picture of Kebab Kitchen had been splashed on the front page after a food inspector, who happened to be Lucy's old high school rival, had eaten at the restaurant's hummus bar and then dropped dead in the parking lot. The paper's headline wasn't favorable. It didn't take brain science to connect the dots. Everyone who picked up the paper assumed the inspector had died from food poisoning. Lucy and her family had been in a tough spot, and it had taken some sleuthing to uncover the real reason behind the health inspector's death.

"We shouldn't be surprised by this. Do you remember our illustrious local reporter at the Polar Bear Plunge?"

"Stan is hard to miss with that camera constantly around his neck like a dog leash." Lucy froze as realization hit her. "Katie Watson, you're brilliant."

Katie looked confused. "I try. But are you going to tell me why?"

Lucy folded the paper on the hostess stand and handed it back to her. "Stan was on the beach taking picture after picture. At least one of those pictures has to be of all the swimmers in the water. Maybe, just maybe, those pictures can show who else, besides Susan, was closest to Deacon."

Katie's eyes widened as she caught on. "Or, if we get really lucky, who killed him."

Lucy grabbed her purse and stuck her hand inside to search for her keys. "I need to pay Stan a visit at work."

"Wait! Does that mean we're officially looking into things to help Susan? And when I say 'officially,' I mean just between us?"

Lucy had known the answer to that one a while back, hadn't she? As soon as Azad had said he admired her need to help others, especially her friends. "I guess we are. If the mayor is pressuring Clemmons, that means the police aren't the only ones in a hurry to figure this one out."

Lucy strode into the office of the *Town News* exactly twenty-three minutes later. The receptionist, a tiny Asian woman with long, red-painted fingernails and wearing a blazer with square shoulder pads looked up from where she'd been typing on a computer. Lucy didn't know how she managed to use a keyboard with those nails.

"Lucy Berberian to see Stan Slade." She spoke before the woman had a chance to ask.

"Is Mr. Slade expecting you?" The woman picked up her phone.

"I was one of the Polar Bear Plunge swimmers."

The receptionist was smart enough to recognize a story when one walked into the newspaper office. "I'll escort you to Mr. Slade's office."

The woman started to stand when Lucy raised a hand. "Don't bother. I know where it's located."

Lucy knocked on Slade's door once and heard a gruff voice. "Enter."

Slade sat in a smoke-filled office crammed with piles of old newspapers, stacks of papers on his desk, a single chair across from his desk, and camera equipment. He had a muscular build, and a head that appeared to rest directly on his broad shoulders. Stan Slade had left a New York City paper to become Ocean Crest's sole investigative reporter. No one knew exactly why—and his past was a mystery.

He blew out a plume of smoke. "Ms. Berberian. I wish

I could say it's a pleasant surprise." His dark eyes watched her with intensity from behind his black-rimmed glasses.

She eyed his cigarette. "I thought you'd quit by now."

"Why should I?"

"How about the Big C?"

"Other than lecturing me like my mother, exactly why are you here?"

"I saw you on the beach the day of the Polar Bear Plunge."

"It's called reporting." He puffed on his cigarette.

Lucy strengthened her resolve and stood straight. "I'd like to see all the pictures you took that day, not just the ones you published in the paper."

"Why would I show you those?" He rested his cigarette on a fish-shaped ashtray. His leather chair creaked as he leaned back.

How much to tell? Slade was no dummy, and he'd figure things out soon enough. Best to be honest about her request if she had any hope of him cooperating.

"Because I want to know if they show anything that could be used to solve Deacon's murder," she said.

His dark, beady eyes gleamed behind his glasses. "You're investigating again."

"Are you surprised?"

"Nope. I want in on your efforts this time."

"Why would I agree to that?"

He opened a file drawer in his desk and pulled out a fat manila envelope. "I had the best of my digital photographs printed. You want a peek?"

Yes. Yes, I do. He held the thick envelope like dangling fruit, and she reached for it.

He pulled it away. "Not so fast. I want the information you unearth before anyone else." At her arched eyebrow, he went on. "Let's get one thing straight. You have had more success lately solving crime than that detective. Too bad you can't split his salary."

"That's not going to happen anytime soon. But why would I agree to your terms?"

"My readers are fascinated by this story. A man is murdered in plain sight with forty-five swimmers and dozens of spectators watching on the beach. How does that happen?"

How indeed?

Lucy wanted to know the answer to that perplexing question herself.

Stan lit another cigarette even though the first one kept burning in the ashtray. "I don't want to follow you and your sidekick around as you figure everything out, but I do want you to tell me who you think drowned Deacon Spooner first. Deal?"

Lucy eyed the envelope. If she wanted to see what was behind the magic curtain, she had little choice. Even if it meant dealing with the wizard—or an ethically questionable reporter. "Fine. Deal."

Slade spilled the contents of the envelope on his desk, dozens of glossy, eight-by-ten color pictures.

Lucy moved a stack of papers from the chair before his desk and took a seat. One by one, she studied each picture. There were a lot of pictures, and she took her time examining each one. Some were of the group before they entered the ocean, others were of family and friends gathered to watch. A good amount showed the "Polar Bears" running into the water. A dozen more pictures showed the swimmers in the ocean and then running back out.

She spotted herself and Katie. She looked for Deacon in the ocean. It was hard to locate him specifically; all the swimmers appeared like tiny action figures. When she did find Deacon, she noticed the back of a blond female's head. Most likely it was Susan Cutie's, but without seeing her face, she couldn't be certain. From what Lucy could tell, different people were within a ten-foot proximity of Deacon in each picture. It seemed any of them could have reached him.

Disappointment tightened in her gut like a tense fishing line. "It was a mob scene."

Stan's dark eyes were sharp and assessing. "I studied each picture in detail. I didn't find anything to point to a killer. And I didn't capture Deacon going under. No smoking gun."

"And you were sure of this before you handed over the photos and still asked me to keep you in the loop?"

He exhaled a big plume of smoke. "Yup. What can I say?"

Lucy gritted her teeth. She gathered the photos and was about to hand them back when something—or rather someone—caught her eye. A tall swimmer in the water—a man who was at least a head taller than the rest.

Norman Weston.

Deacon's partner at the Sea View was one of the swimmers? How had she not noticed the six-and-a-half-foot man the day of the Plunge? Looking back, Lucy had been terrified of the cold and hadn't paid much attention to the other participants. She'd been too focused on calming her pounding heart and watching the ocean. It was possible Norman had been at the back of the pack. Or that he'd joined the swimmers at the last minute.

Katie had mentioned that the town had required a permit for the Polar Bear Plunge and a list of all the names of the swimmers. Clemmons had demanded the original list as part of his investigation. They needed to take a look at that list. She wanted to confirm that Norman Weston was an official swimmer and hadn't joined the group at the last minute for one nefarious purpose.

At her hesitation, Stan leaned forward in his chair. "What is it? Did you notice something?"

"Nope. Just taking one more look." She handed the pictures to him and pushed back her chair. As she reached for the door handle, he stopped her.

"Don't forget your promise, Ms. Berberian. I believe in quid pro quo."

As soon as Lucy left the newspaper office, she headed straight for Katie's work. The town hall was located in Ocean Crest's center, directly across from the library and a park. A red-brick building, it shared space with the police station but had a separate entrance. Katie worked a stone's throw—or a brick wall—from her husband, Bill.

"What'd you find out?" Katie asked as soon as Lucy walked into her office.

Lucy set down her purse on Katie's desk. "Did you notice that Norman Weston was a swimmer?"

"No. How'd we miss him?"

"He must have been behind us. Or he joined at the last minute."

"All the participants had to be registered. It was part of the permit process. They checked off our names as we showed up on the beach."

Lucy pursed her lips. "And you don't think it's possible someone could have snuck in with the group? The pictures I studied in Stan's office showed a crowd of swimmers in the water like a school of fish."

"Hold on." Katie pushed back her rolling chair, went

to a file cabinet, and whipped out a paper. She held it out to Lucy.

"Are you going to tell me what that is, or do I assume it's a large take-out order for dinner from the restaurant?"

"No, silly. It's a list of suspects."

"I thought Clemmons took the list from you."

Katie wrinkled her nose. "Don't be ridiculous. I have a copy machine."

Lucy took the paper. It didn't take her long to find Norman Weston's name. "He signed up to do the Plunge."

Katie walked around and leaned on the back of her desk, her bright eyes flashing. "So he didn't sneak onto the beach, but that still doesn't exclude him as a suspect. He was at the scene of the crime, which in this case was the freezing Atlantic Ocean."

"No, it doesn't exclude him. And as far as we could tell, Norman and Deacon didn't have a rosy relationship."

Katie tapped her foot. "*Columbo* always says the spouse—or if there is no spouse—the person closest to the victim is the first suspect."

Katie's fascination with crime television always colored her thinking, but in this case, she might be on to something. "But was their business relationship contentious enough to kill?"

Chapter Eight

That evening, Lucy tied her running shoes and headed down the stairs of her apartment and out to the street. She needed to think about what she'd learned so far, and there was no better way to clear her thoughts than her usual run. Dressed in a gray sweat suit and matching gray beanie hat, her breath made puffs of vapor in the cold air. It was dark out, but streetlamps lit her path. She jogged several blocks before she worked up a sweat.

She passed festively decorated houses, each one rivaling the next. Brilliant Christmas lights illuminated houses and yards. Decorated Christmas trees visible through living room windows put her in the holiday spirit, and Santa displays with reindeer and snowmen made her smile. An inflatable Neptune, god of the sea, dressed in a Santa suit with mermaids dressed as elves caught her eye. It may be December, but it was still the shore.

Together with Katie, Lucy had "officially" decided to figure out who drowned Deacon. So far, they had only one suspect in mind. The police had Susan in their crosshairs, but Norman Weston was in theirs. But the flimsy evidence they had was far from enough. Just because Norman and Deacon didn't always quote the same prices for their catering business didn't mean that Norman had murdered his partner. Before they could approach Detective Clemmons, they needed a suspect with a lot more motive to kill than Susan or Norman had.

Lucy made it to the boardwalk ramp, and her running shoes pounded on the boards. It was isolated in the evening, and a cold breeze blew from the ocean. A full moon hung like a Roman coin in the velvet sky and illuminated the ocean in an iridescent glow. The sounds of the waves were constant and calming.

The Ocean Crest boardwalk appeared entirely different during the winter months from the summer season. The small town would triple in size during the late spring and summer, and the boardwalk—an eclectic mix of T-shirt shops, salt water taffy and fudge candy shops, restaurants, and entertainment would come to life. A tattoo parlor, a boardwalk medium, and blacklight minigolf were just a few of the unique offerings.

Lucy would often wave to boardwalk business owners, jog back on the beach, and stop at the jetty to sip from her water bottle and observe the magnificent view when it was warm and daylight.

Lucy approached one of the year-round shops, and the boardwalk's newest attraction, Old Time Photos. The shop was closed for the day, but a large window displayed framed black-and-white photographs she paused to admire. They were of families and groups of people dressed in old-time clothing, from cowboys and Indians to 1920s flapper girls with fishnet stockings and feathered boas, to 1930s gangsters with machine guns and bags of stolen bank money. The new shop was hugely popular, and one of the boardwalk shops that could be enclosed with front glass doors and heated.

Lucy had always wanted a photo of her family and Azad, but getting together to pose was a challenge.

Lucy chugged onward and ran down the boardwalk ramp to the street. Her jogs were time to herself that she'd come to value. Managing a busy family restaurant could be stressful. She'd had to learn a lot since taking over, and she still had a long way to go. Inventory, ordering, payroll, staff schedules, and satisfying customers had been more challenging than she'd expected. Her mother's cooking lessons added another layer of stress, even though she'd come to value spending time with Angela Berberian.

Just as she turned onto her street, she spotted the silhouette of a man dressed in dark clothing and standing on the front porch of Eloisa Lubinski's home. For a heart-pounding moment, Lucy thought Vinnie Pinto had returned for a second break-in attempt.

What the heck?

Lucy unzipped the pocket of her sweatpants and pulled out her cell phone to call the police. The screen lit up and Lucy pressed nine, one . . . then stopped. As the man turned, a shaft of moonlight illuminated the side of his face.

She halted at the end of the driveway, her fingers curling around the phone like talons. "Jake Burns, is that you?"

"It's late. I didn't expect a social call," Lucy said as she poured Jake Burns a glass of milk and offered him a plate of chocolate chip cookies as they sat at Lucy's kitchen table.

The cookies were made by her ten-year-old niece, Niari, Emma's daughter. Niari told her she was taking home economics in middle school and was on a baking kick. She asked if Lucy could be her taste tester. Lucy hadn't minded—it turned out Niari could bake well and took after the rest of her family when it came to success in the kitchen.

Jake slumped in his chair. "I know it's strange, but it's the only time I could get away from the brewery . . . and Susan." He ran his hand through his brown hair and slowly released the thick strands.

"Is there trouble between you two?" Lucy asked.

Jake took a bite of cookie and set it down on his plate. "Not romantically, if that's what you're asking. I'll forever be grateful to your mom for introducing us."

"You should know Susan said the same thing."

He appeared genuine. For once, her mother's match-making had worked.

Jake took a sip of milk. "I don't mean to involve you, but since Susan asked you to stay when that detective came into the bakery to question us, I figured you're involved anyway."

She'd already agreed to help with Katie, but she held her tongue. Still, she needed to set Susan and Jake straight about legal representation. "I told Susan I'm not a criminal attorney. I can't help her legally."

Jake met her gaze. "That's not what I had in mind. Susan may not have wanted to talk to you when you first walked into the bakery asking questions about Deacon's death, but she trusts you. So do I. From what I've heard, you're pretty good at solving crimes."

"Were you honest with Clemmons?"

"I was, but after he left, I remembered something else, and I paid a visit to the station the next day. But I don't think the detective took me seriously."

"What do you mean?"

"I told the detective that I did a lot of business with the

Sea View. The catering hall doesn't have a liquor license, and I deliver kegs of beer for their events."

"I remember your telling Clemmons that in the bakery." She knew this arrangement wasn't unusual. Lucy would have to provide her own liquor if she had her wedding at the Sea View, and she would most likely reach out to Jake's Boardwalk Brewery for help.

"Yeah, well, I met Deacon's business partner that way, a man by the name of Norman Weston. Did you know Norman was also one of the swimmers at the Polar Bear Plunge?"

She'd just learned this fact. "Yes, I did. Did you tell Clemmons?"

"He said he already knew."

Of course he did. Clemmons had the list. "Do you think it matters that Norman was in the water?" She wanted to know his opinion. Jake knew Norman and did business with him.

"Oh, it matters." Jake finished a cookie, then leaned forward in his chair and met her eyes. "Last time I made a beer delivery to the Sea View, I overheard Deacon and Norman fighting. They were arguing pretty fierce, and Norman threatened to kill Deacon."

He had Lucy's full attention now. She pictured Norman in her mind. Tall and friendly, he didn't seem like the physical type, but who knew? He certainly had at least a foot advantage over Deacon.

"What were they arguing about?"

Jake shrugged. "I wasn't able to hear because I dropped the keg and the noise alerted them, but their argument had something to do with the Sea View, for sure."

If Norman threatened to kill Deacon, the business

partners had a more contentious relationship than she'd initially thought. "And you told Clemmons all this?"

"I did. He pretty much blew me off. He knew Norman had been a swimmer, and he said that he had already spoken with him."

Why had Clemmons dismissed Norman as a suspect? Or was the detective keeping Norman in mind as a suspect, second to Susan? Lucy was certain there had to be more to this story.

"I just thought you should know this," Jake said.

"Thanks for confiding in me. Susan's lucky to have you on her side."

A determined expression crossed Jake's face. "Susan needs your help. She's a baker, not a killer."

On that, they agreed.

"You think this will work?" Lucy asked.

"Absolutely. All you have to do is stick with the script and I'll do the rest," Katie said.

They were sitting in Katie's Jeep parked outside the Sea View, and morning sunlight was streaming through the window, warming their cheeks. "I'm surprised the place is even open after what happened to Deacon," Lucy said.

"Business must go on, right?"

"Still, I'm not sure if this will work."

Katie pointed to the paper on Lucy's lap. "Just hold that contract and act like a lawyer."

Lucy's fingers played with the edges of the paper. "I'm a restaurant manager, not a lawyer anymore, remember?"

"I said it before: once a shark always a shark. You can pull this off. Besides, think of Susan."

Katie was right. What was a little bluff when it could help her friend out of a sticky situation? Jake had given them a lead and Lucy's curiosity was piqued. Katie had also been curious after Lucy told her what Jake had said regarding Deacon's business partner. They needed to judge Norman Weston's reaction and they couldn't do it sitting in Katie's Jeep.

Taking a deep breath, Lucy nodded once. "Let's go." They stepped out of the Jeep and entered the front doors to the catering hall.

The Sea View appeared just as it had the first time. The tables around the room were covered with linen table-cloths, matching napkins, silver-rimmed china, and flat-ware. Rather than carnations in crystal vases, there was an arrangement of roses. The ballroom's hardwood floor gleamed from the chandeliers and the sunlight streaming through the French doors that led to a balcony overlooking the Ocean Crest beach and the ocean. It was a weird feeling of déjà vu. Except Deacon Spooner wasn't present to snatch a paper out of Lucy's hand.

"Hello?" Katie called out.

Moments later, Norman Weston appeared from a door at the end of the ballroom. Just as impressively tall as Lucy remembered, he approached with a smile, and Lucy's eyes were drawn to his pencil-thin mustache.

"I was glad to receive Mrs. Watson's call to schedule an appointment. It's nice to see both of you lovely ladies again. Have you reconsidered having your event here?"

"We weren't sure the Sea View was still open and taking reservations," Katie said.

A shadow crossed his face. "Ah, you mean because of the demise of my partner, Deacon?"

The demise? What a strange way to say "dead," "drowned,"
or "murdered."

"We were at the Polar Bear Plunge and saw Mr. Spooner
on the beach," Lucy said. "We're sorry for your loss."

"It's tragic. Deacon and I may not have always agreed
on everything, but we were friends as well as business
partners. The Sea View was recently renovated and I have
to consider paying off the loans. Deacon would have
understood more than anyone that business must go on as
usual."

Katie had used the same phrase. Norman didn't seem
broken up about his partner, but was he putting on a good
show? Or was he relieved his partner was out of the way?

Which led to other questions. Who would inherit
Deacon's share of the Sea View? Had the partners signed
a contract that provided that if one died unexpectedly, the
other automatically received the other's share of the business? Lucy had run across this type of business model for
one of her clients at the Philadelphia firm.

But if Norman didn't get the entire business, who was
Deacon's heir?

"The town is still seeking a venue for the annual Christmas party," Katie said. "And Lucy is still considering having
her wedding reception at the Sea View, but we have our
concerns."

Norman rubbed his hands together. "Please tell me
what concerns you have and I shall address each one."

Katie glanced at Lucy, signaling it was her turn. Lucy
turned to Norman and delivered the line she'd rehearsed
before arriving there. "What I never told you, Mr. Weston,
is that I returned here hours after we first met to ask some
follow-up questions about my reception," Lucy fibbed.

"And I overheard you arguing with Deacon. It grew quite heated and I left rather than interfere."

Norman's smile faded and his mustache seemed to sag. "I see."

Lucy's lie was a risk. She was particularly vague about when she'd returned and when she'd overheard the partners fighting. What if Norman and Deacon had only fought once—when Jake Burns had overheard them during a beer delivery? But Lucy was willing to bet her next paycheck that the partners fought more often . . . a lot more often. Running a catering hall or a restaurant was stressful. God only knew, Lucy's parents still fought.

Norman cleared his thought. "It's true Deacon and I often argued. It's no surprise. You met him. He could be quite disagreeable. We fought over further expanding the business to increase the number of weddings and revenue. Deacon wanted to expand. I wanted to book more weddings to pay off our current loans. I told him that if he insisted on expanding, then I wanted to sell him my share of the business. Deacon was receptive to buying me out."

If Deacon wanted to spend more cash and Norman didn't, then there was much more behind their arguments than normal, day-to-day business stress. Had Norman unwittingly just set forth motive to get rid of his partner?

"The next time we saw you was at the Polar Bear Plunge," Katie said.

"I remember seeing both of you on the beach, too. The Polar Bear Plunge has always been on my bucket list. Even though it was freezing, I'm glad I did it."

"Did you know Deacon was Plunging, too?" Lucy asked.

"I did. Deacon signed up on behalf of the Sea View. When he heard other business owners were participating, many of them partners, he wanted to be sure our business looked good." Norman cocked his head to the side and folded his arms across his chest. "Now why all the questions? None of this is relevant to whether or not the Sea View is a good venue for either of your events."

"It made us nervous," Katie said.

His gaze traveled from Katie to Lucy, and his eyes narrowed. "Wait a minute. Because of the argument you overheard, do you assume I had something to do with my partner's drowning?"

"I never thought you drowned Deacon, but I did wonder if you saw or heard something during the swim," Lucy said.

"Any information you can provide will be helpful. My husband is an Ocean Crest detective," Katie said.

"A detective already spoke with me." He pulled a business card out of the pocket of his golf shirt and read the name. "Detective Calvin Clemmons. If your husband is also a detective, then I assume you know him?"

"Quite well," Katie said. "But that doesn't put our mind at ease regarding the argument Lucy overheard."

"It's unfortunate you overheard us. We tended to get heated at times, but we always moved past it for the benefit of the business. I guarantee the Sea View is a good venue for both of your events."

Katie eyed him. "Ocean Crest is a small town. People talk. I wouldn't want them not to come to the party or feel uncomfortable because of bad gossip."

"Like I said, I had nothing to do with my business partner's death."

"We aren't accusing you," Lucy said. "But do you know who might have wanted to hurt Deacon?"

His laugh sounded hoarse. "Who wouldn't? There's a long list."

"Dislike is one thing. Murder is another."

He sobered. "I'll tell you what I told that detective. Henry Buxbaum had reason to dislike Deacon."

"Who's Henry Buxbaum?" Lucy asked.

Katie answered for Norman. "The new owner of Old Time Photos, on the boardwalk. I issued Mr. Buxbaum a mercantile permit at town hall."

"What would Mr. Buxbaum have against Deacon?" Lucy asked.

"Old Time Photos travels to locations for special events like weddings. Guests love dressing up in period clothing and having their pictures taken. Deacon didn't treat some of the vendors very nicely."

Jake had said the same thing about how Deacon had treated Susan after Deacon had damaged one of Susan's wedding cakes.

"There is another person as well. Clarissa Chase, a former angry bride, who threatened to sue Deacon and the Sea View for ruining her wedding when he double-booked her reception."

"That doesn't sound very nice, but I'd hardly call it sufficient motive for murder," Lucy said.

Norman scoffed. "That's because you haven't had your day to walk down the aisle yet, Ms. Berberian. Never mess with a furious bride."

Chapter Nine

The hissing steam of the latte machine combined with the pungent aroma of ground coffee beans made Lucy's mouth water. After leaving the Sea View, Lucy and Katie had headed straight to Lola's Coffee Shop to discuss what they'd learned so far.

Lucy sat at a cozy table in a wire-backed chair across from Katie, sipping a hot cappuccino. The combination of frothy milk and coffee was one of her favorites. The coffee shop was busy today, and there was a long line of caffeine-deprived customers waiting to be served. Others sat at tables, chatting with friends or sitting alone while working on their laptops or reading the *Town News*. Colorful water-colors of beach scenes hung on the walls and gave the coffee shop a cheery feel, while a large Christmas wreath hung above the doorway and a decorated tree was tucked in the corner. The owner, Lola Stewart, was busy behind the counter stacked with chunky white mugs and chatting with each person she served.

Katie pulled out the sheet of paper from her purse and unfolded it. As she studied it, a frown marred her brow. "I don't believe it."

"Are they on there?" Lucy asked, her voice laced with impatience.

"Yup, both Henry Buxbaum and Clarissa Chase were Polar Bear swimmers."

"Jeez! Was everyone in town seeking gooseflesh glory?" Lucy knew it was a close-knit town and everyone wanted to help the senior center remodel. She just didn't think as many people who had a grudge against Deacon would be on the list.

"I need to go over this list more carefully. We could be overlooking more suspects," Katie said.

"I still don't get either of their motives, a photographer and a bride."

Katie set down the list to stare at Lucy. "You mean you haven't heard all the gossip about Clarissa Chase?"

"No."

Katie cradled her mug and shook her head in disapproval. "Honestly, Lucy. Do you have your head stuck in the sand all the time?"

"What's that supposed to mean?" Lucy didn't thrive on gossip like a lot of townsfolk. She was too busy managing Kebab Kitchen to be concerned with who was divorcing whom, who failed to get their dog license renewed, or who decided to get a perm at the Big Tease Salon.

Katie sipped her coffee. "Clarissa was big news in town; it was all everyone talked about for weeks. She happened to be a fanatical bridezilla during her wedding planning. Everything had to be perfect. She terrorized her bridesmaids, one of them a temporary clerk at the town hall, for accidentally ordering periwinkle shoes instead of light blue to match the bridesmaids' gowns. She gave Beatrice at the Big Tease Salon hell about her updo and had her redo it three times. And she screamed at the seamstress at the bridal shop when she needed an extra day to finish her alterations."

Lucy lowered her cappuccino. "God. Smack me if I ever take out my wedding jitters on innocent people like that."

"Don't worry. I'll be happy to if you start screaming like a banshee."

"Good to know. Go on about the bridezilla."

"When Clarissa showed up for her reception at the Sea View, she had a Mount St. Helen's explosion when she found another wedding party taking place. They say her screaming rivaled the teenagers riding the boardwalk roller coaster. She paid for a front-page ad in the *Town News* saying Deacon Spooner was incompetent and to never book a wedding at the Sea View."

This had happened before Lucy moved back home and she never saw the ad. "Wow! She must have been furious. And Clarissa did the Polar Bear Plunge? Why doesn't Detective Clemmons consider her a prime suspect instead of Susan? Don't tell me he never heard this story."

"It's a good question."

The more Lucy thought about it, the angrier she got. "What the heck is wrong with Clemmons?" Lucy's voice was laced with frustration. "I think it's time I paid him a visit at the station and called him out on this."

Katie set down her mug. Her eyes darted over Lucy's shoulder and a horrified look crossed her features. A trickle of unease traveled down Lucy's spine, and she had a very bad feeling she knew exactly who was standing behind her.

* * *

"You wanted to talk to me?"

Lucy craned her neck to look up at Detective Calvin Clemmons. His brown eyes became flat and unreadable. Bill Watson stood next to him, but his attention wasn't on Lucy. Rather, he watched his wife with a critical squint.

Oh no. Lucy's bravado from seconds ago deflated like a punctured balloon. What rotten luck that the two Ocean Crest detectives had to overhear her heated speech.

With an impatient jerk, Bill motioned for Katie to join him at a separate table. He didn't look very pleased with his wife. Causing marital strife for her friend was the last thing Lucy wanted.

"I was just leaving, if you'd like to have my seat," Katie told Clemmons before leaving to join Bill at another table.

Clemmons occupied the chair across from Lucy. He'd abandoned the seersucker suit today for a collared, button-down shirt and slacks. Unfortunately, he didn't look any less intimidating. She looked at his bushy mustache. It was preferable to meeting his steely stare.

"And I thought things had improved between us, Ms. Berberian," he said, his voice a low drawl.

She wasn't fooled by the mild tone. Her mind churned as she thought of what to say. At her silence, he cocked his head and met her eyes. "Is there something you want to ask me? Or did I imagine you were talking about me?"

Lucy was irritated by his mocking tone. She'd faced opposing attorneys at the law firm on a daily basis and argued on behalf of her clients. Clemmons was no different. He considered Susan Cutie a suspect when there were others he should be looking into. She may not officially be Susan's attorney, but she was her friend.

Gathering her courage, she straightened her spine. "Yes. I want to ask you about Deacon's death."

He rolled his eyes. "Why am I not surprised?"

"Susan Cutie is a friend."

"And your client?"

"Well, no. Not exactly."

"It's a yes-or-no question."

She evaded answering. "I heard you consider her a prime suspect."

"My investigation is none of your business. But I'll answer this one question. Yes, she is."

"Why? Simply because Deacon lied about damaging one of her wedding cakes and she had to provide another one for free? Come on, Detective. You must know that's a weak motive for murder."

"You don't know everything." His response held a note of impatience.

Did he know something else about Susan? A nagging began in the back of Lucy's mind, and her fingers tensed in her lap beneath the table. After several heartbeats, she forced herself to push her doubts aside. Most likely, Clemmons was looking for the easiest answer—the easiest scapegoat to relieve pressure from a panicked mayor. "You're failing to look into other suspects," Lucy argued.

"What do you know?"

"I saw the list of swimmers. Someone else on that list drowned Deacon Spooner."

"Be specific, Ms. Berberian."

What to say without revealing just how much she and Katie had stuck their noses into the investigation? "Norman Weston was Deacon's partner."

"So?"

"They argued something fierce and he threatened to kill his partner. Norman was a Polar Bear swimmer and had opportunity to drown Deacon."

"I take it you learned this from Jake Burns?"

Because Jake told her that he'd also told Clemmons, Lucy figured it was safe to admit. "Yes. Why don't you look into Norman?"

This time, he ignored her question. "Who else?"

"What about Clarissa Chase?"

"The waitress at the Silver Diner? What about her?"

Was Clemmons as unaware of Ocean Crest gossip? Or was he playing dumb?

"Clarissa did the Plunge. She was also an angry past bride who had reason to want to hurt Deacon."

"I spoke with her. She wasn't near Deacon in the water."

Frustration bubbled inside Lucy's chest. He couldn't dismiss a suspect that quickly. "For goodness' sake, how do you know? It was hectic in the water that day. All the swimmers were packed together like sardines."

"We took everyone's statement. Another corroborated that Clarissa wasn't near Deacon."

"Who?" As soon as she asked the question, she knew Clemmons wouldn't answer. His lips could clamp tighter than a clam when it served him.

Lucy wasn't satisfied. She wanted to know *who* had corroborated Clarissa's story.

"Anyone else you and Mrs. Watson feel I should be questioning?"

"What about Vinnie Pinto?" Lucy asked.

"The man Bill Watson caught trying to break in to Mrs. Lubinski's home?"

"He was a swimmer and an attempted burglar."

"What motive did he have to kill Mr. Spooner?"

She figured that was his job to find out. She followed his example and answered his question with one of her own. "Why haven't you spoken to every single swimmer on the list you took from Katie at the town hall?"

"How do you know we haven't?" he asked.

"You haven't spoken to me or Katie." Her irritation was mounting by the second.

"Are you admitting to something?"

"No!"

His mustache turned down in a deeper frown. "Then stay out of my investigation."

"Come on, Detective. We both know Susan Cutie isn't capable of murder."

He pressed his hands flat on the table, his dark gaze capturing hers. "Under the right circumstances, Ms. Berberian, anyone is capable of murder."

Katie and Bill returned to Lucy's table after Clemmons departed. Katie slid into the chair opposite her. Bill didn't take a seat, but stood by the table.

"I take it Clemmons told you to steer clear of this one, Lucy," Bill said.

Lucy was keenly aware of his scrutiny. "I told him I'm minding my own business."

"Uh-huh," Bill said.

Once more, Lucy couldn't help but worry about Katie and Bill. She didn't want to cause problems between them.

Katie touched her husband's sleeve. "Bill, can't you help Clemmons solve this case?"

His brows drew together. "Like I told you, I wasn't assigned to it. I'm busy working another case."

Katie threw up her hands in exasperation. "What other crime can there be in Ocean Crest? Shoplifting? Unpaid library fines or traffic tickets?"

His mouth dipped into an even deeper frown. "No. Drugs at Ocean Crest High."

"What kind of drugs? There were good kids and bad kids who dabbled in drugs when we attended back then. How is it any different now?" Katie asked.

Bill pinched the bridge of his nose. "There's an increase in marijuana use at the school."

"Kids smoking joints in the lavatory? I remember the potheads when we went there, Bill. Nothing has changed."

"I get that. But there's been a big spike in dealing and use. We've gotten a lot of complaints from teachers, parents, and even other students. The complaints reached the governor, and he's made it a priority to clean up the schools. We're unsure if a student is selling the drugs or a local dealer, but it's sufficient to have me assigned to the case."

"Does it matter if it's a student or a local dealer?" Lucy asked.

"It matters legally. A while back, New Jersey passed the Drug Free School Zone. It prohibits dealing or possessing drugs with the intent to sell on school property, within a thousand feet of a school. It's a third-degree offense and carries a three-year minimum prison sentence."

"Can't you do both, arrest a pot dealer and help Clemmons solve a murder?" Katie asked.

"It's not up to me. So I'm off to investigate." He shot Katie and Lucy a knowing look and waggled a finger at them. "Meanwhile, you two listen to Clemmons and let the police handle this one. Okay?"

"We'll try," Lucy said. "But we're concerned for Susan. We don't want to abandon a friend in need."

His expression was one of pained tolerance as he looked at the pair. "That's what I'm worried about."

Chapter Ten

The fragrant aroma of lamb stew filled Kebab Kitchen. Lucy arrived bright and early the next morning to find her mother and her niece, Niari, in the kitchen. Her mother had already been busy cooking.

"Hi, Mokour Lucy!" *Mokour* was the Armenian name for aunt, or mother's sister.

Lucy hugged her. "What a nice surprise to see you in the kitchen, Niari."

Her niece was dressed in her soccer uniform of red jersey, black soccer shorts, and tall red socks. Instead of cleats, she wore slides. Her light brown hair was in a pony-tail and she had a red glitter headband that said, "Go Strikers!" She was a lovely mixture of both her parents—Armenian, Lebanese, and Greek on her mother's side and Irish on her father's side. Her niece played travel soccer and her parents, Emma and Max, drove her all over South Jersey to play.

"You're up and ready early. Where's your soccer game?" Lucy asked.

"It's a tournament in Cape May and we have the first game. Dad's coming to pick me up soon. But until then,

I'm showing Grandma what I learned in home economics class."

"She is a little chef," Angela said, her voice full of pride.

Lucy leaned against the prep table. "You mean unlike me?"

A half smile crossed her mother's face and she pinned a loose curl that had escaped her beehive. "You were different as a child, Lucy."

If different meant she'd avoided the kitchen like the plague, that was accurate. Lucy had always thought it was cruel that she was born into a family who could all cook. Angela was a talented chef. Her father could grill a perfect shish kebab. Her sister, Emma, could whip up a meal for the family in record time. It was a crime that her brother-in-law, Max, didn't like Mediterranean cuisine and was a steak-and-potatoes kind of guy.

She watched her ten-year-old niece spread bite-size, waffle-shaped pretzels on a parchment-lined cookie sheet, then top each pretzel with an unwrapped Hershey's Kiss.

"Are you making chocolate-covered pretzels?" Lucy asked.

"Special holiday ones. They're simple and so good." Niari slipped on oven mitts, opened the oven, and pulled out a tray that had already been baking. The chocolate had melted on the pretzels. Niari quickly pressed red- and green-coated candies into the center of each melted Hershey's Kiss. "I put this tray in the refrigerator for about ten minutes until the chocolate sets." Niari reached beneath the counter to show Lucy a small plastic bag with chocolate-covered pretzels inside. The bag was tied with colorful red and green ribbons. "This is what they look like when I'm done. I give a bag to all my friends."

"What a cute seasonal gift," Lucy said.

Niari untied the bag and handed it to Lucy. "Taste one."

The crunch of the salty pretzel combined with the chocolate was surprisingly good. "Yum. I may put these on the menu for dessert tonight."

Niari's face lit up. "Really?"

"Absolutely. I'll name it 'Niari's Holiday Pretzel Treats.'"

Niari removed her Kebab Kitchen apron, then hugged Lucy. "You're the best aunt. I can't wait to tell my friends. They'll be pea green with envy."

Lucy's heart squeezed with affection. Another benefit to staying in Ocean Crest had been growing closer to her niece. Lucy attended soccer games, babysat, and took Niari for funnel cake and ice cream on the boardwalk. If Lucy had returned to the city firm, she'd miss out on so much.

A meow sounded from the storage room. Lucy froze. "Oh no. Gadoo must have followed me to work." The screen door was easy to push open, and the cat had a knack for sneaking inside. He'd been doing it more often than Lucy would confess.

Angela waved a chocolate-covered spatula. "No cat in the kitchen!"

Her mother had first found Gadoo as a stray, named the cat, and started feeding him in the back of the restaurant. She may have loved the orange-and-black cat, but she was a stickler for cleanliness and never permitted him in the restaurant.

"I'll get him," Niari said, darting off after the cat.

"His treats are on the bottom shelf by the back door!" Lucy called out.

"You spoil him," her mother admonished.

"And you don't? You're the one who kept feeding him

and encouraging him to come around. You still put food outside."

Her mother's expression was one of cold dignity. "You're right. I put it *outside*. You took him into your home."

"No sense arguing. We both had a hand in spoiling Gadoo."

Niari returned victorious. "The treats worked and all I had to do was crack open the screen door and lure him out. Dad's parked outside waiting. See you both later!"

"Good luck!" Lucy and her mother called out together.

Once Niari was picked up for her game, Lucy looked to Angela. It was time to get down to business. "What are you teaching me today?"

"Pilaf."

Lucy cocked her head to the side and regarded her. "Pilaf? That's it?" The Armenian-style rice pilaf was a staple and was served with all shish kebab platters, lamb stew, and grilled sea bass.

"It's not as easy as you think."

It never is.

It had been a tough learning curve, but Lucy had been determined to learn how to cook from her mother. If she was going to manage Kebab Kitchen, she had to tackle the basics of Mediterranean cuisine. Lucy had started with hummus and shish kebab, then tackled the tricky but delicious dessert baklava, and had come a long way.

Although Angela Berberian was a perfectionist in the kitchen, she was also a good teacher. Even more remarkable than Lucy's cooking progress was that Lucy had come to enjoy their mother-daughter time together.

Her mother reached for the remote and turned on the TV mounted in the corner of the kitchen. The catchy jingle for Cooking Kurt's show sounded. The handsome blond celebrity chef with bleached-white teeth grinned as he welcomed his viewers. He folded his arms and his tight chef's coat stretched across his broad shoulders. In the background was a shiny, stainless-steel, state-of-the art kitchen. Her mother was absorbed by the celebrity chef and rarely missed one of his episodes. Her father, on the other hand, wasn't as enamored, and disliked his wife's fascination.

"When is Cooking Kurt's next cookbook coming out?" Lucy asked.

"Hmm." Angela's gaze was glued to the TV.

Lucy rolled her eyes. "Mom."

Angela dragged her eyes from the screen to look at Lucy. "What's wrong?"

"Nothing. I just asked when his next cookbook will be published."

"Oh. I'm not sure."

Angela had all the celebrity chef's cookbooks. They were glossy hardcovers with just as many pictures of Kurt as his food. Raffi Berberian hated all of them.

Her mother sighed, then returned to their task at hand. They went to work melting a good amount of butter in a saucepan, then browning egg noodles.

"The secret is to brown the noodles evenly. Keep stirring." Soon the kitchen was redolent with the delicious smell of frying noodles.

"We use chicken broth, never water, to cook the rice. You need to double the amount of fluid. If you use one cup of rice, then two cups of broth. We are cooking a lot more today so we need to adjust."

Lucy's mind went into overdrive as she worked, and she considered everything she'd learned so far about the latest murder. Her parents had been in business for thirty years and knew almost everyone in town. She was a good source of information.

"Hey, Mom, what do you know about Jake Burns?" Lucy asked.

Angela didn't look up from stirring an industrial-size pot. "He's handsome, a successful businessman, and polite. I knew he would be good for Susan Cutie."

"How did you know?"

"His family has owned that brewery for as long as Raffi and I have owned Kebab Kitchen. After his parents passed away, Jake stepped up like a good son to take over the business."

Lucy didn't miss the censure in her mother's voice. Angela had never approved of her leaving Ocean Crest to work in Philadelphia. Her parents had wanted Lucy to return home after college, marry Azad, and take over the family business together. Lucy had been stupid in love and would have willingly gone along with their plans.

But Azad had broken her heart after college, and Lucy had run instead. In hindsight, Lucy realized it was for the best. Azad had said he wasn't ready to settle down, and truth be told, she wasn't ready yet either. She'd always wonder what else there was for her out there rather than marrying the man her parents had chosen for her and adding another twig to the family tree.

She'd learned a lot since then. Eight years away had given her confidence and worldliness, and she knew that returning to Kebab Kitchen was the right decision. Her friendship with Katie was worth its weight in gold. Her relationship with Niari was special. She loved working with Emma and Sally, and she had many other good friends in town as well. As for Azad, he'd changed as much as Lucy had. They belonged together.

"I'd like to visit Jake's brewery," her mother said. "I need to order some of his Christmas ale for a holiday party I'm planning at Kebab Kitchen. Will you take me, Lucy?"

For all of Angela's independence as a business owner, she didn't drive. She'd failed her driver's license test and had promptly come home and declared the instructor was incompetent. "Sure. I'd like to visit the Boardwalk Brewery, too."

"Good. If things progress as nicely with Jake and Susan as they have so far, I wouldn't be surprised if they end up picking a wedding date before you and Azad."

Alarm bells sounded in Lucy's head. It was no secret that her mother wanted to speed along the wedding. Lucy dreaded the you're-not-getting-any-younger-and-I-want-grandchildren speech.

"Mom," Lucy whined. "You know we aren't in a rush."

"Why not? You're not getting any younger and I want grandchildren."

Lucy inwardly cringed. *Here we go.* "You have Niari."

"I want more."

Lucy knew better than to argue with Angela about Azad, weddings, and children. It was enough to make her run for the hills. She decided to change the topic to something else that had been on her mind, something that could distract her mother.

"Jake is worried about Susan," Lucy said. "The police suspect she killed Deacon. I think it's crazy."

Never looking up from her work, Angela shrugged a skinny shoulder. "Not really."

Lucy dropped her spoon and hot chicken broth splashed over her apron.

"Careful!" Angela said.

"What do you mean by 'not really'?" Lucy asked.

Her mother's expression stilled and grew serious. "Susan Cutie has a dark side. I wasn't sure I should introduce Jake to her, but then I figured everyone deserves a second chance."

"Second chance from what?"

"Susan was married before."

Lucy blinked in surprise. "Married?"

Angela's mouth took on an unpleasant twist. "Felix Shift was a bad man. He was also a cheater and had a string of women."

Lucy let out a breath. "Then Susan did the right thing to divorce him."

"I didn't say she divorced him. She killed him."

Chapter Eleven

"What!?" Lucy stared at her mother in shock.

Angela calmly wiped her hands on a clean kitchen towel and placed it on the wooden worktable. "Felix was found dead in bed after spending the night with one of his mistresses. His heart just stopped beating. The money from his life insurance policy is how Susan opened Cutie's Cupcakes."

"If he had a heart attack from sex with a lover, how could Susan have killed him?" Lucy asked.

"Felix was on heart medication. Some say Susan purposely didn't pick up his prescription from Magic's Apothecary. As a result, he died."

Lucy wrung her own apron in her hands. "That's ridiculous! Felix could have picked up his own prescription."

"Yes, but Susan did it for the five years they were married."

"It still doesn't mean she killed him," Lucy argued. "Maybe she had enough of his cheating and finally decided to stop."

"That's what the life insurance company concluded after they hired their own investigator. They wouldn't have paid Susan if they concluded she had been guilty of murder."

Lucy knew this to be true. One of her firm's clients had intentionally caused a fire that resulted in the death of her spouse. The life insurance company had claimed the policy was void and had refused to pay out.

Susan's past marriage must be what Detective Clemmons had referred to when he said Lucy didn't know everything about her friend. Still, things didn't add up, especially a strong enough motive to kill her husband. And Lucy found it hard to believe that Susan had cruelly forced Deacon underwater until he took his last breath.

"Susan must have been exonerated of all charges if she used the insurance money to open her bakery," Lucy said.

"Yes, but people still gossip. Some old-time locals refuse to buy from her bakery."

"You aren't one of them."

Angela shook her head. "No, I never believed she was guilty." Her expression turned hard. "And even if she was, her shifty husband deserved what he got."

"Mom!" Lucy was surprised at the bloodthirsty comment coming from Angela.

Her mother placed her hands on her skinny hips. "Well, if Raffi ever cheated on me, I wouldn't be forgiving."

"That would never happen." Her parents were both hotheads and often bickered, but they cared for each other. Even her mother's little obsession with Cooking Kurt would never push her father over the edge.

"I'm glad you introduced Jake and Susan," Lucy said. "She deserves happiness after being married to a cheating man."

Angela frowned, her eyes level under drawn brows.

"Let's hope I didn't make a mistake and push Jake toward a murderer."

"I'll take out the trash," Lucy said.

The rice pilaf was finished and soon Kebab Kitchen's staff would arrive to prepare for the lunch shift. Butch and Azad would arrive first, then Emma and Sally. Lucy would work on paperwork in the small office until then.

She went to reach for the trash and lug it to the outside dumpster when her mother grasped her chin and gave her a peck on the cheek. "You're coming along in the kitchen. I'm proud of you, Lucy."

Angela rarely spoke words of praise, and Lucy basked in the attention.

Her mother squeezed her hand. "Now, hurry up and pick a wedding date before I turn completely gray."

So much for praise.

Angela removed her apron and tied it on a hook on the door, then waved to Lucy on her way out. "I'm off to meet your father at Lola's for strong coffee."

Lucy waved. Not long ago, her mother had complained about her father's coffee habit at Lola's Coffee Shop every morning, but after learning Raffi missed socializing at the restaurant after retirement, her mother had decided to join him a couple of times a week.

Lucy tied the trash bag and headed for the storage room and out the back door. She hefted the bag over her shoulder and walked to the dumpster in the corner of the parking lot.

A rumble of a garbage truck sounded from somewhere down the street.

Just in time.

Moments later, a trash truck turned the corner and came

into view. Big black letters on the side of a dingy, white truck read, "Citteroni Sanitation." It stopped at the bicycle rental shop next door and the sound of the hydraulic compactor screeched as it compacted the trash in the back of the truck.

Next, the trash truck turned into Kebab Kitchen's parking lot. She raised her hand to wave to the driver, then froze. Vinnie Pinto was in the driver's seat. Her mind flashed back to when he'd tried to break into her home and she'd called the police. She shivered.

Vinnie noticed her at that exact moment. His eyes narrowed, and his lips curled into what could only be described as a menacing and threatening look.

Two hours later, Lucy was still haunted by Vinnie's expression as she walked along the fence that separated Kebab Kitchen from the bicycle rental shop next door. She followed along the fence, then walked into the driveway of the neighboring business.

Citteroni's bicycle rental was closed for the winter, but the garage was open and the lights were on. In just a few months, the shop would be busy renting bicycles, tricycles, and four- and eight-person surreys to tourists who rode up and down the boardwalk and through town.

"Michael?" She stepped into the garage. A shiny black and chrome Harley-Davidson was on display. Lucy's heart pounded every time she saw the powerful motorcycle. Riding on the back of the bike with its owner was an unparalleled thrill.

Michael Citteroni stood behind a bicycle, where he'd been changing a tire. He was tall and dark and had the looks of a male model. His blue eyes rivaled the Ocean Crest sky on a hot summer day. His faded jeans hugged his legs and rode low on his hips. Despite the cold temperature in the garage, he wore a white T-shirt. A black leather jacket hung on the handlebars of a bicycle.

"Hey, Lucy. Good to see you." Michael's lips curved into a grin. He wiped the grease from his hands on a towel and set it down on a workbench.

"It looks like you're busy," Lucy said.

"Not as busy as Kebab Kitchen has been."

"You spying on me?" she joked.

"Nah. But I do see the cars that come and go. People still need to eat, even when it's cold out. But winter means bicycle maintenance for me."

Michael had taken over the business at his father's urging. She shared a strong kinship and a friendship with Michael. They both had overbearing, ethnic fathers who had expectations for their children that could be stifling. Raffi had handed Lucy an apron on her first day back in Ocean Crest. A waitress was on maternity leave, and family helped family. Likewise, Michael had been pressured to run the bicycle shop.

Michael's father, Anthony Citteroni, had numerous businesses—the bicycle rental, laundromats, and trash trucks. Ever since Lucy was a kid, there were rumors that Anthony was a mobster who used his numerous legitimate businesses to launder his illegal profits from Atlantic City. Lucy had met Anthony Citteroni on numerous occasions. He no longer frightened her, but at the same time, she wasn't entirely at ease around him.

"It may be cold, but I still ride the Harley. It needs some work. Want a ride when it's fixed?"

"You know I'd love it." The wind in her face and the

thrill of riding the Harley-Davidson on the Garden State Parkway wasn't something she'd ever give up. At first, Azad had been jealous, but he'd come to understand her friendship with Michael.

"Hey, Michael. Does your dad still own the trash trucks in town?" She'd seen his name on the side of the truck, but she wanted to be sure he hadn't recently sold the business.

"Citteroni Sanitation is one of his most profitable businesses." Michael didn't need to specify one of his father's *legal* businesses.

Lucy played with a stone with the toe of her shoe. "Do you know one of the drivers, Vinnie Pinto?"

Michael leaned on the workbench. "No, I don't know all his employees. Why?"

"Vinnie was one of the swimmers at the Polar Bear Plunge."

"Where that guy drowned?"

"His name was Deacon Spooner."

"I remember the news. Deacon didn't just drown, right? Someone held the poor guy underwater. And you want to know more about Vinnie because you think he was involved somehow?"

"Well . . . kind of."

He pushed away from the workbench to walk close. "You can be honest with me, Lucy. I know how these things keep you up at night."

No sense hiding it. Michael was a good friend and knew her well. "The police think Susan Cutie did it."

He looked at her in surprise. "The baker?"

"She didn't do it," Lucy said. "She asked me to help find out who drowned Deacon."

"And you think this Vinnie guy had something to do with it instead?"

"Possibly. Like I said, he was a swimmer. He also tried to break into Mrs. Lubinski's home when I was alone in my apartment upstairs."

Michael's blue eyes narrowed and his expression turned fierce. "Hell. Why didn't you just say so? I'll call my dad and ask him to meet us."

Chapter Twelve

"If Clemmons isn't going to follow up with Ocean Crest's most infamous bride, we should," Katie told Lucy over the phone early that morning.

"You want to confront Clarissa Chase where she works?" Lucy asked.

"Why not? She's a waitress at the Silver Diner. We can enjoy an omelet and grill her at the same time. She'll never notice."

After thinking about it some more, Lucy agreed it was a good idea. Clemmons had only interviewed Clarissa once. He'd told Lucy someone had confirmed her story that she wasn't near Deacon in the water, but Clemmons hadn't given a name.

And even if he had, Lucy wasn't convinced. She vividly recalled that numbing, chaotic swim. Who could be sure someone hadn't reached Deacon and pushed him under?

That morning, the Silver Diner had a steady stream of hungry patrons. New Jersey was known for its classic diners, and the Silver Diner was typical. The exterior was a shiny stainless-steel that looked like an oversize trash can, and the inside included pink vinyl booths and fluorescent lighting.

"Just the two of you?" A hostess, a thin high school girl with dyed purple hair and a nose piercing, was waiting with a handful of menus by a hostess stand.

"We'd like to sit in Clarissa's section," Katie said.

The hostess selected two menus, then led them to a cozy corner booth for two. Lucy settled across from Katie and a blast of air blew down her neck. Gooseflesh rose on her arms. She looked up to a vent on the ceiling above her.

"It's freezing in here." Lucy pulled on a light running jacket. "Don't they know it's December?"

"Maybe it's a bad omen."

"Of what?"

"Clarissa's section is frigid. She doesn't want us to ask questions."

"That doesn't make sense. The hostess seated us, not Clarissa."

Katie rested her elbow on the table and whispered, "What if Clarissa knew we were coming and told the hostess to seat us here?"

"For God's sake, how? You're sounding like Madame Vega." The boardwalk medium made predictions like that, not Katie.

"It's not fortune-telling. I don't need to remind you about the Ocean Crest gossip mill, do I?"

"You can't be serious? As far as anyone knows, we're hungry for a waffle."

"*Shh.* Here she comes."

Lucy's head swiveled to see a waitress approach. Curvy, with highlighted auburn hair and brown eyes, she wore a skintight, black, V-necked T-shirt with printed white letters that read "Silver Diner," black leggings, and a red apron. Either she was wearing a Victoria's Secret push-up bra or she was very well endowed, because her cleavage was impressive.

"Hi there. Can I start you off with some drinks?" She pulled a pad and pen from her apron.

"Two coffees with tons of cream," Katie said.

"I'll be right back to take your order." Clarissa turned to leave.

"Wait a sec. We have a question," Lucy said.

Clarissa flipped open her pad and began to read in auto pilot mode. "Today's breakfast specials are cheese blintzes, apple cinnamon pancakes, waffles à la mode, and—"

"It's not about the specials," Lucy said.

Clarissa pursed her lips. "You want to know about something else on the menu?"

"Not about the food either."

"If it's about directions, I'm awful and will get you lost. Ask the manager."

"No. It's about Deacon Spooner's murder," Lucy said.

Clarissa stiffened. She lowered her pad and pencil as her eyes narrowed on Lucy. "That son of a bitch?"

Whoa. If Lucy had any doubts about Clarissa's feelings toward Deacon, they were as solid as cured concrete now.

Lucy cleared her throat. "Yeah, Deacon."

"What do you want to know?" Clarissa asked.

"We know you had past dealings. Something about your wedding?" Lucy hoped the question would inspire Clarissa to speak.

Clarissa's eyes turned icy. "Everyone with ears knows about my feud with that guy. Now, why are you two really here? To eat or to interrogate me?"

"Both."

She turned to leave. "You should get another waitress."

"Wait! The truth is, I'm engaged." Lucy held up her

hand to display her diamond engagement ring. "I'm looking for places to have my reception and the Sea View is one of them. I spoke with Deacon, but things didn't go so well. Then his partner, Norman, gave me a better price. But I thought to talk to others who had experiences before I made my decision."

"You want my advice?"

At Lucy's nod, Clarissa tapped her pad with her pencil. "Don't do it. Evan and I had just exchanged our vows and were in the limo headed to our reception. It was supposed to be the happiest day of my life. It turned out to be a nightmare. Deacon Spooner stood at the top of the stairs and told me to get out. He ruined my life that day."

"Perhaps you overreacted? You married the man you loved, right?" Lucy asked.

Clarissa snorted, an unladylike sound. "Evan left me soon after. I blame Deacon."

"That seems like a stretch," Katie said.

"Does it? Deacon didn't just ruin my day. He stole my down payment. I was bitter afterward. Extremely bitter. I couldn't let it go. I took out a nasty ad in the *Town News* and it still wasn't enough. Nothing short of the Sea View going bankrupt would satisfy me. Evan claimed he couldn't deal with me anymore. He ran away with a coworker."

"I'm sorry," Lucy said.

She ceased tapping on her pad and directed her full attention on Lucy. "No sorrier than me. My advice to you is not to have your wedding reception there. The place is cursed."

Lucy decided it was time to bring up another topic. "We were swimmers at the Polar Bear Plunge. We saw you there."

"It's not a secret. But you can't pin the drowning on me. I wasn't near the jerk."

Clemmons had said the same thing. He'd also claimed there was a witness to back up her story. Lucy still found this suspicious. If she had been determined enough, she could have pushed swimmers aside to reach Deacon.

"Besides," Clarissa said, "word on the street is, the police consider Susan Cutie a suspect."

"She didn't do it," Lucy said.

Clarissa eyed her. "You sure about that?"

Clarissa's tone told Lucy that the waitress knew something. Something critical. Lucy's heart hammered in her chest. "What do you mean?"

"I returned to scream at Deacon many times after my doomed reception. I naively thought he would return my down payment. I had to sue him to get a portion of that money back. During one of those visits, I overheard Susan and Deacon fighting in the kitchen."

Lucy knew all about the damaged wedding cake and assumed that was the argument Clarissa was referring to.

"Susan threatened Deacon with grave harm."

"You overheard Susan threaten Deacon over a damaged cake?"

Clarissa's face screwed into a confused expression. "They weren't fighting over a damaged cake. They were arguing over Susan's reputation. Deacon told prospective brides that her cakes were awful. Susan was hollering something fierce that Deacon's lies caused her to lose a lot of business. He laughed in her face. That's when she threatened to bash his head in with a rolling pin."

Lucy glanced at Katie. From her friend's parted lips and stunned expression, she knew she was just as surprised. This must be what Clemmons had referred to when he said there was more to Susan's motive than Lucy knew. After Clemmons had questioned Clarissa, he must have learned about the damage to Susan's business and her retaliatory threat toward Deacon.

"Susan's our friend," Lucy said dumbly. "I can't imagine her killing anyone."

Clarissa's gaze sharpened. "Maybe you don't know her as well as you think. As far as Deacon is concerned, Susan beat me to it. If I could have drowned the bastard, I would have."

Lucy and Katie both ordered waffles à la mode, with strawberry ice cream for Lucy and chocolate for Katie.

"This is so decadent," Katie said. "How many calories do you think are in one of these Belgian babies? I'm thinking that combined with the ice cream, there are more points on this plate than in Weight Watchers' entire daily intake."

The combination of the Belgian waffle and the strawberry ice cream was an incredible sugar shot. Lucy wondered why she hadn't indulged in this breakfast treat before. She'd have to take Niari out for breakfast one day.

"Don't think of the calories. We deserve a treat after what we learned this morning," Lucy said. "But we'll have to ask the hostess for our check. I don't think Clarissa plans on coming back to our table any time soon."

Clarissa had delivered their plates, then traipsed off without a backward glance. Clearly, their conversation about Deacon was as dead in the water as he had been.

Lucy cut a large piece of waffle, scooped up a good dollop of strawberry ice cream, then shoved it all into her mouth. She took her time chewing before swallowing.

"I'm still stunned about Susan. I never pegged her for the violent type."

"Deacon maliciously damaged her business with lies. Brides want the best, especially if they're paying a lot of money for a wedding cake. Wouldn't you be mad if someone spread bad rumors about Kebab Kitchen?"

Lucy lowered her fork. Looking at it from Susan's perspective, Lucy admitted she would be angry. When Stan Slade printed that innuendo about the town health inspector being poisoned to death after eating at the hummus bar, Lucy had been furious. She'd wanted to wrap her hands around Stan's thick neck and squeeze.

Lucy reached for her water glass. "I guess you're right. But just because Susan screeched at Deacon and threatened him with a rolling pin doesn't mean she'd actually kill him."

"I'm not saying she's guilty, only that she had motive. Clemmons must know this by now," Katie said.

"Clemmons insisted that I don't know everything about Susan. At first, I was worried; then I thought he was bluffing and dismissed it. You said he's under pressure from the mayor to find the killer before the crime affects holiday tourism. But we're not at a dead end."

"What are you thinking?" Katie asked.

"I'm thinking we should have a chat with Henry Buxbaum, the owner of Old Time Photos. He's the only other person Norman mentioned who hated Deacon. Want to go for a boardwalk jog later today?"

A faint glint of humor lit Katie's eyes. "Good idea. How about three o'clock? It's your break time at the restaurant, and I can get off early."

* * *

When Lucy returned to Kebab Kitchen later in the morning, Sally was already there. The linen truck had delivered a stack of pristine white tablecloths and Sally was in the process of covering each table. With a flick of her wrists, a billow of linen covered one of the tables.

"Hey, Sally. Why are you here so early?" Lucy asked.

"I could ask the same of you."

"I'm the manager. I have stuff to do in the office."

Sally leaned on the table and faced her. "By stuff, do you mean work on your investigation?"

Lucy eyed the waitress and friend. Sally had worked at the restaurant for years, and she knew each of Lucy's family members as well as her own.

"What makes you think I'm investigating?" Lucy asked.

Sally's brows rose in twin arcs. "I know the slight signs. Coming in early, or leaving early. Hushed phone calls with Katie Watson. And surfing the internet for addresses not related to food. No sense hiding it from me."

"Fine. Katie and I had breakfast at the Silver Diner and spoke with Clarissa Chase."

"The pissed-off bride?"

Lucy wasn't surprised Sally had heard of Clarissa. According to Katie, everyone in town had heard of the feud between Clarissa and Deacon. But Sally was even more attuned to Ocean Crest gossip than the average person. She was a walking encyclopedia of townsfolk and knew all the locals who passed through the restaurant's doors. She remembered things about each customer that Emma and Lucy couldn't, such as the birth of a baby, a sweet sixteen, the facts of a troublesome divorce.

"Did you find out anything?" Sally asked.

Lucy reached for a tablecloth on the stack and shook

it out. "Mostly that more people than I thought disliked Deacon Spooner."

"But you don't think Susan killed him?" It was delivered more as a statement than a question.

"I don't. She had good reason to dislike him, but I still can't believe she drowned the man in cold blood . . . or freezing, cold water."

Sally captured a free end of the tablecloth and helped Lucy cover the next table. "Be careful, Lucy. You know I've always supported your sleuthing in the past, but this whole thing is disturbing. Something strikes me as odd. A man is killed in broad daylight in front of the entire town and no one sees a thing?"

She wasn't the first person to say the circumstances of Deacon's drowning were unnerving. "I'm being careful. No clandestine break-ins or sneaking around. Katie and I are visiting people during business hours."

"Good. That puts me at ease. And I'm not the only one."

"You mean Azad?" Lucy asked.

Sally shrugged. "Sure. But I was thinking of your parents. Raffi and Angela would have a fit if they thought you were focusing your time on crime-solving rather than wedding planning."

Chapter Thirteen

Running with Katie had its challenges. Katie's longer legs were harder to keep up with and Lucy had to quicken her pace to match her stride. Running hadn't come easy to Lucy, but she'd been training for months now and her stamina had increased.

They made it to the boardwalk ramp. It was a cold afternoon, and they both wore long sleeves and sweatpants, but soon enough they took off their beanie hats and gloves and shoved them into their pockets.

On their left were the boardwalk shops, and a cool breeze blew off the beach from the Atlantic Ocean on their right. Lucy breathed in the scent of salty air. A lone seagull circled above. In just a few months, dozens of seagulls would circle the beach and swoop down as tourists ate hot dogs, popcorn, and French fries and dropped food or missed the trash cans.

"We need to do this more. You want to be in shape for the wedding," Katie said. "And I need to fit into a matron of honor dress."

"You're tall and thin. Everything looks good on you."

"You're going to look beautiful. I picked up some more wedding magazines for ideas."

"Oh brother." The fashion magazines showed glossy covers of ridiculously tall and rail-thin models in billowy gowns. "Not one of those models is petite."

"It's all in the tailoring."

"That's a nice way to say a seamstress is going to have to cut off yards of expensive silk."

"Whatever it takes."

Together, they jogged past shops closed for the day, including Madame Vega's fortune-telling salon, the tattoo parlor, and a T-shirt shop. Soon, Old Time Photos came into view.

Norman Weston had said the proprietor, Henry Buxbaum, was also a photographer who worked at the Sea View, taking photographs of wedding couples.

They slowed to a stop. Framed sepia pictures of tourists in old-fashioned costumes hung on the walls and in the window: people dressed as Union soldiers, outlaws, flappers, American Indians, saloon girls, distinguished families, mobsters, and bank robbers.

Inside the shop, a family dressed as hillbillies were having their picture taken. A man holding a camera was positioning each family member. Green-eyed, with a tumble of blond hair, he looked friendly as he moved efficiently and raised his camera to snap pictures.

"Bad timing. Henry's busy. We aren't going to be able to talk to him," Katie said.

"It's not a waste. It's surveillance. Plus, it gives me an idea," Lucy said. "We haven't had a Berberian family Christmas photo taken. Now that I'm engaged, Azad should be included, too. I just need to sell the idea to my parents that a themed photograph would make for a great Christmas picture."

Katie gave her a sidelong glance. "Lucy, you sneaky

girl! Why didn't I think of that? You can snoop while getting a unique family photo."

"I'm surprised you didn't think of it. You're usually on top of these things, with all the crime-fighting TV shows you watch."

"You're learning from me." A note of pride laced Katie's voice.

Lucy poked her in the arm. "Don't get a big head."

"Still, I wish I could come along."

A thought occurred to Lucy and she shook her head. "It's for the best if you don't. I saw the way Bill looked at you in the coffee shop when Clemmons sat down in your seat. I don't want to cause any more trouble between you and Bill."

"Oh, posh. Bill doesn't dictate all my actions. Plus, you're my best friend. I think he's used to us getting into scrapes."

"That's what I'm afraid of."

"What a good idea for a family Christmas picture, Lucy," Emma said.

It was the following day, and Lucy and her sister were flipping through photo albums of sample pictures of people dressed in old-time costumes. The photos were a mixture of sepia, black-and-white, and color prints.

"I'm still surprised Mom and Dad went along with it so easily." Lucy glanced at her parents, who were talking to the owner of Old Time Photos. She needed to chat with Henry, but in private.

Emma turned a page. "Niari convinced them. Leave it to a preteen to persuade her grandparents of almost anything. Max was even easier. She has her dad wrapped around her pinkie."

Max was the self-professed king of real estate in Ocean Crest. He'd introduced Lucy to Mrs. Lubinski and was responsible for getting her the upstairs apartment, a place within walking distance of Kebab Kitchen that was within her budget.

"Look at this one." Emma pointed to a picture of a group dressed as 1930s gangsters. "Azad would make a perfect gangster."

Lucy laughed, and Azad, who had been checking out the fake antique bar and empty bottles of Jack Daniel's on the bar shelves, turned to catch her gaze. With his dark hair and eyes, he'd look striking as a cowboy *or* a gangster. The image was enough to make her pulse race.

Niari came over, her blue eyes shining. She held a feather headband and placed it on her head. "I like this one. What do you think, Mokour Lucy?"

"I think you'd make a great saloon girl. You just need a dress and fishnet stockings and you're set," Lucy said.

An excited look crossed her niece's face and she grasped Emma's hand. "Lucy's right. Help me pick out an outfit that fits, Mom."

Emma shot Lucy a helpless look as her daughter dragged her toward the back, where the wardrobe room was located.

Raffi waved Lucy over to where he stood with Angela, talking with Henry. "This is our youngest daughter, Lucy, and the newest manager of Kebab Kitchen."

"Nice to meet you." Up close, Henry appeared to be in his midthirties with fair skin, blond hair, and a lanky build. He had delicate features that were pretty enough to border on the feminine. He extended his hand, and Lucy found it soft and slightly damp.

"We're looking forward to having our family picture taken. Your place seems like a lot of fun," Lucy said. "How long have you been here?"

"Only a few months. I looked at all the Jersey shore towns and settled on Ocean Crest's boardwalk. There is a diverse mix of shops on this boardwalk and I knew an old-time photo shop would fit right in."

"Do you take other photographs?"

"I've been known to take odd jobs here and there, like birthday parties or anniversaries."

"How about weddings?"

A cloud crossed his face. "At times. Why do you ask?"

Lucy opened her mouth to explain, but her mother beat her to it.

"Lucy just became engaged," her mother said, a note of unmistakable pride in her voice. "To the young man over there." She motioned to where Azad stood.

"Ah, congratulations are in order," Henry said.

"Thank you." The anxiety in his voice had been clear. Why? Was he thinking of his experience at the Sea View? Norman had said Deacon had mistreated the workers, including Henry when he'd taken the pictures.

Henry picked up a framed picture from the wall. "Your parents picked the gangster theme, just like this one."

Had they heard Emma suggest it, or had they picked it all on their own? Lucy turned to her dad. "Gangster? Not western like John Wayne? I know how much you like watching those westerns."

"I suggested it," Angela said. "Your father looks like Al Capone. Short, dark, and heavy."

"Mom!" Lucy said. "That's not nice."

"Why not? It's true."

Raffi turned to Angela. "You chose it because you want to stand behind the bar like a gangster's wife and rule over the family."

"Dad," Lucy drawled.

"Whatever the reason," Henry interrupted smoothly, "it's one of our most popular themes. The wardrobe room is in the back. Pick what you like and what fits, then come out and we can get started."

"Good idea." Lucy grasped both her parents' arms and steered them toward the back. "Everyone is already getting dressed. You two need to stop bickering. It's a Christmas picture, remember? The season is about peace."

After ushering her father toward his room, she kept her hand on her mother's arm and steered her toward the opposite door. The wardrobe room was packed with all types of costumes—colorful flapper dresses, saloon lady dresses, hillbilly overalls, Indian leather outfits, and an array of fishnet stockings, feathered headdresses, and headbands.

"This place is girl heaven," Emma said as she reached for a bright pink feather boa.

Niari held three feathered headbands, pink, blue, and yellow. "I can't decide on a color."

"Try them all on to see which looks best," Angela said. Her prior bickering with Lucy's father was forgotten as she became engrossed in the selection of hanging costumes.

After Lucy dressed in a fuchsia saloon barmaid dress, fishnet stockings, and a feathered headdress, she looked in a full-length mirror. "You look like a madame," Emma said.

Lucy burst out laughing. She did look like a femme fatale. Her dark curls were styled across her shoulders and the dress was laced tight. She felt quite attractive. What would Azad think?

By the time they finished, the sisters were dressed similarly, but in different-colored dresses. Emma chose bright yellow. Niari wore a demurer pink dress. Angela chose a different-styled red dress with a pleated neckline and satin gloves that reached her elbows.

Azad was the first to emerge. She'd been right. He looked devastatingly handsome in a pinstriped suit that accentuated his broad shoulders and trim waist. A hat completed his look. His eyes flared when he spotted her.

"Wow! You look amazing. I think I want to buy this dress for you."

His expression made her pulse pound. "Thanks. You look like a sexy gangster."

"I never thought of a gangster as being sexy."

"Maybe I should have said one of Capone's lackeys. Or hitmen. You could pass for both."

He laughed. "I'm happy you invited me for the family photo."

She cocked her head to the side and regarded him. "You've always been family. Especially for my parents." Kebab Kitchen had been his first job as a teenager in high school. He'd worked his way up from dishwasher to busboy to line cook. Now he was the head chef. Her father had once said the restaurant was in their blood. She'd always thought she was exempt, but she'd come to realize her father was right.

It was in their blood. Azad's, too. He'd left to work as a *sous* chef in a fancy Atlantic City restaurant, but had come back home to Kebab Kitchen.

And to her.

She was grateful.

"And what about you?" Azad asked. "Am I family?"

She held up her hand and showed off her diamond. "I'd say this makes us legit."

Azad lowered his head to kiss her. At the touch of his lips, her senses heightened pleasurably. Hidden behind the curtains, she leaned into the kiss and pressed her hand on his chest. She could feel his heart beat strong beneath the costume.

Just then, Raffi emerged from the dressing room. "Oh, sorry!"

Lucy and Azad jumped apart, but from the look on her father's red face, he was more embarrassed than they were.

Lucy's gaze took in her father's getup and burst out laughing. Her mother was right. He *did* look like Al Capone.

"That bad?" Raffi asked.

"No, Dad. It's perfect."

Before he could respond, Angela appeared. "He is perfect."

Rather than be offended, her father took her mother's arm and kissed the back of her hand. "You look lovely."

Angela's expression softened as she gifted him with a warm smile, and her parents walked toward the bar. Lucy shook her head at their obvious affection and trailed behind them with Azad.

"I'll never get them," Emma said as she joined Lucy's side.

"Even after all this time, they just like to give each other a hard time only to make up soon after."

"It's exhausting. I swear, it's because they work together."

Lucy's stomach tightened at the thought. She worked with Azad. Would they end up like her parents?

God, she hoped not. Even though Raffi and Angela loved each other, she didn't want her parents' marriage.

Henry clapped his hands. "Everyone, get in your places and I'll start shooting."

Fifteen minutes later, Lucy looked at the completed digital photo of her family. Her mother was behind the bar, a serious look on her face, her gold cross shining. Her father leaned on the bar, holding a revolver. Max was next to Emma with Niari sitting on the bar between them. Lucy was seated on the bar as well, and Azad leaned against it. It was unique and perfect, and she'd hang it on the wall of Kebab Kitchen behind the hostess stand for the Christmas season.

"It will take about twenty-five minutes for the pictures to print, then another ten for me to frame the large one. Who would like to wait?"

"I will," Lucy was quick to volunteer. "I'll meet you all at the restaurant." The perfect opportunity to question Henry had just landed in her lap.

Chapter Fourteen

After her family departed, Lucy hoped to talk to Henry, but he hurried into a back room to see to the printing.

Left alone, she studied the framed pictures on the wall. Her lips curled in a smile as she went from picture to picture to see babies dressed as hillbillies, a bachelorette party dressed as saloon girls, and a group of retirees from the senior center dressed as cowboys and Indians. She spotted her landlady, Eloisa, as an Indian maiden and laughed out loud.

She moved on, studying each one, until one picture caught her eye. It was an image of Henry and Deacon. She leaned closer, studying the black-and-white print. Both were dressed in western gear. A sheriff's star was pinned to Deacon's leather vest and he wore a large-rimmed western hat. Henry had on a plaid shirt, jeans and chaps, and a smaller hat. A bottle of whiskey was on the bar next to two shot glasses. They both looked happy. She reached for the frame and removed it from the wall to study it more closely.

"Everything is printing and should be ready quickly." Henry froze as he spotted the framed picture in her hand. "Where'd you get that?"

Lucy waved at the wall. "Is this you with Deacon Spooner? The man who was drowned?"

Henry's mouth drew downward. "I should have taken that down."

"Is that a yes?"

"He was my uncle."

She experienced a stab of surprise. His uncle? That would explain why they'd posed together for this photograph. Who would have guessed? Other than the fair hair, they didn't look alike. Deacon had dark eyes, and his features were coarse and pockmarked, Henry's more refined. Their builds also were dissimilar. Henry was lanky, and Deacon had been stocky.

Which led to another thought. Why hadn't Norman Weston mentioned that Henry was Deacon's nephew? Was it possible he didn't know? Norman had said Henry and Deacon had argued over business. What kind of business argument could result in Henry wanting to kill his uncle?

Lucy grew aware of Henry staring at her. "I'm so sorry for your loss," she blurted out.

"Thanks. His death was unexpected."

Unexpected, not a shock.

She cleared her throat. "You look familiar. Were you one of the swimmers at the Polar Bear Plunge?" Thanks to Katie's list, she already knew the answer, but she was careful to school her expression into one of innocence.

Henry looked at her with renewed interest. "Yeah. Were you a swimmer, too?"

"I was. It went well until the very end. Your uncle's death was distressing."

"Yes, it was."

"Were you with him in the water?"

Henry's green eyes flashed. "No! Whoever was next to Deacon was the one who drowned him."

"I didn't mean it that way. I was just wondering if you saw anything suspicious?" she asked.

"No."

"Do you know of anyone who would have wanted to harm your uncle?"

"My uncle wasn't perfect. But who is?" Henry's eyes narrowed to slits. "Why are you asking me all these questions anyway?"

He was getting defensive and shutting down fast. "No reason. I'm just curious."

His expression hardened and he turned away. "I didn't see a damn thing. If I did, I would have told the police." He snatched the framed picture from her hands and headed for the back room.

Soon after, he appeared and thrust an envelope at her. "Here are your pictures. Your parents already paid."

She accepted the envelope. She wondered if he'd felt the same sense of happiness when he'd first had his family photograph taken with Deacon.

What had gone bad between uncle and nephew?

"I can't believe they're related," Katie said.

"I was just as surprised. Henry and Deacon look nothing alike," Lucy said.

After Lucy had updated her friend over the phone about her encounter with Henry Buxbaum, Katie had rushed over to Kebab Kitchen. Lucy had been folding a pile of freshly delivered napkins into swans and set aside a stack of napkins to meet Katie by the cash register.

"I don't get it. Why didn't Norman tell us that Deacon

was Henry's uncle? All he said was that Deacon didn't treat the vendors at the Sea View well, including Henry when he showed up to take wedding pictures."

Lucy gathered up the napkins and set them on a larger stack on a nearby table. "I thought the same thing. Maybe Norman didn't know."

"I guess it's possible," Katie said. "Henry's name is on the list of Plunge participants. Do you think he killed his uncle? He was there and had opportunity."

Lucy tapped her foot. "I don't know. Henry didn't say that he disliked Deacon. They both looked friendly and happy in the picture, but that doesn't mean there wasn't an underlying problem between them. Along with Clarissa, we need to keep Henry on our suspect list."

Katie walked behind the register to study the Berberian family's old-time photograph, which Lucy had just hung. "It's a great picture." Her brow furrowed in concentration, then she wrinkled her nose. "Except for the fact that Azad is aiming a gun at your head."

"What?"

"Take a look for yourself."

Lucy joined her to study the picture. Sure enough, Azad was leaning on the bar, a bottle of Jack Daniel's in one hand and a gun in the other—which was aimed directly at her head. Lucy stood at the bar next to Emma, and both sisters seemed oblivious and were smiling at the camera.

"I can't believe no one noticed," Lucy whispered.

"Maybe Henry was mad at you for asking questions about Deacon and he positioned Azad that way," Katie said.

"No. I asked Henry questions *after* the picture was taken."

"Hmm. Then maybe Azad did it on purpose."

Lucy looked at her incredulously. "No way!"

"You don't think it was subconscious on Azad's part?"

"Why would Azad do that, consciously or subconsciously?"

"Maybe he's still jealous of your occasional motorcycle rides with Michael Citteroni. Or he's mad you're investigating another crime."

Lucy rolled her eyes at both of Katie's theories. "How about it was an accident?"

Katie shrugged. "Whatever."

Lucy felt the need to explain. "Azad knows I'm just friends with Michael, and he's confident in our relationship. As for crime fighting, Azad told me to help Susan as long as I stay safe. We've been safe. Having a picture taken while asking Henry questions is safe. Eating at a diner and talking with Clarissa is safe."

Katie's lips twitched in humor. "Don't get your panties in a knot. I was just teasing you."

And Lucy had fallen for her friend's teasing hook, line, and sinker. She knew just how to get back at her friend. She picked up a pressed napkin from the pile and held it out to Katie. "How about you help me finish folding these napkins into swans?"

A nervous look crossed Katie's face as she glanced at the pressed cloth. "You are intent on punishing me for what I said, aren't you?"

"Absolutely. Now don't get *your* panties in a knot."

Late that night, Gadoo settled on Lucy's lap as she sat on her pink sofa, her legs tucked beneath her. The cat purred as she stroked under his chin.

"Things just don't add up, Gadoo. Suspects are crawling out of the woodwork," Lucy mumbled. "First Clarissa, then Henry." And for some reason, she wanted to know more about Vinnie Pinto. He had taken the Plunge, but he had no connection to Deacon and no motive to want him dead. But something about the man made her very uneasy, and it wasn't just because he'd broken into Eloisa's house. The look he'd given her as he drove his trash truck into Kebab Kitchen's lot still gave her the shivers.

Gadoo tilted his head so that Lucy could better scratch behind his ears. Lucy found petting her cat had a way of relaxing her after a busy day at the restaurant. "And as for my friend Susan, nothing makes any sense. Why would Susan ask for my help, then hide things from me?"

The cat lifted his head and his yellow eyes looked at her as if to say, *How should I know? That's for you to find out.*

"Susan had to know I would find things out eventually. My mom knew about her marriage to Felix Shift. I suspect Clemmons already knows about Deacon ruining her reputation as a wedding cake baker and her retaliatory threat to bash his head with a rolling pin. What else am I missing? Other than Clarissa and possibly Henry, is there someone else out there?"

More purring.

Then a low growl alerted her that she was no longer alone. The door to the stairs leading down to Eloisa's living area was cracked open.

Cupid stuck his smushed snout into the crack.

If the shih tzu was here, that meant Eloisa was close by and—

"What are you doing brooding on the couch by yourself?" Eloisa pushed open the door and walked in. So much for privacy. Dressed in striped pink pajamas, Eloisa's hair was in pink curlers, and she wore pink slippers with pink pompoms. Despite the overwhelming pink, it was the simplest getup she'd ever seen her landlady wear.

She didn't mind her landlady, and was willing to help if she needed to pick up a prescription from Magic's Family Apothecary or take her to visit a friend. They had come to an understanding, and the door wasn't locked. But Lucy didn't like the prying.

"I'm not brooding. And I'm not by myself," Lucy countered.

"Oh? A cat doesn't count as companionship. Where's your hot chef?"

"He's closing the restaurant."

"Isn't that your job?"

"The dining room is, but not the kitchen. That's Azad's domain."

Her critical gaze scanned Lucy's apartment. "It's looking kinda bare here. Where's your Christmas tree?"

Lucy shrugged a shoulder. "Azad's taking me to get one. Would you like to decorate it with us?"

"If he'll be here with you, yes."

She found her landlady's fascination more than annoying. "What? I'm not enough?"

"You're okay. But I want to see his muscles bunch when he lugs a heavy tree inside."

Lucy burst out laughing. She wanted to see Azad's muscles bunch, too. "What happened to your men from the dancing lessons at the senior center?"

"Not enough of them to go around. And the guys who are still kicking don't look like your fiancé."

"I'll take that as a compliment, I think."

Eloisa joined her on the sofa, and Cupid jumped into her lap. The dog's beady eyes focused on Lucy. "Why are you moping? Are you still thinking about Deacon Spooner's drowning?"

Lucy sobered. "It's hard to forget. Plus, the police consider my friend, Susan Cutie, a prime suspect."

"Your baker friend?"

"Yes."

Eloisa stroked the little dog's head. "Maybe the police are right in this case. How well do you really know Susan?"

That was what Clarissa had said about Susan. Lucy still found it hard to believe. Susan didn't drown Deacon . . . couldn't have drowned him.

Lucy changed the subject to something else that had been bothering her. "What about Vinnie Pinto?"

"What about him?" Eloisa asked.

"Did Vinnie know Deacon?"

"Not that I know of. He never mentioned Deacon to me, but then again, I haven't been on the best of terms with Vinnie." She rested her hand on Cupid's head. "Why are you asking questions about Vinnie? Do you think he drowned Deacon?"

"No. Even though he was there that day, I don't know of any connection he has to Deacon, so no motive. If he did, I'd hope Detective Clemmons would consider him a suspect, and not just Susan. But Vinnie still gives me the creeps. I'm the one who called the cops when he broke into this house. I still don't understand why you didn't press charges."

"I told you, Vinnie has a gambling problem and his bookie will most likely take care of him."

"That's bothering me, too, and doesn't put my mind at

ease. I asked my friend, Michael, to find out more about Vinnie."

Eloisa blinked. "Your motorcycle-riding friend knows Vinnie?"

"No, but his father does. Vinnie works for Anthony Citteroni; he drives one of his trash trucks."

Eloisa took a breath, and a rare expression crossed her face—worry? trepidation? —but it was gone in a flash, replaced with a wagging finger in her face. "Mr. Citteroni is not to be trifled with, young lady."

Anthony's reputation preceded him. Lucy wasn't surprised that Eloisa knew of him.

"I've met Mr. Citteroni on a couple of occasions. I'm hoping he'll have information about Vinnie." Lucy didn't add that the couple of times she had met Anthony Citteroni in person, her anxiety level had doubled.

"Still, be careful," Eloisa said. "What better way to dispose of a body than in one of those trucks?"

Chapter Fifteen

"You haven't forgotten about our outing, have you?" Angela Berberian's voice blared over the phone the following day.

Lucy held the cell phone between her neck and the crook of her shoulder as she cracked open her patio door and carried a mug of steaming coffee outside. It was a chilly morning, but the sun was shining. The ocean glinted in the sun and Lucy squinted.

"What outing, Mom?"

"You're supposed to drive me to visit Jake at his brewery this morning. How could you forget?"

Lucy burned her tongue on her coffee and cursed under her breath. "Shit."

"What was that?" Her mother's voice was shrill.

"That wasn't at you, Mom," Lucy was quick to explain. "I admit that I forgot, but it's not a problem. I'll pick you up in half an hour."

Forty-five minutes later, Lucy picked up her mother. Angela glared at Lucy.

"You're late."

"It's not my fault. Azad called," Lucy fibbed.

Her mother's face softened and her lips curved in a smile.

Any mention of Azad and her mother's ruffled feathers were smoothed.

"How's the wedding planning coming along?" Angela asked.

Not good. The owner of the reception site I was considering was drowned not more than ten feet from me. I haven't had time to think about other venues because I've been busy trying to figure out who murdered Deacon Spooner, and Katie has been obsessed with showing me glossy fashion magazines advertising crazy-expensive wedding gowns modeled by tall, superskinny models.

"It's coming along well." Lucy hoped her voice sounded confident.

Her mother nodded and reached across to pat Lucy's hand.

Crisis averted.

Lucy turned into a parking lot. Jake's Ocean Crest Boardwalk Brewery had a shiny new neon sign. The brewery had grown in popularity, and its new, polished look attracted people of all ages, both millennials looking for the newest craft beer and older folks who wanted to drink and relax with friends.

Lucy stepped out of the car. "The place looks really nice."

"Jake has done well for himself," her mother said as they opened the door to the brewery.

Large vats of fermenting beer lined one wall like shiny sentinels keeping guard over the place. Tubes and pipes ran from the vats into smaller vessels. On the opposite wall, stacks of empty kegs, two rows high, waited to be filled and delivered. A small bar area where customers could sample micro beers was tucked away in the corner.

Craft beer was serious business.

Jake appeared from around one of the vats to greet them. "Ladies! What a pleasure. Can I get you a tasting?"

He was dressed in a blue-and-white flannel shirt and khakis. His hair was styled in a rakish look and a brown lock fell over his forehead.

"Hi, Jake. You know my mom," Lucy said.

"Of course. If it wasn't for the lovely Mrs. Berberian, I wouldn't have met Susan."

Angela blushed. Actually blushed. Lucy stared. Her mother wasn't one to fall for cheesy praise, but Jake was good-looking and had a certain charm. It must have worked on Susan as well.

"Your brewery is impressive. I have no idea what all this equipment does," Lucy said.

"Craft brewers have always been around, but they've made a comeback in recent years. Thanks to all that equipment, we have the ability to make unique blends in small batches. Customers love it." He waved a hand toward the tall, stainless-steel vats. "Those are hundred-year-old barrel fermentation tanks. After the beer is ready, bottles or kegs are shipped to our suppliers."

He walked to the corner bar and pulled out two barstools. "Please sit, and I'll pour you some samples."

Lucy and her mother settled on the stools, and Jake poured four small, frosted glasses and set them on a rectangular tray before Lucy. He repeated the pour for her mother.

Lucy sampled the first beer. It was smooth, and she detected a hint of cloves and cinnamon, but she wasn't a beer connoisseur and couldn't identify everything. "This is good. I'm tasting a hint of cloves and cinnamon, but what's the other hint of flavor?"

"It's my Christmas ale. You're right about the first two, but it's also spiced with nutmeg. Do you like it?"

"I do."

"I experiment with different twists. My customers tell me which are successes and which are just okay. I can then brew bigger batches of the favorites. Large breweries can't connect with their customers this way."

Lucy was beginning to understand. Azad liked beer and he would have his opinions. She made a mental note to bring him here.

"I want to order a half keg of the Christmas ale. I'm having a small Christmas dinner and party at the restaurant," Angela said.

Kebab Kitchen didn't have a liquor license, but her family's gathering would be in the restaurant after-hours. Angela still loved to cook, and she usually invited a select number of townsfolk to celebrate the season.

"Last time we talked, you mentioned that you deliver kegs to the Sea View for weddings and events," Lucy said.

"That's right. I think I told you about my last experience."

Yes, he had. He'd overheard Norman and Deacon fight, then Norman threaten Deacon. "Have you made any deliveries since . . . since—"

"Since Deacon Spooner's death?" Jake asked.

More like murder, but Lucy held her tongue.

"Most events were booked up to six months in advance. Despite what happened to Deacon, Norman still has to honor those contractual obligations, and he remains in business. I delivered a few kegs just yesterday."

Lucy understood. Prior arrangements needed to be

upheld or the Sea View could be sued for breach of contract. A lawsuit was the last thing Norman Weston needed now. As for accepting new business, she couldn't blame Norman, could she? He still needed to earn a living, and running a small business was hard. Lucy had learned that in the past year she'd been managing Kebab Kitchen. An owner couldn't just close its doors, not when the Sea View could easily default on its loans.

Lucy ran her finger down her frosted glass. "How is Susan holding up?"

Jake's face fell and he glanced away. He picked up a rag and began to wipe down the clean bar. "She's not so great. That detective rattled her the last time he spoke with her. We're both grateful you were in the bakery then, Lucy."

Lucy bit her bottom lip. She wasn't sure if she'd helped Susan much.

Jake set aside the rag and captured her gaze. "But if you really want to know how Susan is doing, she's in my office."

Susan was here? Now? "Where is your office?" Lucy asked.

Jake pointed to a path past the big vats. "Down that hall past the ladies' room."

Lucy pushed back her chair and headed to where Jake had motioned. She spotted the sign for the ladies' room, a stick figure of a woman dressed in a skirt and holding a beer in her right hand. She came to a closed door that could only be Jake's private office tucked in the back. She turned the handle and opened the door.

As she stepped inside, she saw Susan was *crying*.

* * *

Susan sat behind Jake's desk. A pile of used tissues littered the surface of the desk and a box was in the corner.

Lucy crept forward. "Susan? What's wrong?"

Susan looked up. Her nose was as red as Rudolph's as she blew it, then met Lucy's gaze. "Oh, Lucy. I'm a mess."

"What happened?" Lucy's heart rate escalated at her friend's distress. "Did you have a fight with Jake? Or something else?"

Susan sniffled and blew her nose in a tissue. "No, Jake's great."

"Then what has you so down?" Lucy asked.

"Detective Clemmons paid me another visit to ask questions. He ended up telling me not to leave town. I'm afraid, Lucy." Susan's voice quivered as she held Lucy's gaze.

Lucy tried hard not to cringe. There was only one reason Calvin Clemmons would instruct Susan not to leave town. He may not have enough to make an arrest, but he was close. She wondered if the county prosecutor, Marsha Walsh, was encouraging Clemmons. If so, Susan was in bigger trouble than they had thought.

Other questions arose. Clarissa had said Deacon Spooner had done much worse to Susan than to make her pay for a ruined wedding cake. He'd damaged her reputation as a wedding cake baker, the most profitable part of her business.

And then there was Susan's prior marriage to Felix Shift, which had ended with her husband's untimely demise. The life insurance money had allowed Susan to open Cutie's Cupcakes.

Lucy had a lot of questions for her friend.

She pulled out a chair across from Susan and sat. "Clemmons wouldn't tell you not to leave town over a ruined wedding cake. I know there's more, Susan. More you haven't told me."

Susan sniffled. "You know about my former husband, Felix, don't you? I'm sure your Mom must have mentioned it."

No sense denying it. "I do."

"Whatever you're thinking, I didn't do anything wrong. I may have wished my cheating husband harm, but I didn't kill Felix."

Lucy had told her mom the same thing. "I believe you, but others may see it differently. Especially because the life insurance payout helped you."

"I won't deny it. Bakery equipment is expensive. Commercial ovens and mixers are pricey, plus I needed rent money for the shopping strip to open Cutie's Cupcakes. But it doesn't mean I purposely didn't pick up Felix's medication with the intent to kill him. I was planning on leaving him for his infidelity. Why should I continue to pick up his meds?"

"I'd do the same."

"Not everyone believes me like you. I overheard Gertrude Shaw and Francesca Stevens whispering in church that they won't touch my baked goods."

"Don't let their cruel words hurt your feelings. Gertrude and Francesca are notorious gossips."

"But they're on the township committee, and others may feel the same about my bakery."

Her mother had said the same, but Lucy didn't want to mention that to Susan. There were more pressing matters she did want to discuss—things to do with the murder. "What about when Deacon spread rumors about your bakery? Rumors that damaged your reputation as a wedding cake baker?"

"God, you know about that, too."

"I wish you'd told me yourself. Instead, I learned it from someone else."

"From whom?" Susan choked on a sob and reached for another tissue to blow her nose. "Oh, what does it matter now? It's true. Deacon did spread cruel rumors about my cakes. You of all people know that I take pride in my work."

Lucy felt bad for her friend, but stopped herself from reaching out to touch Susan's hand. She needed her to talk. "Everything I've tasted from your bakery has been delicious. I'm confident Deacon was lying. But as far as Detective Clemmons is concerned, you hid something, because you never mentioned either of those things to him when he first questioned you."

A panicked look crossed Susan's face. "I couldn't! I was afraid it would look bad. The truth is, I was near Deacon in the water and we exchanged words. Bad ones."

"How bad?"

"Deacon told me that he'd bad-mouthed my bakery to three other brides this month, and that it was just a matter of time before Cutie's Cupcakes went out of business."

"That's awful. What did you tell him?"

Susan bit her bottom lip and sagged in her chair. "I told him that I hoped he'd drown."

"Oh, Susan. You didn't!" Lucy looked at her friend in dismay.

Susan ran her fingers through her blond hair. "I did, but I didn't really mean it. He was just so *mean*." She sniffled and reached for another tissue and blew her nose. "You believe me, don't you?"

"What I believe doesn't matter. In the future, you

shouldn't talk to Detective Clemmons without an attorney present."

Susan's expression turned desperate. "You think he'll come around again?"

Absolutely. If any of the swimmers had overheard her exchange with Deacon, they would spill the truth.

All except Jake. He must have heard her threaten Deacon with drowning and he hadn't said a word to the police. How far would he go to protect his girlfriend?

Lucy realized Susan was waiting for her answer. "I think there is a good chance Clemmons will want to talk to you again. You should contact Clyde Winters."

"Who?"

"He's Ocean Crest's sole criminal defense attorney. He mostly handles DUI cases in municipal court, but he's competent and can represent more serious crimes. I've recommended him to others. Clyde's older, but still good."

"I was hoping you'd do it for me like last time, Lucy."

"Last time was different. I stayed as a friend, not your attorney."

At Susan's crestfallen expression, Lucy spoke up. "Susan, I want to help. But I've never been a criminal defense attorney, and I'm managing Kebab Kitchen now."

"I understand, but can you still investigate on your own? With Katie's help? You're pretty good at it."

"I'll keep my ears open, but I can't promise anything."

She'd been doing a bit more than keeping her ears open, but she didn't want to get Susan's hopes up. The truth was, Lucy was afraid for Susan. Things were looking worse and worse for her friend.

Chapter Sixteen

"Oooh! It smells like Christmas." Lucy's boots crunched on the snow-covered path and she pulled down her knit hat to cover her ears. Azad had driven her to the Christmas tree farm early in the morning, and sunlight glinted off the pristine snow. Numerous paths lined with Douglas firs, Scotch pines, and spruce trees made for a vast selection of trees. She inhaled the fresh scent of evergreen as they headed for one of the paths.

Azad took her gloved hand in his own. "I'm glad we're doing this together. Your first Christmas in your new apartment is special."

Lucy's fingers curled around his in her knit glove. "I've never had a real Christmas tree."

"Really?" Azad glanced at her in surprise as they walked down the dirt-lined path. "Raffi and Angela never had a real tree when you were growing up?"

"Nope. We had the same fake tree for almost ten years. Every year it lost a few more of its plastic needles. Emma and I would have to cover the bare patches with garland and tinsel."

"You don't know what you're missing. There's nothing like a fresh tree for Christmas."

She smiled up at him. "I'm looking forward to decorating it with you this year."

"Me too. I never thought tree trimming would be romantic until now." He leaned down to give her a kiss, and her toes curled in her snow boots.

As they continued onward, they passed a family with two young girls as close in age as she was to Emma. Lucy watched as a worker sawed the trunk of a tree. Soon, the tree started to fall, and the father caught it before it hit the ground. The tree was dragged to a machine, run through a belt, and came out the other end skinny and netted. The girls' excitement as the tree was tied to the top of the family's minivan made Lucy grin. She may not have had the same experience picking out a tree with Emma, but the holiday season was magical and she had many fond childhood memories of celebrating the season with her sister.

Azad led Lucy farther down the path, and they passed tree after tree. The selection seemed a bit overwhelming to her. "What do I look for?"

"Whatever catches your eye. Just make sure it will fit nicely in your living room."

Soon after, she spotted the one—a lovely Douglas fir. She took off her knit gloves and felt the needles. She eyed it for size. It would fit perfectly in her apartment and not hit the ceiling.

"This is the one!"

Azad joined her to study the tree. "Good choice. Wait here and I'll go get someone to cut it down for us." He hurried off to find a worker.

Lucy planted a hand on the tree. She thought of it as her tree now and didn't want anyone else to claim it until Azad returned with help. She imagined how she would decorate it. Her mother had given her a star from her grandmother's house, and it would look perfect on top of—

"Who would think Deacon's death would cause so much trouble?"

Lucy froze at the sound of a woman's voice that came from the adjacent row of trees. The voice was familiar, and Lucy parted an evergreen branch to peek.

Clarissa.

She was with a man, but his back was to her and she couldn't identify him. What was Clarissa doing here? And who was that with her?

"Yeah, even dead, the jerk is causing problems," he said.

Lucy took a quick, sharp breath. She recognized that voice. She'd heard it not long ago.

Henry.

He turned, and her gaze took in the fair hair that brushed his forehead. He wore a corduroy jacket and hiking boots, and his hands were shoved in his pockets.

She had no idea that Clarissa knew Henry. What were the two doing together?

Clarissa's face looked pinched, either from the cold or disgust. "Deacon should have helped you invest in Old Time Photos when he was alive."

"I never expected him to help with my business. My uncle put Scrooge to shame. He always told me I wouldn't get a cent from him while he was alive," he said in a harsh, raw voice.

"But now there's a trust fund. He can't deny you any longer," Clarissa said.

"It's not that easy," Henry said. "The trust says I don't get all his cash outright, but have to wait until I'm forty-nine before I get everything. Forty-nine!"

"Your uncle tormented you when he was alive. Don't

let him get to you now. Look on the bright side. At least he's finally dead," Clarissa insisted archly.

The trill of a cell phone made Lucy jump. She ducked low and scrambled to pull her phone out of her purse. The last thing she wanted was for Clarissa and Henry to know she'd been eavesdropping.

"Hello?" she whispered, her voice a bit hoarse.

"Lucy? It's Michael. You okay?"

Had Clarissa and Henry heard her phone ring? Lucy sneaked a peek between branches, but the couple was gone.

She tried to calm her racing pulse. "I'm fine. The call just took me by surprise. What's up?"

"I talked to my dad. He wants to meet us at Mac's Irish Pub tomorrow night. I can pick you up at nine."

"The pub? Not a restaurant?" She expected a fancy Italian restaurant, like the last time she'd met Anthony Citteroni for information. Or by a municipal lot on the edge of town, where his trash trucks were parked at the end of each day.

"He specifically said the pub. He also said he knows who killed Deacon Spooner."

"I'm gobsmacked! First, you overhear Henry and Clarissa. Then Michael calls you and says his father knows who killed Deacon. What's next?" Katie's voice rose an octave over the cell phone.

"I'm just as surprised." Lucy gripped her cell phone.

As soon as she'd overheard Clarissa and Henry at the tree farm, she'd excused herself from Azad to go to the ladies' room. She'd immediately called Katie and spilled everything. Thank goodness the tree farm had a real ladies' room, not a porta-potty. Lucy shut the door of one of the three stalls and leaned against the door. Hopefully, no one would come inside while they were talking.

"Who do you think Mr. Citteroni believes is the killer?" Katie asked.

Lucy hesitated as she pondered this question. "I have no idea. I plan on asking him about Vinnie, but what if he mentions Henry or Clarissa?"

"Who would have guessed that Henry's the recipient of his uncle's trust fund? Or that Clarissa and Henry are buddies?"

"I wonder if they're more than just buddies. They seemed very comfortable with each other. And both of them had a motive to kill Deacon."

"We need to find out more," Katie said.

Voices sounded outside. Lucy's heart pounded like a drum, and she cracked open the stall door to be sure no one else had entered the ladies' room. Relief washed over her when she realized the voices were coming from outside. Still, she couldn't afford to linger.

"I can't talk long," Lucy said. "I'm at the tree farm with Azad, and I don't want to take the chance of ruining our date."

Katie chuckled. "Yeah. Yeah. I get it. No sense upsetting your hunk of a chef by letting him know you were snooping."

"It has nothing to do with me eavesdropping. And I told you before, Azad knows I'm helping Susan. But I still want our night out to be special. We plan on decorating tonight."

Katie sighed over the phone. "Nothing like a gal's engagement period. It's all peaches and roses. I miss those days."

"What's that supposed to mean? You and Bill have something special."

"We do. But a night out lately has been watching movies on our living room couch with me wearing yoga pants and an old T-shirt."

Lucy didn't like the solemn sound of her friend's voice. "Since when do you act like an old lady? We'll go shopping. Then I'll help you plan a special date night."

"Sounds good. Meanwhile, enjoy *your* special evening."

"Thanks. I will." Lucy ignored the sarcasm and was just about to end the call when Katie said, "Oh, and Lucy—"

"Yes?"

"Good work, Sherlock. Can't wait to hear what Mr. C says."

"No, no. Only white lights should go on a tree," Eloisa said.

"Why? I want to have flashing, colored lights." Lucy stood in the center of her living room holding a box of Christmas lights in her hand. "What's the difference?"

"You want your tree to be balanced, don't you? White lights are classier."

"So are colorful ones. And it's my tree," Lucy whined.

Ugh! She sounded like a petulant child, but who knew her landlady would be so particular about tree lighting? She seemed carefree about everything else in life, especially her clothing. Today she was wearing a gold sweater with an elf holding a gift, a red sequined skirt, and striped red-and-green tights—a holiday clash, in Lucy's opinion.

Azad must have sensed the tension over the decorating. He smoothly intervened to take the lights from Lucy and then hand each of them a box of globe ornaments. "I'll make this easy by using *both* colored and white lights. But afterward, how about we all place these ornaments on the tree where we like them? That way, each of you will have a say in the decorations."

"See? He's reasonable," Eloisa said.

Good grief. Azad could have handed each of them a roll of toilet paper to decorate the tree and her landlady would have happily complied.

As for the tree itself, Azad was right. A real tree looked and smelled wonderful in her living room. The lights could be seen from the front window. Unlike Lucy and Eloisa, Gadoo and Cupid were getting along. Gadoo was batting his paws at a string of garland, and Cupid was chewing his bone while lounging on Gadoo's cat bed.

"How's your friend Susan?" Eloisa asked. "I went by her bakery this morning for my favorite Danish and the store was closed."

Lucy had picked up a red globe ornament and was headed for the tree when Eloisa's comment caught her off guard. "It was?"

"You didn't know?"

"I saw her the other day at Jake's brewery. She was crying."

"Well, I don't think her bakery is permanently closed. Edna said she saw Susan working in the shop later that day. She must have opened late."

That was good news, but it didn't ease all Lucy's concerns. Susan always opened at five thirty in the morning. The bakery did a brisk morning business for doughnuts, muffins, and Danishes. Deacon's murder must have affected Susan's business.

"Detective Clemmons asked Susan not to leave town." Lucy went to place the red ornament on a low branch, then changed her mind. Gadoo could reach it, and she didn't want broken glass ornaments, or for her cat to get sick. She moved it up four branches.

Eloisa placed her hand on her hip. "That detective really thinks Susan drowned that man at the Polar Bear Plunge?"

Lucy bit her bottom lip. "It looks that way, but I don't believe it. Others had strong motive."

Azad lifted his head. "You know something."

Once more, Lucy's tension tightened, but for an entirely different reason. Azad had been supportive lately, but she still was hesitant to involve him or her landlady. She decided transparency was best. "I didn't intend to eavesdrop, but people have a bad habit of gossiping around here. It happened earlier today."

Azad eyed her with interest. "Where? At the Christmas tree farm?"

"I overheard people talking after you left to get a worker to cut down my tree. Turns out the owner of Old Time Photos, Henry Buxbaum, was Deacon's nephew and the recipient of a trust fund. Then there's that bride, Clarissa Chase, who placed an ad in the *Town News* complaining about Deacon because he ruined her wedding day. I think Henry and Clarissa are in some kind of relationship."

Eloisa whistled through her teeth. "Sounds like motive to me. Deacon Spooner didn't have a lot of fans, did he? Anyone else have motive?"

Lucy fidgeted with another ornament, a blue bell this time. She wasn't sure how much to tell. She didn't want to make anyone—especially Azad—worry. Taking a deep breath, Lucy decided the truth was best. "I'm meeting Mr. Citteroni tomorrow night at Mac's to find out. He may know who killed Deacon."

Azad didn't comment. She knew he worried. Plus, Azad and Michael hadn't had a rosy relationship in the past.

But Azad had also come to accept that Michael was her friend, and claimed he didn't mind that she occasionally rode on the back of his motorcycle.

But that friendship didn't extend to Michael's father. Anthony Citteroni had a sketchy reputation. "Are you going to try to talk me out of meeting with Mr. Citteroni?" Lucy asked.

Azad shook his head. "No, I support your efforts to help a friend. But I can't promise that I won't worry. I don't want anything to happen to you."

She gave him a brief kiss. "I promise, I'll be careful. I'm not chasing down criminals. Just meeting Mr. Citteroni to ask him questions at a public bar. Then I'll meet with Bill or Detective Clemmons and tell him all I know. Absolutely no risk."

Chapter Seventeen

Michael Citteroni held open the door of Mac's Irish Pub for Lucy. As soon as she stepped inside, the tantalizing smell of fried bar food wafted to her. What was it about fried mozzarella and chicken wings that lured people like fish biting on a line?

Her gaze was drawn to the mahogany bar and the customers seated on barstools. Two bartenders were busy mixing drinks and pouring beer. Mac's was a hometown favorite and boasted a large selection of microbrews and classic beers on tap. Tables were occupied by locals drinking beer and watching a large television mounted above the bar. A Christmas tree decorated with ornaments of Philadelphia sports teams—Eagles, Phillies, Flyers, and 76ers—stood in the corner. Ocean Crest may be in South Jersey, but its residents rooted for the Philadelphia teams.

"Thanks for arranging this meeting with your dad," Lucy said.

Michael led Lucy to the tables in the back of the room, passing a pool table where two couples were playing a game. "The truth is, I didn't like hearing that one of my dad's employees tried to break into your landlady's home. If my dad can help somehow, it's worth meeting him."

She initially wanted to meet with Mr. Citteroni to learn more about Vinnie Pinto. Vinnie creeped her out, and not just because he broke into Eloisa's house when Lucy was home alone, but because of his ominous look when he drove the trash truck into the restaurant's lot. Both experiences had unnerved her. Then Michael had said his father knew who killed Deacon, and Lucy's interest in meeting Mr. Citteroni had increased tenfold.

Michael chose an empty table near a low stage. A band was scheduled to play Christmas pop songs tonight and equipment was set up on the stage. Until the band began to play, this isolated spot was the quietest.

He pulled out a chair for her, but before she could sit, the front door opened, and Anthony Citteroni walked in. Short, heavyset, and balding, he had a brick-end chin, swarthy skin, and dark eyes. He wore a khaki trench coat, and Lucy couldn't help but wonder if he had a gun hidden beneath it. Despite the warmth in the room, a shiver traveled down her spine.

Anthony approached, and Michael nodded at his father.

Lucy took a calming breath and smiled in greeting. "Thank you for meeting me, Mr. Citteroni."

"Please sit." Mr. Citteroni's voice was low and gravelly and reminded Lucy of Marlon Brando in *The Godfather*.

He took off his trench coat to reveal a gray sport jacket and button-down white shirt. No tie.

And, thankfully, no weapon.

The pub's bubblegum-chomping assistant manager approached and set down cardboard coasters with popular domestic beer brands before each of them. Lucy knew Candace from high school. "Hey, Lucy. What will you all be having?"

They ordered, and Candace sailed away toward the bar to fetch their drinks.

Anthony folded his hands before him and met Lucy's gaze. "You want to know about Deacon Spooner's death."

He wasn't a man to mince words. "Yes. The police think my friend is responsible."

"And you do not?"

Lucy's gut tightened as she met his eyes. "Susan Cutie could never hold someone down and drown them."

"People are capable of many things, Ms. Berberian. Good and bad." His voice, though quiet, had a warning undertone.

Clemmons had said something similar. Still, despite everything she'd learned about Susan—that she'd been married and there had been talk of her killing her husband, and that she'd threatened Deacon after his cruel gossip had damaged her bakery business—Lucy believed in her friend's innocence.

So who did the nasty deed? She leaned forward, eager to hear what he knew.

Candace returned and set down frosty mugs of beer before her and Michael and a glass of red wine for Mr. Citteroni. Lucy's foot bobbed anxiously beneath the table until they were alone once more.

"You also want to know about my employee, Vinnie Pinto," Mr. Citteroni said.

Her mind whirled at the change in topic from Deacon's murderer to Vinnie. She wanted to know about both, but as far as she knew, Vinnie wasn't connected to Deacon. She'd once learned that Mr. Citteroni liked to play with people's emotions, like a puppet master with his marionettes. He had information she needed, and if she wanted it, she had to play along.

Lucy ran a finger down the frosty mug. "Did you know Vinnie did the Polar Bear Plunge?"

Mr. Citteroni took a sip of his wine. "Of course. I told him to."

"You did?"

"He went for the same reason you participated. All the local business owners must show support for the senior center. It's good business sense."

"You didn't want to do it yourself?"

He laughed, a low sound that made the hair on the nape of her neck stand on end. "I do not like the cold."

She also knew from past experience that he didn't do his own dirty work either.

Now, where did that thought come from? Anthony Citteroni wasn't a suspect. He had no reason to want Deacon dead. At least, none that she knew of.

"My dad first asked me to do it," Michael said, "but I don't like the cold either. Dad must have got him to take my place." Michael turned to his father. "Isn't that right?"

Mr. Citteroni nodded once. "Vinnie wasn't fazed at all, but he also knew he had little choice. He has a nasty gambling problem."

Eloisa had told her about Vinnie's gambling addiction. Would Vinnie have been fired if he hadn't agreed to swim? Or did Vinnie swim to keep his job in order to pay off his gambling debts? Or was it for other nefarious reasons?

Lucy decided to cut to the chase. "You said you know who killed Deacon."

"I have my suspicions. I also have my sources."

She knew not to ask. For a man who had numerous town businesses, but who spent the majority of his time in Atlantic City, Anthony Citteroni knew more about what occurred in Ocean Crest than the worst gossips.

She leaned forward, eager to hear a name. "Who?"

Mr. Citteroni sipped his wine and took his sweet time before answering. "Vinnie has a criminal record. Burglary and assault."

He was back to talking about Vinnie. Why? What did he have to do with Deacon?

As for Vinnie's criminal record, she wasn't surprised to hear he had one. Even though Vinnie had a key as a former property manager, he didn't have permission to enter Mrs. Lubinski's home. A respectable property manager would have turned in the key when he lost his job.

Anthony tilted his head to the side and regarded her. "You do not seem shocked at this news."

"Not really. Vinnie broke into my landlady's house when I was home alone. He didn't get to steal a thing because I called the police. Mrs. Lubinski already told me that he has a gambling problem and that he probably wanted to rob her to pay off his debts. He must have confronted a homeowner, which resulted in the assault charges."

Anthony shook his head. "The two charges were separate offenses on different days. The assault happened here, at this pub."

This was unexpected and took her by surprise. "The assault charge had nothing to do with one of his burglaries?" Lucy asked.

"That's correct. It was a bar fight here."

"A bar fight? Here? Who did Vinnie fight?"

Anthony's brooding gaze locked with hers, and for a split second, her heart dropped in her stomach and she knew.

He nodded in confirmation. "Deacon Spooner, of course."

Chapter Eighteen

"Vinnie got in a fight with Deacon at Mac's Pub?" Lucy asked.

"That's right." Mr. Citteroni eyed her over the rim of his wineglass.

Lucy pressed a hand on the table. "Do you know why?" Up to now, Lucy hadn't known Deacon and Vinnie even knew each other. But the fact that the two men had brawled changed everything.

"Over money," Mr. Citteroni said. "Vinnie had been Deacon's property manager when the Sea View was closed for renovations. Vinnie's duties were to check on the place and make sure the electric and heat were not turned off during construction. A surveillance camera revealed that he helped himself to some of the valuables."

"When you say valuables, what exactly do you mean?" Lucy asked.

"Expensive bottles of liquor left after a catering event and a stash of cash hidden in Deacon's office. My sources cannot say precisely how much cash Vinnie stole, but I assume it was significant. What is curious is that Deacon never called the cops to have Vinnie arrested and never filed charges."

"That doesn't make sense. If Vinnie stole a lot of cash, why didn't Deacon report the robbery?" Lucy asked.

"There is only one explanation. It was in Deacon's best interest not to report the crime," Anthony said.

How could being robbed have been in Deacon's best interest? And why didn't he call the police and have Vinnie arrested? Another question arose: Did Deacon's business partner, Norman, know about the robbery, or that the police weren't called?

"Rather than have Vinnie arrested, Deacon fought Vinnie here?" Lucy asked.

"That's what I'm told, but there is one way to verify my theory." Mr. Citteroni waved at their waitress, and Candace left another table to approach theirs. "Do you need refills?"

"No," Mr. Citteroni said. "We'd like a word with Mac if you don't mind."

Candace popped a bubble. "It's a busy night, but I'll tell him."

"Hey, Mac!" Candace called out in a booming voice that made Lucy start in her seat.

Seconds later, Mac MacCabe approached their table. A tall man with long brown hair tied back in a leather thong, he had a large belly from drinking too much of his own beer. He wore a white T-shirt with MAC'S IRISH PUB printed in green letters beneath a large, green shamrock. The man carried a clean bar rag in his left hand.

Michael and Mr. Citteroni shook hands with Mac, and Mac leaned down to brush Lucy's cheek with a kiss. "Good to see you all. Now, what can I do for you?" Mac said.

"Do you remember the night Vinnie fought with Deacon?" Anthony asked.

"Sure do," Mac said, scratching the two-days' worth of scruff on his chin. "I called the police myself."

"What were they fighting about?" Lucy asked.

"It was hard to make out conversation in between fists flying and men grunting, but it had to do with something about money, and that if Vinnie couldn't pay up with interest soon, Deacon was going to make him pay in other ways. I didn't stand by to hear more. I called the police because I didn't want my bar broken up."

"Thanks for the information," Lucy said.

"Anytime." Mac tossed the bar rag over his shoulder and returned to the bar.

"See? Their feud had to do with money. It always does," Anthony said.

Lucy couldn't help but wonder if Mr. Citteroni's illegal affairs had tainted his point of view. People didn't always argue over money, did they?

"Mac mentioned something about interest," Lucy said. "If Deacon decided not to have Vinnie arrested for stealing, but had charged interest on the stolen cash instead, then Deacon was blackmailing Vinnie in a weird sort of way. Vinnie must have already spent the money he'd stolen, most likely gambling."

Mr. Citteroni nodded. "That's right."

"Vinnie couldn't pay back this stolen cash plus interest. It was an illegal 'loan' of sorts, and there would be no records."

Anthony leaned forward. "Yes. Go on."

Lucy quickly connected the dots. "The only record would be Deacon himself. And if Deacon was dead, the loan from the stolen cash would be forgotten."

"That," Anthony said, "sounds like motive for murder to me."

* * *

"Thank God it's Friday." Katie collapsed on Lucy's couch. It was the following afternoon, and Katie worked only half days on Fridays, so she'd come to visit before Lucy had to head back to Kebab Kitchen for the dinner service.

"I brought a couple more wedding magazines." Katie dropped a stack on the coffee table.

"Seriously? I haven't even flipped through the last batch." Lucy pointed to the magazines. "And that stack is a lot more than just a couple."

Katie shot her a serious look. "You need to get with the program. Or are you delaying wedding planning?"

"It's not like I'm doing it on purpose. I've been busy at the restaurant and sleuthing."

"I'll cut you some slack because of the sleuthing," Katie said as she slipped off her shoes and curled her feet beneath her on the couch. "I was nervous about your meeting with Mr. Citteroni and surprised by what you've learned. Clarissa, Henry, and now Vinnie. Who do you think has the strongest motive for murder?"

Lucy handed Katie a glass of water, then joined her friend on the couch. "Vinnie. He was caught stealing cash on the surveillance video. When Deacon confronted Vinnie and demanded his cash back, it was too late. Vinnie had probably gambled it all away the same day. Rather than have him arrested, Deacon blackmailed Vinnie and made him pay back what he stole, probably with high interest."

Katie sipped her water. "We can't overlook Clarissa or Henry. She hated him, and it's no secret she wished him dead."

"Yes, but is a double-booked reception sufficient motive for murder?" Lucy had been contemplating this all day.

"You heard her at the Silver Diner. She blames Deacon

for more than a botched reception. She blames him for her failed marriage and basically said he ruined her life. There's no accounting for crazy."

"True. But Henry inherited a trust fund. Money is a big motive." She was sounding more and more like Anthony Citteroni.

"Deacon wasn't well-liked, was he?"

"He was a sourpuss when we met him," Lucy scoffed. "We need to tell Detective Clemmons everything. Maybe then he'll consider other suspects besides Susan. I just need to figure out how. Clemmons doesn't like it when I stick my nose into his business." Her memory of their conversation at Lola's Coffee Shop was fresh in her mind. She'd come a long way with the detective, but she knew he didn't like her crime-solving tendencies.

"I can leak word to Bill. He's busy at the high school busting a pot dealer right now. But he'll be at the town Christmas tree lighting tonight. The festive mood should make it easier to tell him about our snooping efforts. You're going with me, right?"

Lucy had forgotten all about Ocean Crest's tree lighting. Her meeting with Michael and his father had distracted her. Her parents had agreed to work at Kebab Kitchen tonight so that she could attend. "Uh, I haven't forgotten."

"Liar."

"Okay, maybe I have. I've been sidetracked."

Katie waved a dismissive hand. "I'll pick you up at seven."

Lucy returned to the restaurant for the dinner shift. She had a lot of work to do before going to the tree lighting with Katie. Ordering food from their suppliers had to be completed. Payroll was an endless task. And they were short a waitress, which meant Lucy would pick up the slack as needed. Azad waved her over on her way to the office in the storage room.

"Want a taste?" Azad dipped a clean spoon in a commercial-size pot and held it out for her.

Lucy let him feed her and slurped in a quite unladylike fashion from the spoon. "Hmm. That's the best avgolemono soup I've ever tasted." The Greek egg and lemon soup had orzo pasta, lemon, and eggs. Lucy had never made it with her mother, but it was one of her favorite soups.

His dark eyes gleamed. "Good. It's on the menu for tonight."

"You'll have to be sure to step into the dining room and greet our . . ."

"Lucy!"

Lucy started as Sally swept through the swinging kitchen doors. "Stan Slade is asking to see you."

Lucy's stomach tightened in dread. "Stan?"

"You know . . . Mr. Slade from the *Town News*," Sally said.

"Oh, I know. Is he here to eat?"

"He placed an order." Sally waved a check in the air. "But he definitely has that reporter-at-work vibe about him."

Lucy groaned. "Just great." She trudged into the dining room. She knew why he was here. They'd struck a deal. In exchange for glimpsing pictures he'd taken of the swimmers at the Polar Bear Plunge, she'd agreed to share any information she'd unearthed about the murder.

Good luck with that. She was no closer to finding the killer.

Stan had requested a maple booth in a corner, away from the hummus bar. Smart man. A steady path of customers made their way to and from the hummus bar to sample Azad's different specialties, and sitting anywhere near there would not be private.

Stan sipped a soda. The only expression he made as she slid into the booth opposite him was to raise one dark eyebrow above his black-rimmed glasses. "You haven't come to see me, Ms. Berberian. I was starting to get worried."

"I haven't forgotten our agreement, but I don't have anything to share."

"Now why do I find that hard to believe?"

"I don't know. It must be your untrusting nature."

Stan didn't take the bait. "Word on the street is that Susan Cutie is in a hotbed of trouble."

It was hard to steady her erratic pulse. "Susan didn't drown Deacon."

"Is she your friend?"

"Yes."

"Then why haven't you dug around more to find the real killer?"

Her voice was filled with genuine frustration. "Believe me, I'm trying."

Stan pushed his glasses up the bridge of his nose. "Fine. I believe you."

Lucy thought about how she could use Stan. Maybe she could use him and get him off her back at the same time. "Maybe you can help. I want to know more about someone in town."

"Give me a name."

"Clarissa Chase."

"The pissed-off bride? Everyone already knows about her. She ran a disparaging ad in the *Town News* about Deacon Spooner and the Sea View."

"Clarissa was a participant in the Polar Bear Plunge. She also has a lot of rage. I'd like to know if she has a criminal background."

"Why waste my time? Don't you think the cops already looked into her?"

"Maybe. But I'd like to know more about her. You have experience digging around, right?"

Chapter Nineteen

The Christmas tree lighting in the park at the center of town was one of Lucy's favorite events of the season. She had dressed in a sweater, jacket, scarf, hat, gloves, and boots. Katie was dressed similarly as they crossed a street and walked to the park, where a large crowd was already assembled. A gentle flurry of snow had fallen earlier and the evergreens glistened beneath the park lights.

This year's tree rivaled Rockefeller Center's. A tall, full spruce, it was truly beautiful. Dressed in red-and-green sweaters and Santa hats, carolers from the local school gathered in front of the tree. At the choir director's signal, they burst into "Deck the Halls."

The lighting wasn't for another hour, but there were plenty of activities to entertain families and their young children. Santa sat in a large, stuffed, green throne in the center of the park gazebo. A line of red-cheeked children wearing winter coats and mittens eagerly waited to sit on St. Nick's lap to tell him everything they hoped to receive Christmas morning. Two women dressed as elves helped manage the line, and they gave each child a candy cane and a coloring book on his or her way out of the gazebo. Santa's wagon and two reindeer had arrived and were situated behind a small white fence where people could observe them. A horse-drawn sleigh that could fit six riders circled the perimeter of the park.

"Do you think Mr. Citteroni will be here?" Katie asked as she stood next to Lucy in a line for a booth that served both mulled wine and Jake's Christmas ale. Another booth served hot chocolate for the children.

The line moved, and Lucy walked forward with Katie. "I'm not sure," Lucy said. "But Michael said he'd come late."

Katie eyed her. "I still don't get it. After Vinnie stole a stash of cash from Deacon, why didn't Deacon report the crime?"

The question had been bothering Lucy all day. Why would Deacon insist that Vinnie pay the stolen money back plus interest? Did Vinnie murder Deacon in order to avoid paying it back?

Katie leaned closer to Lucy to avoid being overheard. "Do you think Deacon's business partner, Norman, knew about the stolen cash?"

"I don't know, but that's been on my mind as well. If the stolen cash happened to be business profits, how could Norman not know?"

"What if the money had nothing to do with the catering business?"

"Then Norman may or may not have known about the theft."

They reached the front of the line where Jake, wearing a red reindeer sweater, was busy serving his ale while another worker handed out mulled wine. Jake chatted with each customer. He had a natural charm that reminded Lucy of Azad as Kebab Kitchen's chef made his rounds in the dining room to greet customers.

"Hey, ladies," Jake said. "What would you like?"

Lucy asked for Christmas ale and Katie requested the mulled wine. "Will you two come to my brewery soon? I have new brews with cranberry and spices that I'd like you to sample."

"We'd love to. Is Susan here tonight?" Lucy asked.

His smile faded. "No. She said she's not in the holiday mood. I plan on seeing her as soon as my shift is over."

"Tell her I'm thinking about her, and I'll visit the bakery soon," Lucy said.

"Will do." Jake waved at them as the next customer in line stepped up.

Katie sipped her mulled wine. "He seems devoted."

"I'm glad. Susan needs all the support she can get right now." Lucy sipped her ale. "This is delicious. No wonder there's such a long line."

Katie took a long drink. "I like my wine. You think Jake will be upset if I go for seconds and not ask for his Christmas ale?"

"Heaven forbid."

Katie's expression changed from humor to one of horror. "Oh no."

Lucy lowered her cup. "What?"

"Is that who I think it is?"

Lucy followed Katie's gaze and froze. A shiver traveled down her spine that had nothing to do with the cold. The slender woman with brown cropped hair and a strong chin was someone she'd met more than once at Kebab Kitchen, and who had never brought good news.

County Prosecutor Marsha Walsh.

"What's she doing here?" As soon as the words left Lucy's lips, she knew. "The police must be close to an arrest."

A flash of relief crossed Katie's face. "Here comes someone we can ask."

Once more, Lucy followed Katie's gaze to see Bill walking toward them, a cup of mulled wine in his hand. Clearly, he wasn't on duty tonight.

"Hi, ladies," Bill said cheerily. "Are you ready for the tree lighting?"

The song ended and, seconds later, the carolers burst into singing "Jingle Bells."

"We were ready, but something, or *someone*, ruined our festive mood," Katie said.

He lowered his cup and shot them a suspicious look. "What's that supposed to mean?" His grin faded as he studied Katie first, then Lucy. "Come to think of it, why do you two look so serious? You're not talking murder-solving, are you?"

Lucy forgot all about their intention of informing Bill of what they'd learned. Things had changed, and fast. "Now that you brought it up, can you tell us why Prosecutor Walsh is here?"

Bill's brows shot up into his hairline. "You saw her?"

"I can't imagine she has an abundance of Christmas spirit." The times Lucy had met the prosecutor face-to-face at the restaurant, Marsha Walsh had warned her not to interfere in active investigations, and then she'd turned around and ordered hummus and shish kebab. It was frightening and maddening.

"She's in town to oversee an arrest, isn't she? Susan Cutie?" Katie asked. "Clemmons has convinced the prosecutor that she's guilty."

Bill turned to his wife. "Clemmons hasn't convinced Walsh of anything. He's simply presented the facts. Walsh decides if there is sufficient evidence for an arrest and prosecution."

Katie's lips thinned. "Can't *you* convince either of them that they're wrong?"

"There could be other suspects," Lucy added, her voice tight with strain. Vinnie and the missing stolen cash came to mind. And Clarissa and Henry. The two were most likely having an affair and had motive to want to kill Deacon over a trust fund. How could she tell Clemmons without revealing they'd been asking questions?

Bill ran a hand through his hair and let out a puff of air. "I'm not the detective on the case, Katie. There's only so much I can do. But the truth is, Susan does look bad."

"How so?" Lucy asked.

"Clemmons and Walsh know about Susan's deceased husband. Charges were never filed, but it still doesn't look great. Clemmons also knows that Deacon's bad-mouthing about Susan's baking harmed her business. But what truly looks bad is that other swimmers overheard her fight with Deacon in the water the day of the Polar Bear Plunge. She may not have threatened to drown him herself, but she was near him, had motive, and hoped he'd drown."

Crap. The way Bill summed it up, things did look bad for Susan.

"How much time does Susan have?" Lucy asked. *How much time did she and Katie have to find the real murderer?*

Bill shrugged. "I don't know."

"But Marsha Walsh's presence in Ocean Crest isn't a good sign, is it?" Katie asked.

"It's not," he agreed.

The carolers ended the song, and the mayor stepped up to the microphone. His tap on it caused a burst of static. "This year, a student from Ocean Crest Elementary School will light the tree. Let the holiday season in Ocean Crest officially begin!"

The mayor was handed a portable electrical box, and an eight-year-old girl came forward to flip a switch. The tree erupted into a hundred-foot cone of light. The choir began to sing "We Wish You a Merry Christmas."

The crowd gasped as thousands of brilliant lights shone like stars in the darkened sky. For a second, it was almost blinding.

And that was when Lucy met Prosecutor Walsh's gaze.

"Ms. Berberian."

Lucy's face felt as if it would crack with the effort to smile as she faced the county prosecutor. The woman had asked to speak with Lucy alone. Bill and Katie stood in the distance, watching the Santa's reindeer behind the fence. Katie glanced back, a gleam of interest in her eyes, but Bill shook his head and took his wife's arm to stroll along the fence.

Lucy returned her attention to the woman. "Hello, Ms. Walsh. Are you enjoying Ocean Crest's tree lighting?" She took pains to appear calm, but inside, her stomach churned.

Lucy had previously looked into the prosecutor's record. Walsh was whip-smart, and she never brought a case to trial unless she had sufficient evidence to ensure a jury conviction. As a former attorney, Lucy grudgingly admired her.

Walsh lowered a cup of hot chocolate. "My evening depends on one thing. Are you going to be trouble?"

Lucy's eyes widened with fake alarm. "Whatever do you mean? I'm here enjoying the Christmas spirit, just like everyone else in town."

"Let's not beat around the bush. You took part in the

Polar Bear Plunge, and you've been asking questions about Deacon Spooner's murder."

What was it about the woman that frightened her, but raised her ire at the same time? Lucy took a breath in an attempt to calm her racing heart. "You're right. I was there. But as for asking questions, I've done nothing wrong. Customers come into Kebab Kitchen and like to gossip. I can't control that."

Walsh pursed her lips. "I'm not talking about town gossip. I'm specifically referring to your visit to Norman Weston at the Sea View. Your sidekick, Mrs. Watson, was present as well."

Oh no. As Deacon's business partner, it shouldn't come as a surprise that Walsh and Clemmons had interviewed Norman. He must have told her everything during questioning.

She was aware of Walsh watching her and waiting for her answer. Lucy had learned that the truth was much better than any story she could come up with. "First, Katie is not my sidekick, but my matron of honor in my future wedding. We went to the Sea View to ask about holding my wedding reception there." Lucy held up her left hand to display her engagement ring. "I'm recently engaged."

Walsh cocked her head to the side as she studied the ring. "I see. I believe congratulations are in order. Who is the lucky groom?"

In the past, the woman had an uncanny ability to change topics from food to crime. Would she do it again, only with wedding questions?

"Kebab Kitchen's chef."

"Ah, as I recall, his Mediterranean cooking is exceptional. I'll have to visit soon," Walsh said.

Do you have to? Or is it an excuse to check on me?
"Anytime, Ms. Walsh."

The prosecutor flashed a crocodile smile. "On another note, after speaking with Norman Weston, I do believe your questions far exceeded simply inquiring about the cost of a reception hall for a wedding."

Once again, the woman's method of questioning took Lucy off guard. What precisely had Norman told her and Detective Clemmons?

"You were also present when Susan Cutie was questioned by Detective Clemmons. I call that additional interfering," Walsh said.

Lucy raised her chin and met her gaze. "How is that interfering? Susan asked me to stay with her." If only the detective or the prosecutor would look into other suspects, Lucy and Katie wouldn't have to. But that wasn't something Lucy wanted to bring up. Now that Prosecutor Walsh was involved, she needed concrete evidence of Susan's innocence before approaching Clemmons.

The prosecutor took a step closer, until Lucy could see the intelligence and determination shining in her dark eyes. "You can argue with me all night, Ms. Berberian. I just have one piece of advice: Stay out of my investigation or there will be consequences."

"The prosecutor warned you to stop sleuthing?" Katie asked.

"I believe her exact words were 'Or there will be consequences.'" Lucy's nerves were still tight after her confrontation with Marsha Walsh.

Katie tugged her knit hat over her ears. "Sorry. I wanted to stay with you, but Bill told me I had to listen to Walsh."

"No, it's for the best." She didn't want to do anything to jeopardize Bill's position as detective.

"You okay?" Katie's brows drew together in concern as she looked at Lucy.

Lucy scanned the crowd of townsfolk as everyone seemed to be enjoying the holiday mood. "Sorry, but I lost my festive spirit and want to go home."

"Hey, how about I walk you? Bill won't mind, and it looks like Azad will be busy serving hot chocolate for a while."

"You sure?"

"Yup. What are friends for? How about we go to my house, have a glass of wine, and watch old *Columbo* episodes? I'll even bake chocolate chip cookies, although they'll be from a tub and not homemade."

"Sounds great." Her friend always knew how to make her feel better.

Together, they crossed the street and headed away from the park and the ongoing festivities. The lights of the park faded as a flurry of snow began to fall.

"It's quiet and pretty," Katie said.

"Yes, it's—"

A blur of movement caught Lucy's eye, and she halted and nudged Katie's arm. "Look who else is calling it quits. It's Clarissa."

As they watched, Clarissa left the park, crossed the street, and headed in the opposite direction from where Lucy and Katie were headed.

"Where is she going alone?" Katie asked.

"Who knows? I still can't get over that she and Henry are close," Lucy said.

"It doesn't look great for her, especially if Henry got cash from Uncle Deacon's trust fund."

"I want to ask her about it," Lucy said.

Katie shot her a disbelieving look. "Here? Now?"

"Why not?"

"We have nothing to lose," Lucy said. "Except Prosecutor Walsh's attention."

Katie grabbed her hand. "She left with Bill. I changed my mind. Let's go."

Chapter Twenty

Lucy and Katie were careful to stay in the shadows as they followed Clarissa down the street. They ducked behind parked cars, vans, and in doorways as they went.

"Where's she going?" Katie whispered.

Lucy shook her head to indicate she had no idea. The streetlamps cast long shadows on the snow-covered street. Coming from a cheerful and noisy crowd in the park, it was eerily quiet.

After a brisk walk, Clarissa came to one of the town's stoplights. She looked both ways, then crossed the street and headed for a small shopping strip where Ben's Barber Shop, Magic's Family Apothecary, and Cutie's Cupcakes were located. As far as Lucy could tell, the strip was empty.

"It looks like she's headed straight for Susan's bakery," Lucy said.

Did Clarissa plan on knocking on the side door to speak with Susan? Jake had said Susan wasn't up to attending the tree lighting. Was Susan alone inside her bakery?

But rather than head for the bakery, Clarissa turned down an alley between the barbershop and the apothecary and disappeared from sight.

"Where the heck is she going?" Katie asked.

As they approached the entrance of the alley, Lucy slowed, and Katie nearly bumped into her. The streetlights only cast enough light to see halfway down the alley. The deepest part of the alley was dark and she couldn't see a thing. Thankfully, Clarissa halted in the middle and they could still see her.

She spotted the shapes of two large recycling containers. Several trash bags were piled on top of each other beside the containers. If they crouched low and sprinted, they could make it there without being seen. Lucy touched Katie's shoulder, then pointed to the containers. "Let's get closer."

Katie shook her head.

"We have no choice. We can't see or hear from here."

Katie hesitated, before nodding. For someone who encouraged Lucy to investigate local crime and who loved watching crime TV shows, Katie often got cold feet when it came to taking risks.

Lucy's heart pounding in her chest, they crept forward and made a beeline for the recycling containers and pressed their backs to the cold, plastic receptacles. The pile of trash bags offered additional coverage. A puddle of melted snow seeped through the knees of Lucy's jeans as she knelt on the ground. She wrinkled her nose at the stench of refuse. Trash collection wasn't until later in the week, and both the garbage bags and recycling containers smelled like rotten eggs.

They peeked around the containers to see a figure appear from deep in the shadows of the alley to join Clarissa. The figure paced and walked forward a few feet, just enough for a shaft of light from the streetlight to shine on his blond hair.

Henry.

"Clarissa," Henry said. "Did anyone follow you?"

"No."

"Good. I've been waiting a long time and was afraid you wouldn't show."

"I promised a girlfriend that I would go with her to the tree lighting, and I had to wait until she went home before I could get away," Clarissa said.

Henry gave Clarissa a brief hug, then stepped back. "Are you all right?"

Clarissa pushed a lock of auburn hair from her face and looked up at him. "I am now."

Just like at the tree farm, their familiarity spoke volumes. *They must be lovers . . . had to be lovers.*

Clarissa shifted her feet. "The county prosecutor is in town. I saw her standing in the hot chocolate line."

"I suspected she'd come around," Henry said. "A murder in this town is serious and would get her attention."

Clarissa began to pace. "I'm worried. That detective is bad enough, but a county prosecutor makes me even more nervous."

Henry shook his head. "No need for concern. As long as she's not onto us, it's good news."

The more Lucy heard, the more it sounded like they were guilty. Why else would they be so nervous about Walsh's presence in town? And even more important, why meet in a dark back alley to talk about it?

A rat scurried across the lot and crept close to Lucy and Katie—or, more likely, to the trash and its food source. Lucy watched, fingers tense, as the rat came closer, then ran right over Katie's boot.

Katie let out a screech, then slapped a hand over her mouth.

"What the hell was that?" Clarissa said.

Lucy exchanged a horrified look with Katie. What to do? Make a run for it? Or face them?

The chances of them sprinting from the alley unrecognized were slim to none. They really didn't have much of a choice. Lucy stood on shaky legs and stepped away from the recycling containers and garbage bags. "It's just us."

Clarissa's voice echoed through the alley like a gunshot. "You two!"

"I know her," Henry said, pointing to Lucy. "I took her family Christmas picture at Old Time Photos."

Clarissa's eyes narrowed and she planted her hands on her hips. "I know both of them. They came to the diner to ask me questions about Deacon. They must think they're Ocean Crest cops."

Lucy didn't bother to deny or admit their accusations. "Are you a couple?"

"And did you kill Deacon Spooner?" Katie asked.

Lucy wanted to slap her hand over Katie's mouth. Her friend had an uncanny knack for asking forthright questions. The problem was, they could be facing stone-cold killers!

"No. We aren't a couple. What made you think that?" Henry asked.

Lucy wasn't about to admit that she'd first eavesdropped on them at the Christmas tree farm. Watching them now only reaffirmed her initial belief. "Why else would you secretly meet in a dark alley?"

Clarissa shot her a nasty glare. "To talk. *In private*."

Henry took a step forward. "They're snooping because they think we're lovers who conspired to kill my uncle."

"It does look strange, finding you two meeting in secret while everyone else is at the tree lighting," Katie said.

"We went to Ocean Crest High School together. We were prom king and queen. We've been friends for years," Henry said.

Clarissa struck Lucy as a pretty, popular type in high school—popular enough to be prom queen, like the snobby cheerleader who'd been prom queen when Katie and Lucy had graduated. But Henry seemed a more subdued type than the football captain who'd been their prom king.

"You both did the Polar Bear Plunge," Katie pointed out.

"And you both had reason to dislike Deacon," Lucy said.

Henry met Lucy's gaze straight on. "I never said I disliked my uncle."

Lucy had discovered Henry and Deacon were related from the picture at Old Time Photos, but Henry didn't know she'd learned about the trust fund. She decided there was nothing to lose at this point.

"We know Deacon was your uncle and he left you a trust fund," Lucy said.

Henry's brows shot up into his hairline. "How do you know that?"

Katie spoke up. "My husband is a cop."

Clarissa scoffed. "You know why I disliked Deacon, but what you don't know is that Deacon treated Henry horribly and never helped him as a kid after his dad died."

Henry's face fell. "And he didn't give me any financial help to open Old Time Photos on the boardwalk. My uncle used me to take wedding photos for cheap. He told brides he had a connection to a photographer who would give them discounts on their wedding albums just to ensure the brides would book their weddings at the Sea View. I never received my full fee."

What a jerky thing to do. The more Lucy learned about Deacon Spooner, the less she liked him. But Henry's admission, no matter how disturbing, was motive.

"So you both had motive to off Deacon Spooner." Katie pointed out exactly what Lucy had been thinking.

As Lucy watched the pair, she remembered something else Clemmons had told her when she'd spoken with him in the coffee shop. He didn't believe Clarissa was a suspect because another swimmer had said that she wasn't near Deacon in the water. Lucy thought that defense was insufficient because it was a free-for-all in the water that day. But now, facing both Clarissa and Henry, she had an uneasy feeling as to *who* had told the detective that Clarissa had not been close enough to kill.

"What about you, Clarissa?" Lucy asked. "Detective Clemmons said another swimmer told him you weren't near Deacon in the ocean. I have a feeling that person was Henry." Lucy turned to Henry. "Am I right?"

Henry lifted his chin. "It was me, but I didn't lie. I didn't see Clarissa anywhere near Deacon."

"And you watched her the entire time?" Lucy asked.

"Well . . . it would have been hard to do that." Henry's brows drew downward. "You really do think we drowned Deacon, don't you?"

"Did you?" Katie asked.

"No!" Clarissa and Henry cried out in unison.

"We hated him and talked about giving the bastard his due," Clarissa said, "but we didn't drown him. Someone beat us to it."

"Do you believe us?" Henry asked.

"Why do you care what we believe? Shouldn't you be more worried by what the cops think?" Lucy said.

"Sure we are. But we also know you two have a good

track record for solving town crime. The fact that you followed us and not the cops reaffirms this fact," Clarissa said.

"I'll give you 5 percent of my trust fund if you help us," Henry said.

Lucy shook her head. "That sounds like a bribe to me."

"It's not a bribe. I'm offering to pay for your time. How about 10 percent?"

Lucy held up a hand. "Just stop. We're not Sherlock and Watson."

"You could have fooled us." Clarissa pointed to Katie. "And isn't her last name Watson?"

Katie shrugged. "A weird coincidence."

"I don't believe in coincidences. Only results." Clarissa eyed them both. "You two must have a reason for involving yourselves in Deacon's murder, and don't try to tell me you have the town's interest at heart. There must be something or someone else."

Clarissa caught Lucy's flinch. "It's some*one*, and I bet it's that baker chick."

Lucy straightened her spine. "Her name is Susan, and she didn't kill anyone."

"Well, neither did we. You're one smart cookie, Lucy. So why don't you help all of us and find the real killer?"

Eloisa was home when Lucy opened the door that night. Her landlady wasn't alone. Azad's voice came from the kitchen. He was sitting at the table with Eloisa, drinking coffee. Gadoo was curled up on a chair and Cupid was snoring in his dog bed. As soon as the cat saw her, he stretched, then jumped down from his chair to rub against Lucy's leg.

Azad stood to give Lucy a kiss. "Hey. I looked for you

after my hot cocoa shift ended to walk you home, but you had already left."

Lucy pulled off her knit hat. She had already hung her jacket on a coatrack in the hallway. "Sorry. Katie walked me home."

"I would have waited for Azad," Eloisa said.

Rather than roll her eyes, Lucy ignored her. Azad pulled out a chair for her. Eloisa set a steaming mug before her. "Thanks."

Azad studied her, his dark eyes roaming her face. "What's wrong?"

He could always read her like an open book, and it was hard to hide anything from him. She saw no reason to lie to him, or her landlady.

Lucy cradled her mug and let the warmth seep into her cold fingers. "The county prosecutor was at the tree lighting. She told me to butt out of investigating Deacon's murder."

"She's probably afraid of you," Eloisa said.

Lucy eyed her. "How so?"

Eloisa lowered her mug. "Well, you have a good sleuthing track record. You make her office look bad."

"She's right," Azad said.

"I guess I never looked at it that way."

"I have a feeling you still want to help your friend, Susan," Azad said.

"I do."

Azad tilted his head to the side and watched her. "Then what's my lady going to do about it?"

Lucy gave him a smile. "There are other suspects, including an angry bride, Deacon's nephew, and his business partner, Norman Weston. I just wish Detective

Clemmons and Prosecutor Walsh would look at them and not just at Susan."

Azad reached out to squeeze her hand. "I have faith in you, Lucy."

A warm glow flowed through her, and she returned his affectionate squeeze. No matter how worried the prosecutor made her feel, she had wonderful support from Azad, Katie, and even Eloisa.

"Azad's right," Eloisa said. "Don't be so depressed. Besides, there's an upcoming dance at the senior center to raise more funds for the renovations. Azad said he'd escort both of us."

"It just might cheer you up," Azad said.

"Okay. I could use some cheering up. Although I have to warn both of you that I haven't been in the holiday mood much lately," Lucy said.

Eloisa raised a finger. "But there's one more thing to get through before the dance. Deacon's funeral is tomorrow."

Lucy bit her bottom lip. "I forgot about that." Ever since her grandmother's funeral in the middle of winter, she'd dreaded them. She'd been close to her Armenian grandmother, and she had bad memories of standing in the snow, shivering and waiting until the coffin was lowered into the frozen ground.

Eloisa arched an eyebrow. "The funeral is a good opportunity."

She'd never consider a funeral any type of opportunity, let alone a good one. "How so?"

Eloisa met her confused look. "You can learn a lot. Nothing like watching people to see whose tears are real or fake."

* * *

"Do you want to stay the night?" Lucy asked.

"Do you want me too?" Azad asked.

Lucy leaned into Azad's embrace as they stood just inside the entrance to her apartment. He'd escorted Lucy upstairs after Eloisa had announced she had a yoga class at the senior center early the next morning before the funeral and was going to bed.

Now they were alone. At last.

Azad's cologne and unique masculine essence filled her senses, and she placed her hands on his broad chest. She could feel his heart beat strong beneath his cotton shirt.

Looking up into his dark eyes, her lips curled in an inviting smile. "I'd like that, Azad."

He kissed her forehead, her eyelids, her lips. The touch of his lips was a delicious sensation, and his kiss sang through her veins. He lifted his head, his dark eyes seeking hers as he pushed a wayward curl behind her ear. "I'd like that, too, very much. But I also know you had a stressful evening confronting that prosecutor, then Clarissa and Henry, too."

Once they were alone, she'd told him what had happened in the alley. She no longer feared he'd be upset at her sleuthing. He understood her and, most important, he accepted her.

"I'm feeling better now. Much better." In hindsight, she wondered why she ever hesitated to resume a romantic relationship with Azad. He'd been part of her life for a long time. They may have had their differences in the past, but he'd proven himself time and time again. She wanted to be with him.

She could feel his uneven breathing on her cheek as he held her close. Reaching up on tiptoe, she kissed him. He hesitated for the briefest second before kissing her back, more passionately this time. His hand moved down the length of her back, pressing her to him, and she melted against him. He swept her into his arms, kicked the stairway door shut with a booted foot, and carried her into her bedroom.

He lowered her to her feet on the carpet. This time, it was Lucy who shut the bedroom door.

Chapter Twenty-One

The parking lot of the Catholic Church on the corner of Ocean Avenue and Shell Street was full. Inside, a sea of black crammed the pews as Lucy, Katie, and Eloisa made their way down the aisle to search for a place to sit.

Ocean Crest was a close-knit community and many showed up to pay their respects when one of their own passed away. Katie halted by a pew, and people shuffled down to make room for the three of them.

The funeral hadn't yet begun, and Eloisa nudged her arm. "Your hot chef spent the night."

Oh God. This wasn't something she wanted to talk about with her landlady, especially sitting in a church, waiting for a funeral to start.

But it had been nice to wake up next to Azad this morning. He'd sat with her on the patio with their matching Ocean Crest tourist mugs filled with coffee and watched the sun kiss the ocean. Gadoo had sat next to Azad. The cat was stingy with his affection, but he had taken a liking to Kebab Kitchen's chef. Afterward, Azad had quietly snuck down the stairs and left, but apparently, he hadn't been quiet enough.

Eloisa's gaze focused on the pews in front of them. "Would you look at that?"

Lucy turned to see where Eloisa was looking. "What?"

"Isn't that Susan Cutie sitting right behind Detective Clemmons?"

"She's right," Katie said.

Lucy craned her neck to see around the tall man sitting in front of her. "I see Susan. She's with her boyfriend, Jake."

"He's handsome. How did she find him?" Eloisa asked.

Eloisa made it sound like Susan was unattractive. Lucy had always thought Susan was pretty, with her cornflower-blue eyes and delicate features.

"My parents introduced Jake and Susan," Lucy said.

"Lucky gal," Eloisa said, her eyes focused on Jake.

Before Lucy could comment, Katie nudged her arm. "Look who else just showed up," Katie said.

Mr. Citteroni entered the church. Michael was by his father's side, and Vinnie Pinto trailed behind them. Even though Vinnie worked for Anthony Citteroni, she would never have guessed that they would attend Deacon's funeral together. Especially after what Anthony had told her. Nothing the mobster did was by accident.

So what is he up to?

Vinnie wore black cargo pants and a black blazer that looked about two sizes too big. It was a step up from what she'd seen him wear when he'd broken into Eloisa's home, but she wasn't fooled. He was far from a model citizen. He was a burglar and a thief and had stolen cash from Deacon.

So, why was Vinnie at Deacon's funeral? Was he there to draw attention away from himself as a murder suspect?

Did he believe a murderer wouldn't attend the funeral of his victim?

Or had Mr. Citteroni forced Vinnie to come? But to what end?

She watched as the trio sat, Vinnie between Michael and his father. Vinnie's shifty gaze scanned the crowd, as if he were looking for the fastest way out of the church.

Lucy turned her attention back to the rest of the people. She spotted Henry in the front row, sitting beside a woman in her sixties with brown hair and a conservative black dress. She must be his mother, and the pair appeared to be Deacon's only family in attendance. Norman Weston was also in the front row, and even sitting, he was the tallest man in the church.

"Both Norman and Henry had motive to want Deacon dead," Katie whispered. This was turning out to be a strange funeral. "The only suspect missing is Clarissa."

Lucy glanced at the wide church doors. "I don't think she'll be coming. Everyone knows how she felt about Deacon."

Lucy's gaze kept returning to Vinnie. He fidgeted in his seat, seeming uncomfortable in his ill-fitting suit, and even more uncomfortable sitting between Mr. Citteroni and Michael.

The priest stepped up to the altar and the organist began to play. The funeral was about to start.

Just then, Michael looked back and met Lucy's gaze. He tilted his head in Vinnie's direction, and Lucy knew her friend well enough to understand the message.

This time, Mr. Citteroni was the puppeteer and Vinnie was his marionette.

* * *

"You sure about this?" Katie asked.

"I am," Lucy said. "Michael's look told me all I need to know. His father brought Vinnie to the funeral to talk to us."

Lucy and Katie filed out of the packed church and waited by the side. Even with the sun shining, it was a chilly afternoon, and Lucy clutched her wool peacoat close. They didn't need to wait for Eloisa. She'd met a friend from the senior center and was getting a ride home.

At last, Michael, his father, and Vinnie stepped out of the church. In the sunlight, Vinnie's complexion could only be described as ashen. The trio halted by them.

"Hi, Lucy. Hi, Katie," Michael said.

Mr. Citteroni's mouth curved in a half smile. "Ms. Berberian and Mrs. Watson. Perhaps we should speak by my vehicle."

Vinnie stood silently, his gaze darting from Katie to Lucy.

They made their way through the church parking lot. Lucy looked for a black Cadillac, black Mercedes, black BMW, or another high-end model that a mobster would drive. Maybe he even had a bodyguard dressed as a chauffeur?

But when Mr. Citteroni kept walking, she was truly confounded until she spotted his "vehicle." She tripped. Michael caught her arm.

A garbage truck with the letters CITTERONI SANITATION painted on the side was parked in the last spot of the lot.

"This is your car?" Katie asked, a note of surprise in her voice.

Mr. Citteroni's face was grim. "I didn't say 'car.' I said 'vehicle.' Vinnie has a work shift to cover."

Vinnie remained silent.

They followed around the side of the truck, where they were shielded from the view of anyone lingering outside the church or making their way through the parking lot to their car.

Mr. Citteroni turned to Vinnie. "I had a nice, long talk with my employee and he has something to tell you. It's not what I had initially expected."

"I robbed Deacon Spooner," Vinnie blurted out.

Lucy took a quick breath and shot Katie a sideways glance before returning to look at Vinnie. "Okay."

"I was his property manager and never turned over the key," Vinnie went on. "Deacon never changed his locks. It was like taking candy from a baby."

Just like Eloisa hadn't changed her locks. Lucy wanted to holler at him, but held her tongue. She needed more information. He was obviously petrified of his employer for him to be spewing a confession.

"How much money did you steal?" Katie asked.

"A good amount."

"How much?" Lucy pressed.

"Thirty thousand. All in hundred-dollar bills."

Lucy's jaw gaped. *Thirty thousand?* A quick glance at Katie and Michael revealed they were just as surprised.

Where the heck did Deacon get that much cash? Back then, the Sea View was being remodeled, and that would have taken most of the business's money. She recalled that Deacon's partner, Norman, had said Deacon was going to pay him off for his share of the business. Was he planning to use that cash?

Vinnie ran a hand down his face. "It wasn't even in a safe, but in a suitcase, and stashed under a bookshelf in his office. I thought I had scored big."

"I'd call that a big score," Katie said.

"Yeah, but then Deacon turned up at my home with a gun."

"What?" Lucy asked.

"Deacon had a hidden security camera in his office. He showed me the clip on his cell phone and I knew I was screwed. You see, I'd already spent the money, paying off my bookie and then hitting the blackjack tables in Atlantic City over the weekend."

"You spent thirty thousand dollars in one weekend?" Katie asked.

Vinnie shrugged, as if losing that much cash wasn't that big a thing. "What can I say? Sometimes I'm lucky. Other times, not so much."

"I bet you're unlucky more often than not," Katie said.

Vinnie placed his hands on his hips and glowered at Katie. Lucy turned the conversation back on track before further words were exchanged. "What happened when Deacon caught you?"

"He demanded the cash, and when I told him I didn't have it, I expected him to call the cops." Vinnie's expression grew grim, as if he was recalling the conversation. "Deacon demanded I pay it all back with interest. He gave me six months. When I told him that I couldn't possibly pay back that much cash that fast, he said the weirdest thing. He told me I should rob others just like I robbed him. So I started doing that."

Lucy's lips thinned. "You tried to rob my landlady, Eloisa Lubinski, that night I called the cops."

Vinnie met her gaze straight on. "That's right."

Lucy recalled that night. Vinnie had given them a lame excuse, that he wanted to talk to Eloisa about participating in the Polar Bear Plunge. Lucy hadn't believed it then, and she was glad she'd heard him break in and had called the cops.

"Did Deacon ever say where he got so much money?" Lucy asked.

"No, but one crook can spot another. That much cash stuffed in a suitcase can only mean one thing. It wasn't by legal means. Maybe he was selling drugs on the side."

"Drugs? You think he sold drugs through the catering business?"

"Who knows?"

Lucy mulled this over. The more she considered it, the more it made sense. Why did Deacon stuff thirty grand in a suitcase and store it in his office rather than put it in the bank? She also wondered if Norman knew about the money, and if he was also part of an illegal conspiracy.

Let's get back to the murder.

"So, Deacon had you in a bind and you killed him over it," Lucy said.

Vinnie scoffed. "I thought about it, but I didn't kill him. That's one crime you can't pin on me. But whoever drowned the guy did me a big favor."

Vinnie wasn't the first person to admit they were glad Deacon Spooner was dead. Clarissa was quite open about it as well.

Mr. Citteroni, who had stayed silent during the conversation, nodded at Lucy. "Do you have any more questions for Vinnie?"

"You brought him to the funeral just for me to ask him questions?" She was still surprised. Anthony didn't owe her anything, but he'd been helpful . . . very helpful. She glanced at Michael. Maybe he held more influence over his father than she'd thought.

Michael seemed to read her mind, and he shook his head. "I had nothing to do with it."

"I promised my son I would help." Mr. Citteroni stepped away from the truck and nodded once at Vinnie. "You can go to work now."

Lucy and Katie returned to Katie's house after the funeral to decompress and discuss what they'd just learned in the church parking lot. As soon as Katie had tossed her purse on the counter, she'd opened the freezer and taken out a plastic container of frozen cookie dough.

"I'm still trying to process everything." Lucy pulled out a stool at the kitchen counter.

The oven timer dinged, and Katie pulled on a pair of oven mitts and pulled out a tray of chocolate chip cookies. "Chocolate eases stress," she said.

"I always knew you were smart." Lucy inhaled the delicious smell.

Katie placed two cookies on a paper plate and handed it to Lucy. She picked up a hot cookie and took a bite. Heaven. The chocolate melted in her mouth. "Yum. This is better than any after-funeral luncheon."

"I heard the luncheon was a tray of sandwiches from Holloway's Grocery. We didn't miss anything. Besides, we learned a lot more by talking with Vinnie. By the way, didn't Vinnie look like he was going to pee his pants when Mr. Citteroni glared at him? I think it's the only reason he sang like a canary."

Lucy choked on her cookie. "You sure have a colorful way of describing things."

"Do you believe what Vinnie said?" Katie asked.

"About him breaking in to the Sea View and finding a suitcase stuffed with hundred-dollar bills?"

"Not that. Do you believe Vinnie's story that he didn't kill Deacon?"

"What about Vinnie stealing cash and killing Deacon?" A male voice sounded from the doorway.

Lucy froze, a second cookie halfway to her mouth.

Katie took a quick breath, and she dropped her half-eaten cookie on her plate. "Hey, Bill. You're home from work early."

Bill strolled into the kitchen, his expression taut. Ever since he'd been promoted to detective, he no longer wore a police officer's uniform, but a gray suit and a striped blue tie.

He dropped his car keys on the kitchen counter, then leaned against it. "Well? What have you two gotten yourselves into now?"

"We didn't stick our noses into anything," Katie blurted out. "Mr. Citteroni approached us."

Bill pushed away from the counter and stood straight. "Mr. Citteroni? What in God's name did *he* have to tell you? Most people around here avoid him like the plague, and for good reason."

Lucy didn't like the direction this was going. She hated causing marital strife between her best friend and her husband. "Vinnie Pinto works for Anthony Citteroni," Lucy said.

Bill turned to her. "So?"

Lucy tried not to shrink beneath his blue gaze. Bill was her friend, too, but when he was in cop mode he could be intimidating. "Vinnie was the man who tried to break into Eloisa's home the night I dialed 9-1-1. You showed up, remember?"

Bill's lips drew into a straight line. "I remember."

"Mr. Citteroni made Vinnie talk."

"And why would Mr. Citteroni be so helpful?" Bill asked.

Lucy threw up her hands. "I don't know. Maybe because he knows I'm friends with his son, Michael."

"And did Vinnie confess?" Bill asked.

"Not to murder. Just burglary."

Bill let out a puff of air. "All right, you two. Spill everything."

Lucy talked, and Bill's face grew increasingly grim.

He scrubbed a hand down his face. "I understand that you didn't know Mr. Citteroni would bring his employee to the funeral for the sole purpose of having him speak with you. But still, you two need to let Clemmons handle this. Just because Vinnie says he didn't murder Deacon doesn't mean it's true."

Katie placed a warm cookie on a plate, offered it to her husband, then patted his arm. Bill's tense expression visibly eased at the food and the affection.

"We know that, Bill," Katie said. "We just wish Clemmons would look at all the leads, not just the obvious ones. Both Clarissa and Henry had motive to kill Deacon and opportunity as swimmers. And there's his business partner, too. A man named Norman Weston."

"How do you know Clemmons isn't following up on everything?" Bill asked.

Lucy hoped Bill was right and the detective *was* considering suspects other than Susan Cutie. If only there was a way to confirm it.

"We don't know," Katie said.

"If it makes you feel better, I'll speak with Clemmons and tell him to look into Vinnie. If he was one of the swimmers at the Polar Bear Plunge, maybe others saw him near Deacon before he drowned."

Katie kissed his cheek. "Thanks, Bill. I forgot to ask how your day went. Are you still looking into the drug problem at Ocean Crest High School?"

Bill finished his cookie in two bites. "I am. I'm no longer convinced it's a student who's selling the bulk of the marijuana."

"You think it's an outside dealer? Someone from town?" Lucy asked.

"I hope it's an outsider, but with the help of the principal and staff, we're looking at all the angles. We'll catch the culprit or culprits soon." Bill placed his plate in the kitchen sink. "Meanwhile, you both need to stop meddling in police business. Remember, there's still a murderer loose in Ocean Crest."

Chapter Twenty-Two

Lucy returned to Kebab Kitchen and a bustling lunch shift. The hummus bar needed frequent refilling and Azad and Butch were putting out dish after dish of savory stuffed peppers, tomatoes, and squash with meat and rice in a traditional Armenian dish called dolma.

Other entrees were just as popular, especially the baked scrod stuffed with crabmeat and Mediterranean herbs. Lucy ran around refilling coffee and tea mugs and making sure customers were happy.

Afterward, when the dining room was calm, Lucy made her way into the storage room and selected a crate of fresh eggplants with shiny purple skins.

Butch was mixing a large pot on the stove as she passed by carrying the eggplants. He smiled, and his gold front tooth flashed in the fluorescent lighting. "Hey, Lucy Lou. Another cooking lesson with your mom today?"

Lucy grinned back. "Wish me luck."

Angela was waiting for her by the wooden prep table. She handed Lucy an apron. "The moussaka special sold out last time, and Azad asked if we can help him make more for tonight."

Not long ago, Lucy would have panicked if her mother

sought to serve any of her cooking at Kebab Kitchen. Truth be told, Lucy still was a bit nervous, but she held her tongue. Her confidence had grown after each session.

Lucy tied her apron, then washed her hands. "Are you sure we have enough time to make moussaka for tonight?"

Angela looked at her as if she'd asked a very silly question. "Of course."

Lucy wasn't convinced. Her mother may be able to butter layers of phyllo dough and make trays of baklava in record speed, but Lucy was much slower.

At least she loved what they were to prepare. Moussaka was to Greeks what lasagna was to Italians. She could eat it straight from the pan if her mother would let her.

Angela clicked the remote and the mounted TV turned on, and Cooking Kurt appeared on the screen.

Lucy glanced up. "How come his show is always on?"

"I use something called DVR to record his show. I asked your father to add it to our cable plan," her mother said.

Lucy doubted her father would have added the feature if he knew her mother was going to use it to record the celebrity chef's show.

Kurt wasn't even cooking in the episode, but talking about his new appliances —a shiny, stainless-steel stove with a huge hood, and a gigantic refrigerator with side-by-side doors. No doubt the manufacturers of the appliances had paid him to promote them to his viewers.

Angela reached for the ground beef on the prep table. "For the moussaka, we start by lightly frying the sliced eggplant. Then we prepare the meat sauce."

Preparing moussaka may be daunting, especially if it was going to be on tonight's menu, but Lucy did her best to stand straight and meet her mother's eyes. Angela could sense trepidation.

"What about the béchamel sauce?" Lucy asked.

"We make that last because it doesn't hold well."

Lucy watched her mother carefully as she fried half-inch slices of eggplant in a skillet before taking over the task herself. Next, under her mother's watchful gaze, Lucy browned the meat and onions in olive oil, then added spices and tomato paste. Soon, a delicious aroma filled the kitchen.

"The béchamel sauce is tricky," her mother said. "I'll heat the milk while you prepare a roux by heating butter and whisking in flour. You must constantly mix it, but not let it get too dark."

Lucy concentrated on whisking. She was beginning to sweat. If only Azad didn't need the moussaka for tonight's special, she wouldn't be so nervous. Thankfully, her efforts were successful, and soon they were layering numerous casserole dishes with the eggplant and meat, then topping it with the béchamel sauce. It would take close to an hour before all the trays were ready.

Lucy was taking off her apron just as Sally sailed into the kitchen. "You have a delivery, Mrs. Berberian. It's from Jake's Boardwalk Brewery."

Angela's face lit up and she set aside her oven mitts. "It must be his special Christmas ale."

Clearly, her mother was getting excited about her annual Christmas party. "Is Jake still here?" Lucy asked.

"Yes, but not for long. He said he has a list of deliveries," Sally said.

Jake always seemed busy during the winter season, with weddings, reunions, and holiday parties, but the summer tourist season must be crazy. Jake's Boardwalk Brewery was doing just fine.

"Lucy, you see to Jake while I make sure the moussaka

doesn't overcook." Her mother opened one of the ovens to check on the food.

Lucy whisked off her apron and pushed through the swinging kitchen doors into the dining room to find Jake waiting by the hostess stand. His handcart held a single full-sized keg.

"Hi, Lucy," Jake greeted her. "I have a half keg of my special Christmas ale for your mother."

"Thanks," Lucy said. "How's Susan?" She hadn't seen her friend in days, and Susan had been notably absent at the town Christmas tree lighting.

Jake shook his head and leaned on the handcart. "This murder thing is taking its toll. Yesterday, she told me she doesn't feel like baking. She's *never* said that before."

"That doesn't sound like Susan at all." Lucy couldn't imagine her friend not baking. It wasn't just Susan's livelihood; it was her passion.

"You should stop by to see her. I think it would cheer her up," Jake said.

Lucy nodded. "Of course. I always have a craving for her lemon meringue pie."

Jake pushed the handcart aside and stood straight. "I'll tell her to expect you and to bake a fresh one. Now, where do you want the keg?"

Lucy thought about it. "By the waitress station." It would be easier to serve beer during her mother's Christmas party if the keg was right by the glasses.

The handcart squeaked as Jake wheeled it to the waitress station, then lifted the keg and left it tucked in an alcove. "Tell your mom I said thanks for the business." Jake waved on his way out, the handcart making noise the entire way.

After Jake backed out of the parking lot in his delivery

van, the swinging kitchen doors opened and her mother looked around. "Where's the keg?"

Lucy pointed to where it was stashed away by the waitress station. "I told Jake to put it here."

"Why? It should be in the storage room." Angela marched to the keg and reached down to lift it. The keg didn't move an inch. Her mother rubbed her low back. "This is quite heavy."

"Where's Azad?" Lucy asked.

"He went home for his break before the dinner shift, while we were cooking. Butch left, too. I told them I could handle any stray orders until then. Go get your father. He can move this keg."

Lucy found her father in the tiny office in the corner of the storage room, where he'd been working on this week's payroll. Lucy had learned not to complain when her parent showed up unexpectedly. He may be semiretired, but she'd come to realize her father found helping out fulfilling.

"What's the problem?" Raffi removed his reading glasses and they dangled from a chain around his neck.

"We need to move a keg to the storage room and it's heavy. Azad and Butch are out on break."

Her father was by Lucy's side as they left the storage room, passed through the kitchen's swinging doors, and entered the dining room.

Raffi squatted down to pick up the keg, then promptly dropped it on the tile floor with a thud.

"What's wrong?" Angela asked.

"It's heavy," Raffi answered.

"You used to be able to pick up heavy delivery boxes of food every day," Angela countered.

Her father faced her mother, scowling. "That was a long time ago. If you think it's so easy, you pick it up."

Angela dug her hands into her skinny hips. "I don't want you to hurt yourself. You're stubborn and cranky when you're injured or sick."

"You're stubborn and cranky, even when you're not sick."

Lucy rolled her eyes. "Stop. Both of you. I'll move it."

Her parents' bickering was the last thing she wanted to hear. If anyone overheard them, they'd assume the pair had argued for the past thirty years since owning Kebab Kitchen.

For a heart-pounding moment, Lucy wondered if that was how her relationship with Azad would evolve after they married and ran the restaurant together. A bit of panic tightened her chest. But deep down, she had to believe they would be different—they *were* different. They would have their moments as married business owners, but Azad wasn't her father, and she was *not* her mother.

Lucy grasped the handles on the top of the keg and proceeded to roll it on its edge through the swinging kitchen doors. The keg *was* heavy. Soon, she was panting and sweating. Lucy recalled Jake saying an empty keg was almost thirty pounds and a full keg was one hundred and sixty-two pounds. It felt like a thousand by the time she parked the keg inside the kitchen. They'd have to wait for either Azad or Butch to carry it the rest of the way into the storage room.

Lucy wiped beads of perspiration off her brow. "Mom, how many people do you expect at this Christmas party?"

"Sixty-five. Maybe seventy people."

Lucy looked at her in surprise. "That many?"

"Why else would I order a large keg of beer?"

It would be Lucy's first time at one of her mother's big Christmas shindigs. During the eight years she'd worked at her Philadelphia law firm, Lucy had come home to celebrate Christmas with the family, but she'd never attended her mother's town holiday parties.

"Other than Easter, Christmas is the most important Christian holiday. I invite all the town business owners and their families. We eat, drink, give thanks for everything we have, and share funny stories about tourists."

Lucy's mouth curved in a smile. "You mean you gossip."

"That, too."

"And lots of beer and wine helps."

Angela cracked a big smile and patted Lucy on the back. "I'm glad you're home for good now. Be prepared for a fun evening."

The following morning, Katie showed up at Lucy's upstairs apartment with two large coffees in a cardboard tray from Lola's Coffee Shop.

Lucy took a coffee from Katie as she passed through the door. "You're a godsend. To what do I owe the pleasure of your visit?"

"I made an appointment at Madame Fleur's."

Lucy lowered her coffee before taking the first sip, and her short bark of laughter lacked humor. "The wedding dress boutique?"

"It's difficult to get an appointment. You can thank me later."

Lucy wasn't sure if she wanted to thank her friend or throttle her. "You could have asked me first."

"I didn't want to give you a chance to say no." Katie pulled out her keys from her pocket and waved them in the air. "I'll drive. We don't want to be late."

The insinuation that Lucy's driving was much slower made her frown, even if it was true. Twenty minutes later, they stepped into the boutique.

Madame Fleur's looked like an upscale bordello. Splashes of pink and satin decorated the room—a pink sofa and billowing, satin curtains. Flashy wedding fashion magazines were stacked neatly on round, glass tables. Lucy's heels sank into a thick, white carpet. A doorway with plush, pink curtains led into a separate room where the gowns were stored.

"Welcome!" The curtains fluttered open and Madame Fleur appeared to greet them in a French accent. Her dark hair was styled in a fashionable updo and she was dressed in an ivory suit with a large brooch of a monarch butterfly pinned to her lapel. She looked sophisticated and elegant.

Lucy's mother had once said "Madame" was not French, but used to sell cleaning products back in Trenton.

Madame Fleur looked at Lucy. "Are you the lucky bride?"

"I'm Lucy."

Madame clasped her hands to her chest. "Congratulations on your upcoming nuptials, mademoiselle. A bride's day should be one of the happiest of her life." She led them through the curtain and into a room where what looked like hundreds of dresses encased in clear plastic hung on racks. A separate area with curtained fitting rooms was off to the side. Outside the fitting rooms was a pedestal surrounded by wall-to-wall mirrors for the brides to model dresses.

"I have an ample selection of all types of silhouettes: A-line, sheath, ball gown, mermaid, and trumpet. Select three dresses, and I will choose one that I think you will like based on your tastes and figure. After trying on each one, you will step on the pedestal and we can see how lovely you look," Madame said, then left them to shop.

The racks were filled with satins, charmeuse, chiffon, organza, tulle, and lace. Some gowns were ivory, others pure white. Some had delicate beadwork with seeded pearls, corset bodices, or sheer overlays. The selection was overwhelming.

"Modern or traditional?" Katie asked.

"More traditional, I think," Lucy said.

After almost an hour, they picked three dresses and swept aside a fitting room curtain to find a large area with plenty of hooks to hang the heavy gowns. "Stay," Lucy told Katie. "I'm going to need help getting into these."

But Madame appeared out of thin air with a handful of underthings to help Lucy suck in her stomach and push up her breasts, before slipping the first billowing gown over her head and fastening it in the back. The dress was a size too big, but Madame pulled it taut and secured it with big clips in the back. "Of course we will order the right size, but it will need a bit of hemming."

It needed more than a bit of hemming. The dress was made for a six-foot model. Madame whipped out a pair of high heels in Lucy's size and helped her step up on the pedestal. Lucy turned this way and that as she looked at her image in the multiple mirrors.

"Oh, Lucy," Katie said with a sigh.

Lucy's feminine vanity surfaced with a vengeance. Wearing a ball gown silhouette with capped sleeves, a corset bodice, and a full satin skirt, she felt like a fairy-tale princess. What were the chances the first dress would be the right one? "Thank you, Madame Fleur. It's so pretty," Lucy said.

"No need to thank me, mademoiselle. My job is easy when the model is as lovely as you."

Maybe it was a line from an experienced saleswoman, but Lucy was buying it all the way to the register.

"Who is the lucky man?" Madame asked.

"His name is Azad. He is the head chef at my family's restaurant, Kebab Kitchen, and I'm the manager."

"Ah, you work together in a family business."

An undertone in Madame's voice captured Lucy's interest. Plus, her slip into a North Jersey accent was unmistakable. "You have experience with a family business?"

"I used to own my bridal salon with my ex-husband."

The use of the word "ex" to describe her husband told Lucy she'd been right to sense a note of warning. "How was it?"

"I won't lie. Working together and living together is why we divorced. But that doesn't mean you and your handsome chef will suffer the same fate."

Madame reached into a basket and pulled out a gauzy veil. She placed it on Lucy's head and secured it with an elegant tiara of diamonds and pearls. "I think you should select a long veil. It adds much more elegance." The French accent had returned.

Lucy stared wordlessly as she took in the entire ensemble—the veil, the tiara, and the dress. Madame's words had reignited her insecurities, not so much about Azad, but about their future together in Kebab Kitchen as married business partners.

Would they bicker like her parents?

Or would they end up like Madame Fleur and her ex-husband, divorced and bitter?

Oh God. Panic rose in Lucy's chest, and the gown she'd

thought lovely and perfect moments ago now felt as heavy as an anvil on her shoulders. The corset bodice was laced way too tight, and she struggled to draw breath. She swayed on the pedestal in the borrowed high heels.

"Can I take this off?" Lucy asked.

"You want to try on the second gown?" Madame asked.

Fortunately, Katie must have sensed her friend's distress. She gripped Lucy's arm as she stepped off the pedestal. "No, thank you," Katie said, her tone polite. "I think it's enough for the first day. We both have to get back to work. But we promise to return soon."

"What was that about?" Katie demanded.

"I think I had a panic attack." Lucy collapsed on her couch, tucked her feet beneath her, and rested her head back on the cushion. As if sensing her distress, Gadoo settled beside her on the cushion. Lucy absentmindedly began stroking his soft fur.

"Let me guess. You think you and Azad will end up divorced like Madame Fleur and her ex-husband." Katie handed her a glass of ice water.

Lucy sipped the water. For a brief moment, she'd thought she might pass out on Madame Fleur's fitting room pedestal. "Something like that. I'm also worried we'll end up nagging each other like my parents."

"Your parents are in a different league. Clearly they care for each other but are just a little hotheaded."

"A little?"

A shadow crossed Katie's features. "I've always wished my parents were like yours. Mine never told me they loved me as a kid. I knew they did, but it was never spoken. Emotions were never expressed in my house."

Lucy had known Katie since elementary school. Their families had been as different as night and day. Lucy had grown up in an ethnic household and had brought hummus and pita the first day of school. Katie had packed peanut butter and jelly on white bread. When others had started to make fun of Lucy, Katie had asked to switch lunches. They'd been best friends ever since.

Angela and Raffi had told Lucy and Emma that they loved them every day before school and when they stepped off the school bus. As a teenager, Lucy had thought this was a bit too smothering, but she'd grown to value her family and their affectionate nature.

"Has Azad ever said he's worried about continuing to work together after you're married?" Katie asked.

"No. He's never whispered a word. But maybe that's because his parents didn't work together."

"He basically grew up in Kebab Kitchen and knows your parents. Maybe you need to ask him," Katie said.

"I know you're right. We're supposed to go to a fund-raising dance tonight at the senior center with Eloisa. I'm just hesitant to say anything. He's been supportive about everything at the restaurant. He's even been supportive about our sleuthing."

Katie's lips thinned. "That's more than I can say about Bill."

"Bill's trying to protect us. There is a murderer roaming free in town."

"We're not doing any risky business." Katie wagged her finger at Lucy. "As for Azad, you know I think you two are perfect for each other. If you don't want him, your landlady will take him."

Lucy lifted her head from the cushion. "Is that supposed to help?"

"No. It was supposed to make you laugh. Talk to him, Lucy. I think you'll find it's the best way to warm your cold feet."

Chapter Twenty-Three

"How do I look?"

Lucy's gaze swept Eloisa from head to toe. Her landlady was wearing a full-length, red dress with sparkly sequins and matching red sequined shoes Dorothy from *The Wizard of Oz* would have coveted. A feathered headband completed the outfit.

"You look fabulous," Lucy said.

Eloisa tilted her head to the side as she examined her. Lucy tried to stay still beneath her sharp, brown-eyed stare.

"Well, I wish I could say the same for you, young lady."

Lucy glanced down at her outfit. "Why? What's wrong with what I'm wearing?" She felt highly self-conscious and a little offended. She'd rummaged through her closet before settling on her own outfit. Her light blue dress flattered her figure and her heels made her legs look long. Well, at least *longer*. At five-foot-three inches, she'd never be statuesque like Katie. But the heels definitely helped. She'd even taken time to style her shoulder-length curls with just the right amount of gel to prevent frizz—never an easy feat because of the ever-present humidity at the Jersey shore.

"You could do with something a bit shinier," Eloisa said.

Lucy bit her tongue to keep from suggesting Eloisa had enough bling for both of them. Gadoo sauntered over and rubbed against her leg. Cat hair clung to her silk stockings. She tried unsuccessfully to wipe it away.

"Cupid wouldn't rub against your leg and leave behind all that cat hair."

Rather than argue, she said, "Gadoo is affectionate."

Eloisa pursed her lips. "Hmm."

Lucy changed the subject from pets to the dance. "I've been looking forward to tonight. I've never attended a senior center holiday party."

"The center has been hosting this holiday party for a decade now. This year, we sold over eighty tickets." Eloisa's voice was full of pride.

"Wow! That many?" Ocean Crest may be a small town, but people always seemed to get together to support a worthy cause. The turnout was impressive, and locals must have invited friends from out of town. The ticket sales, combined with the money raised from the Polar Bear Plunge, would help fund the much-needed renovation.

The doorbell rang, and Lucy opened the door to find Azad on the porch. He looked quite handsome in a blue, button-down shirt and gray slacks. Across his forehead, a lock of hair fell that gave him a rakish look. Whenever he stood right before her, all her misgivings melted away. But Katie's words were fresh in her mind. So was her panic attack at the bridal salon. She needed to talk to him.

Azad grinned as his gaze took in her dress. "How are the two most lovely ladies in Ocean Crest?"

Eloisa batted her fake eyelashes. "Ready to dance."

Lucy smiled. "Ready for a night out."

Azad offered an arm to each of them. "Your escort awaits."

They'd decided Azad would drive Lucy's car instead of his Ford truck. It was much easier to get in and out of in a dress and heels. Less than fifteen minutes later, Azad parked in the senior center parking lot.

The lot was crammed with cars. Some were even parked on the grass. "It's crowded," Azad said.

"Biggest party of the year. The decorating committee has been hard at work. The DJ will play lots of Sinatra. Hope you can dance in those shoes, Lucy," Eloisa said.

Lucy wasn't much of a dancer, but she didn't think it would be a problem.

After waiting in a line at the door, they handed their tickets to a smiling lady with hennaed auburn hair, pearly white dentures, and thick glasses, then stepped inside the main room.

The senior center had been built in the fifties and was sorely in need of updating, but the decorating committee had worked wonders. It looked as if Christmas had exploded inside. Two tall Christmas trees, one on each side of the double doors, were decorated with silver and gold ornaments. A garland was strung between doorways, and a large evergreen wreath hung above the hardwood dance floor.

A band was on the elevated stage, playing oldies. Young and old couples danced on the wooden floor. Lucy recognized many of the guests as regular customers at Kebab Kitchen. Others, she didn't know at all.

"I see Wayne and he's without a dance partner," Eloisa said. "I'd better snag him before my competition swoops in and takes him." Without a backward glance, she was off like a shot.

Lucy shrugged as she looked up at Azad. "I guess we can—"

He clasped her hand and headed for the dance floor. "It's a waltz."

Lucy attempted to tug her hand free. "Wait! I don't know how—"

"It's easy. I'll show you."

Azad placed his hand on her waist, took her left hand and set it on his waist, then took her free right hand. Then he swept her into motion.

Panic pierced her chest. "Azad, I'm not sure—"

"I'll lead. Just follow my steps. Step, slide and step. That's it. It's not hard."

Lucy's heart pounded so loudly in her chest, she wondered how he couldn't hear it. She glanced up at him and took in his chin, the encouraging curve of his lips, his dark eyes. He smiled, and the tempting dimple in his cheek made her breath catch.

"When did you learn how to waltz?" she asked.

"I learned after college."

After college. They'd dated in college, and it was after— a week after graduation—that he'd broken up with her. It had taken years to dull the heartache, and their breakup was one of the reasons she'd fled Ocean Crest and taken the city firm job.

No sense wallowing in the past. They were together now. Her diamond ring glinted in the overhead disco ball, reminding her of their renewed commitment.

"Did you take ballroom lessons?" She wanted to know more.

"Not exactly. There was a club next door to the Atlantic City restaurant where I worked. Tuesday nights were ballroom dancing nights. Sometimes I would go after work and watch. Eventually, I tried it a couple of times."

"Who was your partner?"

He chuckled. "A fifty-year-old housewife whose husband had no interest in dancing. We danced, nothing more."

She was surprised, but not because he'd danced with a housewife. Azad liked to cook and work out at his gym after shifts. She never thought he would enjoy ballroom dancing.

Lucy concentrated on the steps. Azad was a good teacher and she caught on quickly. "What other dances did you learn?"

"Not too many. Just the foxtrot and the tango."

A soft gasp escaped her. She didn't know a single ballroom dance. "I have a lot to learn tonight."

Azad lowered his head. His lips brushed her ear and sent a shiver down her spine. "Good thing you have an eager teacher."

Whoa. The innuendo was unmistakable. She felt a swooping pool in her lower stomach. He could make her heart pound so easily.

Still, she couldn't forget the gripping panic that had consumed her at the wedding boutique that morning. Gathering her courage, she looked up at him. "Hey, Azad, are you worried about working together after we're married?"

"No, why? Are you?"

His fingers tightened on her waist as she contemplated how to bring up her fears. "I'm worried we'll turn out like my parents."

"What's wrong with them?"

"You know . . . they bicker a lot."

His lips curved in a tempting smile. "I'm not worried about that at all."

"Why not?"

"We aren't them. We're our own individuals. Do you act or feel like them now?" he asked.

"No, but . . . you know what they say. No matter how hard we try, we always turn into our parents."

"Our experiences are unique and have shaped us into who we are. Your parents came to this country when they were in their early twenties. We graduated from high school here. Our entire upbringing and our lives have been different. We are our own, unique selves."

The way he explained it made sense. They were both first generation Americans and had lived lives completely different from their parents'. They grew up with MTV, attended public school, and had lifelong American friends of all ethnic backgrounds. They both had college degrees, and Lucy had a law degree. It changed who they were, and they were unique.

"I feel better about it. Thanks, Azad."

"Hey, it's natural to have cold feet, but when that happens, call me, and I'll come over in a flash and warm them."

Put like that, what lady could resist his offer? Certainly not Lucy.

The band continued to play. Together, they whirled across the floor, and she felt light as air. There really was something to be said about a skilled male lead. Waltzing was actually *fun*. Who knew?

She smiled up at Azad, then out of the corner of her eye, she caught Eloisa dancing with a man she recognized.

If Azad's hands weren't tight on her waist, she would have tripped and fallen on her face. Because dancing with Eloisa was a very tall, thin man—an all-too-familiar one.

"What the heck is Eloisa doing dancing with Norman Weston?"

"Who is he?" Azad pulled her close on the dance floor to whisper in her ear.

Lucy focused on the steps of the waltz while watching the couple a few feet away. "That's Norman Weston. Deacon's business partner. He's one of the suspects I told you about. I wonder how Eloisa knows him."

"One way to find out. Let's get closer."

"Really?"

"I support your sleuthing. Besides, I'll be watching to be sure it's safe." Azad took her hand and led her over to where Eloisa and Norman were dancing. He tapped Norman on the shoulder. "Excuse me. May I have a turn?"

Eloisa parted from Norman and nearly jumped into Azad's arms. "I'd love to."

Lucy nearly rolled her eyes, but then she caught Eloisa's look. Her meaning was loud and clear.

It took you long enough to catch on.

Holy cow. Eloisa did know Norman, and she had set this up perfectly. Her landlady may be a bit eccentric, but she was smart as a whip.

Lucy took advantage and met Norman's eyes. Fortunately, he took the cue.

"Would you like to dance?" Norman asked.

Lucy gave him her most charming smile. "I'd love to."

The music changed from the waltz to a slow dance. Thank heavens she didn't have to know any fancy steps. Still, Norman was tall, and even with her heels, Lucy had to crane her neck to look up at him.

"How are things going at the Sea View?" she asked.

Norman woodenly shifted his feet. He wasn't as smooth a dancer as Azad. Or had her question made him nervous?

"The truth is, I'm thinking of putting the business on the market."

"Really? I remember you mentioned selling your share of the business to Deacon. I'm sorry that won't happen now."

Norman missed a step. "Yes . . . we . . . that is, obviously, no longer an option."

Time to ask some pressing questions. "Do you know where Deacon would have found the money to buy you out? You had just finished renovating the Sea View. I would think money would have been tight."

Norman's eyebrows drew together. "I never asked Deacon where the money would have come from."

Her body thrummed with anticipation. "I think you knew."

Norman halted suddenly, and another couple nearly collided with them. He glowered at her. "Do you want to dance, Ms. Berberian, or ask me questions?"

She raised her chin. "Both."

"Perhaps we should take this elsewhere?"

"Perhaps we should," she said.

He walked off the dance floor and she was hot on his heels. He stopped by the end of the refreshment table and turned to face her. He waited until a man chose two plastic cups of lemonade and walked away before speaking. "Why don't you just say what you are dying to ask?"

Lucy didn't miss the reference to "dying." "When did you find out that Deacon had a suitcase of cash stashed in his office?"

He stared and his eyes narrowed. "How do you know about that?"

"I know a lot more than you think I do."

"You don't beat around the bush, do you?"

"I find it's better to be straightforward."

"Fine," he snapped. "I didn't find out about the cash until after."

"After Deacon's death?"

"No. A week after Deacon offered to buy out my share of the Sea View. As far as I knew, we were both strapped for cash after the expensive renovation. I wanted to know if Deacon was serious about his offer or just jerking me around. You never could tell with him."

"What do you mean?"

Norman's voice was laced with bitterness. "There was no love lost between us. I wouldn't have been surprised if Deacon was playing a cruel joke. I burst into his office to confront him, and that's when I caught him with that suitcase of cash. He was counting a stack of hundreds on his desk. The idiot didn't even bother to lock the door."

Lucy imagined the scene. She wondered who was more shocked, Norman at seeing the cash for the first time, or Deacon at being discovered. "You must have been shocked."

"Shocked is an understatement. I've never seen that much cash in one place. The only explanation was drugs. Deacon was dealing drugs out of our business."

"How do you know it was drug money?"

"A suitcase stuffed with Ben Franklins? Where else could it have come from? I guarantee you it wasn't from catering. Business wasn't *that* good."

Lucy's first thought had been that it was drug money as well. Vinnie had suspected the same thing. "Did you confront Deacon about it?"

Norman's hands fisted at his sides. "Damn right I did. I told him that if he planned to buy out my share of the business with illegal drug money, I wanted nothing to do with it. I refused to go to jail, and that's exactly what would have happened if Deacon had been caught dealing drugs, then paying me with illegal funds. The cops would think I had something to do with it."

"Did you know that the money in Deacon's suitcase was later stolen?" If Norman found Deacon's stash of cash, did he have something to do with the robbery? Did he know that Vinnie had tried to steal the money? Had he tipped Vinnie off?

Norman's mouth gaped. "Stolen? No, but I'm not surprised it happened. It was probably a drug competitor."

Lucy tried to judge whether he was being truthful or not. Norman seemed genuinely surprised. It was possible he had no idea that Vinnie had stolen the money from Deacon. And if Norman had no idea about that, then he wouldn't have known that Deacon had been blackmailing Vinnie to pay back the cash plus high interest.

All she'd learned was that Norman's dislike for Deacon ran deeper than she'd initially thought.

"First he deals drugs out of our business," Norman said, "then he inadvertently tries to involve me in criminal activity by buying out my share of a legitimate business with drug money. Then it's all stolen by a drug competitor. After years of working with an arrogant and selfish business partner, I'm not surprised he was murdered. I'm glad for it, too."

Norman's hatred for Deacon was crystal clear and provided a motive for murder. As for opportunity, he was one of the Polar Bear swimmers. Lucy craned her neck to meet his glare. "Are you confessing?"

"No. I didn't kill him."

Each suspect denied the evil deed. The question was: Which one was lying?

"Did you learn anything useful?" Azad asked.

"Quite a bit. Thanks for helping." Lucy handed Azad a glass of wine and joined him on her pink couch. After returning from the dance, Eloisa bid them good night and Azad joined Lucy in her upstairs apartment.

Azad sipped his wine. "I know you and Katie are like Holmes and Watson. But we're a pretty good team, too."

She took a sip of her wine and set down the glass on the coffee table. She curled a leg beneath her and faced him. "Yes, we are."

"Although, I have to give some credit to your shrewd landlady," Azad said. "She started dancing with Norman Weston. It was easy for me to interrupt their dance."

Lucy picked up her glass and ran her finger down the smooth edge. "Norman admitted to hating his business partner but denied killing Deacon. It seems to be a common theme."

"And he did the Plunge, too?"

"Yup. Another detail all the suspects have in common."

Azad looked to be in deep thought. "If your suspects all have solid motives and opportunity, maybe a couple did it together."

She looked at him in surprise. "You mean two people drowned Deacon?"

Azad shrugged. "Why not? Deacon was in his late fifties. He wasn't old or weak. Wouldn't it take a good amount of strength to drown him?"

She hadn't considered that possibility. A couple could have conspired drowning Deacon. But which couple?

Clarissa and Henry were an obvious choice. They'd known each other since high school, attended their prom together, and still maintained a friendship. But that didn't mean they were the guilty ones. Lucy had learned long ago not to jump to hasty conclusions. Vinnie and Norman were still strong suspects. And how did Susan fit into everything? Lucy needed time and a long jog to sort everything out.

"Thanks, Azad."

"For what?"

"For thinking of something Katie and I hadn't even considered."

Gadoo leaped onto the sofa and curled up next to Azad. The cat purred contentedly as Azad stroked under his chin.

"How'd you get Gadoo to like you so much?"

Azad grinned. "Cats have great sense. They don't trust just anyone."

She cocked an eyebrow. "You sound so sure."

"I am. You made the right decision to be with me."

Lucy couldn't help but laugh at his teasing tone. "Is that right?"

Azad took her wineglass and set it on the table. He leaned close and brushed his lips against hers. "So right. Let mc show you."

And he did.

Chapter Twenty-Four

Lucy slowed from a jog to a brisk walk on the beach. It had snowed lightly last night and a thin coating of white dusted the sand. She'd come prepared for the cold this morning and wore an Ocean Crest High School hoodie, running tights, and a Philadelphia Eagles knit hat and gloves.

She swept the snow off the stone of a jetty overlooking the Atlantic Ocean and sat. A cold breeze made her cheeks tingle, and she pulled her hat lower to fully cover her ears. She'd frequently come here in the summer, but she hadn't visited the jetty in weeks because of the cold. But today was different, and she needed a place to think. The ocean was calm this morning, and the sun peeked through the clouds to glisten off the sparkling water. She breathed in the brisk ocean air.

No matter the season, the view was magnificent. The mesmerizing pull of the ocean was Mother Nature's way of clearing her thoughts. If only the waves could speak to her and tell her who had killed Deacon.

This was where it happened—where Deacon was drowned and washed ashore. A murderer was on the loose in Ocean Crest and the ocean held the key.

If only she'd dug up something useful . . . and her current list of suspects hadn't changed. She thought back to the day of the Polar Bear Plunge.

Susan and Jake were standing together on the beach. Susan swam to represent Cutie's Cupcakes and Jake participated for the Boardwalk Brewery.

Norman Weston was here that morning, too. He had motive as Deacon's business partner in the Sea View. The business partners disliked each other, and when Norman discovered Deacon's suitcase of cash, it only added fuel to the fire. Norman was certainly physically strong enough to hold Deacon underwater.

Vinnie Pinto was a swimmer. Vinnie's employer, Mr. Citteroni, hadn't given him much choice *but* to participate in the Polar Bear Plunge. But had Vinnie been secretly happy to be in the water with Deacon? It offered him the perfect opportunity to drown the man who had been blackmailing him to pay back stolen cash plus interest. If Deacon was dead, there would be no evidence of the loan and Vinnie would get off scot-free. Lucy still thought he was the strongest suspect.

But both Clarissa and Henry had motive. Clarissa hated Deacon for ruining her wedding and blamed him for her divorce. Henry was Deacon's nephew, and even though he didn't receive any help from his uncle when he was alive, Henry received a trust fund after Deacon died. Both Henry and Clarissa were swimmers and had opportunity.

Azad had offered insight. Could two of the suspects have joined forces to get rid of a hated enemy?

But which two?

Clarissa and Henry already knew each other, and if their secret meeting in a dark alley during the town Christmas tree lighting was any indication, they were an obvious pair.

But Lucy knew from experience that obvious didn't always mean guilty.

According to Clemmons, Susan Cutie was most likely the killer. Deacon had damaged her business reputation and cost her money. Plus, she'd threatened the victim more than once. It didn't look good for Susan.

But Lucy wasn't convinced that Susan was a killer. She stood and stretched her legs. She sipped her water bottle. Her morning jog and the jetty hadn't relieved all her stress. Whether one person drowned Deacon or two, she was still no closer to finding the killer.

Despite the cold, Lucy was sweating by the time she ran the length of the boardwalk and made it to the street. Her cell phone rang.

She unzipped a pocket in her running pants and pulled out the phone and recognized Katie's phone number. "Katie?"

"Where are you?"

"I'm jogging and just left the boardwalk. What's up?"

"Stop by Cutie's Cupcakes on your way home," Katie said.

"Why?"

"Things got worse for Susan. You're gonna want to see this."

Lucy made it to Cutie's Cupcakes in record time. She'd jogged the entire way to the small shopping strip where the bakery was located. The holiday lights that had previously lit the doorway were dark. Thank goodness, the "Open" sign was prominent in the window. Pushing open the door, Lucy stepped inside.

Katie was standing at the counter, talking to Susan.

"Hey, Lucy," Katie said. "I'm glad you came."

"Hi, Lucy," Susan said.

Lucy wondered what Katie's ominous phone call had been about, but then she noticed.

The shelves were nearly empty. On an average day, the refrigerated shelves held cupcakes, cookies, and muffins of all different flavors and colors. The holiday cupcakes she'd seen only two weeks ago were gone—no *Sesame Street* characters wearing elf hats, cakes with red and green icing, and, no cookies with red and green M&M's.

Even worse, the rotating refrigerated pie display case was bare except for a sad-looking chocolate peanut butter pie with only two slices left. So much for buying a slice of lemon meringue.

Lucy looked to Susan. "What happened to all your baked goods?"

Susan shrugged. "No sense keeping the shelves full. Business is normally slow in the winter."

Lucy didn't believe Susan for a second. The bakery was always busy. Granted, it may not have a steady stream of tourists in the winter like it did in the summer, but it was never *empty.* Every time Lucy had stepped into the place, there was at least one customer. The tempting smell of freshly baked cakes and pies was mouthwatering and better than any sales pitch.

"But it's the holiday season," Lucy countered. "Where are all the Christmas cookies and cakes?"

Susan's expression crumpled and she sniffled. "Oh, Lucy. I can't lie to you. The truth is, I don't have the urge to bake."

Lucy's chest ached at her friend's anguish. She walked around the counter to touch her arm. "Are you that worried about things?"

At the affectionate touch, Susan broke down even more. Fat tears streamed down her cheeks. "I can't help it. I jump every time the bakery door opens. I keep thinking that detective is going to burst in here and put me in handcuffs and charge me with Deacon Spooner's murder."

"Lucy's right." Katie reached in her purse and handed Susan a tissue. "You have to relax. Clemmons would have made a move if he had enough evidence."

Susan loudly blew her nose. "You think so?"

"I do," Lucy said.

"I agree," Katie chimed in. "The county prosecutor was at the town Christmas tree lighting. She would have given Clemmons the green light to make an arrest if she was certain they had a solid case."

Susan looked at Katie in horror. "The county prosecutor is here? In town?"

Lucy shook her head at Katie over Susan's shoulder. It was obviously the wrong thing to say. Susan's pale complexion turned nearly white.

"What Katie meant to say," Lucy was quick to add, "is that it's standard procedure for Prosecutor Walsh to visit town events like the tree lighting. It makes for good relations. Her presence here may have nothing to do with Deacon's murder."

Lucy didn't believe that to be true, but why worry Susan? The poor woman looked like she was going to faint, and the bare shelves of her bakery suggested she was already under massive stress.

Thankfully, Katie caught on. "Lucy's right," Katie said. "No sense worrying."

Susan sniffled, then threw the sopping tissue into the wastebasket under the counter. "Thanks for the reassurance. I don't know what's wrong with me lately. I can't seem to get back to normal. I'm afraid it's putting a big strain on my relationship with Jake."

"Jake has been worried about you, and he wants to help," Lucy said.

"I'm sorry I don't have any lemon meringue for you, Lucy. If you come back later this week, I promise to make you a pie."

"Don't do it just for me. I want you to go back to baking for yourself. The townsfolk depend on you, too."

"You think?"

"Absolutely. Christmas is only a couple of weeks away. Everyone loves your holiday cookies and pastries."

"Then I'll do my best not to disappoint anyone."

"What you need is a ladies' night out," Lucy said.

"I saw a flyer for a holiday house tour tonight. Will you go with us?" Katie asked.

"Great idea!" Lucy said.

Susan cracked a smile. "Sure. Maybe a fun night out with the two of you is what I need to forget my problems."

Chapter Twenty-Five

Katie was waiting for Lucy at the corner of Ocean Avenue by the boardwalk ramp. A small crowd had gathered beside a waiting tramcar. The holiday house tour was one of the only times the tram was driven off the boardwalk.

Lucy strained to see above the crowd. "Where's Susan?" She hoped her friend's stress and worry wouldn't make her back out.

"I don't see her. Wait! There she is." Katie pointed past a couple and Lucy spotted Susan waving.

Lucy gave Susan a tight hug. "I'm glad you came. I have our tickets." She waved the holiday house tour tickets in the air.

"Are you kidding? I wouldn't miss this. I've been looking forward to tonight all day," Susan said.

Susan had put on makeup and her eyes were bright. She looked better than Lucy had seen her in a while . . . at least since Deacon's death. Lucy was glad. Her friend needed some Christmas cheer. They all wore knit hats, down coats, and warm boots.

Together, the trio headed for the tram. In the summer, the bright yellow-and-blue tramcar motored up and down the Ocean Crest boardwalk. A Jersey boardwalk fixture, it carried twenty passengers—mostly senior citizens, parents, babies in strollers, or tired tourists—from one end of the boardwalk to the other. Two college students dressed in matching yellow-and-blue tops and black shorts worked the tram, one to drive it and the other to stand in the rear and collect the three-dollar fee. The loudspeaker would endlessly blare, "Watch the tramcar, please!"

Tonight, the tramcar would be used to drive them from house to house. Instead of a young high school driver, the operator of the tramcar was the mayor, Theodore Magic. In his seventies, his uniform matched the bright colors the college student operators normally wore, but instead of summer wear, he had on a yellow-and-blue jacket, black slacks, and a blue hat. A twig of holly was tucked into his lapel. The tramcar was decorated with a garland and red bows. At the front of the vehicle was a large evergreen wreath.

"I'll be your driver for the Ocean Crest Holiday Home Tour," Theodore said cheerfully. "We'll make several stops tonight to see our very own lovely decorated homes. Please climb aboard."

Passengers piled aboard. Lucy slid across the plastic bench to make room for Katie and Susan.

Lucy recognized many of the locals. The two spinsters, Edna and Edith Gray, who owned Gray's Novelty Shop on the boardwalk, sat just a few rows away. Lucy enjoyed perusing their store for sweatshirts and unique shell jewelry by local artists in the summer. Katie waved at Gail Turner, the receptionist at the town hall. Candy Kent, the attractive blond widow who owned Pages Bookstore, chose a seat by herself by a window. Lucy motioned for Katie and Susan to sit far away from Gertrude Shaw and

Francesca Stevens, the town's worst gossips. Both were members of the Ocean Crest town council.

Theodore climbed behind the wheel and the tram was off. It was a cold evening, but not frigid. Thankfully, Lola Stewart—owner of Lola's Coffee Shop—had brought along a commercial-size thermos of hot chocolate, and she passed along Styrofoam cups to each passenger. Lucy cradled the hot brew in her hands.

Rather than the endlessly repeated recording "Watch the tramcar, please!" Christmas music played from the loudspeaker.

"This is so nice. Thank you again for inviting me." Susan's cheeks were pink and her eyes held the customary sparkle Lucy had missed lately.

"Where's Jake tonight?" Lucy asked.

"Working."

"This late?" As far as Lucy knew, the brewery wasn't open too late.

Susan shrugged. "He said he had some last-minute business."

"I understand. Azad goes in after-hours sometimes to prepare certain specials that need extra time."

"Why are you two complaining? I'm glad Bill's working the late shift at the station," Katie said. "This is our *ladies'* night out, remember?"

Lucy shook her head. "We're not complaining. Just talking, but you're right. I say we toast to our special evening out together." Lucy raised her cup of hot chocolate. Susan and Katie obediently raised their cups to tap Styrofoam.

"We're coming to our first stop!" Theodore announced. "Katherine Templeton's home is delightful."

They climbed off the tram and headed for the front

door. Mrs. Templeton, the town's retired librarian, was waving from the porch. The house was a traditional Colonial built in the 1950s, with white columns wrapped in pine and three windows on the second floor. It was similar to many of the Ocean Crest homes built during that time, but what made it stand out tonight was its decorations.

Mrs. Templeton loved Christmas. Snowflake lights hung from the eaves. Colorful lights decorated all the trees, but a massive evergreen stood out from the rest, covered from top to bottom with colorful, blinking lights and topped with a huge yellow star. In each window of the home, an electronic candle was lit. The garage door was open and inside was a full-size, illuminated nativity scene that glowed brilliantly at night.

"I've never seen a garage decorated before," Katie said.

Lucy's eye was drawn to the nativity. "It's certainly unique."

The inside of the home was just as lovely. The foyer had a small white pine tree, and the spindles of the railing leading to the second floor were wound with pine and anchored with metallic bows. A much larger fir tree was in the living room. Mrs. Templeton handed out trays of freshly baked gingerbread men that smelled and tasted delicious.

Christmas cards featuring pictures of her grandchildren were displayed on a glossy black piano. A row of nutcrackers stood guard on the fireplace mantel, along with handmade stockings with each of her grandchildren's names embroidered in gold thread.

"Wow! My decorating is highly inadequate," Katie said.

"You're not the only one. I thought the tree I decorated with Azad and Mrs. Lubinski was pretty. Now I need to rethink some things," Lucy said.

"I haven't even put up a tree yet this year," Susan admitted. "I haven't been much into the Christmas spirit."

Lucy didn't want Susan's happy mood to veer back to depression. "Don't worry. There's still a lot of time."

The group walked around and observed the decorations while nibbling on gingerbread. Soon, it was time to climb back onto the tramcar and head to the next house.

The entire street was decorated, and although all the houses seemed lovely, only a few were on the tour. Everyone appeared to be watching as the tram passed by houses, except Gertrude Shaw and Francesca Stevens, who seemed to be too busy gossiping to take in the lovely sights.

Lucy rolled her eyes. Some things would never change.

After visiting several more houses, everyone's mood grew lighter and happier. By the time they reached the last house, the trio was fully in the Christmas spirit.

The tramcar turned onto Oyster Street and entered the newest development in town. As soon as the builder had finished the first home, Lucy had promptly dubbed them "the McMansions of Ocean Crest." The houses were newer, bigger, and ostentatious, and not of a clear architectural style. They were also too big for their postage-stamp-size lots.

They stopped in front of a home with a stone driveway and multiple chimneys, dormers, columns, and a three-car driveway. They must have hired professionals to decorate the trees and the outside of the house; what looked like thousands of lights hung from the three tiers of eaves. A huge lit-up Santa sat in a sleigh full of gifts and seemed ready to lift off the front lawn.

Katie's eyes sparkled. "You think one of those gifts is for me?"

"Depends what you told Bill you wanted," Lucy said.

"Oh, please. He's been too busy at work, trying to bust a pot dealer."

"Then you need to make a list."

"I'll keep that in mind, honey. What'd you tell Azad you wanted?" Katie held up a finger. "Wait. Let me guess. It wasn't a wedding."

Lucy glared at her friend. "Katie!"

"Well, you *are* taking a long time to pick a reception hall. Should I be worried?"

"Don't be ridiculous. Just because I'm not on *your* schedule doesn't mean I'm dragging my feet."

"Girls," Susan chided. "No arguing. Look at the decorations."

Lucy and Katie fell quiet as they took in the brilliance of the outside lights. The tram came to a complete stop and they piled out.

Three evergreen wreathes in a vertical row decorated the front door. The top wreath was festooned with a large gold bow and pinecones.

"The decorations inside the home are quite different from the outside," Theodore said. "The owner, Emily Sefton, is a talented crafter and loves unique and handmade decorations. I think you will be quite surprised."

As soon as they stepped inside, they were met by their hostess. Mrs. Sefton was an elderly lady, the wife of a financial investor, and welcoming. She wore a red suit with an elf embroidered on the lapel. Her short, round stature reminded Lucy of an English Brown Betty teapot.

"Welcome! Everyone, please come inside and get out of the cold."

The group followed her into a grand foyer. Lucy's eyes were drawn to not one, but two Christmas trees. For a tasteful touch, a large, glass cylinder filled with painted holiday decorations of silver and gold sat on a hall table. Candles of fresh balm gave out a wonderful smell.

The house didn't have the quaint feeling of the older homes, but Theodore was right. The inside was uniquely decorated and lovely. The guests trailed Mrs. Sefton, eager to see the rest of the home. Instead of a garland, thin tree branches and birch bark made a rustic mantel display. And rather than evergreen, numerous wreaths were handmade out of magnolia leaves. She had created her own festive snow globes by filling lanterns with white and red berries and eucalyptus leaves.

The dining room table was decorated with crisscross strands of gold and silver ribbon over the top and sides, and the entire table looked like a large, wrapped gift. Christmas china decorated with holly and evergreen and fluted crystal goblets gleamed beneath a crystal chandelier.

"How charming," Susan said.

"I never knew Mrs. Sefton was so talented," Katie said.

Lucy wandered to the parlor, where more homemade decorations were on display. A huge Douglas fir was by a second fireplace. A hand-sewn tree skirt matched the fabric of a footstool. A tiny village with little houses, a North Pole, a popcorn factory, and a toy factory sat on a bed of fluffy, fake snow. Embroidered Christmas pillows of reindeer and angels on the couches welcomed one to sit and relax in front of a fire. A small, hand-painted sleigh sat on an end table and was filled with oranges and cinnamon sticks.

Lucy moved to the mantel to study pictures of Emily's family, and as she reached for one of Emily and her two grown sons, she heard voices and footsteps enter the parlor.

"Can you believe Susan Cutie's on this tour?"

"Maybe she wants townspeople to keep coming to her bakery."

"I wouldn't buy a doughnut from her. It could be poisonous."

"No, she only drowns people, not poisons them."

A cackle of laughter followed.

Lucy froze. She was in the corner of the room, and the huge tree was blocking her from the two gossips. She stood still, the picture in her hands.

"Well, she's quite audacious if you ask me. If I was Susan, I'd lock myself away in my shop."

"The police just might do it for her."

Lucy's fingers itched to pick up one of the oranges from the hand-painted sleigh and throw it at the gossiping women. Thankfully, Susan was in the dining room with Katie and hadn't overheard them.

Theodore Magic stuck his head in the doorway. "The tram is ready to move along, ladies."

Lucy waited until the two magpies left before she joined the group.

Both Katie and Susan were laughing and smiling at a blow-up Santa in the neighbor's yard. He was dressed in a Hawaiian shirt and holding a suitcase ready for his vacation. Lucy soon forgot about the mean, gossiping biddies. All that mattered was the lighthearted mood of her two friends.

"I'm sad this tour is almost over," Lucy said.

Katie nudged her arm. "It's not over yet. I'm thinking we should enjoy some wine at my house. Bill's shift won't be over until midnight. We can drink as much as we want and pass out on my couch."

Lucy cracked a wide smile. "That sounds perfect."

Once back on the tramcar, they sang Christmas carols

and enjoyed more hot chocolate until the tram returned to the spot where they had first gathered and parked. With a plan in mind, they stepped off.

A police car pulled up and stopped nose-to-nose with the tramcar. Lucy blinked at the bright headlights. Everyone gathered by the curb.

"What's going on?" Katie asked.

The car door opened and Detective Calvin Clemmons stepped outside.

Lucy's stomach bottomed out in dread as Clemmons approached. She knew . . . knew before he said . . .

"Susan Cutie, you are under arrest for the murder of Deacon Spooner."

Chapter Twenty-Six

"Wait!" Lucy pushed through the crowd to reach Susan. Detective Clemmons had her friend in handcuffs and was leading her away.

Clemmons glared down at Lucy, and his mustache twitched with annoyance. "Stay out of this, Ms. Berberian."

"Lucy!" Susan twisted in the detective's grasp to glance back. With her hands cuffed behind her, she winced at the discomfort, and panic flared in her blue eyes. "You have to help me. You're the only one who can, now."

Lucy pressed forward and focused on Clemmons. "You're making a mistake, Detective."

The detective's lips thinned. "Ms. Berberian, if I have to arrest you for interfering with police business, I will."

Lucy wasn't deterred as she trailed behind. A uniformed police officer opened the car door as the detective led Susan toward the backseat cage that prevented any criminal from reaching the officers in the front as they drove.

Except Susan wasn't a criminal.

"Not a word, Susan!" Lucy shouted out. "I'll call Clyde Winters. Don't speak until he arrives at the station."

Clemmons shut the door. Without giving Lucy a backward glance, he settled in the driver's seat and drove away.

Silence descended on the crowd. Even Gertrude and Francesca stood still as statues.

Katie broke the deafening silence. "I think we need that glass of wine."

"Red or white?"

"Either."

Lucy had called Clyde Winters and he was on his way to the police station. He would ensure that Detective Clemmons and Prosecutor Walsh followed all the rules.

Lucy accepted a glass of white wine from Katie. "Susan needs our help now more than ever."

"I knew there was more to Prosecutor Walsh's presence in town than to attend a tree lighting. Clemmons wouldn't have made an arrest without consulting in depth with her. That lady doesn't like to lose."

Lucy's fingers clenched the stem of the wineglass and took another sip. "Don't remind me."

Katie sank onto the sofa and patted the cushion next to her for Lucy to join her. "As soon as Bill comes home, we can ask him."

Two glasses of wine later, the door opened, and Bill stepped inside. Both Lucy and Katie jumped to their feet.

"What can you tell us about Susan's arrest?" Katie asked.

Bill held up a hand. "I knew this was coming. Can I take off my jacket first?"

Katie sprang forward to take his coat and hung it on the coatrack.

"I told Clemmons about Deacon's dealings with Vinnie," Bill said, "but there was too much evidence and witness testimony against Susan. People heard her threaten to drown Deacon right before entering the water at the Polar Bear Plunge. To be honest, she does look guilty."

"But—"

"How well do you two know your friend?" Bill asked.

"I just can't imagine it. How could she have drowned a man so much bigger than herself?" Lucy asked.

"Do you think she could physically have done it?" Katie asked.

"Susan was a baker. They have to pick up heavy bags of flour and sugar and remove commercial-size cakes and pies from the oven on a daily basis. She's young and strong."

Lucy hadn't considered Susan's occupation. *Crap.* Susan's upper-body strength would be used against her. Prosecutor Walsh wouldn't miss the detail, and Lucy could imagine her opening statement to a jury:

Envision a woman who handles heavy equipment all day long for her occupation. Now envision her pushing a man, a hated enemy, underwater until his lungs filled with water and he stopped breathing . . .

"How long until fresh coffee?" Emma asked as she pushed through the swinging kitchen doors into the restaurant's kitchen.

"I'm brewing it now." Lucy flipped the switch of the restaurant's ten-gallon coffee urn to brew. Within minutes, she breathed in the aroma of freshly brewed coffee.

She needed the caffeine more than usual after witnessing Susan's arrest last night. The brand of coffee they purchased was from a local Jersey shore distributor and customers loved it. Years ago, her parents had started serving the coffee in small carafes that held four or six cups for each table, depending on how many coffee-drinkers sat there. The waitresses liked it because they didn't have to run around refilling cup after cup, and the customers liked it because they didn't have to wait for a refill. Lola Stewart's cappuccino's might be Lucy's favorite beverage, but a cup of Kebab Kitchen's coffee was a close second.

"Careful, there."

Lucy turned away from the urn to see her father walk up. "It smells so good, Dad."

"Every time I used to brew the coffee, I helped myself to a cup. Before I knew it, I was drinking twelve cups a day."

"You're kidding! That's a lot of caffeine."

"That's what the family doctor said. I tried to go cold turkey and give it up entirely, but I had a horrible headache and even had shaky hands. I went back to two cups a day and I've stuck with that ever since. Even when I go to Lola's Coffee Shop to meet friends, I don't drink more." He eyed her single cup next to the urn. "So, be careful that you don't fall into the same trap I did when I managed the restaurant full-time."

"Thanks for the warning, Dad."

A grin overtook his features. "I also want to tell you that I picked a vendor for a computerized inventory system from one of the estimates you gave me."

She licked her lips and watched him. "You did? What made you finally pick one?"

He shrugged. "I don't like the fact that you have to stay late every Saturday night."

She eyed him suspiciously. "Azad spoke with you."

Her father shrugged. "What if he did? I thought you'd be pleased."

Lucy wasn't just pleased. She was thrilled. Inventory was time-consuming, and if she missed ordering an item, it could pose a big problem for Azad and Butch when they went to prepare their specials. A while back, she'd been annoyed that it took Azad to make her father see reason. But now it didn't matter. They were a team.

"I am pleased, Dad."

"Good." Raffi kissed her cheek. "I'm headed to Lola's to meet the guys now." He winked. "Don't tell your mother."

"My lips are sealed." She ran her thumb and finger across her lips like a zipper.

As Lucy waited for the coffee to finish brewing, Butch walked by on his way to the storage room. "Hey, Lucy Lou. That smells great. Mind filling me a cup?"

"On the house," Lucy teased.

Once the light changed from "brewing" to "hot," she filled several carafes and helped Emma and Sally deliver them to waiting customers. As the afternoon wore on, Lucy found it difficult to concentrate on greeting customers. She excused herself and headed to the small office in the corner of the storage room. Ordering waited. But she couldn't focus on the mundane task of comparing suppliers' prices either.

She kept picturing Susan's horrified expression. Her friend was sitting in a jail cell accused of murder. How was Jake taking his girlfriend's arrest?

The desk phone rang and Lucy picked it up. Before she

could say hello, a male voice sounded. "I did what you asked."

Lucy recognized Stan Slade's voice. She didn't bother to greet him either. She sat up in her chair, her pulse pounding in heightened anticipation. "And?"

"Clarissa Chase doesn't have a criminal record."

Lucy sagged in disappointment. She'd first asked him to look into Clarissa by chance, but after following her from the tree lighting to an isolated back alley and eavesdropping on her conversation with Henry, she'd suspected there was a lot more to her than just a mad bride.

"Are you sure?" Lucy asked.

"Do you think I don't know how to dig into someone's background?" His voice dripped with sarcasm.

She didn't know what to think. Stan had left a newspaper job in New York City to become head reporter of a small Jersey shore paper. No one really knew why. Had he quit from stress? Or been fired?

Lucy clutched the phone. "Sorry. I was just hoping for something more."

There was a pause, and Lucy thought she heard Stan lighting a cigarette, inhaling, then blowing out. "Just because I didn't find anything," he said, "doesn't mean she didn't commit her first murder in the ocean that day."

Was he trying to make her feel better? Either way, his logic was correct. There was always a first time, and Clarissa was still a suspect.

Lucy hung up the phone. She rubbed her temples and tried to go back to her work. A low knock sounded on the office door and made Lucy start in her chair. "Come in."

Sally stood in the doorway. "We all heard what happened last night. You okay?"

As a longtime waitress, Sally wasn't just an employee, but close to the Berberian family and a good friend.

"I'm fine. Susan Cutie isn't. I plan to visit her in jail later today."

Sally sat on the edge of the desk. She wore her apron with a pad for taking orders sticking out of one of the pockets and had a pen tucked behind her ear. "I know how you are, Lucy. You're a good friend, but you carry around a lot of guilt. Susan's arrest isn't your fault."

Sally understood that Lucy had an inquisitive mind when it came to solving town crime, especially when one of her friends was involved. "I know, but you should have seen her face when the detective cuffed her and led her to a police car."

"You can't solve every crime, honey."

Lucy rubbed her temple. "But this one is truly troublesome. I was in the ocean when Deacon Spooner drowned."

Sally sighed. "I can only imagine how horrific the scene was. Do you have any leads?"

"I have suspects, but not too many leads. Lots of people didn't like Deacon. And many of them were there in the water, too."

"Anyone seem more guilty than the rest?"

"They're all alike because they all have motive."

"Hmm. Seems to me you have a group problem."

"What does that mean?"

"It's kind of like waitressing."

Lucy's interest was piqued, and she leaned back in the squeaky desk chair. "How so? I'm not catching on."

Sally folded her arms across her chest. "When it's really busy and customers are seated at the same time in my station, I need to decide which ones to serve first. They all look hungry and ready to order. It sounds like a random decision, but I've learned from years of experience that it isn't. Customers that I attend to right away aren't the most vocal ones, but the ones who sit quietly and look patient. Those are the ones who are usually in a rush and need my attention first. Sometimes, they're like boilers ready to blow. If you don't attend to them, they get angry."

"You think the most obvious suspect isn't usually the one who's guilty?"

Sally shrugged. "It's not an exact science, only what I've learned from human behavior from waiting on people for over ten years. The obvious person is not always the most troublesome."

Lucy considered Sally's wisdom. All types of people walked into the restaurant. Her father had often said psychiatrists should have to work in the restaurant business before hanging out their shingle.

"Thanks, Sally."

"No problem. You know where to reach me if you need to." Sally winked, then closed the office door behind her.

Lucy tapped her pen on the desk blotter. So, who was the most obvious suspect? She'd always believed it was Vinnie. She'd even asked Bill to tell Clemmons about her suspicions about him and it hadn't worked out. Maybe she was wrong. Maybe Vinnie was telling the truth when he'd stood next to his boss, Mr. Citteroni, and insisted he didn't kill Deacon.

That still left Clarissa, Henry, and Norman. But maybe there was another suspect. A mystery one.

Chapter Twenty-Seven

Lucy expected Susan to be tearful and desperate—maybe even hysterical—but the woman facing her across the interrogation table was strangely calm. Susan's face was almost emotionless. She sat still, her hands cuffed to a metal ring in the center of the table.

Lucy had previously visited other inmates in the Ocean Crest jail, and she was familiar with the place. The room where they processed and fingerprinted those recently arrested was painted a dingy white. A duct-tape line on the floor indicated where a person should stand to have their picture taken. A separate locked door led into a room with four cells. All the cells were currently empty except for Susan's. Just outside the cells was a table where inmates could meet with visitors or their attorneys. It was depressing and dismal, and every time Lucy came here, she wanted it to be her last.

"Lucy came just as you asked," Clyde Winters said as he settled in a metal chair beside Lucy and across from Susan.

Rail-thin and bald, Clyde had an abundance of age spots on his neck and hands. He also had a warm smile that put others at ease.

"Mr. Winters said your police questioning went well," Lucy said.

Susan's blue eyes were dull. A lock of blond hair hung in her face. Because Susan's hands were shackled to the table, Lucy wanted to reach out and tuck the tress behind her ear.

"It doesn't matter anymore," Susan said. "The prosecutor and that detective think I'm guilty. They have witnesses who heard me threaten Deacon more than once, and saw me near him in the ocean. Even a good attorney can't change that." She looked at Clyde. "No offense."

"None taken," Clyde said.

"You were my only hope, Lucy."

Lucy's stomach tightened. She wanted to help her friend, but the responsibility was overwhelming. "I did my best. I still haven't given up, but—"

"But the evidence against me is too much." Once more, Susan turned to Clyde. "How long do I stay here?"

"A couple of days. Then you'll be taken to the larger county jail to wait arraignment."

"You mean I'll be carted off to the county jail to be with all the real murderers?"

Lucy opened and closed her mouth, unsure what to say. She cleared her throat. "Susan, is there anything you can tell us, anything at all that might help?"

"Lucy's right," Clyde said. "Now is the time. Even if you think it's not important, I may be able to use it for your defense."

Susan shook her head. "You know it all. The good and the bad. I disliked Deacon. He hurt my business and would have continued to do more damage if he hadn't died. It was weeks since my last wedding cake order. I threatened him in return more than once. But I didn't drown him at the Plunge."

"If it's any consolation, I never thought you did."

"I appreciate your support. Jake's too." Susan shook her head. "But I told Jake to go away."

The change in topic caught Lucy off guard. "Jake?"

"He came to visit me earlier today. I told him I wanted to end our relationship."

"Why did you do that?"

Susan's calm facade finally cracked and a sob escaped her lips. She lowered her head, her hair falling forward around her face.

"Jake's devoted to you." Susan was fortunate to have a man who stood by her side through this mess. Bill would be with Katie. Lucy was confident Azad would support her.

Susan lifted her head. A fat tear slipped down her cheek. "Don't you see? That's why I did it."

The threat of being incarcerated with hardened criminals didn't upset her, but breaking up with her boyfriend did? Lucy was fascinated and wanted to find out more. "What did Jake say?"

"He refused to see reason. He told me he's with me until the very end."

Lucy didn't return to the restaurant as planned, but made one more stop. She parked her car next to Jake's van and stepped inside the Boardwalk Brewery.

Jake was behind the bar, serving a couple with a sampler of beer. The brewery looked the same as the last time she'd visited with her mother. A flashing, neon "Open" sign was in the window. A tall stack of kegs was on the wall by the door. The industrial-size tanks of beer were to the right of the bar. Hoses connected large and small tanks. A surfboard was mounted above the bar for decoration.

Jake waved when he spotted her. Lucy took a seat at the opposite end of the bar from the couple, and Jake approached.

"I went to see Susan," Lucy said without preamble.

"I was there earlier today. Thanks for sending Mr. Winters. I told him I'll cover his fees."

"That's nice of you. At first, Susan was unexpectedly calm. Then she broke down after she told me she tried to end her relationship with you."

She watched the play of emotions on his face—disappointment? anger? —but then they were gone and he flashed her a weak smile. "Susan's under stress and didn't mean it."

It had sounded like she meant it to Lucy. Was Jake so in love with Susan that he refused to accept it?

"Do you want a drink?" Jake asked.

"No, that's not why I—"

A loud crash made Lucy jump and whirl around on her stool. The couple had accidentally knocked over a keg on their way out the door. Another keg beside it began to wobble, and with a cacophony of noise, the tall stack of kegs fell like dominoes on the concrete floor. The couple jumped back. The woman covered her mouth with her hand, her eyes wide with horror. The man apologized profusely.

Jake rushed from behind the bar. Lucy was on his heels and reached for one of the kegs. Even empty, it wasn't light.

"They weigh close to thirty pounds empty." Jake lifted two at a time. Rather than stack them on top of each other,

Jake decided to line them up two rows deep by the wall. "You don't have to help."

"Of course I'll help. It's a good workout."

Together, and with the couple's assistance, they managed to straighten the kegs. Once each keg was in its proper place, the couple left and Lucy was alone with Jake.

"I'll have to find a place for them away from the door. It's too easy to knock one over," Jake said.

"You use all these kegs?" Lucy rubbed her lower back.

"I do. On a normal weekend, I supply beer for weddings, anniversaries, and birthday parties. And this weekend is the township employee Christmas party at the VFW. Your friend, Katie, placed a big order."

Had Katie finally found a venue? Lucy had forgotten all about the upcoming holiday party for town workers. With everything else that had been going on, including Susan's arrest, who could blame her?

Katie chose a maple booth in the corner and settled on the bench. She plopped her oversize handbag on the table. "I need a break from work. The arrangements for the Christmas party are overwhelming."

Lucy set down a tray of clean glasses. "I was surprised to hear you picked a place."

"I only recently settled on the VFW Hall. I ran into Jake at Lola's Coffee Shop and mentioned it to him. The hall is large and I have a caterer, and Jake's supplying all the beer."

"What's the problem, then?"

"All the other details. Decorations. Music. Catering. I'm a township clerk, not a party planner. I think Susan's arrest is putting a damper on everything, including my enthusiasm."

Lucy couldn't agree more. It was difficult to concentrate on her management duties with her friend in jail. "I'll help however I can."

"How about seeing the place with me tomorrow afternoon? Can you get away?"

"I'll make time. What else do you need?"

Katie rested her elbows on the table. "Feed me. I'm starved. What's today's lunch special?"

Lucy slipped into the booth across from her. "Fresh swordfish shish kebab and rice pilaf."

"Sounds delicious and healthy."

"I'll place your order, and one for Bill to go. My mom has a container of baklava with Bill's name on it, too."

"He'll love both. I think you and Angela spoil him and he'd rather eat here for every meal."

"My mom would love it. She says Emma and I don't eat enough. I think she'd be happy if we gained ten pounds."

"Bill would happily put on the weight if it was from Azad or Angela's cooking."

"Talking about Bill, have you had a chance to talk to him since Susan was arrested?"

"I have. Clemmons believes he had ample evidence for the arrest." Katie hesitated, then bit her lip. "I think he's right this time."

Lucy gaped. "You can't seriously believe Susan killed Deacon?"

Katie twisted the straps of her handbag. "I don't know what to think. Susan threatened Deacon not once, but twice. Maybe she did do it. But then I think about everyone else. Clarissa and Henry both hated Deacon, too. Henry's statement that Clarissa wasn't near Deacon in the water sounded bogus to me. But I know your bet is on Vinnie Pinto."

"It was, but who knows? Norman Weston had both motive and opportunity, too."

Katie sighed. "We're no closer to finding the killer, and Susan stays in jail."

Lucy grimaced, then tapped her fingers on the table. "I need to talk to Clemmons, but I want to be sure I approach him when the prosecutor isn't around."

"Don't go to the station. I overheard Bill say Marsha Walsh is spending a lot of time there overseeing everything to be sure all the *i's* are dotted and the *t's* crossed before the arraignment."

"She doesn't trust her own detective?" Lucy asked.

"She knows Clemmons can rush the paperwork, and any mistakes can cost her in court."

Smart lady. Lucy had always been a bit intimidated by Walsh, but she pushed that fear aside now. "I only have one good shot to talk to Clemmons. I don't want to waste it. Where do you think I can catch him alone?"

Katie sat straight in the booth. "Oh, I have a good idea."

Lucy waited outside Lola's Coffee Shop. She'd spotted Detective Clemmons walk inside at least thirty minutes before. Was he drinking his coffee inside and chatting with the locals? She didn't want to engage him inside. Gossip would travel like wildfire if anyone heard a hint of their conversation.

At last, the door opened and Clemmons walked outside. He held a cardboard tray holding four cups of coffee in one hand and a bag of doughnuts in the other. The coffee and doughnuts were most likely for the officers back at the station.

Clemmons walked to his car and placed the coffee on the hood as he reached inside his jacket pocket and pulled out his car keys.

Lucy swiftly approached. "Those doughnuts aren't from Cutie's Cupcakes. They won't be as good."

Clemmons halted. "Well, hello, Ms. Berberian. I never thought of you as a stalker."

That was a bit offensive. "I'm not a stalker," she protested.

"That's debatable." He lifted the bag of doughnuts. "Well, I won't argue with you about the taste of these. Cutie's has the best baked goods around."

Lucy shifted her feet. Time to get down to business. "I want to ask you a question."

"Ah, I presume you're going to ask about Susan Cutie's arrest. You haven't learned to stay out of police business?"

She ignored his question. "The last time we talked, you said you knew things about Susan. Things I didn't."

His gaze was serious under even brows. "I remember our conversation, and I meant what I said."

"Well, I meant what I said, too. Others had motive to kill Deacon and were in the water that day. Like Clarissa—"

"I told you, there was an eyewitness who said Clarissa wasn't near Deacon in the water, whereas Susan was."

"You're referring to Henry Buxbaum. He's Clarissa's friend—"

"From high school. We know."

"And that Henry—"

"Was Deacon's nephew and has inherited a trust friend. We know that, too. The police do investigate, Ms. Berberian."

Her throat tightened a fraction. "Then you should know

his statement is unreliable. Both Clarissa and Henry disliked Deacon for their own reasons."

There was much more she wanted to tell him. About the back-alley meeting between Henry and Clarissa. And Norman's feud with his business partner. She picked the most relevant. "What about Vinnie Pinto's habit of breaking into homes using old keys from his prior days as a property manager?"

He gripped the bag of doughnuts. "Bill Watson already told us about Vinnie's illegal habit."

"Yes, but did he tell you one of the places Vinnie burglarized was Deacon's office?"

Clemmons's mustache twitched. "I suspect it was you who gave us that tip as well."

"Why don't you follow up and ask Vinnie about it?"

"We did. Vinnie denies breaking into Deacon's office. Without a police report, there's no evidence." He gave her a calculated look. "You're an attorney, Ms. Berberian. You should know hearsay doesn't hold up well in a murder trial."

Crap. Vinnie may have spilled everything to her in front of his scary mob boss, but he'd denied all knowledge when questioned by the police. It was clear who Vinnie feared more.

This conversation wasn't going as she'd wanted or planned. She'd thought to tell him about each suspect, and make him second-guess Susan's arrest.

Instead, he was making her second-guess herself.

"Again, leave the crime fighting to the professionals, Ms. Berberian."

She didn't expect him to make this easy. A nagging feeling settled low in her stomach. She sucked in a breath and looked up at him. "Do you still hold a grudge against my family? My sister never treated you fairly back in high school."

Emma had dated Calvin Clemmons, then cheated on him with a close friend. Not very nice of Emma. Her parents had never approved of Clemmons either. But that was a long, long time ago.

He peered at her. "Your sister was a piece of work back in high school. But I'm a professional."

Lucy tried another tack. "Susan's not just anyone. She's a town fixture and a good neighbor."

He sighed and set the bag of doughnuts next to the coffee on the hood of his car. "Do you think I enjoyed having to arrest her?"

The crack in his normally cold facade took Lucy off guard. She'd understood he was doing his job all along, but she never knew he'd found it difficult.

Another thought occurred to her. Everyone had pressure from a boss. God knew, Lucy had to deal with difficult partners at the city firm. She still had to deal with her father at the restaurant whenever she wanted to make the slightest change. Katie had to please the mayor at the town hall. Michael Citteroni had to placate his father in the bicycle shop.

Detective Clemmons was no exception.

Katie had warned her that the county prosecutor had been spending time in the police station and overseeing everything to make sure the case against Susan was wrapped neatly with a tight red bow. "Did Prosecutor Walsh pressure you to make the arrest?"

"Nobody pressures me or makes me do my job, but I'll say this: Detectives have to work with the county. Walsh is very well respected and has a lot of influence."

"In other words, the deck is really stacked against Susan."

"Let's just say it's good Clyde Winters is representing her."

Lucy didn't think her nerves could tighten any more. "Your investigation is concluded, then?"

Clemmons gave a terse nod. "Unless I have reason to believe otherwise."

Something flashed in his eyes, but it was gone as swiftly as she'd seen it. Was he asking her to give him a reason? Or was she imagining it?

Chapter Twenty-Eight

The Veterans of Foreign Wars Hall, otherwise known as the VFW Hall, was near the end of town and close to the lifeguard station on the beach. Two plumbing trucks were parked out front. Katie's Jeep was parked next to them and she was standing outside talking to a man in worn blue overalls.

Lucy grabbed her purse from her car and joined Katie. "What's going on?"

Her friend's expression was grave. "This is Frank Malvern, owner of Malvern Plumbing. A pipe burst inside and flooded the kitchen."

Frank, a swarthy man with deep crow's feet around his eyes and a goatee, shifted his booted feet on the blacktop. "I can stop the leak and replace the pipe, but the damage is extensive. The pipe must have burst on Friday and no one discovered it until Monday. It will take weeks to dry the place out and replace the kitchen."

Katie groaned. "There goes the town Christmas party."

"Sorry, ma'am. I have to get to work." Frank left them to enter the building.

Lucy hated to see things go wrong for her friend. "I'm so sorry, Katie."

She shook her head. "I think we're going to have to skip this year's celebrations."

"No way! We'll think of something." Lucy knew how important the annual holiday party was to her friend, and to many town employees. Coworkers often stopped by the town hall to ask Katie about the details.

"How? Trying to find another venue under this short notice is a nightmare. Everywhere is booked for holiday parties and events. Trust me," Katie said, "I've called around."

Lucy believed her. The Jersey shore, even in the winter, was busy during Christmas time.

Katie's shoulders sagged in defeat. "I can't reserve decorations like balloons, or music, or even food until I have a hall." A tear rolled down her cheek, and she swiftly brushed it away. "I'm sorry. I'm not a crier."

Lucy's stomach sank at her friend's distress. She hugged her. "Don't worry about acting tough around me. Cry and let it out, Katie."

Katie choked on a sob. "I feel worse that I never even asked you how things went with Clemmons."

Lucy tightened her hug. "Don't worry about Clemmons."

"It didn't go well, then?"

Lucy sighed and reached in her purse for a tissue to hand to Katie. "He's just doing his job. But he did surprise me by admitting that he doesn't like the fact that Susan is behind bars."

Katie blew her nose. "Really? I guess even Clemmons likes Susan's doughnuts."

They both laughed. "I guess so."

"Please don't worry about your party. We'll think of

something." Then Lucy did. "Wait! What about Kebab Kitchen?"

"What about it?"

"We can have the town employee Christmas celebration there. My mother has an annual party for all the business owners and their families. Why not combine the guest list?" In hindsight, she was surprised she hadn't thought of it earlier.

Katie crinkled the tissue in a fist and looked at her. "Really? You think your mother would agree?"

"The restaurant has seating for one hundred and fifty. She's already ordered a keg of Jake's Christmas ale. We'll just order more. As long as we don't go over the fire code, I think I can convince her. Besides, I'm the manager now. I have some influence."

This time, Katie hugged her. "You're the best, Lucy. It will be perfect."

As soon as she walked into Kebab Kitchen later that afternoon, a delicious aroma of grilled lamb wafted through the air and reached Lucy's nose with a distinctly comforting perfume. It was early afternoon, and the kitchen was bustling, with a full staff hard at work. Azad and Butch efficiently worked together to put out food. The cook's wheel was full of checks, and Azad spun the wheel as he read customer's orders out loud to Butch, who helped prepare each dish.

Sally and Emma were buzzing around the dining room serving hot plates of food. Her father was in the office and her mother was in the back of the kitchen, preparing her famous rice pudding.

"Everything okay while I was gone?" Lucy asked her mother.

Angela stirred a commercial-size pot with a spoon. Strands of hair escaped her signature beehive from the kitchen's ever-present humidity. "A customer asked about our gluten-free menu."

"The new menus are at the printers. Meanwhile, we can accommodate him."

Azad had brought up the subject of a gluten-free option a couple of months before. Lucy had been on board immediately and thought it was a great idea. More and more people were going gluten-free, whether it was because of a food allergy or just a desire to eat healthier, and Lucy wanted to offer the option at Kebab Kitchen. She'd run it by her father, expecting a "discussion," but Raffi had surprised her by quickly agreeing.

Lucy couldn't help but wonder if her father's quick approval was because Azad had suggested it.

"Sally handled it well. She told the customer our new menus will feature a full gluten-free section, and she suggested items he could order today. He was satisfied."

Her mother glanced around the worktable. Lucy anticipated her need, reached for a clean rag, and handed it to her. Angela nodded, then efficiently proceeded to clean off her worktable. Lucy had grown accustomed to her mother's cleanliness as she worked. Her mother's lessons had taught her more than just about cooking, but how to run a safe, sanitary kitchen.

"Mom, I want to ask you something. Katie is having problems finding a place for the township employee holiday party. The VFW recently flooded and won't be ready in time. I suggested Kebab Kitchen. Maybe we can combine your party with hers? What do you think?"

Angela halted in her task. "Have both parties together here?"

"Yes."

Seconds ticked by as her mother pursed her lips in thought. Then, at last, her face broke into a smile, and she nodded once. "I like Katie and want to help. Business owners and township employees all work together from time to time, and it will be nice to have even more people at Kebab Kitchen. Christmas is a time of giving."

Lucy clasped her hands to her chest. "Wonderful! Katie will be so happy."

And relieved. Her friend could relax, and Lucy would be able to help much more if the restaurant was the venue. Lucy's mind churned as she kicked into her role as manager. Combining parties meant many more people. She'd have to sit down with Azad to discuss the menu, then order more food from their suppliers. She'd need to visit Jake's Boardwalk Brewery to order more kegs. Other items came to mind—holiday decorations, creative varieties for the hummus bar, and—

"We can officially announce your engagement to Azad before all our guests."

"What?"

"Your engagement." Angela stirred the tall pot, oblivious to Lucy's sharpened tone. "I've been wanting to have an engagement party for you both. A large holiday party is the perfect opportunity."

"Mom, I don't think—"

"Oh, I know Katie is your matron of honor, and she has been working hard to help and has even taken you dress shopping, but I want to do more, too. Raffi and I couldn't be any happier you have finally come to your senses regarding our Azad."

Our Azad.

She knew her parents loved Azad, had always wanted him for her. From the first day of her return, they'd been quite vocal, and it had nearly made Lucy run for the hills.

But this took it to another level. She wasn't prepared for what her mother had suggested.

Azad had gone a long way to ease her fears regarding their continuing to work together as a married couple. She loved him, and happily wore his diamond on her finger. But this was different.

She had no desire to stand on a rooftop and shout out an announcement to all those people. She was a private person. It was bad enough that gossip traveled like wildfire in this small town. Many people already knew about the engagement, but not *everyone*. She didn't like public attention, had never liked it.

Lucy opened her mouth to tell her mother a flat-out no.

Her mother held up the spoon. "Before you tell your mother no, you should ask Azad's opinion. It's not just all about you now, Lucy."

Lucy snapped her mouth shut.

As much as she hated to admit it, her mother was right. Azad did have a say. She hadn't picked a wedding date yet. He'd never pressured her; that wasn't his style. Azad wanted her to be happy. But was she being fair to him?

A pang of guilt pierced her chest. "I don't like the idea, but I'll talk with Azad. Don't get your hopes up yet."

"Fair enough."

Lucy eyed her suspiciously. That was too easy, and she didn't trust her parent. Not one bit. What did her mother know that she didn't? If Angela ever learned of Lucy's panic attack at the bridal boutique, her mother would panic herself and call the family doctor.

"One more thing. I had planned a visit to your cousin, Nora Garabedian, tomorrow, to invite her to my Christmas party. She lives at the Seashell Inn, where she works. Raffi can't drive me. Can you?"

Lucy hadn't seen her cousin in a while and would like to catch up with Nora. "Sure, I'll take you."

Her mother pulled her down and planted a kiss on her forehead. "Good. But talk to Azad first. I'm looking forward to hearing what he has to say."

Lucy found Azad in the storage room, lifting heavy boxes that had been delivered by their Mediterranean food supplier. Muscles bunched beneath his chef's coat as he picked up a box to place it on one of the stainless-steel shelves. Another heavy box followed.

Lucy halted in the doorway. A warm feeling flowed through her as she watched him. She felt like an overheated and hormonal teenager staring at the star quarterback in the high school hallway. Azad had always been in good shape and lifted weights at the gym, but he looked even better working. Her father used to do the heavy lifting, but since his retirement, he hadn't been able to do what he used to. Once more, she was grateful for Azad's help.

"Thanks for doing that for me."

He turned from his task to spot her in the doorway. "Hey. I've been thinking about you."

Her cheeks grew warm. *Was he thinking about her the same way she'd just been thinking about him?*

"Oh?" Was all she managed to croak out.

"The Beach Bums are coming back to town tomorrow night. Want to go?"

The band was a local favorite and often played at

Ocean Crest during the season. They performed cover songs and their originals, too. "Sure. When will they be at Mac's Pub?"

"They're not playing there, but beneath the boardwalk bandstand."

"The boardwalk? Won't it be freezing?"

"No. There will be space heaters. Those big ones you see at outside bars."

She'd seen the tall space heaters at restaurants and bars. Toasty and warm, people gravitated to them during cold days.

"A lot of local crafters will have tents set up selling holiday items, too," Azad said.

Lucy loved the local crafters. She didn't have a crafting bone in her body, but she wanted to learn one day. She'd have to start by buying a glue gun. "It sounds like fun. I'd like to pick up a few festive items to decorate my new apartment."

His grin made her heart pound. "Your parents said they'd cover. I'll pick you up at six. Dress warm."

He went to reach for another box when she recalled why she'd sought him out in the first place. "Wait! I want to ask you something."

He pushed the box aside to look at her. "What's on your mind?"

"Katie's been having trouble finding a place to have the township employee holiday party. I offered to host it at Kebab Kitchen and combine it with my parents' party. My mom agreed."

"Sounds like a great idea."

"It will mean a lot of work in the kitchen."

"I'm on board."

"My mom . . . she wants to . . ."

"Azad!"

Lucy started just as Butch walked into the storage room. "Sorry, I didn't know you were here." He looked at Azad. "The fishmonger delivered the wrong fish. You said striper, he delivered mackerel. What do you want to do with it?"

A crease appeared in between Azad's eyebrows. "Mackerel? That won't work at all with the menu I'd planned." Azad shoved the box farther back on the shelf. "I'm coming." He was halfway to the doorway when he halted, as if remembering Lucy was still there. "Sorry. What did you want to ask?"

"Never mind. You have more important things to worry about now. We'll talk later."

Azad must have sensed her inner turmoil because he said something to Butch, then turned back to her. "Butch can wait. What did you want to talk about?"

Uncertainty made her voice break slightly. "It's silly, really. Mom wants to . . . she wants to . . ." How to say it? Would he agree?

"Spit it out."

"My mom wants to announce our engagement at the big combined holiday party."

"Knowing Mrs. Berberian, I'm not surprised."

She watched him for any outward reaction, but his expression wasn't one of horror or protest. "Well? What do you think?"

"I think you wouldn't like that."

He mentioned her feelings, but there was no mention of his. "You know I don't like public attention."

He nodded once. "You don't want everyone in our business."

"Exactly."

"Katie's been gung ho about wedding planning. But from what I can tell, you haven't been that excited," he said.

Whoa. She detected a hint of worry in his voice then. "Azad, I . . ."

"I thought you were worried we'd turn out like your parents."

"I was. But you put my mind at ease about that." This was different from the panic attack she'd had at the bridal salon. But she was still uncomfortable with her mother's plan.

"But there's more that worries you?" It was a statement more than a question. "You haven't wanted to set a wedding date. Should I be concerned?"

It was true. She hadn't. She'd been content with their engaged status. But her feelings had more to do with what was going on in town and with her incarcerated friend than with her fiancé. "It's been hard for me to be excited about wedding planning when Susan's in jail."

"I'm going to guess you haven't given up on your friend."

She sighed. "I don't want to, but things don't look good right now."

"Things can change. Have faith." He reached out to take her hand in his. "I want to be sure that's all that's going on here. Just reassure me of one thing. Are you happy?"

She searched his face. She knew every angle and curve, the arch of his eyebrows, the exact shade of brown of his eyes—not as dark as coffee, but a deeper shade than chocolate.

She took a deep breath. The familiar smells of Mediterranean spices and herbs filled her lungs. She was content with her job as manager of Kebab Kitchen. She hadn't been content at the law firm, and upon her return to Ocean Crest, it had taken her a while to realize she was exactly where she wanted to be. Looking into his handsome face, she knew, deep down, that she was more than just content with her fiancé.

She loved him with all her heart.

"I am happy. I love you."

His worried brow eased. "Then how about we set a date?"

This was a different sort of question. "I want everything to be perfect, but not in the sense that you would think. I don't want one of those fashion-magazine weddings or a ritzy catering hall. I want our friends and loved ones to celebrate with us. I want to feel sand between my toes and the ocean breeze to loosen my salon updo. I want to eat shish kebab straight off the skewer and sticky baklava with my fingers. I want to walk from the reception and dance on the beach. I want us to be us."

His grin was devastating. "Lucy Berberian, that is the sweetest thing you've said in a long time."

Her heart danced with excitement, and she was glad she'd summoned the courage to talk with him. "On second thought," she said with a smile, "I think we should let my parents go ahead and announce our good news at the party."

Chapter Twenty-Nine

"Are you sure Cousin Nora lives on this road?" Lucy asked.

Angela peered out the window as Lucy drove. "It's been a couple of years, but this is how I remember it."

Lucy turned off a main road, gritted her teeth as she crossed a narrow, one-lane bridge, her tires rumbling over patched asphalt, and wound around a curve to come to a wide, smoothly paved street. They passed a sign that read, "Welcome to Rock Harbor." The Jersey shore had numerous small towns, and each had its own municipalities and police stations.

They made it to Main Street, with a row of tiny, charming shops—a coffee shop, a boutique clothing store, a pet store, and a paint-your-own-canvas salon to name a few. A ticket stand, which reminded Lucy of an old-fashioned movie theater booth, advertised train rides on an old steam engine. Soon after, Lucy drove over railroad tracks and spotted the large, black steam engine.

"Make a right here," Angela said.

"Are you sure? Following the GPS would be better to—"

Angela pointed to the right. "My memory's better. Just turn."

Lucy wasn't so sure, but she made the turn anyway. Then she nearly slammed on the brakes, her eyes wide. "Wow! I didn't expect this."

Dozens of well-kept Victorian homes came into view. Quaint and lovely, they took Lucy's breath away.

"See? I told you it was nice here," Angela said.

"Nice" was an understatement. One-hundred-year-old oak and sycamore trees lined a wide street. At first glance, it looked like Cape May, but it was even older, and the houses were spaced out a bit more and had expansive lawns. She imagined they would be lush grass in the summer. Lucy knew how difficult and expensive it was to grow perfect grass in a beach town. The soil tended to be sandy.

Lucy was more than eager to spot her cousin's bed-and-breakfast now, and she scanned the street. She located it a second before her mother. "There it is!"

The Seashell Inn was meticulously maintained and looked like a dollhouse, with a turret, large bay windows, iron railings, and an old, wraparound porch. Several of the windows were stained glass. The house was painted a lovely robin's-egg blue, and the delicate wood trim was accented a bright green. A large Christmas wreath hung on the front door.

"Isn't it lovely?" Angela asked.

"Does Nora own it?"

"No. Nora's a year or two younger than you. Old Man Sherman owns it. Nora has worked for him for only a couple of years."

"Who's Sherman?"

A vee formed between her mother's eyebrows. "I'm not quite sure of the connection, but I think Sherman's an old friend of Nora's family. Nora needed a job and Sherman needed the help. The inn is unique because even though it's Victorian architecture, it has a Mediterranean decor. Nora prepares Greek omelets and Mediterranean breakfasts and lunches for the overnight guests. She's quite the cook, almost as good as me."

Almost as good as me. Lucy didn't miss the reference.

Lucy had to see inside. She couldn't picture a Victorian with Mediterranean decor. How did Nora pull it off?

"Nora's also talented at reading coffee cups. She can read your fortune from the grounds of your Turkish or Greek coffee."

Lucy had heard of the fortune-reading talent, but other than her great-grandmother, who had died before she was born, no one else in the family had it.

They parked in a small lot behind the inn, then climbed the steps to the porch. It was even bigger than she'd thought. Each of the four white rocking chairs had a chair pad with a Persian design. From the front of the house, a visitor had a lovely view of the Atlantic Ocean. She imagined a room in this place would cost more than a shiny penny during the summer season.

The door was open and they stepped inside. The foyer was furnished with a tufted Persian rug and a mahogany end table holding a lantern with an Arabic pattern to welcome guests.

"Lucy! Horkour Angela! How long has it been?" Nora addressed Angela as *horkour*, which translated as father's sister, or aunt, in Armenian.

Lucy looked up a winding wooden staircase to see a young, smiling woman descending.

"Too long," Lucy's mother said.

Nora reached them and gave both a big hug. She was

pretty, with shoulder-length brown hair and hazel eyes. Dressed in tights and a purple sweater dress, feather earrings, and matching purple suede boots, she looked chic and fashionable.

"It's wonderful to see you again, Nora." Before Lucy could take a step farther, a little white dog was at her feet, tail wagging.

"Don't mind Trixie."

Lucy bent down to pet the top of Trixie's head. "She's adorable. What kind of dog?"

"A Havanese mix, and a rescue. Trixie's not much of a guard dog; she loves everyone who steps through the front door."

Trixie sniffed the hem of Lucy's pants with ardor. "She must smell Gadoo."

"Unique name for a cat." Nora knew Gadoo's name meant, simply, "cat."

Nora led them into a sitting room. Two more exotic rugs were scattered across the hardwood floors. A coffee table held a mother-of-pearl backgammon set, ready to play. With a bench covered with colorful red, gold, and green pillows for seating, a pair of matching upholstered red chairs, and a side table with a hookah in the corner, the room definitely had a Mediterranean feel. Lucy sat in one of the chairs, and her mother sat beside Nora on a settee.

"Can I get you something to drink? Coffee or tea?" Nora asked.

They asked for coffee. Lucy was tempted to ask for Turkish or Greek coffee to have Nora read her fortune, but they weren't there for that purpose. Another time, for sure.

But Nora was a mind reader, because she returned with a tray that held small porcelain cups, much smaller than any teacup. Each was etched in a blue-and-gold design and was solid white inside. A small copper pot with a long handle sat on the tray, and steam curled from its surface. She poured three cups of a dark brew and handed one to Lucy's mother, then one to Lucy. A plate of baklava was also on the tray.

Nora and Angela took their coffee without cream or sugar. Lucy added one lump of sugar, raised her cup, and sipped. She'd had this type of coffee before at her mother's and numerous relatives' homes. It was stronger than any American coffee, but once you grew accustomed to it, it was velvety and delicious.

Nora reached for the baklava. "I use finely chopped pistachios, not walnuts." She looked at Angela. "I know you make the best, but see if you like it." Nora gave each of them a Waterford plate with a square of baklava.

Lucy took a bite. The phyllo dough was flaky and the pistachios added a delicious and different layer of flavor. The baklava melted in her mouth. "Hmm. I'll have to try swapping out walnuts for pistachios myself."

"You've been baking?" Nora didn't try to mask her surprise.

"Lucy's been baking and cooking," Angela said, her face beaming with pride.

Lucy stared, unnerved at her mother's praise. Angela was stingy with compliments. "I'm no cook, but I'm learning." She looked around. "The inn is beautiful. You're probably packed all summer long."

"We try to keep it full. We have lots of receptions, corporate gatherings, even sorority girls' weekends." Nora sipped her tea. "I'm happy to see you both, but I wondered if there was a certain reason for your visit when you called."

"We are having a big holiday party at Kebab Kitchen. We'd love for you to come," Lucy said.

Nora's face brightened. "How nice. I'll have to tell Sherman to get coverage for me."

"How is he?" Angela asked.

"Feisty as ever. He's probably in the library, if you want to see him."

"I haven't seen him in years." Angela rose and left to find Sherman, leaving Lucy alone with Nora.

"Now we can talk about the good stuff. I've heard you're engaged. Tell me about him."

Lucy lowered her cup. "He's our head chef, Azad Zakarian."

Nora dimpled. "How's that working out? No pun intended."

"I get it. Working together has its challenges. We've known each other forever, but I went away to work in the city for years, and when I came back, we kind of hit it off again."

"That fast?"

"Well . . . there was a lot of drama in between." Like a murder charge, but who was counting?

"Hmm. We haven't seen each other in a while, Lucy, but I sense something's wrong."

Lucy found herself wanting to talk to someone. Maybe it was better that Nora lived a few towns away and not in Ocean Crest. She could open up to a friend, a cousin, and not fear it would get back to her mother or Azad, or the entire blasted town.

"Things are a bit tense. My mother wants to announce our engagement at the upcoming holiday party. At first, I wasn't so sure. Azad asked if I'm dragging my feet by not picking a wedding date."

"Are you?"

"I guess it's been true, but not because of Azad. I've had a lot on my mind. My good friend and the local baker has been arrested for murder. I feel weird planning my wedding when Susan is sitting in jail and her own romance is on hold."

Nora's feathered earrings swung as she shook her head in dismay. "I've heard about the Polar Bear Plunge murderer. But is that really the reason you're dragging your feet?"

"I love Azad."

Nora nodded, as if she'd never doubted her. "A lot of couples and honeymooners spend time at this inn. I've seen quite a few things and have had to give impromptu couples' therapy more than once."

Lucy could picture her cousin like another Lucy—the Lucy from the *Peanuts* cartoon, hanging out in her little hut, charging Charlie Brown for therapy by the hour. There was something calming about Nora Garabedian that made you want to spill your guts to her.

"May I read your cup?"

Lucy shifted in her seat. She'd thought it would be fun to have her cup read when her mother had first told her of her cousin's talent, but now, faced with the question, she wasn't sure. It wasn't as if she was superstitious. She'd had a stint at Madame Vega's fortune-telling salon on the boardwalk in the past. Madame had read her tarot cards and her palm and had been frighteningly close with her predictions, but Lucy wasn't entirely convinced of the occult.

But this was different. She'd grown up knowing about coffee cup reading, and it was part of her culture. The practice was old, very old, dating back to the sixteenth century, and was favored by Ottoman sultans. Even her mother believed in the stuff. Nora was her cousin, and Lucy had already concluded that she was easy to talk to. What harm could come of her reading a few coffee grounds?

"Okay. Sure. Just don't tell me how I'll die," she joked half-heartedly.

"You know it doesn't work that way."

Nora took her cup from her, placed the saucer on top of it, and handed it back to her. "Now swirl the cup and saucer clockwise three times and repeat, 'Whatever is my situation, let that appear in my cup.'"

Lucy covered her cup with its inverted saucer and carefully swirled it three times, repeating Nora's words, "'Whatever is my situation, let that appear in my cup.'" Then Lucy flipped her wrist so that now the cup was upside down on the saucer. Soon, a dark rim of coffee began to appear at the cup's perimeter where the thick liquid seeped into the saucer. Lucy knew it would take a few minutes for the grounds to set.

"How does it work?" Lucy asked.

"The portion of the cup closest to the handle will show your love life. To the left of the handle will reveal your present, and to the right your future."

"Did you always know you had the talent?"

Nora looked pensive. "I used to sit by my grandmother's side as she read cups. My interest really grew when I was eight. She used to show me the cups and I'd try to see what was written there. I remember the first time she looked at me in surprise. I was ten, and I predicted something bad would happen to one of her friends. I made the mistake of telling them both that I saw sickness. My grandmother was furious with me when her friend left."

"Why? You were young and didn't know better."

The fringe of Nora's eyelashes cast shadows on her cheeks. "Her friend was diagnosed with lung cancer and died six months later." Nora's gaze lowered. "My grandmother never let me look at a cup again unless we were alone."

Lucy pressed a hand to her throat. "That's horrible. It could have been a coincidence."

"I thought about it a lot after that. I also swore to keep life-and-death readings to myself from then on."

Lucy lowered her gaze to her inverted cup. Maybe her initial hesitancy was for a good reason.

"Don't worry. I haven't read anything like that in a long, long time. Want to back out?"

Lucy shook her head. "No."

Nora picked up Lucy's cup and showed it to her. Lucy could see a muddy sediment of coffee grounds in her cup. It looked like a brown glob, and she wondered how Nora could make sense of it.

"I'm curious. What do you see in that?" Lucy asked.

"It is important to read a whole impression, not just individual symbols." Nora tipped the cup toward a beam of sunlight streaming in from an overhead window. "For your present, I see a fish. You have advanced in your career, but not the way you initially thought."

That made sense. If you'd asked Lucy where she'd thought she'd end up a year ago, she would have believed that she'd make partner in her Philadelphia firm. Her life had taken a much different path for sure. Never would she have thought she'd end up as the manager of her family's restaurant. And even more confounding, she never would have thought she'd be happy working at Kebab Kitchen.

"I can almost see the fish now. But what does it say about my future?" Lucy was curious to hear more.

Nora tilted the cup this way and that, her brow furrowed. "For your future, I see a hurricane. It will leave behind destruction, but the outcome will result in calm."

"A hurricane doesn't sound good, especially at the Jersey shore." Lucy thought her cousin wouldn't read bad outcomes.

"It's not unusual to see turmoil, but your future will definitely be resolved and . . . wait!" Nora hesitated, her gaze eerily intent on the cup. "I see an *achk*, or eye. It is located just beneath the hurricane, but I see it clearly now. See?" Nora held out the cup to Lucy.

At first, Lucy wasn't sure what she was seeing other than a glob of dark, brown grounds, but then she saw it. The eye was small. The hair on her nape began to stand on end.

She knew what an I-see-an-*achk* meant. It was an ancient symbol throughout the Middle East and the Mediterranean. The good eye was a talisman that warded off jealousy or bad feelings from others. Her father, who never believed in cup or tarot reading, or any other form of superstition, still had a talisman of a protective eye pinned to the visor in his car.

Even Lucy was raised to believe in that talisman.

"Is it a good eye or an evil one?" She almost didn't want to ask. At Nora's silence, Lucy raised her gaze from the cup to her cousin. She knew the answer immediately. "Who is responsible for the bad eye?"

"I can't tell that. I can only warn you that you must be careful. An evil in Ocean Crest is close to you."

Once more, trepidation made Lucy's gut tighten. She was glad her mother wasn't present.

"There is still your love life to read in your cup," Nora said.

Maybe she didn't want to hear this after all. If her future wasn't peaches and roses, then what would her love life show?

"For your love life," Nora said, "I see fire. Passion and love go hand in hand for you."

Azad did bring out her passionate side. When it came to their wedding, it certainly had brought out all types of emotions so far.

"This is a good reading of your life." Nora set down her cup on the saucer.

"Yes, and it's accurate, too. We have lots of passion, but we've had some bumps in the road, especially with the wedding stuff."

Nora tilted her head to the side and studied Lucy. "Wedding planning is stressful and daunting. You need to think about what type of wedding you two want, not what everyone else wants or expects."

Her cousin's advice struck a chord. She'd been concerned with pleasing Katie and her parents, rather than thinking—really thinking—about what type of couple they were and what would make her and Azad happy.

"You're so right," Lucy said.

"And if that doesn't work," Nora said, "maybe what you need is a quick weekend getaway with Azad. You are welcome to come here to stay. You'd be surprised how much it will help."

* * *

Her mother had turned on the radio as soon as Lucy turned on the car's ignition. Lucy was grateful her mother was distracted, surfing the stations. Her thoughts were occupied with Nora's predictions after reading her cup.

An evil in Ocean Crest is close to you.

A killer still roamed free. Nora had to be referring to him . . . or her. Thank goodness the rest of her cup reading had been positive.

"Did you get along with Nora?" her mother asked.

"We did. I hope to see her again soon." Lucy decided to keep her cup reading to herself. Knowing her mother, she'd panic if she learned Nora had seen the evil eye in her cup. Angela just might tell her father. They'd watch her like a hawk from then on, and try to give her a curfew.

Her mother finally settled on a radio station. "Cooking Kurt is being interviewed about his newest cookbook."

Really? As if watching the muscular celebrity chef wasn't enough during their cooking lessons, now Lucy had to hear him boast about his baking talents? The interviewer, a woman who Lucy had heard ask tough questions of a local politician, was asking soft questions now, gushing over Kurt's every word.

Lucy lowered the volume on the car radio as she turned onto the Garden State Parkway.

"Why'd you do that?" Angela asked.

"I've been thinking about what you said about announcing my engagement to Azad at the upcoming Kebab Kitchen holiday party."

"Did you ask him like I told you to?"

Lucy shrugged, hoping to appear nonplussed. "We talked."

"By your expression, I can only assume you've maintained your stubborn opinion."

"Mom," Lucy whined. "That's not true." Ever since she'd talked with Azad, Lucy had been doing a lot of thinking, and Nora's reading had reaffirmed her initial idea.

"Well?"

"I want to be the one to announce our engagement to all our friends."

"Really?" The shock in her mother's voice made Lucy smile.

"Yes, really. Azad thinks you and Dad are going to make a speech. But I'd like to surprise Azad with a champagne toast. What do you think?"

"I think we are going to need a lot of champagne. Now, turn the volume back up."

Chapter Thirty

A steady stream of customers flooded the restaurant the next day. Even though Lucy was busy with her duties, she kept thinking of her decision. Once she'd made up her mind to surprise Azad at the holiday party by raising glasses of bubbly and announcing their engagement, a shimmer of excitement hummed in her veins. Her biggest challenge was to keep her excitement hidden and her ultimate plans secret from Azad.

She'd also been looking forward to their night out. Her parents were covering the dinner shift so that Azad could take her to see the Beach Bums beneath the boardwalk bandstand. Lucy was ready when he showed up that night. She'd dressed in a Christmas sweater with a Santa, jeans, and warm boots. Her assortment of Christmas sweaters was growing. Azad looked casual in jeans and a flannel shirt. He looked good in a chef's coat, sport jacket and tie, or well-worn jeans.

Azad took her hand. "I've been looking forward to spending time together all day."

They walked up the boardwalk ramp hand in hand. A cool breeze blew from the ocean, but it was toasty beneath the heating lamps. The band hadn't started playing yet, but was warming up beneath the bandstand. An assortment of tents was set up on both sides. Local artists and crafters sold art, jewelry, crafts, and beach clothing. Jake's Boardwalk Brewery had a tent. Canvas flapped in the ocean breeze as shoppers walked from tent to tent.

Lucy stopped to admire a small, hand-printed sign that said, "A happy home needs coffee, tea, and friends."

"This is perfect for my kitchen," Lucy said.

"Then it's yours." Azad pulled cash from his wallet and handed it to a woman in her sixties with dyed black hair. "Can you please hold this for us until the end of the evening?"

The saleswoman gave him a sassy wink. "Sure thing, honey."

"You didn't have to do that," Lucy said.

"Why not? I think it will look great in *our* kitchen."

Lucy didn't miss his use of the words "our kitchen." Her heart did a pitter-patter, and she wanted to tell him her news right then and there, but she bit the inside of her cheek to keep quiet. She wanted her plans to be a surprise.

Azad led her to Jake's tent, where a young, pimply faced college student was serving customers. "Where's Jake?"

"He couldn't make it. Something about visiting his girlfriend."

So, Jake was spending as much time as he could with Susan before she was shipped off to the county jail. Lucy wondered how Susan was handling his visits. She'd been adamant about wanting to break up with Jake and saving him the trouble of standing by her side during a murder trial, and worse—if she was convicted—having to visit her in prison. Lucy's stomach sank at the thought.

Azad ordered cranberry ale and handed Lucy a paper

cup. Glass wasn't allowed on the boardwalk. He must have sensed her melancholy mood, because a concerned look suddenly filled his eyes. "Oh no you don't. Please don't let depressing thoughts ruin our special evening, okay?"

He was right. This was their date night and she wouldn't let morbid thoughts dampen their fun. There was nothing she could do about Susan's situation at the moment. She should focus on having an enjoyable evening. "I promise to smile. How about we check out the rest of the tents?"

They wandered past booths of pottery, hand-drawn caricatures, and jewelry made of tiny seashells and black string. The last tent didn't have sides. A crowd of onlookers gathered before an artist with an assortment of spray paint. The artist slipped on a mask, then proceeded to use the cans of paint to create an image of the shoreline during the summer with a sailboat, a lifeguard stand, and a patch-work of colorful beach blankets on a sunny day. Working at lightning speed, he turned the canvas into a lovely painting. Lucy could almost feel the summer sun kissing her cheeks.

"Wow! He's amazing," Lucy said.

"Do you want his picture?"

"Nah. I'll stick to my wooden kitchen sign. I mean *our* sign."

Azad flashed a wide grin, then tugged her toward the bandstand. "Quick. The band is starting."

The Beach Bums was a talented cover band, and they didn't disappoint tonight. They began with "Rockin' Around the Christmas Tree."

Four large heat lamps kept Lucy toasty warm. After two beers and a full set of eight songs from the band, she was ready to talk to Azad.

She looked up at him. "Hey, Azad?"

"Hmm."

"I found a place."

"Pardon?"

"The perfect place for our wedding. My cousin's bed-and-breakfast. Well, it isn't exactly Nora's, it's Sherman's, but it's lovely and overlooks the ocean and fits us to a T."

Her heart pounded as she waited for his answer.

He watched her. "Tell me about it."

"Well, it's not ritzy or glamorous, but it's an old Victorian home and quite beautiful. It has Mediterranean decor, but, surprisingly, it works. The wraparound porch with its rocking chairs is lovely, and you can watch the ocean waves as you sit and relax."

"When can we see it together?"

"You sure you want to? It's a small town, with an old-fashioned steam train and a single strip of shops."

"I'm sure," he said. "It's also a short walk to the beach where we can take off our shoes and feel the sand between our toes and have an ocean breeze mess up your expensive updo, all while we're dressed in our wedding finery, remember?"

She gifted him with a smile, then kissed him. "I remember."

"We'll have to take Katie to see the place at some point. God knows, we'll have to convince her. It wouldn't surprise me if the Ritz-Carlton is on her reception list for you to tour," Azad said.

Lucy laughed. "Leave Katie to me."

"I've been wanting to take you shopping," Katie told Lucy as she parked her Jeep in front of A Second Pleat. The consignment shop was new to town, in a shopping strip across the park. Katie had left work early for their excursion and had babbled with excitement the entire car ride.

Lucy opened the door and stepped out of the Jeep. "Why? You know I'd rather have you over to watch old episodes of *Murder, She Wrote* and open a bottle of wine."

Katie joined her, and they walked to the front door. "You're acting old."

"Not old, just tired from running around the restaurant all day."

"Too bad. We need to get dolled up for the big holiday party at Kebab Kitchen. This consignment shop is perfect. You'd be shocked at what the rich women purge from their huge, walk-in closets. Gorgeous dresses, most of them designer, that they simply grow bored with wearing. Sometimes, they don't even wear them once and the price tags are still on."

"I can't imagine."

"Check out the sexy number on the mannequin."

Lucy glimpsed in the bay window where four mannequins were displayed. Each wore a different dress. The first had on a vintage wedding gown from the eighties, with enough lace and frills to make three gowns. A long white veil that looked a tinge off-color from age was perched atop the mannequin's head. The second and third mannequins displayed sequined dresses—one in black and one in white, straight from the nineties, and the fourth wore a Chanel suit the color of Pepto-Bismol. All the mannequins wore superhigh heels in varying colors.

"Don't be picky," Katie said, waving a hand at the window display. "I like the new owner. I handled Mandy's mercantile license at town hall."

Lucy stepped onto the porch. "Let's see what Mandy can do for us."

Mandy Furrer was steaming a hanging taffeta skirt when they walked inside her shop. With curled blond hair that could only be achieved with a curling iron and a can of Aqua Net, Mandy wore a tight black pencil skirt, a purple silk blouse, and matching purple stilettos.

Mandy's smile was wide. "Katie! How wonderful to see you. And you brought a friend."

"This is Lucy." Katie made the introductions. "My oldest and best friend from Ocean Crest High School."

"Ah, the delights of OC High. I graduated way before you two. Go Pirates!" Mandy chimed out the name of their school's mascot.

"Gah, were you a cheerleader?" Lucy asked.

"Never. I played French horn in the marching band."

"Really?" Mandy didn't seem the band type, more like one of the popular girls on the cheerleading squad.

Mandy patted a fat, blond curl. "I didn't dress like this back then. Now, what can I do for you two today?"

"We need to get dolled up for the holiday party at Kebab Kitchen. All business owners are invited. Did you get your invitation?"

"I did. I'm looking forward to devouring the baklava."

"My mother's specialty," Lucy said.

"I want something sexy to wear," Katie said. "I need to keep Bill on his toes."

Mandy gave her a knowing look. "Always a good idea. It's too easy to fall into yoga pants and sweats after your work routine. We can't have our men take us for granted."

"Heck no," Katie agreed.

Lucy did a mental eye roll. Katie had complained of falling into this rut not long ago.

On second thought, Lucy hoped this wasn't in her future. It wasn't unusual for her to be tired at the end of a workday and want nothing more than to collapse on her couch, put up her feet, and cuddle with Gadoo. Running around the restaurant could be exhausting, and summer season was coming fast. Mandy's advice was full of wisdom.

"I'll need something sexy, too," Lucy blurted out.

"I just received new inventory," Mandy said. "Some great pieces from the ladies on Oyster Street. You two peruse the racks and I'll bring out some special items." Mandy sailed into the back room.

Katie nudged Lucy. "Did you hear that? Oyster Street is where all the rich socialites who want a piece of the Jersey shore are moving."

One of the McMansions had been on their holiday house tour. Lucy had always thought the houses were ostentatious, but the donated clothes could be fabulous.

Together, Lucy and Katie flipped through clothes on racks and selected a few pieces to try on, just as Mandy appeared before them holding up two dresses. One was a black cocktail dress with a long slit up the leg, the other a slinky red number with a deep décolletage.

"I have a good eye for size and fashion and picked these out for both of you." Mandy held up the cocktail dress for Katie's perusal. "Katie, this black dress will fit you perfectly and will accentuate your fair complexion and long legs."

"It's hot!" Katie relieved her of the dress.

Mandy turned to Lucy with a sly wink. "Lucy, this red number will look stunning with your raven hair and olive complexion. I guarantee it will turn your beau's head."

Lucy blinked. She didn't want to look like a street-walker. "I'm not sure . . ."

"Don't be a ninny," Katie urged. "Azad will drool."

Mandy thrust the dress at Lucy, then pulled back the curtain on one of the fitting rooms. "You said you wanted sexy. Try it and see."

Moments later, Lucy was staring in the fitting room mirror. Mandy was right when she said she knew sizing. The dress fit every dip, valley, and curve. The swell of her breasts above the bodice was much more revealing than she'd ever worn. Still, she had to admit the dress did look good on her. It didn't even require alterations—not even a hem, which she was used to having to pay extra for. Whoever had originally owned the dress must also have been petite.

The curtain was swept aside and Katie stood at the entrance. She clapped her hands to her chest. "It's gorgeous and the perfect dress to wear to announce your engagement to the world!"

"I hope so. Is it too much? I want Azad to be happy."

Katie's eyes traveled her from head to toe before meeting Lucy's gaze in the mirror. "Oh, he'll be happy all right."

"You're not putting my mind at ease."

"Trust me. You look great. Now all you need are superhigh heels and the right accessories. It's going to be a night to remember."

Chapter Thirty-One

"Any thoughts about reception halls?" Katie asked from where she lounged on Lucy's couch.

She sat forward to pour herself some merlot. "Let's not ruin a perfectly good bottle of wine."

They'd left the consignment shop with their purchases and headed straight to Lucy's apartment to relax. Who knew shopping could be so exhausting? After trying on dresses, they'd sifted through jewelry, fancy evening purses, and then shoes. At Katie and Mandy's urging, Lucy picked out a pair of sky-high stilettos with a rhinestone buckle to go with the red dress.

Katie sipped her drink. "I have a new list of reception halls I was going to e-mail to you."

"Please don't." Lucy was pretty sure she knew where she wanted her reception to take place. Her trip with her mother to visit her cousin Nora had been enlightening. The bed-and-breakfast was charming and had a lovely backyard and view of the ocean. She knew that dozens of other wedding details would have to be sorted out. They'd need a tent, a caterer, a florist, and a band, just to name a few, but the setting would be lovely for pictures.

"You're right. I shouldn't e-mail it. I'll print my list at work and we can go over it together in person."

Lucy shot her friend a look. "How about we take a break from wedding planning?"

"Take a break? You know how places fill up, especially if you want a summer shore wedding. You'll have to arm-wrestle brides and tourists for a venue."

Lucy bit her bottom lip. "The truth is, I think I already have a place in mind."

"You do? Where?"

"My cousin's bed-and-breakfast inn. She doesn't own it, but runs it because Sherman, who does, is old and basically retired." She spoke quickly, worried about Katie's reaction.

Katie's eyes held her still. "Seriously?"

"Yes."

"Did you book it?"

"Not officially. Azad hasn't seen it yet."

She pursed her lips. "Well, I guess it's your wedding. Is the place nice?"

"It's a lovely old Victorian and has a fantastic view of the ocean."

Katie lowered her wineglass. "Why didn't you just tell me?"

A pang of guilt centered in Lucy's chest. "I know how hard you've been working to help me, and I didn't want to hurt your feelings."

"Lucy! It's your wedding. I was just trying to help."

"I know that, too. And I'd love for you to see the place with me. I'll also need your help more than ever to plan. There will be a lot of details, not to mention the wedding dress."

Katie sat up as if she'd been jolted with an electrical

wire. "The dress! Now that you have a venue, we need to resume shopping in earnest. Not just Madame Fleur's salon, but others, too."

Oh no. Had she jumped from the frying pan into the bridal salon fire? "Are you sure you have the time?"

"What are best friends for?"

It turned out that getting ready to host the holiday party was much more work than anyone had expected. Lucy and Azad had spent a good chunk of time planning the menu, with Angela's input, of course. Raffi had helped Lucy order food, pay the invoices, and deal with the steady stream of deliveries. Azad, Butch, and Angela had been busy in the kitchen all week long, while Katie and Lucy had added additional decorations. Kebab Kitchen would close early after the lunch shift so that everyone could go home and get dressed.

Despite all their hard work and anticipation for a fun night, a dark cloud hovered over Lucy's head. Susan Cutie remained in jail. The judge had denied bail, claiming Susan was a flight risk.

"What flight risk?" Lucy asked Clyde Winters over the phone while she sat in her chair behind the desk in Kebab Kitchen's small office. In her agitated state, she banged her elbow on the file cabinet close to the desk.

Ouch.

"I don't believe Susan's a flight risk for a second," Clyde said. "I think Judge Hammond is concerned about scaring away tourists if Susan is released. It isn't adequate grounds to deny bail, but our hands are tied."

Lucy knew what Clyde meant. Local judges had a lot of power. It would take weeks to repeal the decision.

Meanwhile, Susan would spend the holiday season in a jail cell.

Lucy hung up the phone and rubbed her elbow. The knowledge that she hadn't been able to help her friend twisted and turned inside her. She needed to pull herself together and focus on one thing at a time. Tonight's party was important to her best friend, the town employees and business owners, and everyone at Kebab Kitchen. She hadn't given up on Susan. She just needed to make sure tonight's party was a success.

Immersing herself in work was the best way to forget her problems—at least for a short time. She left the office and headed for the dining room, where she picked up a clean rag and energetically began to wipe down the hummus bar.

Bins of freshly made hummus of various flavors—lemon pucker, extra garlic, black bean, artichoke, and traditional—would be featured in the hummus bar for tonight's party. Tables had been moved in order to accommodate the rest of the food, which would be served buffet style. A white tablecloth, chafing dishes and warmers to make sure the food stayed hot, and serving utensils had already been arranged. Azad had prepared a Mediterranean delight of moussaka, shish kebab, grilled striper with Mediterranean herbs, tabbouleh, and lentil soup with kale. Additional sides of rice pilaf, freshly baked pita bread, and grilled vegetables would appeal to the guests.

In the back of her mind, Lucy had hoped to have Susan's cakes, cookies, and pies beside Kebab Kitchen's baklava. She realized now that her hope was only wishful thinking.

Lucy was cleaning the sneeze guard on the hummus bar when Emma and Sally approached.

"We have spiced eggnog. And Jake delivered the rest of

the kegs of beer early this morning. He said he'll be late to the party because he wants to visit Susan in jail as long as he's allowed," Emma said.

"Poor guy. I admire his loyalty. It's hard to find a boyfriend like that," Sally said.

Sally had never married, but she frequently dated. Lucy had always thought she was single by choice, but maybe she wanted to settle down after all.

Lucy looked around the dining room. "Where did Jake put the kegs? Last time I put one in the kitchen, my mom had a conniption."

"Don't worry," Emma said. "They're all in the storage room, safe and sound. Crisis with Mom averted."

"Good. Meanwhile, I need to see about the food."

"Azad and Butch have it all under control, Lucy. Why don't you go home, shower, and change?" Sally said.

"Wait. I can't leave yet. I need to check on the hummus," Lucy protested.

Sally gave her a reassuring smile. "Stop stressing. You worked hard and are superprepared, Lucy. I have a good feeling that the party will be a hit and everyone will be talking about it tomorrow."

As soon as Lucy stepped into her apartment, Gadoo sidled up close and rubbed against her leg. His meow was quite loud.

She scratched the cat behind his ears. "Hello, Gadoo. Are you hungry?" She padded into the kitchen and poured kibbles into his bowl, then focused on getting ready for tonight's big shindig.

Her dress hung in her closet. The little red number that Mandy from A Second Pleat had sworn would bring Azad to his knees. Lucy didn't need Azad on his knees tonight—he'd already proposed, and she wore his diamond on her finger to prove it. Still, she wanted to look her best when she raised a glass of bubbly and publicly announced her engagement to Azad to the packed dining room.

Lucy turned on the shower and washed her hair. She rehearsed what she planned to say out loud as the hot water eased her tension. It was almost like wedding vows. Almost.

Azad and I have known each other since we were teenagers. I fell for him. He broke it off. That's all history, and we're back together.

No. That wouldn't do.

Time couldn't part us for long, and we both realized our grown-up love is much better than teenage infatuation.

Better.

She worked on her speech until the steaming water ran out and her skin pricked from the cold.

Her curly hair always posed a dilemma. Should she wear it up or down?

She decided to leave it down and reached for her trusty spray gel. It was a delicate balance—too much product and it would look crunchy, like one of the punk rock kids at the boardwalk arcade. Not enough gel and the curls would frizz from the ever-present Jersey shore humidity and the heat from the restaurant's kitchen. She was satisfied with the result. Her curls felt soft and brushed her shoulders.

Makeup posed a different type of challenge. She wasn't a pro makeup artist by any means. Applying cosmetics for her daily work routine was mascara and a swipe of lip gloss. Tonight was different—special—and she applied eyeliner, smoky eye shadow, a hint of blush, and a coat of mascara. She slipped into the tight, red dress, and with a bit of a struggle, managed to zip it up the back.

Opening a shoebox, she held up the pair of high heels with the rhinestone buckles. She hadn't worn stilettos since she worked at the law firm and had to attend one of the partners' birthday party at a fancy Philadelphia country club. They'd pinched her toes then. These shoes were no different. But anything that added a few inches to her petite height was worth the discomfort.

She turned this way and that to examine her efforts in the full-length mirror behind her bedroom door.

Nice. Maybe Azad *would* fall to his knees, but later tonight.

Her thoughts turned back to her friend, and she felt a stab of guilt for celebrating when Susan couldn't join them as the owner of Cutie's Cupcakes. Would the bakery close? Would Ocean Crest residents have to go out of town for baked goods at some commercial chain?

A loud meow drew her gaze to her bed. Gadoo had snuck in and lounged on her comforter like King Tut. Another sassy meow, and he cocked his head to the side to say, *you should take this much care more often.*

"Not likely, Gadoo," she said.

With one last look in the mirror, she was off.

"Kebab Kitchen has never looked so beautiful," Katie said.

Lucy straightened one of the lids of the chafing dishes on the buffet table. "Azad outdid himself, too. You'll have to taste the moussaka."

"It smells so good in here. I'm already drooling."

Katie had arrived at the restaurant early so they could make sure everything was perfect before tonight's big event.

"Hey, I know I said this before, but thank you for saving my butt by having the party here," Katie said.

"What are best friends for?"

The dining room was decked out in Christmas delight. Not one but three trimmed trees were artfully displayed in the corners of the dining room. A smaller one was by the hostess stand and greeted customers as they entered. Pine boughs hung on the walls with the occasional mistletoe. A huge balsam wreath adorned with pinecones, berries, and a large red bow hung on the front door and a smaller wreath hung above the cash register. Poinsettias sat on the waitress station. Striped red-and-green tablecloths graced the tables, along with balsam centerpieces with red pillar candles. Ceramic elves greeted customers on top of the hummus bar.

Katie had hired a DJ, and he would set up by the hostess stand and play holiday music throughout the party.

"There's going to be a surprise visit from Santa," Katie said.

That got Lucy's attention. "Really? Is Bill going to do it?"

"Nah. I hired the guy from the Bayville Mall. He poses as Santa every year."

"I know him! I take Niari there every Christmas for her picture with Santa. He looks so real."

"That's because it's his real beard. He starts to grow it out in May." Katie looked Lucy up and down. "By the way, you clean up pretty good."

"You too." Katie's black cocktail dress emphasized her fair coloring, and her blond hair was styled in an elaborate updo.

Katie wandered to the buffet table. "The entire guest list is expected to attend, mostly because of the food."

Lucy straightened one of the red-and-green tablecloths. "Everything would be perfect except for Susan. I can't help but feel horrible."

A pinched expression crossed Katie's face. "Hey, it's not your fault. Neither of us have been able to crack this case."

They stood in silence as voices sounded from the kitchen. Azad and Butch were hard at work putting the finishing touches on all the food.

Katie leaned a hand on one of the tables. "I've been thinking more and more. There's a good likelihood the murderer will be here tonight."

Lucy scanned the dining room and imagined it full of people. "That's a sobering thought. We have enough beer and wine for the entire night. Keep your eyes and ears open. Drunk people have a tendency to talk."

"You think we'll learn something?" Katie asked.

"If we're lucky."

Chapter Thirty-Two

With a half hour left before the guests were to arrive, Lucy ran around making sure everything was ready. Azad and Butch were still in the kitchen and wouldn't fill the chafing dishes with food until the last minute to make sure everything was hot and fresh. The DJ had arrived and set up his equipment and speakers.

Lucy made sure the commercial coffee urn was full, an assortment of tea bags was displayed, and a mound of wrapped silverware in green napkins was in a basket at the end of the buffet table. With one last glimpse in the storage room, a flash of yellow eyes caught her attention.

"Gadoo! Bad kitty. You know not to sneak inside."

A resounding meow sounded, and the cat pounced to her side. She picked him up and scratched beneath his chin, which effectively erased the sting of her words. Kebab Kitchen was only a couple of blocks from her apartment, and the cat frequently wandered the neighborhood. He'd also been following her to work more often lately.

"You're lucky I found you first and not Mom," Lucy admonished him.

She was rewarded with purring.

Lucy filled a bowl with his favorite kibbles, added

water to another bowl, and set both outside the storage room by a stack of crates. She then put him outside and closed the storage room screen door. If the finicky feline wanted to hang around all night, he'd have enough food and drink.

A half hour later, party revelers began arriving and were greeted with holiday music and cups of eggnog. Sleigh bells chimed as the front door opened and closed.

Eloisa Lubinski was escorted by an older gentleman wearing a black-and-white tuxedo, top hat, and carrying a cane. "This is Donald. I met him at the theater."

He looked quite dapper. Was he onstage or in the audience?

Eloisa answered the question. "Donald plays the role of the butler in a *Downton Abbey* show."

That explained the getup. "It's a pleasure to meet you, Donald. Eloisa is my landlady."

Donald gallantly bowed and placed a kiss on the back of Lucy's hand. "The pleasure is mine."

Soon the mayor, Theodore Magic, and Ben Hawkins, the town barber, arrived.

"The food is delicious," Theodore said. "Please pay my compliments to the chef."

"Azad will be out soon enough to greet everyone and join the party. Meanwhile, please sample the Christmas ale from the local brewery. It goes well with the hummus bar."

Theodore rubbed his stomach. "You sure know how to tempt a man, Ms. Berberian."

As the town pharmacist and mayor, Theodore Magic knew his supplemental vitamins from his prescriptions, but he was growing into a political charmer as well.

Guests poured in, and Lucy played hostess and greeted each one. She was happy to see that Angela and Raffi were enjoying themselves. Her mother was serving guests from the chafing dishes on the buffet table, and her father was helping to serve beer from the keg. Both were chatting with the townsfolk they'd frequently seen when they worked full-time at the restaurant.

Next to approach her was Stan Slade. The newspaper reporter eyed her from behind his glasses. "Still no news for me? Not even about Ms. Cutie's arrest? I'm surprised at your lack of ingenuity, Ms. Berberian."

"I'm surprised at your lack of investigative reporting," she fired back. By now, she knew not to be insulted by Slade's lack of tact. She had a list of suspects with motive and opportunity, but no real leads she was comfortable giving the reporter.

"Touché," he responded. "I have a delicate stomach. What do you recommend from the buffet table?"

"Start with the shish kebab. As long as you aren't a vegetarian, I've never received a complaint from others about grilled meat."

Fortunately, Slade wandered off without causing a scene.

Bill approached Lucy and Katie. "I finally have a lead at Ocean Crest High School. I've been working with the staff and principal to track down and bust the marijuana ring."

"Good for you!" Katie said. "When can we go out and celebrate?"

"Soon. Meanwhile, you two should know that Clemmons is coming to this party. He has a fondness for your mother's baklava."

"And a fondness for arresting the wrong person," Katie said.

Bill eyed his wife. "Don't make a scene. He's not entirely to blame and you two know it. The evidence against Susan Cutie couldn't be ignored."

"The prosecutor couldn't be ignored either," Lucy said, a note of sarcasm in her voice.

"It's all the same," Bill said.

Lucy grudgingly admitted Bill was right, but she didn't have to like it. Out of the corner of her eye, she saw her father start to serve beer from the keg. Lucy had decided to use the waitress station as a makeshift bar. As more and more guests wanted to sample Jake's ale, she knew it was a good decision to place the keg close by.

Soon after, Butch came through the swinging kitchen doors carrying a second keg. He tapped the keg and Raffi reached for more glasses. Her dad would be busy all night.

Lucy continued her tour of the dining room and greeted guests along the way. She hadn't intended for the town holiday party to be a form of advertisement for Kebab Kitchen, but many people were thrilled with the food and said they'd return with their friends.

She'd have to thank Azad later.

The sleigh bells chimed above the front door once more, and Michael entered with his father. Lucy hurried to greet them. "I'm glad you're here."

"Wouldn't miss it," Michael said. He'd changed from his usual jeans and T-shirt to dress slacks and a button-down, long-sleeved shirt.

"Kebab Kitchen and Citteroni's Bicycle Shop have been neighbors for over twenty years," Mr. Citteroni said. "We are happy to come." He leaned down and lowered his voice. "Any news on our ocean killer?"

Lucy bit her lower lip. "Other than my friend sitting in jail?"

"I was sorry to hear about that. I guess my initial assumption about Vinnie was wrong."

Was it? She still wasn't convinced that Vinnie wasn't the murderer. A thief could be a good liar.

Hours later, everyone continued to have a grand old time. "It's going well. Maybe we can have the holiday party at Kebab Kitchen again next year," Lucy told Katie.

Katie had just stuffed a large piece of pita bread in her mouth. She chewed and swallowed. "I'd owe you my first-born."

"Nah, wouldn't want your baby. Maybe your approval of my cousin's bed-and-breakfast for my wedding reception."

"I promise to keep an open mind when I visit."

What else could she ask for? "Remember, I still need your help with a lot of other wedding details."

Katie gave Lucy a thumbs-up. "You bet."

A draft from the front door caught Lucy's attention, and she turned to see Jake step inside.

"Jake! We're so glad you came," Lucy said.

"I wasn't going to, but Susan told me I shouldn't live like a hermit just because she's behind bars."

What were they to say to that?

Dark circles appeared beneath his eyes, as if he hadn't slept well in days, and his hair was mussed, as if he'd repeatedly run his fingers through the brown locks in agitation. His normally neat appearance was lacking. His button-down shirt was wrinkled and his khakis had a stain on the pocket. Susan's incarceration had clearly affected him.

Not knowing what to say, Lucy reached out to touch his arm. "Your beer is a hit. My dad's already on the third keg."

"Good to hear."

"You want one?" Katie asked.

"Nah. I can drink my own beer anytime. Is the eggnog spiked?"

Lucy grinned. "Sure is. No kids here tonight." She was quick to fetch him a glass of eggnog.

Jake was pulled away by the mayor and a group of men. Lucy overheard them ask him about specially flavored micro beers. Others peppered him with questions.

Lucy sipped her drink. "Something's off with Jake."

Katie shrugged. "Can't blame the guy for being distracted. His ladybird is in jail."

She couldn't fault Katie's reasoning, but as she watched Jake, he extracted himself from the group. He walked to the far end of the waitress station, glanced both ways, then pushed through the swinging doors into the kitchen.

What the heck?

Why the kitchen? Did he want to talk with Azad or Butch?

Then she remembered Jake's kegs of beer in the storage room. He'd delivered the kegs earlier that morning. Maybe Jake wanted to check on his supply.

Or maybe he wanted to make a fast exit through the back storage room and go home. If Azad was in jail, she'd be bereft and not in a party mood.

"Excuse me," Lucy said. "Time to make my rounds of the kitchen. Be back in a flash."

She made a beeline for the kitchen as fast as her stilettos would allow. She wasn't used to wearing high heels, and she was proud of herself for keeping them on this long.

The heat of the kitchen struck her like a hot wave, and she felt her cheeks flush. She spotted Azad hard at work behind a grill.

"Everything okay out there?" he asked. "I'm about ready to go out and party."

"Please go and have a beer. All the guests are eager to talk food." Even through the swinging kitchen doors, she could hear the noise from the party.

He beamed as he took off his apron and hung it on a hook in the corner. "I'll be sure to bask in the attention. Did you need something?"

"Did you see Jake pass through here?"

"No."

No surprise. Azad had been hard at work, his back to the pathway leading to the storage room. It would have been easy for Jake to sidle on by unseen. Azad waved as he left the kitchen to join the party.

Lucy walked through the abandoned kitchen with one purpose in mind: to find Jake. She passed the prep table and the walk-in refrigerator.

And halted at the entrance to the storage room.

Jake was there all right. And he wasn't crying or fleeing through the back doors.

He was pulling wads of cash from one of his kegs.

Chapter Thirty-Three

"Oh my God." Lucy stood stock-still. Her eyes widened as she watched Jake pull out what looked like a stack of Ben Franklins from one of the kegs.

"Lucy." Jake froze, his complexion turning a shade red. His hand was halfway in the keg like a kid caught red-handed reaching into the cookie jar.

Her mind flashed at warp speed as she processed what she was seeing. "What are you doing?"

He pulled his hand from the keg, his fingers empty this time. "You shouldn't be back here."

"It's my family's restaurant. *You* shouldn't be back here."

He stood, and his eyes became as flat and unreadable as stone. His shock at being discovered had disappeared and his voice was cold when he answered. "What I mean is that this is none of your business. Turn around and go back to the party. You didn't see a thing."

A cold wave entered the room at his frigid tone. Lucy ignored his demand as she noticed more now. A canvas bag was at his feet and he was removing money from the keg and stashing it in the bag.

"Why is there cash in that keg?"

Jake shook his head. "I didn't want to involve you, Lucy, but you keep sticking your nose where it doesn't belong."

Noise and music from the party sounded all the way back to the storage room. "I hardly call walking into my storage room sticking my nose in your business. Where did all that cash come from? Are you a drug dealer?"

He tore his fingers through his hair. "It's not what you think."

"Enlighten me."

He cinched the top of the sack all the while holding her stare. "Most don't consider marijuana a bad drug anymore. More and more states are making it legal to buy and sell. New Jersey politicians are slow to come around. I'm just taking advantage until then."

She gaped at him. *Holy crap.* Jake must be part of the drug ring that had been selling to Ocean Crest High School students. *He* was one of the dealers Bill Watson was looking to bust. "You're selling pot? Why, for heaven's sake? You have a profitable brewery."

He motioned to the stainless-steel storage shelving. "You manage a business. You should know why."

"No. I don't."

He looked at her as if she was a simpleton. "Business taxes are sky-high. It's tough enough for my Boardwalk Brewery to make it through the winter in this town. Tourist season is only three months out of the year. I had to supplement my income. There's no shortage of suppliers in Atlantic City. Once I started selling, it was hard to ignore the cash. I didn't have to look outside the town for a market."

"By market, do you mean our vulnerable high school kids?"

His lips thinned. "Those bratty kids are spoiled and

have more money these days than we did as kids. If not me, someone else would cash in."

"I can't believe you'd do such a thing." It was the last thing she'd expected him to say. She'd thought he'd mention tax evasion or something else, but not selling marijuana to teenagers.

He shot her a look of disbelief. "Oh please. Get off your high horse. I'm not the only one in town."

"You mean Mr. Citteroni?" she blurted out, then immediately regretted it. She should have known not to mention Anthony Citteroni's name. Ever since she was a kid, she'd heard his illicit activities involved gambling, not drugs.

"No. I didn't mean Mr. Citteroni. Others have their fingers in the trade," Jake said.

She wondered who, but pushed the thought aside. She still couldn't believe Jake sold drugs to kids and then used his brewery business to launder and hide the cash. He'd fooled everyone about his character, even her mother, who'd introduced Jake and Susan.

What would Angela Berberian have to say about Jake now?

Lucy's gaze darted back to the keg by his feet. "Why on earth would you bring a keg stuffed with cash here?"

"I didn't have much of a choice. I was worried the cops were on to me and would search the brewery. I needed to get it away until I could move the money and pay my suppliers in Atlantic City."

He was talking about Bill Watson, who was close to busting the high school dealers. "So, you brought that keg to Kebab Kitchen? What if we had tried to tap that keg and found the cash?"

"I wasn't worried. I hid this one behind boxes on your shelves. Plus, I modified the keg myself. It would have still worked if someone did try to tap it. There's a hidden compartment inside to stash the cash. The rest holds beer. Brilliant, isn't it?"

Despite everything, Lucy had to admire the ingenuity of Jake's criminal design. She guessed the keg weighed close to the same whether it was stuffed with cash and beer or just filled with beer. No one would notice, especially her father or Butch, who didn't handle kegs on a regular basis.

"Now, like I said, you should turn around and go back to the party and act like you never saw me. Think of Susan. You wouldn't want to upset her even more by turning me in to the cops, would you?"

His twisted logic made sense.

Poor Susan.

Lucy had failed to find the real killer, and if she was responsible for having her boyfriend arrested, Susan would suffer even more. But there were other things to think about, like Bill's efforts to bust the drug-dealing creeps and . . .

Another thought crept into Lucy's head, and she couldn't believe she hadn't suspected it right away. Jake had admitted he'd been supplementing his business with drug money for some time. The fact that he'd modified a keg in order to stash illegal cash was proof that he'd been at this for a while.

And a large amount of cash, like the stuffed canvas bag Jake held, sounded unnervingly familiar. Illegal drug money wasn't all that was at stake here.

As their eyes met, she felt a shock run through her. "It was your money that was in a suitcase in Deacon Spooner's office, wasn't it?"

Chapter Thirty-Four

Jake's expression shuttered. "I don't know what you're talking about."

"Oh, I think you do." Lucy spoke with quiet, but desperate firmness. "Deacon had a suitcase full of hundred-dollar bills, just like the money in that canvas bag." Her gaze whipped to the bag, then back to his face. "You said yourself others in town are selling marijuana. You must have been partners with Deacon Spooner."

"Partners with Deacon!" Jake scoffed. "No way! That scumbag stole that cash from me."

Jake's eyes widened a fraction as he realized what he'd revealed.

"How on earth could Deacon have stolen cash from you?" Lucy asked.

"I delivered beer for receptions and parties at the Sea View. It just so happened that my modified keg was delivered there by mistake."

She was about to ask how when he said, "It's hard to find good hired help. I learned my lesson and make my own deliveries now."

Lucy's thoughts churned as she sorted everything out.

"Are you saying that Deacon discovered the cash inside your special keg by mistake?"

"That's exactly what I'm saying. At first, I was worried Deacon would call the cops. Eventually, they'd figure it all out and I'd be arrested."

"But he didn't, did he? He kept the money instead."

Vinnie had first told Lucy about the cash-filled suitcase he'd found when he'd broken into Deacon's office. Lucy had assumed Deacon had been involved in something illegal.

Never in a million years had she suspected the money had belonged to Jake. He'd fooled everyone, including Vinnie, Mr. Citteroni, the police, Katie, and especially Susan.

"Why wouldn't Deacon call the police when he found your keg?" Lucy asked.

Jake's eyes glittered with anger, and his fists curled into tight balls at his sides. "Bastard said he wanted in on my marijuana dealings, and that he'd consider the keg cash his first cut. He kept the money. *My* money. I was furious!"

"I bet you were. Thirty thousand dollars isn't pocket change."

Jake's eyes narrowed to slits. "How the heck do you know the amount?"

"Does it matter?"

He shook his head. "I guess it doesn't matter now. Not only did Deacon steal my money, but he knew my secret. A witness was a loose end I couldn't afford. I had to do something."

Oh God.

Jake's face turned dark, and a malicious, calculating glimmer shone in his brown eyes. She took a step back and glanced over her shoulder. Holiday music and conversation reached her. She needed to get out of here. But she needed to know the truth.

She pointed at his chest. "You did do something. You drowned Deacon at the Polar Bear Plunge."

His mouth pulled into a feral snarl. "What was I supposed to do? Let that bastard steal from me without consequences or blackmail me forever?"

Had Susan known about her boyfriend's criminal nature? Had she known he was dealing drugs, or that he was stashing bundles of drug money in one of his kegs? The last time she'd spoken to Susan was when she'd visited her in jail with Clyde Winters. Susan had been uncharacteristically cold and distant, and when they'd mentioned Jake, she'd insisted she wanted to end their relationship.

Had she suspected something?

Lucy started to back out of the storage room. "How'd you manage it without anyone seeing? Like Susan."

"It was crazy in the water. I was a lot stronger than that older weasel. It didn't take long. Susan was in front of me in the water and didn't see a thing."

"You'd let Susan take the fall for you?"

His hard expression wavered. "I like Susan. I feel bad about that."

"You feel bad? That's it?" Her outrage at his selfishness made her breathless and her fingers fisted at her sides. How about horribly guilty? And willing to put the woman he loved above himself?

Only he hadn't loved Susan. Not really. He loved the lure of cash more.

A lady's peal of laughter pierced the storage room and the thrum of party revelers echoed in Lucy's head like a swarm of bees. Azad had left to join the guests long ago. Not another soul was in the kitchen.

Her stomach sank as the full impact of her precarious position hit her. She'd have to scream louder than she'd ever screamed before and pray someone—anyone—would hear. Taking a quick breath, she opened her mouth . . .

Jake reached down to pull something else from the keg. A shiny black revolver, now aimed at her chest. "Don't even think about screaming, Lucy. It's time to go."

Chapter Thirty-Five

Lucy's pulse raced as her gaze darted to the revolver Jake aimed at her chest. "You can't be serious."

"Oh, I'm dead serious. I gave you a chance to turn a blind eye and go back to the party, but now it's too late. You know too much. Get moving."

When she didn't obey, he grasped her arm and spun her around until her back was to his chest. He placed a hand over her mouth, forcing her out the restaurant's back door.

Panic rioted in her chest, and her high heels skidded against the asphalt. The moon behind a cloud was dim except for a streetlamp that faintly illuminated her car and Jake's van in an eerie, yellowish glow. The reflective letters on the side of the white door read "Jake's Boardwalk Brewery."

Jake dragged her toward the van. Lucy struggled the entire way, but his hold was merciless as he dug the muzzle of the gun into her back.

"I'm sorry to treat you this way, Lucy, but you're now a loose end and leave me no choice," he said, breathing heavily into her ear.

She swallowed hard, and her eyes darted to the fence separating Kebab Kitchen from its business neighbor, Citteroni's Bicycle Shop. If only Michael was inside, maybe he'd notice something was amiss. But Michael and his father were at the party.

Her heart pounded, and she struggled to keep her wits. She needed to think clearly now.

He dragged her to the rear of the van, where the double back doors were already open, and she saw half a dozen kegs held in place by bungee cords. He must have been ready for a quick escape.

"Get in," he ground out.

No way!

She knew, without a doubt, that if she got in his van she was as good as dead. She'd attended a women's self-defense course when she'd lived in the city, and the instructor had spent a good chunk of time spouting the dismal statistics of the number of women who'd survived an abduction.

"Once you're in the car," her instructor had said, "the chances you'll be found alive are slim to none."

She'd also heard enough of Katie's warnings after she'd binge-watched some of her favorite crime-fighting TV shows.

Fight with all you've got! Katie would say.

So Lucy did.

She bit down on Jake's hand covering her mouth, then lifted her heel and slammed it down on his leg with all her strength. Her stiletto ripped his pants and dug into the tender flesh of his instep.

Jake howled in anger.

A rush of satisfaction coursed through her. High heels were good for something!

Lucy twisted away and tried to make a mad dash back into the storage room. From there, it wasn't far into the kitchen, then the dining room, where half the town was indulging in food and alcohol.

But Jake lunged forward to grasp her arm. "No, you don't!"

Crap!

A second later, there was a howl of feline fury. Jake screamed in pain and released his grip.

From a stack of crates outside the storage room, Gadoo had leaped onto his chest and raked his claws down his face. Jake dropped the gun, and it skittered across the asphalt. With his other hand, he tried to yank the cat off him, but Gadoo nimbly jumped down and scurried out of reach.

Lucy lunged for the gun, then sprinted into the storage room. Like a track star, she leaped over the keg, landed on one high heel, then sprinted through the kitchen. Gasping, she burst through the swinging kitchen doors and into the dining room.

The room was even more packed than when she'd left, full of well-dressed, well-fed, and on their way to well-drunk revelers.

Lucy came to a screeching halt. "*Jake's the murderer!*" she shouted at the top of her lungs.

The activity in the dining room halted like a cannon had exploded. All eyes turned to her.

"Lucy?" Azad came forward, his expression one of shock mingled with concern.

Relief washed over her, and she took a step toward him just as Jake burst through the swinging doors. Lucy whirled, dread pooling in her stomach. Ugly gashes bled down Jake's face from Gadoo's claws, and he had a panicked, wild expression in his eyes.

Lucy did the only thing she could think of. She pointed

the gun squarely at his chest. "Jake Burns, you are under citizen's arrest for the murder of Deacon Spooner."

All hell broke loose after Lucy's shocking outburst. Detective Clemmons dropped his eggnog; it splashed on the carpet and the glass rolled under a table. Bill swallowed a lump of shish kebab and scurried to Katie's side.

Lucy rushed to speak. "Jake drowned Deacon at the Polar Bar Plunge over stolen drug money."

Lucy knew her explanation sounded garbled, but something must have made sense because the two detectives immediately turned their attention to Jake.

"I didn't have a choice!" Jake hollered. "And Deacon deserved it."

The crowd gasped in unison. Bill started forward and cornered Jake between the waitress station and his kegs. He began to read Jake his rights.

Clemmons approached Lucy, his eyes fixed on her. "Can I have that, Ms. Berberian?"

Lucy looked down and realized she was still clutching the gun. "Oh, of course." Pointing it muzzle down, she handed the weapon to Clemmons.

"Stay here. We'll talk later. Okay?" Clemmons asked.

"Okay."

Clemmons joined Bill to lead Jake Burns out of Kebab Kitchen and into a waiting patrol car. Someone must have called the police.

"Please tell me you're okay." Azad held out his arms, and Lucy gladly stepped into his embrace. His strength and warmth were just what she needed.

"Now I am."

He exhaled a deep breath. "Do you have to keep single-handedly facing killers?"

"I swear, I didn't plan it this time."

He raised her chin with a forefinger and kissed the tip of her nose. "For a brief second, when you didn't come back out, I thought you had cold feet about your parents announcing our engagement."

"Trust me, that wasn't it at all. I was going to hand out glasses of bubbly champagne and announce our engagement myself."

"Really?"

"Yup. Sorry it was ruined."

He kissed her lips. "I don't care about that. I'm just glad you're safe." He raised his head and flashed a grin at someone over her shoulder. "Looks like I'm not the only one."

Katie's face was flushed, either from wine or excitement or both. "Well, the surprise visit from Santa was nothing compared to this."

"This party is either going to be a hit or a flop tomorrow according to the Lola's Coffee Shop gossip mill," Lucy said.

"A hit, for sure. Ocean Crest residents love gossip, and you gave them enough to last through the entire summer season."

"We can only hope." Lucy laughed. The aftershock of her fight-or-flight response kicked in and her hands were a bit shaky, but Azad's presence combined with her best friend's humor was just what she needed.

Katie thrust a glass of wine in her hands. "Drink. There's nothing like wine to calm bad nerves. You did good, Lucy. You also happened to break Bill's big pot case. He'll never live it down."

"Don't scare me. I already have to talk to Clemmons."

"He's already coming back inside," Katie said. "Probably to ask you to give a statement."

The guests stepped back to give the detective wide passage through the dining room.

She couldn't tell by Clemmons's expression if he was furious or not. She straightened her spine. It wasn't like she'd planned on walking in on Jake and his modified keg. And she certainly never wanted to have a gun thrust in her back, a hand clasped over her mouth, or to be dragged across a parking lot by a killer intent on abducting, then murdering her.

She shuddered anew.

"Detective Clemmons, now you can let Susan Cutie go," she told him before he had a chance to speak.

The detective's mustache twitched as he looked down at her. "When I agreed that Susan's doughnuts were superior and that I missed them, this wasn't exactly what I meant."

Lucy let out a hoarse laugh. "Trust me, this isn't what I meant either. But Susan is innocent."

He flashed an uncharacteristic grin. "For once, I'm happy to agree with you."

Chapter Thirty-Six

The heavenly smell of fried dough filled Lucy's senses as soon as she opened the door to the bakery. The scene displayed before her was just as enticing to the eyes.

The bakery case was loaded with a delectable assortment of cupcakes, cookies, doughnuts, and pastries. Colorful holiday pastries featured Christmas trees, Hanukkah dreidels, elves, and Santas all decorated with red, green, and gold icing. But it was the tall, rotating case of pies that drew Lucy's gaze like a magnet. Every shelf was full of mouthwatering pies—apple, blueberry, chocolate peanut butter, lemon, coconut cream, and her all-time favorite, lemon meringue.

"Merry Christmas!" Susan's eyes lit up as she spotted Lucy, and she sped around the counter to sweep Lucy into a big hug.

"Merry Christmas, Susan." Lucy squeezed her back. "I wanted to check on you to make sure you're okay."

Susan's shoulder-length bob was styled and she wore light makeup. She looked pretty and content.

It had been a week since Jake's arrest and Susan's release. A week during which the town was relieved that the murderer was behind bars, but sad that one of their own had been the Polar Bear killer. Lucy had been more than a bit worried about Susan.

Her friend had been wrongly arrested and incarcerated, and had been deceived by someone she'd loved. How was she taking it?

"I won't lie," Susan said. "It hasn't been easy. I still miss Jake terribly. But I've rediscovered my love of baking. It's amazing how work can make you temporarily forget difficult problems."

Lucy thought it would take a lot more than just work to get over what Susan had lived through, but held her tongue. Her friend was strong and would be okay. Plus, Lucy and Katie were determined to help her. All the townsfolk were.

"I've also been doing a lot of thinking as I've been mixing batter and cookie dough," Susan said.

"Oh?"

"I sensed something was off with Jake even before I was arrested. I had a lot of time to myself in jail to think."

Susan *had* acted strangely in jail, especially when she'd wanted to break things off with Jake. Lucy had thought it was because she didn't want to put a loved one through a murder trial, but maybe there had been more to her behavior.

"What do you mean?" Lucy asked.

Susan sighed and leaned on the bakery counter. "I kept thinking back to the day of the Polar Bear Plunge. I wasn't glued to Jake's side. He kept pushing me in front of him in the water. So much so that I lost sight of him for a bit. I just thought it had been the cold temperature or fear of the water, but looking back, it didn't make sense. Jake was a strong swimmer. Much stronger than me."

Jake had said that Susan was in front of him in the

ocean and didn't see him reach for Deacon. Susan's version of the story made sense.

"And when I was behind bars," Susan continued, "I thought it was best to break up with him. But he kept insisting he'd keep visiting me, no matter how many years I would be sentenced to prison. At first, I thought it was loyalty and love, but he acted so weird. Rather than tell me that the truth would set me free, he behaved like I was already declared guilty by a jury." Her blue eyes darkened with pain. "Now I know the truth. He never loved me, but was content for me to serve time in jail for a murder *he* committed."

Lucy's heart ached from her friend's acute sense of loss. She wished she and Katie could have figured it all out sooner. "I'm so sorry. Jake fooled a lot of people. Even my mom. She feels bad for setting you two up."

Lucy's mother had been horrified after Jake was arrested. She prided herself on being a good judge of a person's character, but Jake had fooled her, too. Lucy carried her own guilt. If she hadn't stumbled upon Jake in the storage room transferring his cash from a keg, would anyone have known?

"Tell Mrs. Berberian it's not her fault, and I don't blame her. Jake Burns was a talented liar," Susan said, a note of sadness in her tone.

"Well, thank goodness he's behind bars and you are free."

"Thanks to you, Lucy."

"I really didn't do anything."

"I'd call escaping a killer and then putting him under citizen's arrest in a room full of oblivious and drunken holiday partiers a heroic deed."

Lucy cracked a smile. "Well, if you put it that way . . ."

Susan opened the pie case and removed one of the pies. "I know it's not enough of a thank-you, but how about a lemon meringue?"

"How about you package that pie to go? I didn't just come to check on you, but to invite you to Christmas dinner at my home. That pie will make a perfect dessert."

Susan smiled and reached for a cardboard take-out container. "I'd love to come. Are you cooking?"

"I plan to. I hosted Easter last time. I think I've finally learned how to be the perfect hostess." She lowered her voice. "Although I have to admit, having a chef as a fiancé is a big help."

Christmas Day arrived with a pretty snow flurry. Lucy was hard at work in her apartment kitchen with Azad at her side. Eloisa Lubinski rushed in and out of her apartment all day to help with small details and to set the table. Cupid came and went with her. To everyone's pleasant surprise, Gadoo and Cupid were getting along. Both dog and cat shared the same couch cushion.

"It smells good in here," Eloisa said.

"Lucy's been working hard," Azad said as he slipped on oven mitts and removed a pan from the oven.

"Lucy or you?" Eloisa asked.

"Both of us," Lucy was quick to add.

Two hours later, her family and closest friends arrived, including her parents and Emma and Max with Niari, Sally, Michael, and Susan.

Susan's lemon meringue pie was already in a box in the refrigerator, but she brought along a dozen holiday decorated cupcakes and enormous chocolate chip cookies.

Lucy put the cupcakes in the refrigerator and eyed the cookies. "I want to skip straight to dessert."

"I won't tell if you sneak a cookie," Susan said.

Lucy groaned as her mother walked into the kitchen. "I'll leave you two alone," Susan said.

"Traitor," Lucy whispered.

Susan winked as she left the kitchen.

Her mother opened the oven, stuck a meat thermometer in the roast lamb, then nodded in approval. "You know that I would have come to help."

"I know," Lucy said. "But Azad and I have it under control."

The kitchen light reflected on her mother's gold cross. "Hmm. I supposed you two have to get used to cooking together after you're married."

Lucy hadn't considered two chefs in the kitchen after they tied the knot. They would bring home food from Kebab Kitchen after working a long day, but she held her tongue. No sense starting an argument with her mother on Christmas Day.

"Sit. Have a drink. Relax." Lucy ushered Angela out of the kitchen. "Dinner will be served soon."

Azad was on it in a flash and handed Angela a glass of white wine. Her mother took it from him with a smile. "Thank you, Azad."

Lucy suppressed the urge to roll her eyes. She was learning not to comment whenever her mother dealt with Azad. If his charm worked on her, who was Lucy to argue? It had the desired result.

Azad made sure the lamb roast was perfectly cooked. Lucy had prepared the moussaka and was thrilled when Azad gave her a thumbs-up. "See? It looks great."

Soon, all the dishes were spread out on the dining room

table in a Mediterranean Christmas feast. The lamb and moussaka. Green beans in a light tomato sauce, tabbouleh, and, of course, hummus and fresh pita bread.

Raffi raised his glass of Armenian cognac, the special drink that Michael Citteroni had obtained just for him. "Merry Christmas!"

Lucy raised her own glass of wine. "Azad and I have our own announcement. We've decided our wedding reception will be at Cousin Nora's Victorian inn."

"Really?" Her father and mother asked in unison.

"I thought you wanted a fancy reception hall," Emma said.

"Nah," Sally chimed in. "I could have told all of you that wasn't Lucy's style."

"How the heck do you know?" Emma asked.

"Because she's a beach lover," Michael spoke up.

"And how do you know that?" Azad asked.

"She spends half her time sitting outside on her balcony watching the ocean even though it's freezing outside in December," Eloisa said.

Niari chimed in. "And because Mokour Lucy stayed in Ocean Crest at the Jersey shore and didn't go back to Philadelphia."

"And because she's good at helping out her friends," Susan said, a note of happiness in her voice.

Lucy laughed. Her friends and family all had their own opinions.

She loved them all.

She gazed around her table. "You're all right. You each know me so well." She raised her glass. "Cheers to all! I think this is the best Christmas so far."

Chapter Thirty-Seven

"It really is lovely," Katie said.

"I thought so the first time I saw it," Lucy said.

Lucy, Katie, and Azad stood on the porch of the Seashell Inn. Her friend was thrilled the first time she set foot on the shell-lined driveway. Azad seemed transfixed as well. From their vantage point, they could see the pristine beach and ocean. It was a chilly December afternoon, but they hesitated before going inside.

"I can picture your veil blowing in a gentle sea breeze and the skin kissing your cheeks. Seagulls soaring above and the ocean in the background."

"I never knew you were a poet," Lucy said.

"Don't ruin the mood. You have my approval." Katie turned to Azad. "What about you?"

"I like it a lot. I especially like it because Lucy does," Azad said.

Katie sighed. "You are such a charmer."

Azad grinned from ear to ear.

Lucy rolled her eyes. "Don't give him a big head."

Azad chuckled. "Now, all we have to do is pick a date the church is available and hope it's good with your cousin Nora, too."

"What do you think about a summer wedding?" Lucy asked.

Azad looked at her in surprise. "You want a wedding during tourist season at the Jersey shore?"

"I want to take off my high heels and walk barefoot on the beach during our reception, remember? It just so happens that's during the summer season."

"Well, who am I to deny us both that?"

Katie jumped up and down. "Ohh! The pictures will be beautiful. I'll have Bill clear the beach of tourists for the photographer."

"How will he manage that?" Azad and Lucy asked in unison.

Katie waved a hand. "Leave it to me to convince Bill."

Lucy wasn't so sure. The last time Bill had cleared the beach was when Deacon Spooner's body washed ashore. She shivered just thinking about it.

"As long as it's not another crime scene, we're okay with it," Azad said.

"Please don't say that," Lucy said. "Things at the Jersey shore have been unpredictable. You never know . . . you just never know."

Author's Note

I grew up in the restaurant business, where my Armenian American parents owned a restaurant for almost thirty years in a small South Jersey town. I worked almost every job—from rolling silverware and wiping down tables as a tween, to hosting and waitressing as a teenager. My mother was a talented cook, and the grapevine in our backyard was more valued than any rosebush. I'd often come home from school to the delicious aromas of simmering grape leaves, stuffed peppers and tomatoes, and shish kebab.

But growing up in a family restaurant definitely had its pros and cons. As one of the owner's daughters, I'd often get last-minute calls from my father to waitress or hostess when another worker was sick. I used to grumble about it as a teenager, but I always showed up. Family came first. But there were plenty of great times, too, and my tips paid for my prom gown. Some of my favorite scenes in the book are straight from my memories—temperamental chefs, busy busboys, and gossipy waitstaff can be quite entertaining.

My *Kebab Kitchen Mystery* series also takes place at the Jersey shore. Ever since I was a little girl, my parents vacationed there. We now have two girls, and we still take them to the Jersey shore every summer. As I wrote the books, I pictured my fictitious small town of Ocean Crest at the Jersey shore. I heard the seagulls squawking and pictured them circling above the beach. I felt the lapping of the ocean waves and the sand between my toes, and imagined the brilliant Ferris wheel on the boardwalk pier. I pictured myself in Ocean Crest—minus the murders, of course.

I loved writing this book, and I'm happy to share my own favorite family recipes with you. Enjoy the food!

RECIPES

AZAD'S MOUSSAKA

¼ cup extra-virgin olive oil
1 large finely chopped onion
2 pounds ground beef
4 tablespoons tomato paste
½ cup red wine
½ cup chopped parsley
¼ teaspoon cinnamon
Salt and freshly ground pepper to taste
2 large eggplants
¼ cup vegetable oil
¼ pound butter
6 tablespoons flour
1 quart full-fat milk
4 beaten eggs
⅛ teaspoon grated nutmeg
2 cups ricotta cheese
1½ cup fine bread crumbs
1 cup grated Parmesan cheese

For the ground beef:
Heat ¼ cup extra-virgin olive oil in a skillet and cook the onions until they turn transparent. Add the ground meat and cook until fully cooked. Transfer the meat to a large strainer set over a bowl and drain off any excess fat. Return meat to the pan and heat. Add the tomato paste, wine, parsley, and cinnamon. Season with salt and pepper to taste. Stir and simmer over low heat until all the liquid has been absorbed. Remove from heat and set aside.

For the eggplant:

Cut unpeeled eggplants into ½-inch-thick slices. Lightly salt the slices and let them sit for five minutes. Heat ¼ cup vegetable oil in a separate skillet. Working in batches, fry the eggplant slices until they are golden brown on both sides. Set eggplant slices aside on sheet pan lined with paper towels to absorb the oil. Preheat oven to 375 degrees F.

For the béchamel sauce:

In a saucepan, melt the butter over medium heat. Add the flour and cook, whisking constantly, until the mixture is smooth. In a separate saucepan, bring the milk to a boil and add it gradually to the butter-flour mixture. Whisk constantly. When the mixture is thickened and smooth, remove it from the heat. In a bowl, whisk together beaten eggs, nutmeg, and ricotta cheese. Add it to the béchamel sauce and whisk until smooth.

Putting it all together:

Spray an 11-x-16 pan with nonstick cooking spray. Sprinkle lightly with bread crumbs. Layer half the eggplant in pan, then add half of the meat sauce. Sprinkle with bread crumbs and Parmesan cheese. Add the rest of the eggplant and then the meat sauce. Pour the béchamel sauce on top.

Bake for 45 minutes or until the top is browned and bubbly. Allow it to cool for twenty minutes before serving.

ANGELA'S PERFECT PILAF

2 tablespoons butter
1 tablespoon olive oil
½ cup fine egg noodles
1 cup long-grain white rice
2 cups chicken broth

Melt butter in a saucepan. Add olive oil. Add fine egg noodles and fry them until they are lightly brown. Add the rice and the chicken broth. Cover and allow it to come to a boil. Reduce heat to a low simmer and cover. Let cook for ten minutes. Turn off heat and let saucepan sit on burner for additional five minutes. Pilaf will then be ready to enjoy.

SUSAN CUTIE'S LEMON MERINGUE PIE

For the lemon pie:
1 cup sugar
¼ cup flour
4–5 tablespoons cornstarch
⅛ teaspoon salt
2 cups water
3 eggs, separate yolks from whites and keep both
1 tablespoon butter
¼ cup lemon juice
Grated rind of 1 lemon
Pastry pie shell

Combine the sugar, flour, cornstarch, and salt and mix. Gradually add the water, stir, and cook the ingredients over low heat until the mixture gently boils. It should thicken and become smooth. Gradually add beaten egg yolks, constantly stir, and cook over low heat for three minutes. Beat in butter, lemon juice, and lemon rind. Allow to cool on stovetop. Pour custard into the pie shell and cool in refrigerator.

For the meringue:
3 egg whites (reserved from above)
⅛ teaspoon salt
¼ teaspoon cream of tartar
1 teaspoon vanilla extract
6 tablespoons of sugar

It's easiest to use an electric mixer to make the meringue. Beat the egg whites with the salt in a small bowl until light and frothy. Add the cream of tartar and continue to beat at high speed until mixture will stand in peaks, about 4 to 5 minutes. Add the vanilla extract and beat in the sugar, 1 tablespoon at a time. Cover the cooled pie filling with the meringue until it touches the edges of the pastry to prevent the meringue from shrinking. Bake in 425 degree oven for five minutes. Cool and then refrigerate until cold before serving.

NIARI'S HOLIDAY PRETZEL TREATS

Bite-size, waffle-shaped pretzels
Hershey's Kisses or Hugs
M&M's green and red candy

Heat oven to 170 degrees. Arrange waffle pretzels in a single layer on a cookie sheet lined with parchment paper. Top each pretzel with an unwrapped Hershey's Kiss. Bake for 4–6 minutes, until chocolate feels soft when touched with a wooden spoon. Remove from oven. Quickly press an M&M's candy into the center of each Hershey's Kiss. Place the cookie sheet in the refrigerator so the chocolate sets, about ten minutes. Enjoy!

ACKNOWLEDGMENTS

Writers create stories in solitude, but publishing a book is a team effort. I'm thankful for all the wonderful people who have helped me along the way. I will always be indebted to my parents, Anahid and Gabriel, and miss them every day. This series would never have been written if it wasn't for them. My life experiences growing up in the family restaurant were invaluable. They taught me to work hard and never stop believing in myself.

Thanks to my girls—Laura and Gabrielle—for believing in Mom. I'm eternally grateful to John for his never-ending support, encouragement, and love. I'm lucky we get to live this life together.

Thank you to my longtime friend, adopted mother, and grammar queen, Maryliz Clark.

Thank you to my agent, Stephany Evans, for your guidance and for always believing in me.

And a special thank-you to Michaela Hamilton and everyone at Kensington for believing in this series and all their work on my behalf.

A special thank-you to readers, booksellers, and librarians for reading my *Kebab Kitchen Mystery* series. I hope you enjoy the book as much as I loved writing it!

Did you miss the first book in the irresistible *Kebab Kitchen* cozy mystery series? Not to worry! Just turn the page to read the opening pages of

HUMMUS AND HOMICIDE

to meet the lively characters and visit the sweet (but sometimes deadly) beach town of Ocean Crest. All the *Kebab Kitchen* mysteries, and more, are available from Kensington Publishing Corp., www.kensingtonbooks.com.

Ocean Crest, New Jersey

"Lucy Berberian! Is that you?"

Lucy's car was stopped at a red light when the excited shout caught her attention. Her gaze turned to the crosswalk, and she lowered her sunglasses an inch to peer above the rim. A tiny old lady with an abundance of gray curls was pushing a rolling cart filled with groceries. She waved. One of the plastic bags stuck out from the cart and flapped in the breeze.

Lucy glimpsed the name *Holloway's* printed on the bag—the sole grocery store in the small New Jersey beach town. "Hello, Mrs. Kiminski," she called out her open window.

The old lady smiled, revealing pearly white dentures. "You're visiting? Your mama will be so happy."

No doubt her mother and father would be thrilled when they learned Lucy was back, not only for a visit, but longer. Lucy swallowed hard. She'd hit the first stop light out of three in town and already her nerves were getting to her. It felt like a corkscrew was slowly winding in her stomach the closer she came to her destination. And to *him*.

Don't think about it.

The light changed, and Lucy waved as she continued down Ocean Avenue. Parking spots in the town's main street were vacant in late April, and only a few people strolled about. The tourist season wouldn't begin until Memorial Day. A month later and the town would be crammed with seasonal tourists, and a parking spot would be hard to find.

Lucy drove past a ramp leading to the town's mile-long boardwalk, and she spied the Atlantic Ocean between two buildings—a blue line to the horizon. The Jersey shore was in Lucy's blood. She'd been born and raised in Ocean Crest, a tiny town located on a barrier island about six miles north of Cape May. Even off-season the scent of funnel cake drifted from one of the boardwalk shops and through her window. The bright morning sunlight warmed her cheeks, and she spotted the single pier with a Ferris wheel and an old-fashioned wooden roller coaster. Soon the Ferris wheel would light up the night sky and the piercing screams from the coaster would be heard from a block away.

The small ocean town was so different from the rapid pace of the Center-City Philadelphia law firm and apartment she had grown accustomed to over the last eight years. But now that part of her life was done, and she needed to figure out what she was going to do next. When her work had thrown her a curveball, returning home had come to mind. Other than hasty holiday visits, she hadn't stayed for longer than a weekend.

A few blocks later Lucy parked before a quaint brick building with a flower bed bursting with yellow daffodils and red tulips. A lit sign read KEBAB KITCHEN FINE MEDITERRANEAN CUISINE.

A flash of motion by the front door caught her eye as soon as she killed the engine. Gadoo, the calico cat with yellow eyes her mother had adopted when he kept coming around the restaurant, cocked his head to the side as if to say, *What took you so long to come home?* and then swished his tail and sauntered down the alley.

Taking a deep breath, she got out of the car, then pushed open the door to the restaurant.

The dining room was empty and the lights were dimmed. Sunlight through the front windows shone on pristine white tablecloths covering a dozen tables and a handful of maple booths. Small vases with fresh flowers and unlit tea light candles in glass votive holders rested upon the pressed linen. Cherry wainscoting gave the place a warm, family feel. The ocean shimmered from large bay windows and seagulls soared above the water. The delicious aroma of fresh herbs, fragrant spices, and grilled lamb wafted to her. It was only ten o'clock in the morning, well before the restaurant opened for lunch, and that meant her mother was preparing her savory specials.

Lucy walked forward and stopped by the hostess stand. The place hadn't changed since she was a kid. As a young child, her mom carried her around to greet customers and kiss the staff. When she was eight, she started rolling silverware in cloth napkins and refilling salt and pepper shakers. Lucy eyed the cash register behind the counter with its laminated dollar bill showcasing the first cash the restaurant took in as well as the required health department notices that hung on the wall. A low wall separated a waitress station from the dining area, and a pair of swinging doors led to the kitchen. She recalled her days as a hostess and cashier, seating customers and handing them menus, then ringing them up to pay on their way out. A waitress pad sat on a nearby table, and she remembered how excited she'd been as a teenager the day her father promoted her from hostess to waitress. The cash tips had helped pay for her prom gown.

Footsteps sounded on the terra cotta tiles. Lucy turned to see her older sister carrying a tray of sparkling glasses.

"Lucy! What are you doing here?" Her sister set down the tray on a nearby table.

Lucy smiled and embraced her warmly. "Hi, Emma. I've come for a visit."

At thirty-seven Emma was five years older than Lucy. Lucy had always been a bit envious of her sister who was slim and attractive with long, curly brown hair. She weighed the same as she had since college, and she'd never had to worry about how many carbs or pieces of pita bread she consumed. "How's Max?" Lucy asked.

Emma wrinkled her nose. "He's the same. The king of real estate in town. He works a lot and is never around."

Emma tended to frequently complain about her husband, but they had a ten-year-old daughter they adored. "And my little niece Niari?"

"Most of the time Niari's great," Emma said. "She's good in school and likes soccer. But she's also a tween who can drive us crazy. I dread the puberty years to come."

Lucy chuckled. "I imagine we drove Mom and Dad nuts as teenagers."

Emma perched on the edge of a table and crossed her arms. "How's work? I'm surprised you could get away."

Lucy cleared her throat. "Well, that's just it. I have some time to—"

"Lucy Anahid Berberian!"

Lucy whirled to see her mother and father emerge from the swinging kitchen doors. Her Lebanese, Greek, and Armenian mother, Angela, had olive skin and dark hair that she'd styled in a beehive since the sixties. Her Armenian father, Raffi, was a portly man of average height with a balding pate of curly black hair. Both had arrived in America on their twenty-first birthdays, met months later at a church festival, and married soon after. They'd meshed cultures and languages, and Emma and Lucy were first-generation Americans with ethnic roots as strong as her parents' prized grapevine clinging to its trellis.

Lucy found herself engulfed in her mother's arms, flowery perfume tickling her nose. The large gold cross—the one piece of jewelry her mother never left the house without—was cool as it pressed against Lucy's neck. Her mother was a tiny woman, only five feet tall even with her beehive hairdo, but she was a talented chef and a smart businesswoman.

Angela passed Lucy to her father, and Lucy smiled at his bear hug and the light scrape of his whiskers as he brushed her cheek with a kiss. He released her to study her face and grinned. "My little girl, the big city lawyer."

Her mother touched Lucy's arm. "It's Tuesday. Shouldn't you be at work?"

Lucy's insides froze for a heart-stopping moment. "I'm taking a vacation," she blurted out.

Why did she have to sound so nervous? She'd rehearsed the perfect excuse over and over in her car on the way here.

"A vacation?" Angela folded her arms across her chest. Her gaze filled with suspicion as it traveled over Lucy from head to toe, taking in the worn jeans, Philadelphia Eagles T-shirt, and Nike sneakers.

Lucy's attire was far from her normal business wear, but it was surprising how quick a week of unemployment could affect one's desire to dress in anything but yoga pants or jeans.

"It's true," Lucy said. A small streak of panic ran through her at her mother's continuing inquisitive gaze.

"Well, it's about time." Her mother nodded curtly and unfolded her arms from across her chest. "That law firm works you too hard. You only visit for Thanksgiving, Christmas, and Easter. You stay two, maybe three days, and then you're off again. Plus"—she eyed Lucy with an admonishing glare—"you didn't visit last Mother's Day."

Lucy's pulse quickened. Here it was. Her family's ability to layer on guilt. She'd always made an effort to visit for the holidays, but the truth was she didn't always want to come home. The smothering could be as thick as the sugar syrup on her mother's baklava—sticky, sweet, and as effective as superglue.

"You know I had a big case and couldn't take time off. You could have visited me," Lucy said.

"Bah!" Raffi said with a disgusted wave of his hand. "What company makes its employees work so many weekends? And you know we don't like to drive into the city."

Lucy knew crossing the Delaware River via the Ben Franklin Bridge into Philadelphia was like traveling to another country for her parents.

"How long is your vacation?" Emma asked.

"A month." At their stunned looks, Lucy quickly added, "It's really what we call a sabbatical." She wasn't ready to admit she was no longer employed. Knowing her parents, they'd think she was home for good. Why give them false hope?

"You'll stay with us. I'll tidy your room," her mom said.

Heck no. Seeing her parents was good, but living with them was something else entirely. "I'm staying with Katie and Bill, Mom."

Her mom hesitated and glared at her as if she'd been denied access to Lucy's firstborn. Katie Watson was Lucy's long-time friend. When Lucy had called her to tell her that she was coming home and staying for a while, Katie had offered for Lucy to stay with her and her husband, Bill, an Ocean Crest police officer.

"Fine," Angela finally said. "I've always liked Katie, and she comes from a good family."

Raffi cracked a wide grin. "You came at a good time, Lucy. With Memorial Day in less than a month, the tourist season will begin. Millie left to have a baby. We need your help."

Lucy's smile faded. Millie had worked for her parents as a waitress for years. From what Lucy recalled, Millie had married right out of high school and started having kids. Was she on baby number four by now?

"It's her sixth boy," her dad answered as if reading her mind. "We need a waitress. We're already short for today's lunch shift."

Lucy felt as if she were being sucked back into the fold like quicksand; no amount of professional accomplishments mattered. Family helped family, and their expectations could be stifling and overwhelming. It was partly why she'd fled years ago.

But she was older and more experienced now. "Dad, I don't think—"

"You can borrow Millie's apron and Emma's clothes," Angela said.

Good grief. Millie's apron was one thing. But how would she fit into her skinny sister's black pants and white shirt? Lucy was bigger than Emma in every way. From her breasts, to her hips, and definitely her derriere.

Angela pulled out a chair. "Sit. You're too thin." She glanced at Lucy's father behind her shoulder. "Raffi, please bring Lucy something special to eat. We can catch up while we wait."

Her dad disappeared through the swinging kitchen doors.

Lucy rolled her eyes as she sat. Their mother never seemed to notice any physical differences between her two daughters. To her, everyone appeared in need of food.

Emma smiled mischievously as she set a glass of water in front of Lucy. "Good luck," she whispered, then followed their father into the kitchen.

Lucy inwardly groaned as her mother pulled up a chair beside her. She didn't need her sister's warning. She knew what was coming as soon as she spotted the gleam in her mother's eyes. The maternal message was clear. *Let's talk about how old you are and remind you that your biological clock is ticking louder than a pounding drum and that you should be married and birthing my grandchildren by now.*

Her mother patted her hand. "You know I think you work too hard."

Once again, a nagging guilt pierced Lucy's chest for not revealing the truth. "It's okay. I'm home for a while now, remember?"

Angela's face lit up. "Good. We need to focus on finding you a husband."

"Mom," Lucy whined. "I'm not opposed to marriage, but only if the right man proposes. Meanwhile, my career is important to—"

"Posh," her mom said, waving a hand. "A career doesn't keep you warm at night when you get old. Granted, men are far from perfect. Your father is a good example," she said, motioning toward the kitchen, "but he's there."

Lucy wrinkled her nose. She didn't consider herself a romantic, but she'd hoped for more than just *there* when it came to a man.

"I saw Gadoo," Lucy said, hoping to change the topic.

Angela always loved to talk about the cat. "He waits for me every morning by the back door. Actually, he's waiting for his breakfast. As long as I feed him, Gadoo keeps coming."

Gadoo was Armenian for cat. Not very original, but it fit the patchy orange and black calico cat with yellow eyes.

Before long the kitchen doors opened again and her father emerged with a large shish kebab platter and set it before her. Two skewers of succulent lamb and a skewer of roasted peppers, tomatoes, and onions were accompanied by rice pilaf and homemade pita bread. The aroma made her stomach grumble and her mouth water.

Lucy may not have missed her mother's lectures about

husband hunting, but damned if she hadn't missed the food. She picked up a warm piece of pita bread, then stopped. "Is there hummus?"

Her gaze followed Emma's pointing finger. "You have to see our newest addition."

Lucy stood and looked toward the corner of the restaurant where a long sidebar stood. She hadn't noticed it earlier. At first glance, it looked like a salad bar, but instead of lettuce, tomatoes, and salad, bins of hummus were displayed, each tray a different variety.

"Specialties of the house, and all my own flavors. Roasted red pepper, extra garlic, Mediterranean herb, lemon pucker, artichoke, black bean, sweet apricot, and of course, my own recipe of traditional hummus," Angela boasted with pride.

"Customers love it," Raffi said.

Lucy carried her plate to the bins full of the creamy dips and added a large spoonful of traditional hummus next to the pita bread, then returned to her seat. "Wow! Business must be good, Dad." She dipped a piece of pita into the hummus and shoved it into her mouth.

Heaven. The lemon blended with the garlic, chick peas and sesame seed puree perfectly, and the texture was super-creamy.

Silence greeted her. Lucy looked up from her plate to see all three members of her family staring at her. "What's wrong?" she mumbled.

Emma broke the awkward silence. "Dad wants to sell."

Lucy nearly choked on a mouthful before managing to swallow it down. "Sell?"

"Not right away, but I've been thinking about it," Raffi said.

An uncomfortable thought crossed Lucy's mind. Her gaze swept him from his balding head of curly black hair to his sizeable belly back to his face. "Are you sick?"

His brows furrowed. "No. I'm old."

The irony was not lost on her. Less than an hour ago she was hesitant to set foot in the place. But selling the restaurant? For thirty years, ever since her parents had opened it, Kebab Kitchen had been the center of their lives, socially and economically. What would they do without it?

"But I don't understand why—"

"I have no sons or sons-in-law who want it. Emma doesn't have a head for business, and Max is into real estate." Her father eyed Lucy hard, his glare cutting through her like one of his prized butcher knives. "If you'd married Azad Zakarian this wouldn't be a problem."

Lucy's stomach bottomed out at the mention of the man her parents had so desperately wanted her to marry. He was one of the main reasons she'd left to take the job in the Philadelphia law firm. It had taken months, years, to dull the heartache. Her throat seemed to close up as she felt the all-too-familiar pressure from her parents' unreasonable expectations—that the ultimate fate of the restaurant rested upon her shoulders and that she had to be the one to keep everything together. Lucy reached for the water glass and took a big swallow.

"Dad, stop," Emma said. "No sense nagging Lucy. Max has a buyer."

"Who?"

"Anthony Citteroni."

Lucy sat upright at the name. "The bike man next door to the restaurant?"

Every summer, Mr. Citteroni's bike shop rented a

variety of bicycles to tourists. Ever since she was a kid, she'd heard stories that he had mob connections in Atlantic City, and his many businesses were how he laundered money.

"He wants the property," Raffi explained.

"Why?" Lucy couldn't fathom what Mr. Citteroni would do with it.

"He wants to open a high class Italian restaurant, but he's not the only interested buyer," Raffi said.

"A local woman wants to convert Kebab Kitchen into a diner," Emma said.

"Another Jersey diner? The state is loaded with them. And Ocean Crest already has the Pancake Palace," Lucy said.

"Don't forget that Azad's interested," Angela announced.

There it was again. His name.

"Why would he want it?" Lucy asked.

"Azad graduated from culinary school and is working as a sous chef for a fancy Atlantic City restaurant. He wants to buy Kebab Kitchen and keep it the way it is."

Of course, he did. He was perfect. Hand-picked by her parents. He'd started working as a dishwasher for the restaurant when he was in high school. He'd soon worked his way up to busboy, then line cook, and had earned her parents' respect. Not to mention their hopes of a union with their younger daughter. The pressure tightened in Lucy's chest.

She glared at her parents. "What will you do if you retire? Where will you go?"

"We'll stay in Ocean Crest. It's a peaceful place," Angela said.

Raffi waved his hand toward the window and a view of the calm ocean and blue sky. "After all, what bad things happen here?"

Connect with

Visit us online at
KensingtonBooks.com
to read more from your favorite authors, see books
by series, view reading group guides, and more.

for sneak peeks, chances to win books and prize packs,
and to share your thoughts with other readers.

facebook.com/kensingtonpublishing
twitter.com/kensingtonbooks

Tell us what you think!

To share your thoughts, submit a review,
or sign up for our eNewsletters, please visit:
KensingtonBooks.com/TellUs.